The Hungry Bones
The Fifth Alexa Glock Forensics Mystery

"I love novels in which history, geography, science, and a little love intersect. And where surprises turn over with every page. *The Hungry Bones* is the fifth installment in what could also be called *CSI: New Zealand.*"

—Cary Griffith, Sam Rivers Mysteries

"Unexpected plot twists will keep readers turning pages until they reach the exciting ending. Johnson has crafted a compelling story that features little-known history (to American readers, at least) and strong women."

—*Booklist*

"Johnson seamlessly ties the past mystery to the present one, and her rich shading of even minor characters sets this apart from similar procedurals. This series continues to impress."

—*Publishers Weekly*

Praise for Sara E. Johnson

Molten Mud Murder
The First Alexa Glock Forensics Mystery

"Johnson provides a fascinating view of New Zealand and insights into the Māori culture... Armchair travelers will have fun."

—*Publishers Weekly*

"The novel is a page-turner par excellence, with vivid characters and an enthralling plot, all wrapped up in a most charming evocation of New Zealand's landscapes, people, and local politics. I highly recommend this debut novel!"

—Douglas Preston, #1 bestselling coauthor of the Pendergast series

"Johnson gives us a compelling picture of modern New Zealand overlaid by Māori culture with its strict taboos and amazing artifacts. Alexa hopes to stay in New Zealand, and if this leads to a full series, my fingers are crossed that she gets her wish."

—Margaret Maron, *New York Times* bestselling author

The Bones Remember
The Second Alexa Glock Forensics Mystery

"At the exciting climax, Alexa uses her wits, not a gun or martial arts skills, to take out the bad guy. Hopefully, this refreshingly normal heroine will be back soon."

—*Publishers Weekly*

"Ready for some armchair travel with a hint of *Jaws*? Sara Johnson provides the ride in her second New Zealand–set Alexa Glock Forensics Mystery, *The Bones Remember*. Once you discover, with this dauntless forensic investigator, the wilds of Stewart Island, you'll want more pages. And the shark attacks and treachery along the way will keep the pages turning."

—Kingdom Books Mystery Blog

The Bone Track
The Third Alexa Glock Forensics Mystery
"Johnson's wonderful descriptions of New Zealand's natural beauty immerse the reader in her action-packed tale, and the relationship between Alexa and Charlie adds a layer of emotion and regret to the well-plotted adventure. Fans of internationally set mysteries will enjoy this dangerous ride."

—Sarah Stewart Taylor, author of the
Maggie D'arcy Mystery series

The Bone Riddle
The Fourth Alexa Glock Forensics Mystery
"There's much to enjoy. Bonus: those New Zealand landscapes the victim seemed determined to destroy."

—*Kirkus Reviews*

"Forensic technology, a rising body count, and romance abound."

—*Criminal Element*

"Johnson expertly balances her lead's personal and professional lives and maintains nerve-shredding suspense throughout. This gives every indication that Alexa can sustain a long-running series."

—*Publishers Weekly*

Also by Sara E. Johnson

BONE CHILLING

BONE CHILLING

AN
ALEXA GLOCK
FORENSICS
MYSTERY

SARA E. JOHNSON

Poisoned Pen
PRESS

Published by Poisoned Pen Press, an imprint of Sourcebooks
1935 Brookdale RD, Naperville, IL 60563-2773
(630) 961-3900
sourcebooks.com

Cataloging-in-Publication Data is on file with the Library of Congress.

Printed and bound in the United States of America.
VP 10 9 8 7 6 5 4 3 2 1

To my children Scott, Phillip, and Sally and to their wonderful loves: Mary Hannah, Katie, and Joe.

Mehemea ka tuohu ahau me maunga teitei.

Māori proverb: If I should bow my head
let it be to a high mountain.

FAILURE

1. John Ruskin says if you come to danger and turn back, though it may have been the prudent thing to do, your character suffers deterioration; you are to that extent weaker, more lifeless.

2. Sir Edmund Hillary says human life is more important than just getting to the top of a mountain.

3. Charlie Brown says good grief.

4. Mum says dust off and try again.

5 NOVEMBER 1984

It's our second day at Wanaka Backpackers. I'm rereading my ratty Travels with Charley. Steinbeck says to throw it all on paper. I'll start with the naked truth: we didn't make it to the summit of Mount Cook. It wasn't a hard call. Every time I stood, the wind blew me backward. I can take a hint when I'm not wanted.

I think C was relieved.

It was easier to catch up on my writing before the hippies from the States arrived. One has a guitar, and they're all singing Bob Dylan's "Shelter from the Storm," C the loudest.

Something about blowing a futile horn.

Christian often blows a futile horn, but he's my only male cuz, he's a competent mountaineer, and he had the time to climb with me.

xvi   Sara E. Johnson

Tackling Mount Aspiring next is a fitting quest. In the te reo Māori language, Mount Aspiring is Tititea: peak of glistening white. In legend, Tititea is the younger brother of Aoraki Mount Cook. I know this because Rachel straddles Pākehā and Māori worlds. You wouldn't know it with her pale eyes, but she told me, "My heart aligns more with being Māori."

I don't know where I'm going with my scribbling (C calls it that). I'm not the first one to fail climbing Mount Cook, and if we get to the top of Mount Aspiring, I won't be the first to do that, either. Maybe an article on success vs. failure. That depends on whether we have success.

I study the guide book: Day One: Raspberry Flat to Aspiring Hut, Day Two: Aspiring Hut to Lucas-Trotter Hut, Day Three: SUMMIT(!) to Colin Hut, Day Four: back to car.

Steinbeck says in Travels with Charley: "I wonder why it is that when I plan a route too carefully, it goes to pieces, whereas if I blunder along in blissful ignorance aimed in a fancied direction I get through with no trouble."

Chapter One

THURSDAY

The cremains cometh.

That's not what the text said, but that's what it meant. Alexa Glock left the empty lab, eager to do them justice.

A thickset man in a wool coat waited in the nearly empty lobby. Alexa showed him her Auckland Forensic Service Centre badge. "Good morning. I believe those are for me."

The man's eyes skipped from the badge to the carton in his hands. "A most unfortunate situation. Mind you, the mistake has been rectified."

Alexa pulled her lab coat closed. "Are you the owner of Castle Crematory?"

"Yes, indeed. I'm Edward Castle."

Techs and admins scurried into the building, the cold clinging to their coats and scarves. Auckland temperatures had dropped into the single digits last night—almost freezing, an unusual cold snap for the North Island. Mr. Castle stepped aside and gestured with his free hand. "There's no need for this."

Alexa assumed he meant a forensic probe. Or sift. "The family disagrees."

He tucked the carton under his arm and removed various documents from a satchel, pointing out how this matched that. "There's also an ID tag tucked in with the cremains. You'll see as soon as you open them."

Alexa shuddered. Then she got a grip. Cremation was a choice.

"We are offering the family a free urn for their trouble. Either the Fleur de Keepsake or the Weeping Angel." He thrust a touch screen at her. After she signed, he relinquished the carton.

She resisted the urge to shake it. Back in the lab, she opened the box and set the clear plastic bag of coarse, gritty remains on a scale: two kilos. Ashes to ashes, dust to dust.

Yeah. But nah.

A typical crematorium burned a body at 1800 Fahrenheit for two and a half hours. All the soft parts burn away so that only bone and teeth are left. Once cooled, they are pulverized. Ground teeth and bone filled the bag, not ashes. And the identification tag Mr. Castle had promised. Alexa slipped on gloves, undid the zip tie, and fished it out. It listed the correct certificate number and name: Phyllis Carswell.

Last night Alexa's boss, Dan Goddard, had called, upset. His Aunt Phyllis had died, and he'd gone with his mother to Castle Crematory to pick up her remains. He discovered the identification tag didn't match the cremation certificate. "Wrong ashes. Can you freaking believe it? Right away the owner wanted to trade them for some other ashes, but Mum refused to accept them. I told Mr. Castle to deliver them to the lab in the morning. There will be teeth fragments, right? Can you take a look?"

Teeth, the hardest substances in the human body, were Alexa's specialty. She had canceled a date with DI Bruce Horne in order to poke and plan. She'd have plenty of time with him this weekend. They were taking a ski trip.

With. His. Daughters.

The poking took her to Castle Crematory's website. Most reviews were good, but one client complained, "When my partner phoned to ask for their help regarding 'ashes in art' jewelry, Mr. Castle's response was not helpful."

No complaints about receiving the wrong ashes.

She also poked into cremation laws. Only one body can be burned at a time, and pacemakers must be removed or they could explode. Then she lost ten minutes to a Māori-owned company called StardustMe. For a price, a metal token containing a small amount of cremains can be rocketed into space.

The planning of how she would figure out if the cremains were Aunt Phyllis took her to the burn-pit case. She'd read about it in *Forensics Science* and found the journal article online.

Human bone fragments and a single damaged tooth were discovered in a burn pit at a rental property.

Naturally, the police wanted to know who the burned remains came from. DNA degrades at high temperatures, so identification through those means was out. The police turned the tooth over to a forensic odontologist, who analyzed the filling material in the tooth.

Alexa tongued a composite filling she'd had done back in Raleigh, where she had lived before moving to New Zealand. First molar, upper right, dentist's view—tooth number 16 here but number 3 in the States, which has its own numbering system. Silver was old school. Her filling was made of resin—a hard synthetic polymer that matched the color of her natural teeth. Resins withstand extreme heat, and each brand is unique. The odontologist was able to trace the brand of resin in the charred tooth to filling material used in a missing woman's tooth via her dental records.

The person who murdered and burned the woman was never caught. A chill ran up Alexa's spine.

Dan had sent her Aunt Phyllis's records. She had two recent resin-filled cavities. Her dentist used PermaDenta. The Swiss-manufactured resin was new on the market, and the dentist doubted anyone else in Auckland used it. Its primary component was silica.

Alexa poured the cremains onto a paper-covered tray. Some of Maybe Aunt Phyllis wafted up and tickled her nose. She pulled on a mask and scooped some into a paper baking cup. Then she readied a portable X-ray fluorescence device—it looked like a ray gun—and scanned the first batch. Its chemical components would display on the little screen. It took seven seconds to process.

Round one: nada for silica. Round two—the same. Batch after batch was negative. If this wasn't Aunt Phyllis, then who was it?

"Any luck?"

The sudden voice made her wiggle the XRF. She hadn't heard Dan enter the lab. "Not yet."

He frowned at the baking cup. "Is that…?"

"It's a portion of the cremains. I have the brand name of the resin used in your Aunt Phyllis's restorations. If I identify some fragments with the XRF, I'll use the electron microscope to determine whether it's the same brand."

Dan took off his glasses and polished them with his polo shirt. His nose was red, probably from riding his bike to work on such a cold morning.

"People don't realize the fillers in their teeth are mostly made of glass, silica, and ceramic."

He shuffled from one Converse tennis shoe to the other. "How much longer?"

She refocused on Maybe Aunt Phyllis. "An hour or two. What will you do if it isn't her?"

"Our solicitor said no crime has taken place. I'll report it to the Cremation Regulatory Board either way." His shoulders sagged as he walked out the door.

On the twenty-third batch the screen registered $SiO2$ for silicon dioxide. Maybe this *was* Aunt Phyllis. It took ten minutes to winnow the sample to a small positive sample. She took her prize and settled at the electron microscope.

She added the sample to the chamber, turned the electron beam on, and zoomed.

Bingo. Its composition was consistent with PermaDenta. After cleaning up and reassembling the cremains into the plastic bag, she summoned Dan to the lab. "I found fragments of the resin Aunt Phyllis's dentist used in her teeth."

He looked at the bag squatting on the table. "So it's her?"

"It's not like a DNA match, but given the circumstances, I'm certain the remains are your aunt. Mr. Castle is throwing in a free urn for your troubles."

Dan let out a long breath. "I was on my way to see you. An away case just came in."

Her heart sank. No ski trip.

"You can still go." Dan knew she was off to the slopes tomorrow. "Two weeks ago, a couple of ice climbers were crossing a glacier. One of them slipped. When he got up, he saw a skull poking out of the snow."

A skull on ice? What the hell?

"Search and Rescue had to wait for the weather to clear to go in. Snow and high winds, all that. This morning is it."

"Where's this glacier?"

"Mount Aspiring National Park."

She must have looked blank.

"An hour from Queenstown. That's where you're skiing, right? The local police and rangers are headed there now. They need an odontologist to be a part of the recovery team."

"You want me to go to a glacier?" She almost said "glass-ee-er" like Dan but reverted to the American pronunciation.

"It's stable."

"They need a forensic archaeologist."

"These aren't historic remains like Ötzi," Dan said.

"Who is Ötzi?"

"You know, the Iceman. He lived in the Alps thousands of years ago. There's a modern boot and some rope near our skull. Search and Rescue suspect it's a climber who went missing thirty years ago. Teeth will be the quickest way to identify him."

From teeth on fire to teeth on ice. She hopped on board. "Who is this missing climber? Does he have dental records on file?"

"I'll send you the details. You're flying out at noon."

On the drive to her apartment to pack, she thought of her mother's book of Robert Frost poems, left behind and lonely in her storage pod in Raleigh. One poem was "Fire and Ice." How did it go?

> *Some say the world will end in fire,*
> *Some say in ice.*

Chapter Two

Cases popped up fast in Alexa's position as a traveling forensic investigator. She kept a packed suitcase ready, but with the ski trip—and now a glacier—her three-day supply of khakis and button-down Lands' End blouses wouldn't suffice.

The word *suffice* reminded her of that poem again. As soon as she entered her apartment, she looked up "Fire and Ice" on her phone. It was a short poem—probably why she liked it. The final lines were:

> *But if it had to perish twice,*
> *I think I know enough of hate*
> *To say that for destruction ice*
> *Is also great*
> *And would suffice.*

The *pounamu* pendant nestled against her sternum pulsated. She fingered the greenstone spiral nervously as she surveyed the two-bedroom apartment. The dog crate was empty. Her cop roommate Natalie was on day shift, and Kaos was with her, naturally. She wished the German shepherd were here. He steadied her.

She had started packing for the ski vacay last night. *Forever Never* peeked at her from atop folded jeans. The happy-ever-afters of Lucy Score's romance novels appealed to her, plus she studied the tips on how to flirt, but they seemed written in a foreign tongue that her own tongue rejected.

What if Bruce's girls saw her reading material and made fun of her? She took the romance novel out and tossed in her latest forensic journal. She combined work clothes and ski clothes in one bag.

She collected her toiletries and checked her hair: her shoulder-length sable locks were in a tizzy. Each stroke of a brush gave the frizz more confidence. The woman who cut her hair recommended taming it with a spray bottle of conditioner diluted with water, but who had the time? She gathered it in a ponytail and leaned close to the mirror. Her greenish-brown eyes gleamed with energy. She dabbed drugstore gloss on her lips and twirled away.

How does one dress when meeting a glacier? She chose thick leggings, a turtleneck, a cream-colored fleece pullover, two pair of socks, and hiking boots. She stuffed the thin merino beanie that murdered her hair into the pocket of her puffer jacket.

Bring it on, glacier.

She had time to call Ana, who was a forensic archaeologist.

Alexa didn't do friends. This was a deficiency of which she was newly aware, maybe triggered by being alone in the Southern Hemisphere. Her theory was that her brain had been deprived of normal teen interactions during early adolescence. She had been badly scalded shortly after her thirteenth birthday and spent the next two years in and out of hospitals enduring three skin grafts. In between, she was in pain and hunched over. Not BFF material.

Her neural circuitry that connected positive affect with relationships, intimacy, nurturing, and feminine community had shriveled during those formative years.

Or maybe she'd been born this way.

Ana, a fellow Aucklander with a five-year-old daughter, Shelby, was becoming a friend. They were both thirty-eight. They'd worked two cases together. Since then, Ana invited her along to a couple of outings with Shelby, and once, when Ana's mom babysat, they'd ventured to a bar.

Uneasiness hit Alexa. Now that she was dating Bruce, she was neglecting Ana. Being social was complicated. She punched Ana's number.

"Preserving Heritage. Dr. Luckenbaugh speaking."

"It's me, Alexa."

"I was thinking about you. Shelby wants you to take her to Create a Tuatara at the art museum."

"What's a tuatara?"

"A lizard."

Alexa was flattered. No one had ever asked her to co-create a lizard. "It depends. I have an away case and a few questions."

Ana said something to someone and then, "Shoot."

"I'm headed to a glacier on Mount Aspiring. A skull has appeared out of the ice. The DOC rangers think it's a hiker who went missing thirty years ago."

"Whoa, girl. You're headed to a glacier?"

"Yep. Dan said the glacier is stable."

"Glaciers are never stable. They move continuously."

"True, but slowly. You know that expression *glacial pace*?"

"That expression doesn't apply anymore. Take Greenland. Its ice loss is averaging two hundred eighty gigatons per year."

Greenland? Gigatons? Alexa didn't have much time. "A modern hiking boot was found near the skull." When she thought about it—why was the boot near the skull and not on a foot? Did the boot have a foot in it? "Do you have advice for how I should protect the skull?"

"I've never done an ice extraction. I'll contact Gladys Ball. She's a glacier archaeologist."

"There's such a thing?"

"A new field, courtesy of climate change. I'll have Dr. Ball call you. Be careful."

Alexa hated it when people told her to be careful. The expression portended disaster and instilled fear.

At the airport she canceled tomorrow's ticket to Queenstown. Now she wouldn't have to fly with Bruce and the girls. The new arrangement was for the best; it would give father and daughters some alone time. She was nervous about spending time with Denise and Sammie. She had only met them three times total. Ice Skull was a partial rescue.

Bruce would be at work—Auckland Central Police Department—where he led the serious crime division. She reviewed their history as she found a seat in the departures area.

They'd known each other a year.

They dated for a couple months.

She called time-out (and almost bailed).

Now they were re-dating (Alexa's term).

The ski trip was Bruce's idea. They'd been washing dishes at his apartment. "Come skiing with me and the girls," he'd said. "My parents have a villa. Mostly they rent it out, but I've got it for three nights at the end of August."

Daughters were bad enough, but parents?

He looked at her face and laughed. "It will be just the four of us."

"Just the four of us" did not lessen her panic.

"The trip is for Denise's sixteenth birthday."

A dish slid through her wet hands into the dishwasher. She righted it. "Isn't it rushing things for me to go on a trip? You know. With your girls."

"Rushing?" Bruce held her gaze. "I wouldn't invite you if I wasn't serious about you. I want Denise and Sammie to get to know you."

His gaze was the moon, and she was the tide. "We wouldn't, um, share a room, right?"

"The villa has three bedrooms. The girls can do the sharing."

She had doubts. Airport announcements refocused her. She pulled out her phone and punched Bruce's number. A skull on ice was a relationship test. Would he support her call to duty? The intertwining of policing and forensics had brought them together, but the demands of either could tear them apart. She pictured him as the phone rang: tall and fit, dark short hair, salt and pepper at the temples, vivid blue eyes that turned slate when he angered and, given his age of forty-five, were rimmed with crow's-feet, which were sexy.

"Bruce Horne."

"It's me." *Obviously.* Alexa's cheeks flushed. "I'm at the airport. I have an away case."

Silence.

"It's in Queenstown, like your villa is," she said brightly. Or would be when she was off the glacier. She stared at her hiking boots, imagining crampons attached to the soles. "Hopefully, I can meet up with you and the girls tomorrow. Saturday, at the latest."

"What's the case?" His voice was measured.

"Skeletal remains have been found on a glacier. Authorities think it's a climber who disappeared three decades ago. I'll do dental comparisons once they extricate him."

"Ice bones are popping out more and more as the glaciers melt," he said.

That made sense. Global warming pulling the covers back to reveal the dead.

"The villa is empty. I'll text you the code. You can check in a night early. Have the place to yourself."

She let go a lungful of air. Bruce had aced the test.

Chapter Three

At a window seat, midsection of the plane, Alexa checked email
to see if Dan had sent her information about the hiker who had
gone missing. No dental records yet, but he'd sent a link and a
note: Skeleton might be Mark Lyon. Christchurch police will send
you his dental records.

The link was to a *New Zealand Outdoors Magazine* article. She studied the photo of a man with a disfigured nose—
frostbite, maybe—and haunted eyes. The caption identified
him as Sam Coyle. Farther down was another photo of two
shaggy haired young men, arms around each other, a snowcapped mountain in the background, captioned "Mark Lyon
and Sam Coyle honed their mountaineering skills climbing
Arthur's Pass."

Alexa read the article.

MISSING ON MOUNT ASPIRING
by Steven Eckel, 1997

*(Journalist and climber Steven Eckel has been published in
New Zealand, Australia, Canada, and the UK. He writes
to promote the safety of mountaineering and to bring voice
to the ones who never made it back.)*

"We had cut through Quarterdeck Pass and reached Blue
Peak Glacier late morning," said Sam Coyle, an electrician,

*as he recounts the climb that claimed his friend Mark Lyon.
"We thought we were okay, you know?"*

Coyle and I are in a coffee shop in Christchurch on the
two-year anniversary of Lyon's disappearance. He and his
friend were 27 when they'd attempted to climb what many
call the Matterhorn of the South.

"It was steep, maybe 45 degrees. Aspiring loomed above
us. We were roped together, and Mark was leading." At 3,033
meters, Mount Aspiring is the highest peak outside of Aoraki
Mount Cook National Park. Coyle and Lyon had spent the
prior year preparing to summit it, though mountaineers are
discouraged from actually going to its highest point out of
respect for Māori beliefs.

"The winds started gusting, and then an ice slip caught
us from behind. I somersaulted into rocks and ice blocks,"
Coyle said of the fateful August day in 1995. "When I came
to a stop, the rope was severed."

Coyle suffered a broken collarbone, cuts, and abrasions
but would not know this for 48 hours.

"The landscape was completely different. Slabs of ice and
boulders covered the surface. I lost my equipment and goggles
and was on my hands and knees. The wind blew granules of
snow in my eyes. It felt like burning sand. I crawled the length
of the rope that was left. It ended at two enormous slabs of ice. I
knew right then I was looking at Mark's tomb. Mark was gone."

It took Coyle 10 hours to reach Lucas Trotter Hut
and notify a ranger. Authorities speculate that a tower of
glacier ice, a serac, broke loose and sideswiped the climbers.

Those three words: "Mark was gone" have haunted Coyle
every day since. "Imagine telling Mark's mum and dad," he
said. "I'm alive, and their only son is gone. No body then, no
body now."

.Lyon and Coyle grew up in the same Riccarton neigh-borhood in Christchurch. They'd known each other since kindy. Authorities further speculate that Lyon most likely was entombed in a crevasse. Wanaka Search and Rescue teams scoured the area for weeks when weather allowed. Despite the search then, and several the following year, Mark Lyon's body has not been recovered.

"What if Mark didn't die right away? What if he was waiting for me under the ice? There's been more than one day when I've wanted to kill myself," Coyle said. "Mark could climb circles around me, but he's the one the mountain swallowed."

In the two years since, Tititea/Mount Aspiring has claimed two more climbers. One remains missing.

"I wish Aspiring would give us Mark's body, that's all," Coyle said. "It would bring his parents some peace."

Alexa switched her phone to Airplane Mode and speculated that the surviving friend's wish may have come true.

Chapter Four

Alexa tightened her seat belt as the plane landed and reflected on the three main ways of identifying skeletal remains: DNA, dentals, and radiological imaging. The latter two methods relied on antemortem records. DNA could be retrieved from living relatives, but the comparison, if the cold temperatures hadn't degraded the samples, took weeks.

Her money was on teeth.

Her instructions were to rent a car and drive to Heli-Tours heliport. She pulled her suitcase through animated arrivals dressed in outdoors attire and toting ski or snowboard bags.

They weren't on their way to view bones.

The glacier woman had called while she was in the air. The slow car rental line gave her time to call back. When Dr. Ball answered, Alexa explained the situation. "The remains are on Blue Peak Glacier. What advice do you have for extraction?"

"It's unusual for bodies to pop up in the winter. The turnover usually happens after the summer when there is thaw and retreat."

A little kid in line stepped on her boot toe. Alexa frowned, and he stuck out his tongue. "Turnover? What's that?"

"Glacial movement." Dr. Ball's voice was young. "Don't assume who it is. Glaciers carry bodies kilometers from their original location. Is the skeleton in its entirety?"

"Only a skull and boot and some rope have been recovered."

"The skull and femur are the bones most often recovered."

An image of a seal sticking its head out of a hole in the ice popped into Alexa's mind. "How do the bones, um, scatter?"

"Crevasses squeeze closed and apply intense pressure. A body would likely be embedded in deep layers of ice and crushed, chipped, and cleaved over the years as the glacier moves down the mountain. It's more common for people who perish in glaciers to show up at the foot of them. Glacier environments are a unique taphonomic agent, you know," she added. "Bodies decompose from the outside in."

Alexa pried her brain away from cleaving and chipping to taphonomy, the process of body decomposition. Unfrozen remains decompose from the inside out. She looked at the kid in line ahead of her, now eating apple wedges. If he keeled over, the microorganisms and bacteria in his little intestines would start devouring the intestinal walls, and enzymes would start eating surrounding tissue. She caught his eye and smiled apologetically.

"There might be preserved tissue or adipocere formation," Dr. Ball continued.

Grave wax. *Gross.* "What advice do you have for protecting the skull during removal?"

"I suggest cutting a block of ice with the skull in it and transporting it to the morgue. Let it thaw there. I can assist the pathologist on the thawing technique. Whatever you do, go slowly to minimize damage."

Alexa thanked Dr. Ball and disconnected. She licked her top teeth. Teeth would lead the way. Cold and ice could not destroy them.

The Budget attendant recommended a four-wheel drive. "We expect more snow tonight."

A flurry of panic descended as she paid with her Auckland

Forensic Service Centre credit card. She was from North Carolina. Everything shut down when snow was merely forecast.

"Would you like to hire snow chains as well?" the attendant asked. "Only sixty dollars."

Snow chains? What were they? "No thanks."

She found her red Kia Sorento in the outdoor lot and immediately fell in love. It had keyless entry and backup cameras, neither of which her eleven-year-old Toyota Vitz had. She pressed the gas, eager to bring Mark Lyon home.

Chapter Five

Heli-Tours was only a mile from the airport. Snow was heaped in piles on the sides of the road, and the pavement was patchy with ice. Winter in August? That was weird. The farther south she traveled in New Zealand, the colder it got. Also weird. The heliport facilities consisted of a boxy single-story booking office, a hangar, and two sleek helicopters.

Alexa's throat dried as she stared at them. Her past included a helicopter incident that she would rather forget.

A single pickup truck was in the lot. She parked next to it, grabbed her backpack crime kit, and headed for the building. Inside, posters lined the walls: couples posing on glaciers, single-file hikers crossing snowfields, ice climbers straddling walls of blue ice, kids in shorts throwing snowballs. In one, a woman in a wedding gown and parka stood on the edge of a snowy abyss.

Alexa scanned the price boards: Snow Landing: $395. Grand Glacier: $695. Glacier Picnic: $850. Heli Skiing: Please inquire.

No thanks. "Hello?" she called.

A door behind the counter opened, and a bearded man came out. "Ms. Glock?"

She nodded.

"*Nau mai.* Welcome. Call me Kevin." His cheeks were sunburned. The pale outline of sunglasses surrounded his light eyes. "We're closed today so I'm helping the DOC lads out."

DOC was the Department of Conservation. The lads must be the rangers chiseling the ice from the skeleton.

Kevin looked her up and down. "I'm going to outfit you. Medium, eh? What size boots?"

Women's New Zealand shoes sizes were the same as in the States. "I wear an eight." She remembered she had on two pair of socks. "Make that an eight and a half."

He disappeared into a back room and came out with mountaineering boots, gloves, a hooded snowsuit, crampons, and a scary axe attached to a leash. "What's that for?"

He pointed to a spike at the bottom. "Use this to test the snow depth." The top was two-headed. One side was a sharp serrated pick, and the other looked like a digging tool, which Kevin thumbed. "Use the adze to cut steps in the snow." He thumbed the other side. "If you find yourself sliding on ice, use the pick to self-arrest."

"Arrest myself?"

"Drive the pick into the ice to break your slide."

Jeez. "Is it steep where we're going?"

"Glaciers flow downhill. Put on everything but the crampons."

She lifted them by the straps. The stainless-steel points looked like shark teeth. "Do I need a lesson in how to walk with these?"

"Just plunge the points into the ice." He pointed to a changing room.

So, no safety demo. Her hands shook as she stepped in, threaded through, zipped, and buckled. She slipped her hand through the ice-axe strap so that it dangled from her wrist. When she reappeared, Kevin nodded. He had also suited up and now wore aviator sunglasses. Panic. Would she go snow-blind? Her tortoiseshell prescription glasses were not the fancy kind that morphed from clear to dark. "Do I need sunglasses?"

"Sunnies are a must."

"I don't have any."

Kevin's eyes flickered to a display of sunglasses on the counter.

Alexa quickly chose blue wraparound frames, paid seventy-nine dollars—a small price to pay for UVA/UVB protection, she told her sticker-shocked self. She switched from her regular glasses (she had slight myopia) to the sunglasses.

She pulled on her beanie, hugged the crime kit, and waddled behind Kevin to the copter. The helicopter was a black glass bubble. "It's the Squirrel," he said. "Can hold up to six passengers."

She used the landing skid as a step and climbed in next to Kevin, stored the kit under the seat, and willed her heart to slow. He handed her a headset. "Ready?"

"How long is the ride?"

"Twenty minutes. We'll pass three mountain ranges and enter Mount Aspiring Park."

She surveyed the array of gauges, dials, buttons, and switches on the dashboard. "Is Blue Peak the only glacier?"

Kevin laughed as he flicked buttons. "We've got a hundred glaciers in the area. Bonar, Volta, and Blue Peak are the largest."

She located the fuel gauge and felt reassured that it registered full.

She wanted to ask more questions, to stall, but the rotors whirled to life, and the bubble lifted. When she opened her eyes, she forgot to be scared. Queenstown and The Remarkables, the mountains where she'd be skiing, were already behind them as they headed—she searched the dash for the compass—northwest.

Mountains stretched in every direction. At first they were

snowcapped and snow-streaked, patches of black and gray peeking through, and then—as if they'd passed through a magic screen—the mountains were entirely white. Then there were no people. Only emerald lakes, slivers of rivers, jagged peaks, cirques, snowfields, and then a road of ice curving between two mountains. It seemed to be alive, a churning river. She pointed. Kevin smiled and lowered the helicopter so she could get a closer look. Through the headset he said, "That's Mercer Glacier."

The ice was frozen ripples, then waves. Veins of dark rock cut through in places.

Kevin shook his head. "That rock wasn't visible last year."

Mountains enlarged and multiplied. Sometimes the snow was dimpled as if a hundred school kids had trampled it. Other times it was smooth, and sometimes it was indistinguishable from the low white clouds slashed through with ridges and peaks.

"That's Skyscraper," Kevin said through the headset. He pointed to another peak. "That one is Spike."

Who would venture into such an alien landscape? Who had been the climber who discovered the skull? Her stomach told her they were ascending. The fear she'd tamped returned with force. She gripped the seat. When she looked down, the earth had split open, revealing gaping jaws. Interspersed with the crevasses were towering columns of ice, each an evil stalagmite, intent on toppling and spearing.

Alexa thought of Mark Lyon. She hoped he had been killed instantly, and not entombed alive like his climbing partner worried. How had he and the other guy gotten to this frozen hunk of wilderness? "How do mountaineers even get here?" she asked through the headset.

"You can reach Blue Peak by hiking two or three days, or by helicopter when weather permits."

A mountain filled the window. Kevin veered so that they skimmed by it instead of flying over it. "That's her. Mount Aspiring," he said. It dwarfed surrounding mountains and had three knifelike ridges. "Blue Peak Glacier is farther down, on her left flank."

A cloud enveloped them. Gusts of wind buffeted the metal bird. Alexa death-gripped the seat and couldn't see through the swirl of gray. She was sure they'd crash into the mountain. As suddenly as they were in the cloud, they were out of it. She saw a glacier zig, then zag between two steep flanks, widen in a level area, and then spill off the edge at an impossibly steep angle. Blotches of color encircled a crack in the level area. People in red and orange snowsuits, she realized. Five in all.

They set down twenty-five yards away, near another helicopter, and in the shadow of a cliff. The rotor wash blew snow into a localized blizzard. Alexa felt like she was in a snow globe. Kevin cut the engine. The blades womp-womped and stilled as the agitated flakes settled. Vibrations leached from her body until the snowy world was deathly still.

Chapter Six

As soon as she wormed her fingers into the gloves and unlatched the copter door, cold pounced like a stalking polar bear. Panic again. How would she work her camera while wearing gloves? Or examine a frozen jaw? Would her fingers get frostbite if she took the gloves off?

She was out of her element.

She shouldered the backpack crime kit, clutched the crampons and ice axe, and extended first her right foot and then her left onto the landing skid. When she stepped to the ground, her boots broke through three inches of crust. She hopped back to the landing skid.

Kevin rounded to her side. He lined his crampons in front of him. "Toe first." He slipped his large boot into the front binding and then snapped into the heel. "Like stepping into skis," he said. "Do you ski?"

She shrugged modestly. She'd skied three times at Appalachian Ski Mtn. in Blowing Rock, North Carolina.

Kevin tightened the straps. It looked easy-peasy. She eased off the skid, leaned against the copter for balance, arranged her crampons, and stepped in like a pro.

"They're on the wrong feet," Kevin commented.

How was she supposed to know there was a right and a left? She flushed as she switched them. Straps tightened, she breathed deeply. The frigid air made her lungs constrict. She breathed through her nose, which helped. She zipped her suit up to the chin and pulled the hood over her beanie. She stabbed the pointy end of the axe into the snow ahead, which forced her to hunch, and took a tentative step.

"As many tines in contact with the snow as possible," Kevin advised. "The rangers staked a safe route to the remains."

Small yellow flags led to the group of five people, their backs to her.

Alexa stomped straight down. The tines dug into ice. She threaded the axe strap over her wrist and walked alongside Kevin. Peaks surrounded them in every direction but one. A football field away, the glacier slipped over the lip of the world and disappeared.

Kevin followed her eyes. "That's Gloomy Gorge. Need equipment to climb it."

Need a head examination, too, Alexa thought.

He pointed one peak over. "That's Mount Avalanche."

Her chest tightened. "Is there avalanche danger?"

"There's always a chance. But glaciers are a safer terrain than other places because there's less gradient between the air and ground temps."

They had landed to the side of the glacier. It spread before them, gray and crusty at the edges, some bare rock and boulders interspersed with blocks of ice and layers of snow. Wavy ice covered the surface. In random places the ice slit open, revealing an impossible blue, a lucid aquamarine. "Why is it so blue in places?" she asked.

"Glaciers are compressed snow. The denseness absorbs every color on the spectrum but blue."

"It's beautiful."

"It's not a good sign, though. Blue ice is bare ice, stripped down. Should have a coating of snow over it."

The glacier looked healthy to her sun-protected eyes. She wanted to ask more, but Kevin trudged past ice stacked like broken glass, toward the first flag. She took a deep pull through her nose, smelling the air: invigorating and thin, with a hint of peril. She followed Kevin, planting her crampons with each step, ice axe at the ready. The snow creaked. The wind blew. The cold made her cough.

Second flag conquered. She paused, locating the third flag. It was at the edge of the glacier and steeper than she had imagined. Kevin clambered up and onto it. She swung the axe into a chunk of dirty-looking ice, testing it. The adze bounced off. She thrust harder. It caught. She used it as leverage and pulled herself up. Her right boot lodged between ice-coated rocks, and she stumbled. She crawled forward and looked up to make sure no one was watching.

Everyone was.

She stood and steadied herself. Kevin gave her a thumbs-up. She stepped over a foot-wide crack and a series of frozen white-caps. Shy of the pod of people, a single mocha-brown hiking boot lay on its side, a dark lanky material spilling from its innards. A sock, maybe? Rusty crampons were still attached to the sole by frozen leather straps. The boot looked circa modern age.

She stomped her crampons hard in the surface as she approached it. The material *was* a sock—*wool*, she thought, and through a hole she spotted bone. The ankle talus or tarsal, maybe. Detached from the tibia.

Human remains.

She struggled the backpack kit off her shoulders, fished out a yellow marker, and photographed the boot with and without it. A segment of rope coiled beside it like an intestine. Maybe three feet. Nylon perhaps, blue and black twisted together, frayed on either end.

Two park rangers in orange insulated suits, another heli-copter pilot, and a woman in a red Aspiring Guides parka stepped away from a pit they were cutting out when she walked over. Alexa assumed it was where the skull was. The head ranger introduced himself as Rongo and introduced the three others. Duane was his assistant. Kirk was the second copter pilot, and Elke was a guide. All four wore helmets. Alexa's skull suddenly felt like an eggshell. "You saw the foot, then?" Duane asked.

Alexa nodded. "Have you searched the area for more remains?"

A second woman stood apart. She was dressed in a Heli-Tours snowsuit like Alexa's, hood cinched around her face and goggles on. "We aren't searching for more remains at this time," she said.

Her voice was familiar. Alexa swept her hood off so DI Pattie Katakana could see her better.

"Ms. Glock. The tooth fairy. I requested your presence."

They had worked a harrowing case together a couple of months ago. A local principal had gone missing and was later found dead. The Māori detective had been businesslike, com-petent, and extremely private. "How's your arm?"

A deranged woman had slashed Alexa's left forearm during that case. The scar was now a three-inch pink seam. "All better."

The DI scowled at the rangers. "Let's get him out quickly. Families of missing climbers have already called in. They can't be kept waiting a second longer."

Alexa reviewed her mission: Protect the teeth and get the skull—and foot—to the morgue. She readied the camera. One of the rangers sidled up to her. "Got something for you." He held out a clenched fist, turned it over, and opened up. Accented against his dark glove was a perfect incisor. "Human, right?"

It was chisel-shaped, with sharp edges, and had a long single root. "Yes. Did you find it near the skull?"

"More like how did I find it at all, eh? Teeth the color of snow. Even a needle in a haystack is a different color than the hay."

Alexa clumsily extracted a plastic bag from the kit. He let the tooth slide from his hand into it. Alexa tried to log the details, but her Pilot G-2 pen wouldn't work. "What's your full name?" she asked.

"Duane Knight. Wanaka Search and Rescue."

"I need to know where you found it. For my report."

Duane pointed past the skull. "I face-planted near that fissure. Maybe twenty-five, thirty meters that way. That's where it was. I felt like a dentist pulling it out."

Adults have eight incisors. A missing one was visible if someone smiled. How had this one gone walkabout? She tucked the tooth away.

Alexa was ready for the skull. She pulled her gloves off and pulled on latex gloves in case she needed to touch it. She tucked her glue spray into her pocket. The spray was developed by a forensic dentist to stabilize teeth during transport. Then she put the gloves back on, plucked out a few more evidence bags, and hung her Olympus Tough camera around her neck.

"Don't forget this." Duane held out her ice axe.

She grabbed it and joined the DI. "Take a look at what the climber discovered," the DI said.

The others stepped aside.

A square cavity had been excavated at the base of a hillock. Neatly cut striated bricks of ice piled beside it. The depression was large enough to squat in. Alexa searched the bottom, expecting the skull to stare up at her, but the skull poked out of the hillock like a sculpture in relief. The posterior half was still entombed. Alexa's mouth dropped. She hadn't expected tufts of brown hair grazing the forehead.

Skull was Old Norse in origin. *Skalli* meant bald head. This guy wasn't.

She crept closer and knelt. The skull tilted sideways, like a person asking a silent question. *What has happened?* No neck bones were visible; the skull rested between bony shoulder knobs, one of which protruded. Remnants of green material showed through the frosted turquoise ice. Nothing else.

No arms.

No torso.

No legs.

One foot, nearby.

She thought of the musician in Raleigh who had hacked and sawed his ex-girlfriend into parts. Her torso was found one day, her head and leg the next day. A hand had been delivered to Alexa a week later. She had taken fingerprints from it.

But that was human evildoing. In this case, a glacier was the weapon. She officially hated glaciers.

"Get a move on," Duane said. "We're looking at a snow dump sooner rather than later."

Alexa photographed the skull from where she knelt and then dropped into the cavity for a face-to-face. The skull was coconut brown. She gently lifted the frozen wisps of hair. The bulbous forehead was intact. One eye socket was empty. The other was packed with snow like a white pirate's patch. The frontal bone of the right orbit was cracked. The nose cavity was flat. The upper and lower jaw bones were slightly parted, a frozen grimace. No lips hid the teeth.

She hoped Mark Lyon's dental records were waiting in her nice warm inbox. She photographed the skull. Then she zoomed in on the mouth. The jaws weren't open enough for her to see the molars, but she could see a single gap where a premolar was missing. She checked by her feet in case it had just fallen out. The ranger was right. It was worse than trying to find a needle in a haystack. She accessed the visible teeth; overall they looked in good condition.

Before her fingers numbed, her brain registered that John Doe's grimace was toothy. She counted. One, two, three—all the way to eight. He wasn't missing an incisor.

Chapter Seven

A complete set of incisors meant the tooth in the crime kit didn't belong to John Doe Climber. Then to whom did it belong? Mark Lyon's friend had survived. Alexa looked at the rangers and DI Katakana, staring at her curiously. "Eight incisors are present."

"So what?" DI Katakana said.

"Duane found an incisor." DI Katakana looked around the vast snowy landscape like it was an enemy army. "Are you saying there's another body here?"

"Could be another missing climber," the female guide said. Reindeer or Elk. "Might be the foot doesn't match the skull."

That sounded weird, but Alexa knew what she meant. The wind gusted, twirling snow into minitornadoes. Something brushed Alexa's cheek. She looked up. Snowflakes.

"Front is moving in," Kevin announced. "We need to hurry."

Alexa nestled her camera into her parka against her chest and then sprayed the stabilizing glue in the mouth and teeth area, relieved the nozzle hadn't frozen. The spray glue would help prevent damage and fragmenting of the dental remains. She removed her outer glove and touched the cheekbone to test for fragility. There was no sign of preserved tissue or grave wax, which could present in a greasy or crumbly white or gray substance.

The zygomatic felt rock hard. "We need a shelter to protect the remains from the snow," she told DI Katakana.

"No time," she replied. "Just get it out."

Alexa recalled what Dr. Ball had said. She looked up at the rangers. "Can you remove the remains in a single block of ice? It will keep the bones in the right position."

"We can use the chain saw," Rongo said. "Then slip it in a body bag."

While they gathered equipment, Alexa decided to snoop in the area where Duane found the incisor. She hauled herself out and stood, making sure her crampon tines stabbed the ice, and waved to Duane. "Show me where you found the tooth."

"Is it safe for her to walk around?" DI Katakana asked.

Elk or Reindeer piped up. "I'll rope her."

Rope her? What was she? A horse? She left the crime backpack with DI Katakana and patted her sternum to make sure she had the camera.

The guide produced some equipment and instructed her to step into a waist belt contraption with attached leg loops. "Like pulling on pants," she said.

Duane pulled on a harness as well. "I'll lead, you'll be in the middle," he told Alexa. "That's the safest spot for a person with the least experience."

"Try no experience." Alexa got her first leg threaded through, but the crampon of her left boot caught on the loop. The female ranger guided her boot through and pulled everything up and tightened the waist belt around her snowsuit. Even through the padding, the straps cut into her groin. "Is this necessary?" she asked.

"Better safe than sorry if you want to walk in an area we haven't tested," the guide said. She jerked the harness even tighter.

"I don't remember your name," Alexa squeaked.

"Elke, with an *e* at the end."

All she could see of Elke—between helmet and parka

collar—were perfect white teeth and chapped lips. Alexa's eyes must have shown fear.

Elke smiled. "No worries."

Alexa's frozen lips wouldn't smile back. Elke clicked a cara-biner onto Alexa's harness and threaded a rope through it. She did some fancy knots and attached the rope to her own harness. Then she measured a distance of rope by stretching a portion between outstretched hands, made a knot in it, and repeated the process. Duane was doing the same with his bit of rope. "Seven arm spans. I'll be ten meters ahead, Elke ten meters behind. Keep a slack in the rope."

Duane weighed more than Elke, who weighed less than Alexa. Shouldn't he be the anchor? Focus on the mission, she told herself. A human tooth had been found at a certain loca-tion. She wanted to see if there were more, or if the source of the tooth was visible. Meaning: Another skull. The focus worked. She calmed. She heard the chain saw power to life. She patted the camera through the snowsuit and zipped up to her chin.

Elke nodded at Duane, who set off toward the icy drop-off. The fissure—or crack in the ice—was only twenty-five yards away, give or take. Alexa planted her boots firmly and followed, conscious that she was heading downhill, at a steeper angle than she'd experienced walking from the copter to the skull.

Her boots crushed through ridges of snow. Sometimes the ridges were separated by troughs of blue-tinted ice. It was hard, but she was managing it. She was okay. She was walking on a frigging glacier. If only her brother, Charlie, could see her. He was a geoengineer and loved all things rock. Of course a glacier was made of ice and snow, but it rested on rock.

"Here's where I found it," Duane yelled. He was peering in a fissure fifteen feet ahead.

Alexa squeezed the ice axe tightly and increased her speed.

The rope trailing behind her went taut. She felt Elke tug it. She slowed. Her feet slid out in front of her, and she skidded across the last four feet, on her butt, into Duane at the lip of the fissure. *Jeez.* She grabbed his shoulder.

"Whoa. Shit," he said.

Alexa's heart thudded in her ears.

"Everything okay?" Elke yelled.

"All good," Duane said.

She crabbed back a few feet and stood on shaky legs. "Sorry."

Duane started rooting in the fissure.

Then the crust beneath Alexa caved in.

Chapter Eight

She fell. She bounced. She slammed into something hard.

Layers of blue sped by.

Ice axe. Ice axe.

Miraculously, the handle was in her hand. She jabbed the adze into ice, once, twice, a cat clawing, claws catching. She spread her legs, kicked her crampons into either side of a narrow chute, slowing her fall. One foot found a ledge but slipped off, and she was sliding again. Pain pierced her forehead. The weight of her body wrenched the ice axe, jerking her arm socket, her feet scudding along walls of ice. She careened, then jolted.

To a stop.

The ice axe caught on something, yanked off her wrist, clinked, dropped.

Her lungs heaved. Her right cheek was pressed against ice. Her eyes focused on a bubble trapped behind glass. Faint bluish color was everywhere. Snow trickled by her nose. Her feet hung uselessly. Above a void.

Don't look down.

It was quiet, except for someone's ragged breath. She had been swallowed by a crevasse.

She tasted blood. A droplet spilled from her mouth onto the ice at her chin. It spread like a Rorschach card in red and pink.

"Are you okay?"

She jerked at the sound of Duane's voice. Instead of looking up, she turned her head—her neck worked—and looked down.

No.

The chute widened and then narrowed. If she slipped another ten feet, she'd be wedged between walls of ice, her chest constricted.

"Oh, Charlie," she mewled. She craned her neck up and saw the hole her body had punched through the crust almost two stories above. Impossibly far. There was a tantalizing glimpse of sky. Duane's face peered over the edge.

"We've got you," he called.

The harness had saved her life. Then the rope slackened. She dropped a few inches. Her body spun. *Oh, my God.* Icy air blew up from the bowels like from a city sidewalk grate. She spread her hands, groped at slick ice for handles. She settled on the rope with her left hand and a ledge with her right. Contact kept her from spinning. Panic budded, bloomed, threatened to erupt. Her breath came in short pants. She fought against the terror by inhaling lungsful of oxygen. *Get a grip, Glock.*

Deadweight. She was deadweight as she waited. Weighted. What if the rope gave? What if Elke couldn't hold her weight?

A drop of rain or snow plopped on her shoulder. Oh, crap. The glacier was melting. What if it shifted and cleaved her in two?

"We've set an anchor, Alexa." It was a different male voice. One of the other rangers. "I'm securing the crevasse lip."

More droplets on her shoulder. She didn't want to let go of the ledge and start spinning again.

"Can you climb out?" the voice said.

Was he crazy? Alexa spread her legs, found a toehold on one side, nothing but a slick freezer on the other. "Pull me up!"

"You're okay." The voice was calm, authoritative. "Elke is setting up a rescue pulley."

Alexa heard more voices, then nothing. The weight of her dangling body set her groin on fire. She spread her legs, found a toehold with her right, a larger one for her left, and pulled up on the rope to lift herself a few inches, relieving a little pressure on the harness. There. No more dangling. Why was nothing happening? Had they forgotten her? Had Mark Lyon been stuck like this? Had he frozen to death? Cold air sinks. She felt it slicing through her jacket. The human body is 80 percent water. All that water is susceptible to freezing. Was her blood freezing?

Loud panting filled her ears. Her heart beat at a hummingbird rate. She had to get in control. She looked up. Duane stared down. "I'm lowering a pulley attached to a carabiner," he called. "When it gets to you, clip the carabiner into the belay loop on your harness."

TMI. "What?"

"The green loop, right at your belly button."

She couldn't do it. "I'll climb out," she yelled. She looked up to plan a route. A foot slipped. She spun, bumping the icy wall. She flung her arms wide to stop the twirl.

The pulley and carabiner appeared in front of her face. She grabbed it. She looked down and found the loop on her harness. It was a different color from the rest of the harness. Smart. To help climbers in distress. Her hands shook. She had to bite a glove off so her bare fingers could work the release. The lever opened, slipped, closed. She tried again. Open. She snapped the carabiner to the loop. "Okay," she called.

The glove fell out of her mouth.

"Help us out by pulling up on the rope you're attached to," Duane called.

Alexa felt a jerk. She grabbed the rope and pulled with all her might. Pulled and pulled, one glove and one bare hand, one after another, that hand-on-top game kids play. My hand. Your hand. Slap. Slap. Slap. She jerked higher, closer to the irregular rim, to the sky, to life. The passing walls of ice were stratified and beautiful: blue ice, clear ice, sparkling ice. Close to the lip she spotted something red.

"Wait. Stop!"

The pulley ceased. "Are you okay?" Duane called.

Alexa blinked. What the freaking hell? Encased in opaque ice was a human pelvis.

Wearing a Speedo bathing suit.

Chapter Nine

She let go of the rope, spread-eagled her feet to keep from spiraling, whipped the camera out from her snowsuit, and snapped several photos. She felt a jerk. She let go of the camera and clung to the rope. In seconds she was pulled onto the snow like an inert ice fish, the camera digging into her chest, three, four feet. Then there were rangers' hands under her armpits, dragging her farther from the hole.

"Gotcha," Duane said.

She sat up. Rejoiced. Smiled like an idiot at the three people surrounding her: Elke, Duane, and the head ranger, Rongo. Her bare hand pressed hard into granular snow. She dug her fingers in, aware she was sitting on a slight slope. Through a flurry of snowflakes she saw that drop-off, Gloomy Gorge.

A disarticulated pelvis? A red Speedo?

She craned her neck toward where they'd found the skull. DI Katakana, near the closest yellow flag, scowled in stormy fierceness. The helicopter pilot, Kevin, stood next to her.

Elke and Duane helped her stand. "You're bleeding," Duane said.

Alexa didn't know from where. Her hood was askew, half blinding her. Her new sunglasses had miraculously stayed in place. She took a tentative step—pressing the tines firmly into the packed snow—and concentrated on her body. Adrenaline masked any pain, though her forehead throbbed. She touched it with her bare hand and found the source of blood. She was more worried about the camera. It had been dragged through the snow. She tucked it back into the snowsuit. Rongo pointed at a rescue sled he'd pulled over and urged her to lie down on it.

She was tempted. Then the strange image of the pelvis pumped more adrenaline through her veins. She blinked back tears. "I saw…" What exactly had she seen? She swallowed and tried again. "I saw a human pelvis. In a bathing suit."

No one spoke. Then Rongo said she better get checked out by a doctor. "Might be you're concussed." He wrapped an emergency rescue blanket around her shoulders. She grabbed an edge with her bare hand. It was heated. Wind gusted, lifting the blanket. She was alive. Elke and Duane and Rongo had saved her life. She swiped at her nose and looked at Elke. "Falling in that hole?" Tears bullied their way to her cheeks. "I thought… Well, thank you for getting me out."

"No worries," Elke said. "That's our job."

Rongo jerked the empty sled back toward the helicopters.

Duane looked at his retreating form. "Rongo would have lost his job if something had happened to you."

Something did happen to me. Her hands trembled as she unclipped the rescue carabiner/pulley and started worming out of the harness. The chemical blanket slipped off one shoulder, and a crampon tangled in the rope. She fell backward, onto her ass. Quicker than the scream flying from her mouth, she was sliding, legs out in front, the surface oil-slick, toward Gloomy Gorge. Wait. What?

Dammit!

The ground steepened. She was a kid on a saucer, no control, hurtling toward the drop-off.

"Roll over," a man screamed. "Roll!"

The words registered. She flipped to her belly, clawed at the snow, dragged her boots into it, slowing infinitesimally, slip-sliding toward the void.

The rope attached to her waist went taut. The umbilical cord brought her to a halt.

Before she could react, a great weight like an avalanche landed on her back, smothering her body. "Fucking hell. Don't move."

A man's voice.

Rongo had flopped on top of her. Her lungs were in a vise. She turned her face to the side to breathe. His arm was stretched, his hand around the shaft of an axe. The pick end was driven into the snow. The rope jerked again. Rongo released the axe. More of his body weight settled on top of her. Coarse snow abraded her cheek. The sunglasses smooshed into her face. Her glove-less hand dragged along the surface. They were hauled, inch-by-infernal-inch, up the slope.

She felt ashamed. When she saw boots—again—Rongo rolled off. He clambered to his feet and growled, "Mistake to bring you up here."

Alexa stayed prone, one cheek frozen to the ice, afraid to move. Everything she did on this hunk of terror was wrong. She summoned some strength, rolled over, and sat up. Elke and Duane, their faces white, caught her by the armpits and hauled her to a stand. The original rope that had tethered them together—the one she had been eager to shed—had saved her life. Again.

"Let's get to the helicopters before we unclip," Elke said.

She clasped Duane's arm as he rewrapped her in the rescue blanket. Her legs were jelly. "I'm sorry. The ice. I was flying." Tears stung her eyes. She was blind. She groped the sunglasses off and let them fall. "I couldn't stop. You saved my life. How can I—"

"Buy us a beer," Elke said. She retrieved the sunglasses and slipped them into Alexa's suit pocket.

Slowly, they ushered her toward the open-mouthed DI Katakana and Kevin. He pointed to the sky. "We have to leave."

A thunderous clap made Alexa whip around. A hunk of ice the size of a city bus slammed down a cliff one peak over.

"That's Mount Avalanche," Kevin said.

Chapter Ten

DI Katakana rode shotgun with Kevin. Alexa was tucked into the back row of the copter by the rangers. Elke removed the crampons from her boots. She set the crime kit on Alexa's lap.

The body bag containing the skull sat next to her. The boot, wrapped in another body bag, was on the floor below it.

Kevin lifted off the mountainside and flew straight over where the ice had cleaved off Mount Avalanche. Snow dust obscured the view. "That was a massive slip."

Get me out, Alexa thought. She pulled off her remaining glove and pressed her hand against her sternum, feeling for the camera, praying it would live up to its name: Olympus Tough. Her breath came in juddering bursts. Her life had hung in the balance twice, once in the bowels of a crevasse, and once on the edge of an abyss.

She wiggled her toes. The fingertips of her right hand were white and insensate. She made a fist, clenched and unclenched it, and then double-wrapped it in the chemically heated blanket. A gust juddered the copter. They would probably crash.

Why not? In her one year of living in New Zealand, she'd used up all her luck. Māori war clubs. Sharks. Gaffs. Rock slides. Knives. Now falling in a freaking crevasse and hurtling on ice.

Tears trekked across her raw cheeks. She shivered violently and pulled the blanket tighter.

Kevin was on the radio, issuing frightening terms: "limited visibility" and "sustained gusts." He hunched over the steering control. DI Katakana stared straight ahead, motionless. Her lips moved, but no words tumbled out.

Who was Pattie Katakana? Alexa wondered. The first female Māori detective inspector, proficient and aloof. What brought her happiness? Was she praying? Whom did she love?

Whom do I love?

Bruce. She shivered, even as heat radiated from the blanket.

DI Katakana spoke up. *"Ehara i te aurokōwhau, he takerehāia."*

"What does that mean?" Kevin asked.

"Not a leak in the upper lashings, but an open rent in the hull."

"No worries," Kevin replied. "The copter will hold."

"I have faith in your piloting skills. I'm speaking of climate change," the DI said. "These sudden storms. The disappearing glaciers."

They barreled through the tempest and came out the other side, Queenstown sparkling in the distance, the snow delicate and light. When they landed at Heli-Tours, Alexa let go a gallon of air.

Kevin radioed for an ambulance to take the body bags to the morgue. "I'll wait here for them to arrive," he offered.

Light was waning as she and the DI climbed out. She waited for her land legs and clutched her kit and the wadded-up rescue blanket. When her bones and muscles kicked in, she followed the DI to the building and into the dressing room. She wanted to kiss the concrete floor as she sat on a bench and pulled off her boots. "We made it."

The DI didn't answer.

Alexa set aside the kit and blanket and removed the camera from inside her parka. The DI yanked at her snowsuit zipper. It was caught and wouldn't budge. She glared at Alexa. "Everything was fine on that bloody glacier until you showed up."

The words were a slap. Alexa was speechless.

"Blasted zip," the DI said. She yanked and tugged. "You bloody well dropped through the earth. If that ranger hadn't thrown herself into the snow, you'd have dragged her in as well."

She was right. Elke could have died. Rongo, too. Alexa unzipped her suit and fumbled out of it, the cold air of the dressing room chilling her to the bone. Her body asserted itself. Her arms and groin ached. Her right hand tingled. Her forehead throbbed. She walked stiffly to the mirror. Raw cheeks, wild eyes. A hint of defiance. Hair a frantic static.

She was alive. So were the rangers. She held her hair back. The gash in her forehead was an inch wide. She wet some tissue and pressed them on it.

"All you needed to do was access the skull, but, no—you go tramping across Antarctica. What if you flew off that glacier?" The DI took the suit in both hands and ripped the zipper apart.

Heat gathered in Alexa's chest. Her voice erupted. "*You* requested my presence. I didn't volunteer. I was told the glacier was stable." She stood straight and fierce. "I should sue the police department for putting my life in danger."

The DI threw the snowsuit aside and sat on the bench. Her nose was running. Alexa handed her three tissues. Their eyes met in the mirror: Alexa's a sizzling green, and the DI's onyx daggers. Alexa watched them soften.

"I couldn't move an inch to help you."

Alexa sat next to her. "We've got the skull and boot, and I'm okay." Hot shower. Warm bed. Bruce. All three, right now.

"I lost a friend."

"On the glacier?"

"In Mount Aspiring Park. A long time ago. I was doing a four-day outie with the girls from uni. The Gillespie Pass Circuit. A fine day turned into a blustering gale out of nowhere. Helena got separated from the rest of us. We were frantic when we noticed, calling for her. We searched together and when we could, called for help." She bowed her head and squeezed her knees together. "I had the map and compass. Helena didn't have anything."

"Did you find her?"

"It took LandSAR two weeks. Those were the longest two weeks of my life and unbearable for her *whānau*. They found her in the end. Drowned in the Makarora River. What if Helena had never been found? If she was still out there?" She stood heavily. "At the station there's a family that's been waiting thirty years. Find out if our skull belongs to Mark Lyon. The boot brand is enough for a preliminary ID if it matches what he was wearing. Are you able to head to the morgue?"

Alexa wanted to crawl under covers and hibernate. But what if it were Charlie who was missing? She lifted her right hand, wondering if she could use it. The fingertips were pinking up. "I can."

The DI bowed her head. "There's nothing for it but to tell the family exactly what we've got. Body parts."

"Wait," Alexa said. "There are more. When I was in that crevasse, I saw a pelvis." She doubted herself. Maybe it had been an optical illusion—a glacier mirage. She turned the camera on. The three photos were slightly out of focus. She enlarged the best one and showed the DI. A faded red Speedo was frozen to the iliac crests, or wings, obscuring the sacrum. The height of the iliac crests suggested male.

"What is that? Underwear?"

"I think it's a bathing suit."

"The SAR team are going to have to retrieve it."

Not with me, Alexa thought. "There's that incisor, too. The bones might belong to two different people."

The skull on ice emerged in her mind. The mandible and maxilla, the hinged parts of the jaw, opened in a grimace—maybe half an inch wide. "Has Mark Lyon's family released his dental records?"

"I sent them directly to Dr. McKenzie."

Alexa had worked with the pathologist before. "I doubt I'll be able to take X-rays until the jaw thaws." She wasn't sure about postmortem CT scans and frozen remains, either. "We'll take DNA samples to see if the skull and foot come from the same person. That will take time."

"If the dentals match, and the brand and size of boot is what Mr. Lyon wore, that'll be enough. I'll drop by the morgue in an hour or so."

Chapter Eleven

Alexa summoned strength and went to thank Kevin, who stood behind the counter. "I lost a glove and the ice axe," she said.

"No worries." He pushed a mug of tea toward her. "Almost lost *you*. What was it like in the belly?"

She gulped, grateful for the warmth and sweetness of the tea.

He fingered his beard, waiting.

"Snow fell with me. I just remembered that. We fell at the same speed." *Falling at the speed of snow.* She felt it in her stomach, the lurch, the weightlessness, the helpless suspension. "The light was murky blue. I don't know how much deeper that crevasse went, but the passageway narrowed."

"Average depth of a crevasse is forty to sixty meters." He reached under the counter and produced a Whitaker's almond chocolate bar. He tore it open, broke it in half, offered it to her. "Belly of the whale. Like Jonah."

She paused mid-chocolate-chew. *"Moby-Dick?"*

"The Bible. A foreshadowing of Jesus's crucifixion. Don't see how I can keep doing my job, flying tourists to the glaciers."

"What do you mean?"

"My daughter flight-shames me. I don't blame her, the way the glaciers are beating a retreat, and me churning out the fossil fuels to hunt them down. They're slipping through our fingers. It was probably a snow bridge that collapsed under you. That's climate change right there. Never would have given way ten years ago."

Alexa finished the last of the chocolate and drained the tea. "Tell your daughter you helped bring a climber home to his family."

"Nah, yeah. She'll like that."

While the SUV heated up, Alexa called Dr. Ball. "The skull and foot—there were bones in the boot—have been taken to the morgue. Both are encased in ice. And I spotted a pelvis not far away from where the skull was found. We weren't able to excavate it. How should I proceed?"

Alexa drove through a light snow reflecting on Dr. Ball's instructions. Wasn't any different from thawing a thick rib eye.

Chapter Twelve

A middle-aged woman hovered near the check-in desk at the Lakes District Hospital. Alexa sensed her eavesdropping as she showed the attendant her ID. "I'm here to see Dr. McKenzie."

The volunteer's eyes darted to Alexa's forehead. "I'll call the morgue, see if he's available."

Alexa watched the eavesdropper scurry across the lobby to an elderly man. He stood from a bench, head bowed, to hear what she said. Then they looked her way.

Uh-oh.

"Dr. McKenzie is in his office." The attendant handed her a visitor's pass. "It's on the third floor."

Alexa knew the way. She stuck the pass on her fleece and headed toward the elevators instead of the stairs. Three flights felt impossible. She wasn't surprised when the eavesdropper and her companion intercepted her.

"Are you with Search and Rescue?" the man asked.

The hope in his eyes tugged at Alexa's heart. She adjusted the crime backpack to a more comfortable position. "I work with forensics. May I help you?"

"They brought my son's body here," the man said. "I'm Douglass Lyon. My son is Mark Lyon."

The fifty-something woman with him looked beseechingly at Alexa. "I'm Mark's sister, Diane Cottle. We've been waiting hours at the police station. They told us the remains were sent here."

What she had just been through was nothing compared to their ordeal. "We did transfer some remains here."

"Oh, my," Mr. Lyon said. "Mark has come home. I can't—"

"No identification has been made," Alexa said quickly. "DI Pattie Katakana will be here soon. She'll have more information."

"Was he wearing the green coat?" Mr. Lyon asked. "We gave it to him for Christmas."

"A GORE-TEX." The sister smiled. "He loved that coat. And we heard a boot was recovered. Was it a Danner? Mark wore Danners, sized ten and a half."

"I don't know the brand."

Mr. Lyon cleared his throat. "I've waited all these years for my boy to come home."

In the elevator Alexa breathed deeply to regain the iota of emotional balance she had left. She texted DI Katakana, explaining that Mark Lyon's father and sister were at the hospital, waiting for news.

The forensic pathologist's door was ajar. He unfolded his lanky body from a desk chair and stood, smiling at her. "Ms. Glock. We meet again."

When they last worked together, he had mentioned retirement so that he could devote more time to his passions: archaeology and a grandson. "Still not retired?"

"Three months to go. That's a nasty gash on your forehead. What happened?"

She hoped it wasn't still bleeding. "I had a run-in with the ice."

"Would you like me to take a look?"

She almost caved at the warmth in his eyes. "It's fine."

Dr. McKenzie's thick gray eyebrows knit together. "I assume your injury is related to the popsicle downstairs."

Popsicle was morgue-speak for frozen corpse. Humor was

a way to cope with the distresses of the job. "A skull and foot were recovered on Mount Aspiring. Plus, there's a pelvis, but we weren't able to excavate it."

Dr. McKenzie shook his head. "Torn asunder and disgorged by a glacier. It's happening wherever there are glaciers. Two soldiers from World War I just emerged in the Italian Alps."

She took a deep breath. "The pelvis is wearing a man's bathing suit."

The doctor frowned. "People in the throes of hypothermia sometimes strip off their clothes. Paradoxical undressing. The brain interprets extreme cold as feeling hot."

Alexa pictured herself stripping off clothes in front of the rescue team. "I might have just met John Doe's father and sister. They're downstairs. Have you received Mark Lyon's dental records?"

"I have, I have. They won't do much good until we can part the jaw."

"What about CT scans?"

"Ice decreases density. I'm waiting until our specimens thaw."

"Maybe I can take preliminary X-rays."

Dr. McKenzie picked up an old-fashioned desk phone and made a call. "Transfer 4907A and B to the autopsy suite." He straightened the collar of his button-down shirt and pulled on a lab coat. As they descended the stairs to the basement, Alexa willed the bones in her legs to do their job. She clutched the rail and recounted Dr. Ball's thawing techniques. "She suggests twelve hours at ten degrees Celsius, and then another twelve at fifteen, followed by room temperature."

Dr. McKenzie pushed open the door at the bottom of the stairs and held it for Alexa. "I was going to overnight the specimens at eighteen Celsius and then let them sit at room temperature."

Either way, by Sunday morning the jaws would thaw so that Alexa could see what secrets the teeth would reveal. The thought strengthened her to get through the next hour.

Through the glass of the anteroom, she watched a technician wheel a cart holding two oddly shaped body bags into the autopsy suite. He unzipped the larger bag and hefted the hunk of ice onto an exam table. The protruding skull faced the ceiling. The tech stared at it and then removed the hiking boot from its bag and placed it on a second table. The tech nodded at them through the glass and left.

Alexa woodenly pulled on an apron, gloves, and a mask.

"Ready?" Dr. McKenzie asked.

She followed him through the door and made a beeline for the skull, which emerged from the ice like a face surfacing from water. The frozen strands of hair had melted and were now clumped to the bulbous forehead.

Dr. McKenzie shook his head. "I've never seen the likes."

The facial bones glistened in the overhead light. Alexa imagined Mark Lyon's eyes hurting after years of darkness. Photophobia is the term for eye discomfort in bright light, but there were no eyeballs. Just vacant cavities and her punchy thoughts. Alexa swayed a tad. "We also recovered an incisor that isn't from the skull." It was tucked in an evidence bag in her crime kit. "We might be dealing with two different people."

Dr. McKenzie pointed to a greenish fabric through the ice. "Textile remnant, eh?"

"Mark Lyon's father said he was wearing a green coat."

"Let's peek at the boot first."

"Mark Lyon wore Danners," she said.

The leather boot lay on its side, globs of ice attached to the underside and toe. Rusty crampons seemed to claw at the air. She counted the spikes: twelve. They weren't step-in crampons;

they were attached to the boot by leather straps. The darkish woolen sock poked out of the boot's padded collar. The bone was still visible.

"The talus, most likely," Dr. McKenzie said. He tugged the sock to see if it would slip out of the boot.

Alexa thought of the time she and her Raleigh boyfriend had cooked a turkey for Thanksgiving. She had tried to yank the bag of giblets out of the partially frozen cavity. It wouldn't budge, either.

"It's the right boot," Dr. McKenzie observed. He used a magnifying glass to look at the bone through the sock hole. "There's some soft tissue."

She felt queasy. Bones were one thing, but tissue? She prayed the boot belonged to Mark.

"Let's have a look at the brand then," the doctor said.

The crampons obscured the stamp on the sole. The tongue—another place the brand might be stamped—was trapped behind stiff leather laces. Near the metal eyelets on the side of the boot, through the yellow crisscrossed crampon straps, she saw a globe stamped into the leather and a word that started with a *V*.

Her heart sank. This was not a *V* for victory.

Her right fingers throbbed with pain as she took photos. When she enlarged the best image on the screen and added a filter, the brand came into focus: Vasque.

Not good news for Mark's family. She did a quick search. Vasque hiking boots, made in Italy, had been around since 1964.

"Narrows our time frame down, at least," Dr. McKenzie said.

They returned to the skull. Alexa bent close to the bony knob protruding from the ice.

"That's the top of the shoulder," Dr. McKenzie said. "There's a bit of clavicle, too."

There was no neck. Alexa studied the hunk of ice encasing the skull and shoulders. Kevin had said that blue glacial color was a result of layers of snow compacted over the years. She applied this to the seven bones of the neck and figured they had compressed to a flat disk. Her heart compressed. She held on to the table for support.

"What's wrong?" Dr. McKenzie asked.

She wasn't sure how much longer she could stand. "It's been a rough day."

Do it for Mark Lyon's father.

She backed up as Dr. McKenzie extracted a few hairs and dropped them into sample bags. Then he swept the locks to the side. The bulging forehead reminded Alexa that the frontal bone constituted 30–40 percent of facial space.

"Characteristically male," Dr. McKenzie said. "One orbital rim fracture, right side. I'll fetch the portable X-ray for you," he said.

She took photos of the skull and then close-ups of the visible teeth. Then she traded her camera for her dental kit. The neat and orderly elevator, probe, tiny mirror on a stick, forceps, and ruler gave her comfort. Everything in its place. She chose the probe. It slipped from her clumsy grasp, onto the floor. Her fine motor skills were on the fritz. She could do damage. She scrambled for the tool, knew she'd have to sterilize it, and slipped it back in the case.

Dr. McKenzie returned with the machine.

She positioned it next to the ice block. Was it her imagination or was the temperature getting colder? "I'll take a frontal. The others will have to wait."

Fifteen minutes later, she and Dr. McKenzie were back in his office, staring at the dental X-ray on the left-hand side of his computer screen. The right-hand side glowed with a panoramic

X-ray dated June 7, 1994, the last known radiograph of Mark Lyon's teeth, one year before he disappeared.

Alexa pointed at the newer film. She could see a screw. "That's a single-tooth implant."

Her eyes bounced back and forth, comparing the X-rays. The implant was not visible in the 1994 X-ray.

Before Dr. McKenzie reacted, DI Katakana barreled into his office, scaring them both. "What do you know?" she asked.

Dr. McKenzie frowned at her.

"*Aroha mai.* My apologies. The Lyon family is downstairs. I had them escorted to a family waiting room where we can tell them the news."

"The hiking boot is not the brand Mark Lyon wore," Alexa said. "And the dental X-rays are not compatible. Our skull has a single-tooth implant that isn't compatible with Mark Lyon's antemortem X-rays." The revelation was heavy in Alexa's gut, like a swallowed stone. She wanted a different outcome for the family. Instead, their son and brother was still embedded in the bowels of the beast.

That's what she now thought of glaciers: beasts.

DI Katakana took her cap off. "So much hope."

Alexa racked her brain. "Single-tooth implants debuted in the 1970s. That helps us date the skull. It also means John Doe has dental records on file somewhere. When the skull thaws, I'll get better images. I'll be able to play with the balance, contrast, brightness, things like that, and trace the implant to one of the three big manufacturers."

The DI held up a hand. "The tooth the ranger found? Could it belong to Mark Lyon?"

"It doesn't belong to the skull. A strontium isotope analysis will tell us what geographic area its owner lived in when it developed."

"A single tooth is not their boy back." The DI glared at the radiograph. "We need to know whose skull we have. I'll contact Search and Rescue for a list of missing climbers, 1970s onward. Let's go inform the Lyon family."

One last hoop before she crashed.

Alexa made arrangements to meet the pathologist Sunday morning. "Good luck with the thaw," she said.

"Just the tip of the iceberg, eh?" Dr. McKenzie replied.

In the private waiting room, the DI removed her police cap and explained to Mr. Lyon and the sister that she had bad news. They rose in unison.

"The hiking boot is not a Danner like your Mark was wearing." She looked to Alexa. The father and daughter switched their eyes to her.

"It's a Vasque boot, made in Italy." She swallowed to moisten her mouth. "I'm sorry to report the dental records of the remains do not match Mark's."

The father sank into his seat.

"I know how much you wanted it to be your boy," DI Katakana said.

"I took an X-ray of the jaw," Alexa said. "It showed an implanted surgical screw and false tooth."

Ms. Cottle deflated in a slow, sad leak. "Mark didn't have any false teeth."

Mr. Lyon's eyes glistened. "Forty centimeters of snow fell in the two days after Sam came back without Mark. Search and Rescue couldn't get there. Sam should have tried harder after it happened."

"He was injured, Dad."

"*We* should have tried harder."

"There was nothing we could do." Ms. Cottle sounded as if she had repeated these words many times. "Mark was probably already dead."

Alexa flashed back to hanging in the crevasse. What if a slab of ice had blocked the opening after she fell in? Had that been how Mark died?

"I'm sorry" was all Alexa could offer.

Chapter Thirteen

DI Katakana walked her to the SUV. An inch of snow frosted the top. More was falling. The DI dusted it off her windshield. "Are you staying in town?" she asked.

"I'm staying at Alpine Villas."

"Fancy."

She checked; Bruce had texted the address and code, plus: Call me.

"The Junior Snowboard Championship is this week. Already had one boarder charged with intoxication and vandalism. The nutter pulled a fire alarm at a downtown hotel." The DI caught Alexa's eye. "I placed you in danger today. *Aroha mai.*"

Alexa hadn't expected an apology. "It was my fault. I left the secured area. I'm fine. What about the pelvis?"

"A SAR crew will head back when it's safe."

Alexa beeped the door open and slipped in.

The DI gave a curt nod. "Come by the station in the morning."

Alexa turned the heat up and rested her head on the steering wheel as the car slowly warmed. Saying she was fine and being fine were two different things.

Her glacier mishaps would careen out of her mouth if she called Bruce right away. He admired her ability to stay calm, grounded, and scientific. That wouldn't be possible until she processed her near-death experiences. With a glass of wine to ease the journey.

She'd call him later.

The villas, located on Queenstown Road, were only twelve minutes away, and the road was mostly clear. She veered into a grocery store lot, ravenous. She grabbed a trolley and loaded it with sausage rolls, mincemeat pies, and a large frozen pizza. In the bakery she picked up bagels and double-chocolate muffins. She found dark-roast coffee, milk, cream cheese, and bananas.

Snowflakes tickled her cheeks as she loaded her purchases into the boot.

Boot, not trunk in New Zealand. *Trolley*, not cart. *Glass-ee-er*, not glay-sher.

A deathtrap no matter how you said it.

Dammit. She forgot the wine. She returned for two bottles of red and, fully armed, drove to the villas. Just shy of her destination she spotted a restaurant set back from the road. Papa Penguin's Pizza. The lot was full. Through the windows, she saw crowded tables. She envisioned dining there with Bruce, Sammie, and Denise. Laughter. Bonding. Carbs.

Around a bend, the Alpine Villas perched over Lake Wakatipu. The driveway dipped steeply, made a hairpin turn, and then leveled out in front of eight stone-and-wood villas. Light glowed through the glass panels flanking several front doors, including Bruce's, which was number six. A huge silver SUV was parked in front of it. She panicked. Had Bruce's parents made a surprise trip?

His father was a retired barrister, and his mother was Center of Attention. That's how Bruce described her. Her name was Denise. "I hung the moon when we named Denise after her." Bruce had told Alexa this with a dreamy look in his eyes that she'd never seen before. Did everyone want to please their mothers?

No way could she handle an evening with the senior Denise and the barrister.

She found a guest parking spot, grabbed the groceries, and struggled to the door. She knocked. No one came. She typed the code into the keypad and the door clicked. She pushed it open. "Hello?"

No answer. The hallway light must be on a timer.

A dining table was straight ahead, and beyond it, through expansive glass, the lake and mountains were a black canvas splattered with twinkling lights. The living area was to the right, the kitchen to the left. Vaulted ceilings and wooden floors. She turned on the overhead lights. A black-and-white cow-design rug was under the dining table, and a large ottoman of the same fabric sat catercorner to a gas fireplace. All tasteful and impersonal.

She was too beat to be impressed. The fifteen minutes it took to bring everything inside and put the groceries up felt like fifteen hours. She found the thermostat and turned on the heat.

Finally, she hung her coat on one of the hooks lining the foyer and searched for a bedroom.

The primary had an enormous king and an arrangement of photographs on the wall. Smack in the middle was Bruce, arms around Sharla and the girls, who were maybe seven and ten. They wore ski gear, and Bruce smiled proudly.

Sheesh.

She backed out and found a bedroom with a queen bed—no personal photos—and left the room with two double beds for Denise and Sammie.

Music and voices seeped through the wall. Villa 5 was partying.

Her room was a Jack-and-Jill with the girls' room, a shared bathroom in the middle. She had zero practice sharing a bathroom with teenagers. She set her toiletry kit on the counter, then held her hair back from her forehead. The bleeding had stopped, and the skin around the cut was swollen. She popped two Tylenol and headed to the kitchen.

Eat, drink, praise her fortune—*I'm alive!*—call Bruce.

Her body trembled. She closed her eyes. The icy drop-off ran on cinematic repeat in her head. She took several deep breaths to calm down. She stuffed the sausage rolls in the microwave, set the timer, and found a wineglass. Her phone buzzed. Bruce's name flashed on the screen, ruining the sequence of events. "Hello," she said, cheerfully, "I'm in the villa. It's nice."

"Wish I was in front of the fire with you," Bruce said. "Better yet, the hot tub."

Her tongue tied. Plus, she didn't do hot tubs.

"It's only twenty minutes from Coronet Peak, where we're skiing," Bruce said. "How was your day?"

"Fine." Her heart rate accelerated. "How was yours?"

"There was a drive-by shooting in St. John's last night. A duplex. No one was hurt. The family in the attached unit are terrified."

She grabbed the counter to steady herself.

"This is the sixth drive-by in the past two months. Coop and I executed two searches without warrants…"

She stared at the bottles of cabernet sauvignon as Bruce blathered. *Tell him the truth,* the bottles scolded. She sucked in a deep breath and took the plunge. "My day wasn't fine," she interrupted. "I fell into a crevasse."

"You what?"

"On a glacier. On Mount Aspiring." The truth now shared, she grabbed a wine bottle. She prayed for a screw top; it was corked. "The skull I told you about. That's where it was."

His voice was measured. "You didn't mention you were heading to a glacier."

The microwave beeped. The aroma of oily sausage made her salivate. "I was told the glacier was stable. Plus, I didn't want you to worry."

He didn't answer. His anger or frustration pulsed through the radio waves. The silence stretched. She had no energy to defend herself. She put the phone on speaker, set it down, and rummaged through a drawer for a corkscrew.

He sighed. "You fell into a crevasse? Did I hear that right?"

She slammed the drawer. "The snow caved in under my feet."

It wasn't Bruce she had cried out for in the icy coffin. It had been Charlie. What did that mean? "I was roped. The rangers pulled me out." Her groin throbbed. "Afterward, I slipped down this hill, toward a drop-off." She squeezed her hands into fists. Her breath hitched. "A ranger flung himself on top of me."

Stupid. Fat. Tears.

"Who put you on that glacier?" Bruce demanded.

She snatched a paper towel and wiped her eyes. A framed poster on the kitchen wall showed the Coronet Peak ski runs, a dizzying array of crisscrossing arteries with names: Chimney Swoop, Ego Alley, The Hurdle, Dirty Four. She shuddered, took a deep breath, got in Glock Control. "In the crevasse, I saw a pelvis. There are more bones up there, and the skull doesn't belong to whom we suspected."

"Are you hurt?"

"I'm starved."

Bruce laughed. "That's a good sign. I don't like it that you were endangered."

"Your job is dangerous at times," she countered.

"You're right. Raising teenagers can be deadly."

This time she laughed. Tension dissipated. She gave him more details: about the tooth implant and the crushed father and daughter. His steady voice calmed her. "When are you and the girls arriving?"

"Our plane lands at eleven. Will you be free? We're planning to hit the slopes."

Sliding on snow again? "I'll meet you at the villa afterward."

"I need you in my arms," Bruce said.

She disconnected, imagining those arms, holding her tight. The microwave beeped again. She plated the rolls and uncorked the wine. She burned her tongue on the first bite and doused it with wine. Once sated, she poured a second glass of wine and carried it to the living area, switching on the gas fire. She stared into the flames, wondering if she'd even make it until nine p.m. Blue, gold, orange—an amalgam of color drawing her in, sparking the words of that Frost poem again.

I hold with those who favor fire.

Amen to that.

———

Laughter. Music. Thumps.

She tossed the covers back and reached for her phone. Ten p.m. She'd been asleep an hour. The music notched up a decibel.

She staggered to the foyer, pulled her puffer coat on over her pajamas, stepped into her unlaced boots, and clomped next door. Through glass panels she counted three, no, four teenagers sitting around a table, laughing, drinking—maybe beer. The kids looked young, but legal drinking age in New Zealand was eighteen. One kid sucked on a vaping device.

She knocked.

No one looked her way.

She pounded.

A kid put down a bottle, danced to the door, opened it. "S'up?" he said. Sixteen or seventeen, "BFree" across his T-shirt. His longish hair was tousled, parted in the middle.

"I'm from next door," she explained. A whiff of bubble gum—something sickly sweet—wafted in the air. "Your music is keeping me up. Are your parents home?"

A red-haired boy joined him. "Lance," he yelled.

BFree bumped into the kid as he went back to the table. The redhead scowled and followed him. No one turned the music off. It was bouncy, catchy, irritating. A bare-chested twenty-something guy, sideburns down to his jawline, shuffled to the door. He pulled bulky headphones off. "What's up?"

"I'm staying next door. The music is keeping me awake."

He scratched his stomach. "The kids are celebrating the dump."

She felt ancient. Woozy. "The dump?"

"Fresh snow, excellent for boarding. I'm Lance Brown, NZ SNO Z team chaperone and developmental coach. Woke me up, eh?"

"Your music woke *me* up. Alexa Glock. Auckland Forensics."

"Dude. The police," BFree shouted.

"The music?"

"I'll get it," a girl yelled. In a second the music ceased.

Lance swiveled to the kids. "Go to bed, you lot. Super busy day tomorrow."

The girl called, "Big air showoffs. Taking the plungy."

"Hell, yes," Lance said.

Back in the villa, she crawled into bed and turned the mattress warmer on high. Before drifting off she wondered: *Who wears a Speedo on a glacier?*

She heard wailing in the wee hours. Villa 5 again? But no, it was sirens. In the distance and more than one. She flopped down, regretted the sudden movement, pulled a pillow over her head, and burrowed.

DAY ONE

6 NOVEMBER 1984

In my bunk now, seven p.m., writing down the day.

Mount Aspiring Road was unsealed and rutted. Sheep roamed all over. Dodgy stream crossings, sometimes the water went over tires, seeped through the doors. C yelled to floor it. I parked the Valiant at Raspberry Creek. We gapped it along the West Matukituki River, milky blue, ice-capped peaks all around, C singing "American Pie" and dodging sheep shit.

We met a ranger who warned us that avalanche threat was high in the area. "Avoid Quarterdeck Pass. There's a seventy-foot-long crevasse, and a fragile snow bridge forming over it." He also warned us about river crossings. "River crossings cause more deaths than climbing."

Christian talked nonstop. The metric system, the All Whites, McDonald's. I thought about rivers. Up first: Raspberry Creek. Then Matukituki, Rough Creek, and Roaring Cascade.

I reminded myself to undo my chest strap. That way I can worm out of my backpack if I get swept away. We stripped down to skivvies with every crossing. My thighs turned blue every time. Even now, hours later, they tingle.

It started snowing after the Roaring Cascade and the track got gnarly. Roots everywhere. I scrambled up, used my hands. C finally quiet except for grunts and swears. We broke through to where we could see up and down the valley. Everything was covered in snow. The Rob Roy glacier hung above us, a river of frozen dreams.

Aspiring Hut is two rooms. One for cooking and eating with a wood burner, one for sleeping.

The avalanche warning poster freaks me out:

> You have a very small likelihood of surviving a decent sized avalanche: if the fall from being swept over a bluff doesn't kill you outright, expect to suffocate, immobilized in the snow.

A ranger checked in with us. He said a couple Aussies made it to the summit yesterday and it took them ten hours to get down to Colin Hut. Ten hours?

A poem hangs by the door in memory of Major Bernard Head, who made the first ascent of Mount Aspiring in 1909. Here it is:

> What if I live no more those kingly days?
> Their night sleeps with me still.
> I dream my feet within the starry ways;
> My heart rests in the hill
> I may not grudge the little left undone;
> I hold the heights, I keep the dreams I won.

Chapter Fourteen

FRIDAY

Body parts screamed when Alexa crawled out of bed. Tylenol paired with a cream cheese-slathered bagel and espresso worked their magic, although she was disappointed to find a Nespresso machine instead of a French press.

Pods didn't have the same tantalizing smell as fresh ground beans. Plus, only a pea-dab amount came out of the gurgling machine. What was with that?

She found her glasses and stood at the windows in her NC State T-shirt and pajama pants, sipping her inch of coffee. It wasn't snowing, but the deck and hot tub cover had six inches of accumulation. The snow was tinged with gray.

Dirt? Smog? In New Zealand?

She looked down at Lake Wakatipu, jerky and menacing in the dim light. On the far side of the lake, The Remarkables rose sharply. Bruce had said they were "remarkable" because they faced due north and due south, one of only two mountain ranges in the world to do so.

Yesterday's events rushed back as cold seeped through the glass. Charlie. Her baby brother. She had called his name while hanging in the ice tomb. The urge to hear his voice came on strong. Seven a.m. here was two p.m. yesterday in North Carolina. Charlie, a geoengineer, would be fixing a dam or preparing field reports. She let the coffee machine mosh another pod as she dialed his number. She pictured his affable face and hazel eyes, clones of hers, as she waited for a squirt of coffee.

"Lexi? Everything okay?"

Hearing her nickname made her smile. "Charlie. How are you?"

"I'm at work. What's up?"

Falling, hanging, sliding. "What's your latest project?"

"A pedestrian bridge in Riverside Park. Why are you calling?"

She sipped coffee, stalling. "How are Benny and Noah?"

"Ben. I told you he wants to be called Ben. School started last week. Second grade and kindergarten. I can't believe it. They rode the bus together. It broke my heart. Okay. What's wrong?"

She felt a free-falling sensation in her stomach. "I was on a glacier yesterday, and the snow caved in."

"What the hell were you doing on a glacier?"

"Work. A skeleton, I mean, a skull was discovered popping out of the snow. I was part of the recovery team. And then the snow caved under my feet, and I fell in a crevasse. Charlie. I was just hanging in there, in a tunnel of ice. If I hadn't been roped..."

"I can't believe it."

Neither could she.

"Your life was never endangered when you worked in Raleigh. You should come home."

"Where's home? I don't have a home." She was dangling again. She swallowed. Gathered courage. "You're the one I always think about when something happens."

"Move to Asheville. I want the boys to know their aunt."

To be wanted. Her heart swelled. But if she worked at the Western Regional Crime Lab, she'd be pigeonholed into a specialty like she had been in Raleigh. Teeth. Fingerprints. Trace evidence. Her job as a traveling investigator in New Zealand allowed her to get her mitts on everything. "I like it here, glaciers and all."

"A glacier? Really? How about 'know when to say no.'"

"Isn't that a drug slogan?"

"It should be an Alexa Glock slogan."

Her life *had* veered into the danger zone since living Down Under. She asked about Charlie's wife, Mel, and then he asked about Bruce.

"He invited me on a ski trip with his girls."

"You're not going, are you?"

"I'm already here. We've been dating—well, redating—for three months now."

"That's my point. Spending a weekend with the guy's kids after only three months? That's insane."

So now Bruce was *the guy*. She felt confused, torn. Bruce wanted the girls to get to know her. Charlie thought it was a bad idea. Who was right? "I've known Bruce over a year."

"If you pull your love 'em and leave 'em routine, there's kids involved."

That remark was a gut punch.

"Lexi? Are you there?"

The conversation ended tersely. Talking to Charlie had not been the balm she needed. She pushed the cowhide ottoman out of the way and started a Vinyasa Flow to work out her muscles and angst.

She pushed thoughts of the girls away. While she downward-dogged, planked, and held chaturanga, she wondered who the skull and foot and pelvis belonged to. The U.S. had the National Missing and Unidentified Persons system. NamUs used identifiers such as physical features, dental records, DNA, scars, tattoos, and prostheses. She had worked at NamUs during her odontology internship—obtaining, scanning, and coding dental records of missing people into the system.

Timmy Ricci had been her only positive ID. The fourteen-year-old had gone missing from his Wake Forest group home. His house parent said he went for a walk one day and never returned. Nearby woods and Falls Lake were searched, but Timmy was never found.

She held plank until her forearms gave out.

When Alexa had entered the missing boy's scanty dental records two years after his disappearance, the automated system flagged a potential match: a body found in sand dunes at Wrightsville Beach. Timmy's skull had been fractured. The police called it homicide.

Poor kid.

In New Zealand, missing persons information was kept by the police, and dental records were obtained nationally through a network of dentists and internationally through Interpol and the wider network of dental associations.

She flopped on her back but was too antsy for corpse pose.

In the bathroom she checked the gash on her forehead; it looked bad. She dabbed antiseptic cream on it. Her hair immediately stuck to the cream. She coerced it into a ponytail.

The thawing skull popped into her head. What had she read last week? The thawing of the permafrost was releasing dangerous microorganisms and carbon emissions that had been buried in ice for thousands of years.

What danger would be unleashed by the thawing of the skull and foot? None, idiot. A family would finally get answers. If there was any family left.

Khakis, button-down, fleece, thick socks, and boots were her uniform of the day. Plus, coat and beanie. DI Katakana had said to come to the police station in the morning. It was early, but she felt weird in Bruce's family villa. Grabbing a spatula from the kitchen to use as a scraper, she slipped the crime kit over her shoulder and left.

Her nose wrinkled; there was smoke in the morning air.

Chapter Fifteen

She stashed her stuff in the Sorento and trudged on foot up the slippery driveway. Her calves and butt protested. The smell deepened as she crested the drive, standing on the side of the road. A bright-orange fire truck and a police car, lights flashing, blocked the lane of traffic closest to her. A Tesla driver stared glumly ahead.

Conscious of the cars on one side and the steep embankment on the other, she plodded carefully. Something dark—trash, maybe—was in the ditch covered by snow. This was New Zealand. There wasn't supposed to be trash.

Right.

A waft of smoke set her heart racing. Past a curve, the parking lot of the pizza restaurant was full of fire engines and emergency vehicles. She scurried across the road. The restaurant was a smoldering ruin.

"Aw, hell," a voice said.

Alexa turned. The two teen boys from Villa 5 stood behind her. "No more extra-large Italian Stallion. Devo," the redhead said.

The other boy's hair was a disheveled mop. "Like a frigging A-bomb went off." He'd worn the BFree T-shirt last night.

Alexa sniffed. The smoke was tinged with chemicals. Lead or asbestos instead of melting cheese or pepperoni. "We met last night," she informed the boys.

The red-haired one said, "Nah, yeah."

She'd gotten the hang of the Kiwi expression. The meaning hinged on the last word. Yeah, *nah* meant no. Nah, *yeah* meant yes. They walked past, and she followed them to the parking lot.

"Fucking hell," BFree said.

Alexa agreed. The restaurant was a black, smoldering shell bookended by stone walls. Now she and Bruce—and the girls—would never share an Italian Stallion. She mourned her loss.

A sprinkler system had failed. A few pipes, two brick ovens, various knee-high walls, sinks, and toilets had survived the fire. Not much else. A flight of metal stairs on the left led to a second floor that no longer existed.

Caution tape separated the parking lot from the restaurant. A police officer stood guard. Beyond him, a firefighter sprayed into the right corner of the building, smoke rising from the ash. Another perched on an extended ladder above him, dousing the same area. They wore shields and masks to protect their lungs. Standing farther back, a huddle of responders watched.

Alexa nudged up to the tape. Heat still radiated from the charred building. Individual rooms of the restaurant—kitchen, dining, foyer, whatever had been upstairs—were indistinguishable.

A helicopter throttled overhead. The press, probably.

An unmarked car pulled into the lot. Alexa turned, the sudden movement making her wince. Yoga hadn't worked out all the kinks from yesterday's ice follies. DI Katakana, dressed in a dark pantsuit, got out and marched toward the huddle, followed by a male constable Alexa remembered from her first case in the area. Constable Boom or Buff.

She wouldn't be meeting the DI at the station, after all. Alexa searched local news on her phone. *The South Today* came up.

BREAKING NEWS

Emergency services were called to a popular Queenstown restaurant, Papa Penguin's Pizza, just after two a.m. local time (2:00 GMT) Friday. A Fire and Emergency NZ (FENZ) spokesperson said eight emergency vehicles including an aerial unit responded.

"Flames had broken through the roof by the time we were on scene," Queenstown Brigade Chief Ian Ritchie said. "As luck would have it the restaurant had closed hours earlier. Our crews contained the blaze to the stand-alone structure. Local evacuation was deemed unnecessary."

Restaurant owners Kipper and Mattie Parr were unavailable for comment.

Crew remain at the scene, fighting hot spots. Brigade Chief Ritchie said it was too early to determine the cause of the fire or the extent of the damage. "We have called for specialist investigative teams from around the district to assist."

Alexa summed up the extent of the damage: total.

A shout made her fumble the phone.

The ground firefighter waved. Someone shut off the water as two emergency personnel joined him. Another firefighter helped the DI into a bulky yellow coat, helmet, and boots and escorted her to where the firefighter had been spraying water. The firefighter on the ladder climbed down and joined the huddle.

Alexa pressed against the caution tape. The constable she had worked with before quickly intercepted her. "Stay back, ma'am."

His name popped into her head. "Constable Blume. How are you?"

The constable's light-blue eyes widened. "I remember you. Teeth, eh?"

"We've got a body," a fireman shouted.

Chapter Sixteen

Alexa ducked under the caution tape.

"Halt," Constable Blume ordered.

The constable—bossy? He'd been blushing and bumbling when they'd worked together before. But he was right. She was a hindrance and possible contaminator. Plus, her crime kit was in the rental car. She retreated. "Let DI Katakana know that I'm here if she needs me."

He didn't answer.

She sniffed for the putrid steaky smell of burning flesh. Only wet ash and smoke triggered her scent molecules. She used her phone to photograph the firefighters leading DI Katakana around to the rear of the restaurant.

To the body.

A silver Jeep veered into the lot, ran over a cone, and jerked to a halt. A middle-aged man—large and bearded—and woman jumped out. A white ski hat with a fur bobble contrasted with the woman's dark thick hair. She gestured toward the building. Constable Blume intercepted them.

The owners? Or worse—a relative of the deceased? Alexa blinked back tears caused by acrid smoke and snapped pictures of them.

The woman and the man ducked under the tape and marched toward DI Katakana and the firefighters, ignoring Constable Blume. The woman was saying something and gesticulating toward the rubble.

Alexa desperately wished she could hear. A siren made her twirl. A fireman removed cones so an ambulance and a car could enter the lot. Alexa recognized the police photographer, Senior Constable Sally Freeman, dressed in civvies, climbing out of the car. She hung a camera around her neck and grabbed a tripod.

Would the scene still be too hot for her to enter?

Now a rusty compact pulled into the lot. A fireman waved it away. The driver pulled off the road ten yards up, almost in a ditch. She got out, shook her long yellow hair, and slogged toward the scene.

Alexa turned her back and called her boss. Dan was probably still at home, which was biking distance to Auckland Forensic Service Centre. He had one of those folding bikes that looked like it belonged to a kid. He appeared each morning carrying it like a briefcase.

"It's early. Did you retrieve the skull?" he asked.

Alexa rubbed her smarting eyes. "It's at the morgue, thawing. So is a boot with a foot in it. I had a little trouble on the glacier, and there are more bones up there, but that's not why I called."

"Trouble on the glacier? What happened?"

Dan was bird-dog alert to her propensity to act first and rationalize later. "I'm staying at a villa on Queenstown Road— Bruce's villa, I mean DI Horne's—and there's been a fire. Papa Penguin's Pizza Restaurant. It's in the news, and there's a fatality."

"Who is it?"

She watched DI Katakana lead the couple away from the remains, toward the parking lot. "They just discovered it," Alexa said, "five minutes ago."

"Is there a possibility of more bodies?"

She surveyed the ruins anew. "It's possible. The sight is still hot. It's almost total destruction. My services will be needed."

"If DI Katakana puts in a request, I'll start the paperwork. Meanwhile, concentrate on the glacier skull."

Formalities were irksome. Alexa jumped up and down—her toes were cold. The blond woman from the shooed-away car came up, her cheeks bright pink. "Hell. I can't believe it." She was thin, even in an oversize puffer coat, and in her mid-twenties. "I waited tables here last night."

Alexa noted her American accent. "What time did you leave?"

"Closing time. There's my boss." She pointed at the Jeep woman. "Why is there an ambulance?"

"There's been a fatality," Alexa said.

Her grayish eyes widened. "WTF? Who?"

"I don't know."

The woman ducked under the tape and ran toward her boss. It hit Alexa that a lot of people were suddenly without jobs.

For ten minutes she watched the police photographer—outfitted in a helmet, large coat, and boots now—photograph and video the rear area where the body was. Two firefighters stood guard. Alexa would intercept the photographer when she was finished. Sally would know whether Alexa's services would be needed.

Constable Blume escorted the server back to the caution tape. She looked in a trance and headed toward her car.

Alexa slipped under the tape, walked past the protesting constable, and joined DI Katakana and the Jeep couple. The DI glanced at her. "This is Ms. Glock, with forensics. Ms. Glock, these are the owners of the restaurant, Kipper and Mattie Parr."

The man nodded, but the woman didn't even look at her.

"So you thought the building was empty?" DI Katakana asked.

"Yes," Mrs. Parr said. "I don't know who he is."

The DI frowned. "How do you know the deceased is a male?"

Constable Blume materialized by her side and opened his notebook.

"I don't," Mrs. Parr said. Ash clung to the soft white wool of her hat. "This is too much. Papa P's is our livelihood."

"We've a flat above the restaurant," Mr. Parr said. "We let it out. Usually to ski bums."

Alexa looked at the stairs. They had led to an apartment.

"Was someone staying there?" the DI asked.

Mrs. Parr snapped to. "We let it to Graham, but he moved out. Remember? Sudden like. The flat was empty."

A flicker crossed Mr. Parr's face.

"Who do you think the victim is?" DI Katakana asked.

Mrs. Parr looked speculatively at the ruins. "The staff knew we were gone."

"No one was authorized to be in Papa P's after closing time," Mr. Parr said.

"I'll need the name and number for this Graham and all the staff, especially whoever was working Thursday evening. Where were you last night?" the DI asked.

"Two nights ago was our son Dylan's commencement," Mr. Parr said. "Dunedin Town Hall. We stayed an extra day, got home late last night."

A firefighter marched up. "Are you the owners?"

"We are," Mrs. Parr said. "What happened? How did the fire start?"

Soot mixed in with the firefighter's cheek stubble. "I'm Queenstown Brigade Chief Ian Ritchie. It's too early to tell. FRIU is on the way."

FRIU stood for Fire Research and Investigation Unit, which Alexa knew included fire forensics, for which she was not qualified.

"When was your last safety inspection?" the chief asked.

"In June. Everything was up to code," Mrs. Parr said.

The DI pulled Alexa to the side. Before she spoke, Alexa said, "My boss will be in touch with you about me working the fire."

The DI frowned. "I called you to Queenstown because of the glacier skull."

"You'll need an odontologist."

The DI looked toward the ambulance. "We can't move the body until FRIU gives permission. It will be hours. Your priority is the skull identification. Check those missing people records. Find who he is."

A "hot" case superseded a "cold" one, but Alexa bit back her argument. "I'll check in with the police photographer and then leave. Um, that woman who was here? With yellow hair? She served tables last night."

The DI stiffened. "Where is she?"

Alexa pointed. The woman was heading toward her car. DI Katakana ordered a constable to catch her. "Hurry," she said.

The police photographer had finished and was loading her black kit into her car. Alexa told the DI goodbye and caught up with her. "Senior Constable Freeman? I'm Alexa Glock."

The photographer pushed her glasses up the bridge of her nose. "Call me Sally. Teeth, right? Bad scene in there. I hate thermal deaths."

"Will the pathologist need an odontologist?"

Sally wiped her brow. "Absolutely."

"Is it a male or female victim?"

"Can't tell."

Must be really bad. "Can I see the photos you took?"

Sally looked conflicted. "Have you been assigned to the case?"

"My boss is contacting DI Katakana." Or was he waiting for DI Katakana to contact him?

Sally thumbed through photos on the screen. "It's grim."

Alexa took the digital camera, steeling herself, but her back scars constricted anyway. She gasped. Burns were classified by their severity. Her scalding had been third degree and had requited skin grafting.

Memory of the pain coursed through her nerve endings.

Fourth-degree burns present as charred, white skin, and minor bone exposure. In fifth-degree burns, the skin is charred, and bone is exposed. This body was fifth degree to the max.

It was prone on the floor. The skull, in profile, was bowling-ball black. The body ended at the charred buttocks. No legs. The single attached arm bent at the elbow, the wrist contorted awkwardly. No hand. Alexa swallowed back bile. "Where are the other limbs?"

Sally shook her head. "Likely thermally amputated."

Alexa gulped. She scrolled for photos of the jaw and teeth. The last one was a close-up of the skull. A few gray teeth showed through wizened lips. They would need to be protected. The spray glue she used on the glacier skull had been invented to not only stabilize teeth during transfers, but to also help identify victims of fatal burns. Her bottle of the stuff was in the crime kit. *Dammit.* Alexa handed Sally the camera. "The jaw will need to be stabilized before the decedent is moved."

"The fire investigation team know to do it. Autopsy tomorrow morning," Sally said.

Chapter Seventeen

The big SUV was gone from in front of the villa. BFree and team-mates must be on the slopes. She stomped her boots as she unlocked the rental car and retrieved the kitchen spatula. She scraped the windshield with it.

It was harder to scrape away the image of the burned body.

DI Katakana ordered her to work on identifying the skull. She cast a look toward the villa, imagining herself and Bruce in front of the gas logs. Not that they'd display affection. Sammie and Denise would be on alert, she was sure. Her unease about them lessened the farther she drove away from the villa.

The desk clerk at the Queenstown Police Department hitched up his pants. "Ms. Glock. Where's your shovel?"

She laughed. That shovel had been key evidence in the missing principal case. "Good to see you, Sergeant Dryer."

He sniffed the air. "The Papa Penguin's fire, eh? Are you on the case?"

Her jacket and hair must stink. "I'm here because of the skull found on Mount Aspiring. DI Katakana asked me to search records of missing mountaineers. Are they located here?"

"The records are in Wanaka," he said. "An hour's drive, maybe more. Their SAR facility has a library. Journals, logbooks, letters, newspapers, family pleas, bits and bobs."

Wanaka Search and Rescue was where Elke and Duane

worked. She could buy them lunch for saving her life on the glacier. "Are the roads between here and Wanaka clear?"

"What are you driving?"

Kiwis tended to minimize danger, so the question alarmed her. "An SUV."

He checked his computer monitor. "Ow, here you go. 'Snowstorm rolling through after five p.m. Up to twenty-five cm of snow across the Queenstown ski fields.'"

That was about ten inches. She had time to get to Wanaka and back. She returned to the still-warm rental car and called Bruce about the impending snowstorm. His phone was off. He and the girls were probably in the air, but they would get in before the new storm.

The GPS advised State Road six through Cromwell. Traffic was light, and the road was easy until she reached the Kawarau River, where it narrowed and snaked and was separated from the gorge by a flimsy rail.

She slowed to take a hairpin turn and instantly had no traction. She let up on the gas and rode it out, fingers clenched.

Black ice.

Her heart hammered. She crawled along until the road straightened again and depressed the pedal. Wearing hiking boots reminded her of the three-day hike she'd taken when she was sixteen—for gym credits. Twenty-two miles on the Appalachian Trail. She'd befriended a fellow hiker, Joan, a short, feisty volleyball player. They had biology together.

They'd shared a pup tent and talked about boys and tests and the biology teacher. When the weekend trip was over, Joan ignored her. Alexa never understood why.

It hurt, even now.

She looked in the rearview window at her cool new sunglasses. Maybe they would impress Sammie and Denise.

She let her mind dally in Bruceness—his deep voice, his woodsy aftershave, the way his cheek felt against hers, his hands on her skin, causing electric currents. Had her skin always been so sensitive to touch? Or had the nerve endings been dormant until Bruce?

The Wanaka Search and Rescue facility was built into a hillside, bunker-like. Alexa stood in the cleared parking area, watching a fantail bird hop back and forth on a bare branch. The tree, like the others around it, was young and fragile. The snow along the walkway was deeper than in Queenstown, but the sky was still clear. She entered the building and called, "Hello?"

"Be right there," a male voice called.

There was a table in the middle of the room, and the light plywood walls were covered with maps. Letters were tacked to a bulletin board. She read the inside of a thank-you card:

Dear Elke, Manaaki, and Finn,

Thank you for finding our daughter Elizabeth Wade, the American who went missing in the Matukituki Valley. You risked your lives to bring our girl home and you helped us piece together what happened. Now we know she fell and died quickly. That's something to hold on to. We will never be able to hug our free spirit Lizzy again, but at least we have closure.

Vivian Wade
Seattle, Washington

Alexa shook her head, wondered if the Elke in the letter was "her" Elke, then read another.

Kia ora Rescue Crew, especially Don and Poppy,

Tu meke, tu meke for finding me after I slipped down that ridge on Breakaway. I'm recovering quicker than the docs predicted. Ka pai for stabilizing me and treating my frostbite and hypothermia before flying me out. The doc says I had about another hour left before I would have passed on. Lost two fingers, though. Left hand, so all good.

A case of coldies coming your way,
Lenny Bedell
Hamilton

A bald man in a thick red overshirt entered from a hallway. "Don Wood, operations manager. How can I help you?"

"Hello. I'm Alexa Glock. I was part of the recovery team yesterday on Mount Aspiring."

"You're the one who fell down the slot."

What was she, a coin?

"I saw you looking at our trees beside the building. Each one is planted in memory of someone who didn't make it back."

Alexa looked out the window at the dozens of trees. To think one could have been planted for her. *Jeez.* "Are Elke and Duane working today?"

Don shrugged. "Not here. We're all volunteers. There are eighty odd of us."

"I wanted to thank them."

"You can make a donation, eh? Been to a campfire?"

She caught a whiff of her jacket. "A restaurant burned down near where I'm staying. Papa Penguin's."

"I'm gutted. Their loaded veggie? Sweet as. Sergeant Dryer called. He told me to be on the lookout for you. I'm grateful you recovered some remains. A family might get answers. You're wanting the records. Come to the training room."

He ushered her to a large windowless room with tables and chairs facing a whiteboard and pull-down screen. "Cup of tea?"

"I'm good," Alexa said. "How many people are missing in Mount Aspiring National Park?"

"Depends on how far back you go. Our park is popular." He got a faraway look in his eyes. "A wolf in sheep's clothing. That's what we call Aspiring. Not as high as Aoraki Mount Cook, so we get less experienced climbers. Mix that with underprepared trampers—sometimes in jandals or trainers—and the weather."

"Jandals" was Kiwispeak for sandals. Were people crazy?

"New Zealand doesn't have the tallest mountains in the world, but our weather changes faster than anywhere. A bluebird day turns into a snow dump, just like that." Don plucked a clipboard from a shelf. "Here are our most recent deaths."

Alexa set down her tote and skimmed the sheet.

11 December 2024: Anne Shafford, 68,
  Fern Burn Track (tramping)
18 August 2023: Ari Rossman, 21,
  Mt. Aspiring (climbing)
31 August 2022: Mason Katman, 32,
  Volta Glacier (climbing)
05 January 2020: Jeremy Cone, 52
  Mt. Alta (river crossing)

Don gestured to an alcove of bookcases. "But you want the missing, eh? Not the found. How far back?"

She thought of the single implanted tooth in the jaw of the skull. "The 1970s onward."

He gathered an armful of binders and plopped them down in a stack. "Make yourself at home. Copier is over there. Sure you don't want a warm cuppa?"

Alexa changed her mind. "That would be great."

The binder on top of the stack was 1970–1980. She breathed deeply before entering a sad world. The first entry was dated November 1971. A trio of young climbers were missing from Mount Aspiring: Ruth Spitsbergen, 20, Ralph Block, 22, and Warren Euliano, also 22.

Bingo. Ralph or Warren could be her pelvis, foot, or skull.

She skimmed their addresses, phone numbers, and occupations. (Ruth: university student, Ralph: university student, Warren: welder.)

Point last seen was "Northwest flank."

Last seen by Edwin Hill, twenty-one.

A section on the form was titled "Reason for person(s) missing." A fourth member of their group, Edwin Hill, apparently witnessed Ruth slip, catching the other two climbers to whom she was roped off guard. "Dropped ice axes" and "fell long, long, long way" were underlined.

Her heart fell with them.

A form listed each climber's clothing. She skimmed for mention of a red Speedo. No luck. No hiking boot brands were listed, either.

There were no medical files. Contact numbers were listed for each missing climber, followed by a set of number/letter combinations.

When Don delivered the tea, she asked about them. He rummaged through the shelves and returned with an accordion file. "Matches this. Fleshes out the tragedy, eh?"

She untied the string and rummaged through the collection of yellowed newspaper clippings. One of the articles was newer than the others. The headline was "Death Plunge: Mt. Aspiring

Climbing Accident Marked 50 Years On. Edwin Hill Pays His Respects."

The survivor was still alive. That could be helpful. Alexa copied the documents.

She flipped to the next name in the notebook: Clay Tornquist, twenty-five. Reason for missing was listed as "possible slip," Bonar Glacier, no eyewitnesses.

Next was thirty-seven-year-old Clair Stanford. Reason For Missing: Unknown. Last Seen at Lucas-Trotter Hut By: Alec Useff, Harry Marchese, Preston Martin. A journal was listed. Maybe climbers left backpacks and food behind in the huts for their return. And journals.

When she located the corresponding accordion file, she found the dark leather-bound booklet with a gold-ribbon placemark. She sipped the hot sweet tea and flipped, like a voyeur, to the bookmarked page, dated 6 September 1972.

In the days leading up to my Mt. Aspiring climb, male climbers bombarded me with advice. A local rock-jock, Alec Useff, pointed out a direct line up the south face. I tramped with him to Lucas-Trotter Hut at the base of Mt. Aspiring. I got tired of his instructions and warnings. I set my sleeping roll at the far end of the platform.

Alexa wanted to read more, to get to know Clair better, to commiserate over mansplaining, but she only jotted down the contact number and names of the people who had seen her last.

On March 6, 1973, a German woman, twenty-seven, fell one thousand feet to her death on Mount Aspiring. Her companion, Jakob Schein, aged twenty-eight, did not see the mishap. He was the Last Seen By person. Alexa found the accordion file and read a newspaper article about the accident. Jakob heard the woman scream. When he investigated, he saw her red climbing helmet in the snow, and down the slope, he spotted her body. He was unable to reach her. Recovery was delayed because of weather. When they finally reached her, the body was buried in avalanche debris.

Why did people climb in the first place? Alexa could not figure it out.

She imagined being on a mountain, hoping against hope to be rescued, the clouds covering the sun, a storm rolling in, the thunder of an approaching waterfall of snow. Her heart rate increased as she made copies, and she jumped when her phone buzzed.

Bruce's name flashed on her screen.

"Hello," she said. "Where are you?"

"We're here," he said happily. "At the airport. Where are you?"

"Wanaka. I'm searching missing person records. You know, the skull. Did you hear about the fire?"

"The girls are gutted. Papa's is their favorite restaurant."

"That's what people keep saying. Did you hear there's a body?"

"A fire victim? No, I didn't."

"The remains are in bad shape. Facial recognition isn't possible. The police photographer couldn't even determine the sex. I'll probably be assigned to the case."

He paused. "What about skiing?"

"Probably someone will report the victim missing, and identification will be quick." She felt tension through the sound waves.

"Gotta go," he said. "We'll see you soon."

He hung up before she could warn him about the snowstorm.

James Welsh and Bill Gilroy went missing in 1984. Under "Clothing," she noted that Bill wore Vasque boots. She felt a burst of hope as she made copies of the files. They were from

Wellington, which would make follow-up easier. They were last seen the night before by Steven Eckel and Christian Drake.

She also copied the report and the single newspaper article from the file:

MISSING CLIMBERS
Wellington, 11 November 1984

Air and ground searches were called off for two missing climbers in the Mount Aspiring area. "Weather has been horrendous," Amish Castelle, Wanaka Search and Rescue coordinator, lamented. "Our thoughts are with the lads' families."

The climbers, James Welsh, a 21-year-old graduate student, and Bill Gilroy, a 20-year-old college student, both from Wellington, were due out of the area last Saturday. They were last seen 7 November by two other mountaineers, Christian Drake and Steven Eckel, after the four of them had summited Mt. Aspiring. The Wanaka police reported that the pair were climbers of limited experience, though both were members of the New Zealand Alpine Club.

She moved on, the reading both fascinating and horrifying. Several missing persons were listed as possible river drownings. Alexa skipped them.

James and Bill were among eight mountaineers who went missing in Mount Aspiring in the 1980s. She checked the 1990–2000 book and found Mark Lyon, the missing climber related to the father and sister she'd met at the hospital.

She continued until she reached 2010.

Her hand cramped. She stretched her fingers. Twenty-four names and a stack of copies rewarded her work. Could the skull or pelvis or foot or tooth belong to one of them? She'd start calling contact numbers as soon as she returned to the villa. It was noon. Her stomach rumbled.

She found Don rummaging through a cubby in an equipment room. It was loaded with radios, batteries, first-aid kits, binoculars, ice axes, crampons, safety vests, flares, rope, night goggles, and backpacks. She recognized the jumpsuits the rangers had been wearing yesterday.

"All set?" he asked. "You should hit the road, eh?"

"I need a Mount Aspiring National Park map. I want to pinpoint the 'Point Last Seen' locations."

"You're thinking like a SAR volunteer. Interested?"

That would be a no.

She followed him to the entrance. He ducked behind a counter and popped up with the map. She thanked him. "This will help me eliminate some names."

Don answered his phone. After listening, he said, "Give me the details." He paused, glanced out the windows. "Weather's moving in. I'll give the callout. Line up the heli."

Alexa followed his gaze, alarmed to see snowflakes.

When Don hung up, he said, "We've got an overdue climber."

She left in a worried hurry.

Hot air blasted her as she squinted at the road ahead. Still clear, despite the flakes surfing the air. She relaxed, but not enough to stop for lunch.

Outside of Cromwell, the snow turned to pellets and bounced off the windshield. The terrain was flat, but mountains crowded the periphery in every direction. The GPS map named them: Pisa Range, Dunstan Mountains, Mount Difficulty. She worried for the overdue climber.

All the hikers she had just read about were "overdue."

The road gave up the straight and narrow. Below it, the

emerald Kawarau River rushed with kinetic energy. Not a soul was around. Instead of feeling isolated and afraid, Alexa relished the breathing space. That's what her traveling forensic job gave her: breathing space. She felt like a pioneer. A solo explorer.

Did she want to team up with Bruce? It would never be just the two of them. Sammie and Denise stood in the way.

That wasn't true. The girls lived with their mom most of the time. She felt a pang for their loss. Maybe the parents were happier, but she didn't imagine Sammie and Denise were.

It took almost two hours to reach Papa Penguin's. One firetruck, one police car, and a Rescue Response van were left. Constable Blume walked over to greet her. "Hi ya," he said.

"Have they removed the body?"

He brushed snowflakes off his dark jacket. His face was red with cold. "An hour ago."

"Any ID yet?"

"No. The FRIU team are working on their incident analysis. The snow is in our favor, dampening sparks and whatnot."

She envisioned sparks as she drove the short distance to the villa.

They could ignite. Or they could die.

Chapter Eighteen

Backpacks were tossed on the twin beds, a stuffed tiger on one. She recognized Bruce's duffel in the master bedroom. In the Jack-and-Jill bathroom, her toiletries were shoved to a corner of the counter, and her drugstore lip gloss was on the floor.

She was in for it.

The three remaining chocolate muffins were gone, and a fruity scent—body wash or shampoo—lingered in the air.

A reprieve. In law enforcement, a reprieve was a temporary delay or suspension of punishment. That's what the girls' absence gave her.

She ate a banana and a minced pie. Then she spread out the Mount Aspiring National Park map. It encompassed 3,562 square kilometers. She eliminated ten missing persons based on their points last seen—not near Blue Peak Glacier. That left fourteen phone calls to make, five international and nine in New Zealand. She worked her way from 1970 until 2005, figuring the glacier needed a couple decades to rend a body to bones.

By five thirty, dental records had been promised from six sources, and three numbers were no longer in service. The rest of her inquires had been defeated by full mailboxes or no-answers. She left a message for someone from the New Zealand Missing Persons to call her. She peered out the window, into the twilight. Snow fed the hungry black waves of the lake.

Bruce and the girls gusted in, rosy-cheeked, snow on their

jackets, stomping their boots. The entrance hall was full of bodies shedding winter apparel. "Leave your boots here," Bruce told the girls. He wore an All Blacks pompom beanie, which he swiped off.

Alexa pressed her bangs to cover the gash on her forehead and eased off the safety of her stool. "Hi, everyone." Then her mind blanked, her vocabulary depleted.

Bruce looked pleased at the sight of her. "Hi, yourself."

Sammie's eyes were big and blue like Bruce's, and her hair was dark. She shed her red parka, waved at Alexa, and plopped on her butt, loose-limbed. She thrust a large foot at Bruce. He tugged off her boot.

"My sock," screamed Sammie. She grabbed the boot and pulled it out.

Denise's honey-blond hair was fancy-braided, and her ski jacket was a bright pink. She was heavier than her sister, her face fuller, her brown eyes rimmed in violet eyeliner. She ignored Alexa. "After we eat. Please, Dad."

Please what?

"We'll see," he said.

Alexa bit back a laugh at the universal parental response.

"We can't go to Papa Penguin's," Sammie informed Alexa. "It burned down. Can we go somewhere else, Dad?"

Alexa searched the desert and found her tongue. "I bought frozen pizza."

Denise scoffed.

Bruce frowned at his daughter but said, "Be ready to go in thirty minutes."

The girls squealed in unison, "Right and wrong." Then they scattered to their room. Bruce walked over to Alexa, pulled her close, and buried his nose in her hair. "You've been to Papa Penguin's," he whispered.

She should have showered. "You're a good detective," she whispered back. "Um. Why did the girls shout right and wrong?"

"W-H-I-T-E and W-O-N-G-S," he spelled. "It's their second-favorite restaurant."

"What does Denise want to do after we eat?"

"She knows some of the NZ SNO Z snowboarders from school. They're staying in the villa next door. She wants to hang out."

She pulled back. "They play loud music."

Bruce kneaded her shoulders. "Denise is acting twenty, and Sammie is acting ten. The psychologist Sharla takes them to says both are normal reactions to divorce, but it's been over a year now. Time to move on."

Alexa had googled Sharla. She had big hair and sold real estate in Rotorua, where she and the girls lived. Alexa didn't know what to say about regression and progression, so she switched subjects. "The autopsy on the burn victim is in the morning. My presence is required." She braced for his disapproval or an argument, ready to defend herself, her job.

He brushed the hair from her forehead. The gash throbbed under his inspection. He kissed her nose and then her lips. She was surprised at how quickly she succumbed, fire and ice and teenagers fading. She kissed him back, the smell of the outdoors on his skin, his tongue dancing with hers.

"Dad, where's my shoes?" Sammie yelled.

They pulled back. Bruce disappeared.

Alexa hoped to shower before they left for Yin and Yang, or whatever, but the girls commandeered the bathroom. She feared for the safety of her lip gloss.

Bruce had parked his rental Subaru Outback in front of the villa. Denise claimed the front seat because tomorrow was her birthday. Alexa said it was fine. She sat in the back, shivering next to Sammie, smelling rather than seeing the silent black lake: sweet and fecund beyond the villas.

As if he could smell it, too, Bruce said, "Lake Wakatipu has a scientifically proven tide. The Māori call it a heartbeat."

"How can a lake have a heartbeat?" Sammie asked.

They crested the steep driveway. The wipers struggled to keep the windshield clear.

"A Māori myth explains it," Bruce said.

"Just answer the question," Denise said.

"A chief's beautiful daughter was stolen by a giant, the *karara*. That might happen to you if you're not careful," Bruce told Denise. "The chief said that whoever rescued his daughter could marry her."

"Why didn't the chief rescue her?" Sammie asked.

Alexa wondered why the beautiful daughter didn't rescue herself. She found her seat warmer and switched it on high.

"A boss has to know when to delegate," Bruce said. He slowed by the empty parking lot of Papa Penguin's. Cones blocked the entrance. "A young man, Matakauri, loved the chief's daughter. He knew that when the northwest winds blew, the giant would fall asleep. So when the winds blew warm, he set out to rescue her."

Alexa hoped Bruce was paying attention to the road. The snow blew sideways.

"When Matakauri found the giant, he set him on fire. The flames roared. The giant curled up his legs. His burning body sank deep and deeper into the earth, a thousand feet deep," Bruce said. "Then the fire melted the snow on the mountains, which filled in the lake. That's why Lake Wakatipu is in the shape of the giant's body."

Too much snow. Too much fire. Alexa turned off the seat warmer.

"What about the heartbeat?" Sammie said.

"The lake rises and falls every half hour," Bruce said. "The giant's heart is still beating."

"For real?" Sammie asked.

The vibe inside White and Wong's was giddy, the youngish crowd hyped by all the snow. They were shown to a booth. Alexa and Bruce sat across from the girls, his thigh firmly pressed against hers, which only slightly distracted her from her crispy sweet-and-sour pork when it was served.

Sammie kept the conversation lively. She chattered about a science class coding project to make her own galaxy and then about bearded collies. Their size. Cost. Temperament. "Mum won't let me get one."

Alexa, chopsticks poised, said, "My roommate has a dog. A German shepherd. His name is Kaos."

"That's a cool name," Sammie said. "Tomorrow, I want to snowboard instead of ski."

Denise frowned. "You want to copy everything I do."

"What wrong with that?" Sammie said.

"There's a competition going on," Bruce explained to Alexa.

"Qualifiers," Denise said. "Look. That's them."

Alexa followed Denise's eyes. The Villa 5 chaperone with the long sideburns and his posse filled a table by the windows. "I met them last night."

Denise eyed Alexa suspiciously. "You did?"

A chunk of pineapple slipped from her chopsticks. "They're staying next door."

"I *know* SNO Z is staying next door." Denise stared at her father. "Please?"

"Home by ten," Bruce said.

"Ten thirty," Denise said.

"One of them is coming," Sammie said.

It was BFree, the boy who had come to see the burned restaurant this morning. Tonight his T-shirt had a squirrel on it. *Weird*, Alexa thought. There were no squirrels in New Zealand.

He smiled at Denise. "S'up?"

"Hi, Tex," Denise said.

"We're sitting over there. Want to stop by?"

"She's busy," Bruce said. "Family time."

"I can come over later," Denise said, blushing.

The kid turned on a hundred-watt smile. "I'm Tex Zafiro, sir," he said. "I know how family time is important. Denise and I know each other from school."

"DI Bruce Horne. Serious Crime. How are the qualifiers going?"

Tex didn't miss a beat. "The fresh dump is good. Do you board, sir?"

"Ski," Bruce said.

"Easier to get on and off the lifts, that's for sure."

Another boy, the redhead who'd been with Tex this morning, came up. "Hi, Denise."

"How's it going, Cam?"

"Cringy on the powder." He smiled at Alexa. His eyes were the color of southern iced tea. "Is this your mum?"

"As if. You're an effing moron," Denise said.

Cam's face turned as red as his hair. Alexa wanted to crawl under the table.

"Lads," Bruce said, "if you'll excuse us." He waited until the boys returned to their table, waved off a server, and then glared at Denise. "That was rude. To Alexa. To the boy."

"But…"

Bruce's face turned to stone.

"Alexa doesn't even look like Mum," Sammie said.

"Shut up," Denise said.

Bruce continued staring at Denise. After a minute of silence, she took a quivering breath. "Sorry, Dad."

"Not to me."

She glanced at Alexa. "I'm sorry."

"It's okay," Alexa said.

———

Shazam, the movie, didn't hold Alexa's attention. She didn't blame Denise for her effing moron comment, but she was glad the girl was next door with the snowboarders.

Sammie, in tie-dyed PJs, nestled against Bruce at the other end of the couch. She poked Alexa with her big toe. "How long has odon—whatever—been around?"

"A long time." Alexa sat straighter. "Want to hear about the first time a tooth solved a crime?"

Sammie paused the movie and looked at her expectantly.

"Archimedes was an ancient Greek inventor and scientist. He was also a detective and really smart," Alexa began.

"Like Dad," Sammie said.

Alexa flushed as she met Bruce's eyes. "The king at the time ordered a special gold tooth, a crown."

Sammie's blue eyes got bigger. "King Charles?"

Kiwis were obsessed with the big-eared king. "Way before King Charles. The king worried that the goldsmith cheated him, that the tooth wasn't pure gold."

"Cheaters never win," Sammie said.

She thought of that poor woman in the burn pit. *Sometimes they do.* "The king put Archimedes on the case. Archy had to figure out if the gold was pure. He liked to do his thinking in the bathtub, so that's where he went."

"Gross. A naked man."

Alexa avoided Bruce's eyes. "You know how when you get in the bathtub, the water gets higher?"

"Displacement. We learned that in science," Sammie said.

With the TV muted, the music from Villa 5 penetrated the walls. Alexa wondered if the kids, Denise included, were drinking or smoking and how Bruce would handle that. "Archimedes figured if his body displaced water, the gold tooth would, too."

"Then what?" Sammie asked.

She better not blow her story. She never wanted kids, but she wanted at least one of Bruce's kids to like her. "So Archy gets dressed and goes to his lab. He puts some real gold in a cup of water to see how much it displaced, and then does the same thing with the gold tooth. He figured out the crown wasn't pure gold, that it was mixed with silver."

"That's it?" Sammie asked.

"The goldsmith was busted."

"Gold displaces more water than silver?" Bruce asked.

"The other way around," Alexa said. "Even though the mass was the same, silver has a larger volume because it's less dense."

Sammie turned the movie back on.

Bruce gave Alexa a pitying look. She winced when she stood; the aches and pains from the glacier debacle begged for a hot shower. "Good night. I'll see you in the morning."

Bruce followed her to her bedroom. He kissed her tenderly, quickly, and left.

She locked the bathroom door that led to the girls' bedroom and turned on the water. She showered quickly. The doorknob from the girls' bedroom jiggled when she was brushing her teeth.

"Just a minute." She rinsed and wiped her mouth. Then she unlocked the door.

Denise pushed it open. Her hair had come loose from its

braids, and her brown eyes narrowed. "What are you even doing here?" she asked.

Her breath smelled of beer.

Alexa retreated to her bedroom.

Hell if I know.

DAY TWO

7 NOVEMBER 1984

I'm in the Lucas-Trotter Hut—a.k.a. Tin Igloo! If all goes according to my plan (ignoring what Steinbeck said), and the weather plays nice, tomorrow will be summit day.

Aside: The Lucas-Trotter Hut was built in memory of Colin Lucas and Ruth Trotter, who died crossing Breakway in 1970. Not really wanting a hut built in my memory—ha!

I'm beat, but it's a good beat. I want to write this down while my memory is sharp. At first we tramped through beech forest which cut the wind to a peaceful nothing. I thought about the Māori concept of maunga, or mountain, representing their ancestors. The peaks are their ancestors' upoko, or heads. To summit Mount Aspiring, or any Aotearoa mountain, is to stand on their head and disrespect the past. C said that's bullshit.

After the beech forest we came to a wide river. I wasn't ready to strip to my skivvies, so we took a detour to the suspension bridge. After another mile there was another river— this one had a hip-wide cable bridge. It wasn't made for bulging packs with crampons, pulleys, axes, and ropes hanging off. I shimmied sideways. C bounced up and down. My stomach was out of sync for the next half hour.

The track steepened. Scramble time. Three thousand feet of pulling up on shrubs and roots, the track mud, ice in spots, then snow. My arms burned.

No more trees. The snow-glazed tussock was punchy. The wind slapped us round like rubbish. C tripped. Screamed, "My ankle." I chucked my pack, ran to help, but he leaped up, laughed. Does everyone have a cousin like this or am I just lucky? My ears were freezing until I found my hat. Mountains surrounded us like aunts and uncles with open arms. Snow lifted from their ridges in powder clouds. The grandeur was tu meke.

But then there were the endless horizons, the vague path, the false summits. Here's the lowdown:

C yelling, "This is it."

It wasn't.

"This is it."

It wasn't.

Finally! The hut.

One room, fifteen bunks, a cooking bench, privy out back. Two top bunks were claimed by Zittydog Welsh and Bill Gilroy, from Wellington, long hair, baby faces, though Bill has a scar from his cheek to his mouth.

Some Germans tramped in behind us, sunburned noses, zinced lips. "Hallo" and "Guten Tag." The stink of their dried sweat filled the hut as they shed coats and boots and draped their wet socks over the bunk rails. They stampeded to the porch. Two keas strutted and preened along the railing. C tossed them some scroggin. The keas went mad for it. The Germans clapped their big red hands.

The sharp peak of Aspiring lorded over us.

The Germans offered us slices of salami, cheese, and apples, supplementing my freeze-dried spaghetti. They were in high spirits. Lucas-Trotter Hut was their destination. They were done. The Wellies planned to summit tomorrow like us. They studied maps and spoke quietly.

"We'll beat their asses," C told me.

He's compulsively competitive.

We're taking the southwest ridge approach: Bonar Glacier, via the Quarterdeck. Then the steep open couloir to the summit. I laid out my clothes because we'd dress in the dark.

long underwear (wearing)
ski pants
shirt (wearing)
sweater
windshell parka
silk socks (wearing)
wool socks (wearing)
felt booties
boots
silk gloves
down mittens
wool cap
down coat
helmet

I jangled and throbbed. This was the last haunt before we tackled Aspiring. Last year a climber died on the ice couloir. He fell from the top of it. I couldn't get him out of my head.

"Two a.m. wake-up," C announced and dove into his bag.

Every time I closed my eyes, I slipped into white oblivion.

Chapter Nineteen

SATURDAY

The storm had added a few extra inches of snow, some of which invaded the gap between her pant leg and boot as Alexa crossed the hospital parking lot in the morning. It melted into her sock, as chilling as Denise's words.

What are you even doing here?

Alexa had asked her father's "friend" the same thing. Three years after Mom died, her father had introduced his "friend" into their bubble, Pam fluttering about, baking Toll House cookies and offering up trips to the mall.

Charlie, six at the time, flung himself into Pam's arms. His need for a mother superseded his need to please his sister. Alexa, nine, considered Charlie a traitor. Dad, too. She shunned Pam. Told her she didn't belong. When Dad and Pam married years later, Alexa refused to be in the wedding. She watched from the front row, arms crossed over her chest, teary-eyed. Dad had forgotten all about Mom. Alexa had to be the one who remembered her. One of the guests remarked how sweet it was that Alexa cried tears of joy. She ran from the backyard ceremony and sulked under a tree, counting ants, until Charlie brought her a piece of cake.

She had been a jerk.

Then she got a grip. Bruce only had the girls two weekends a month, holidays, and a month in the summer. She could deal.

Denise had been celebrated with pancakes and bacon

whipped up by Chef Dad and a new Golden Orca snowboard. Denise read aloud: "Happy birthday! Love from Mum and Dad!"

Alexa choked on a bacon strip. She had been unable to decipher Bruce's look as she waved goodbye. Irritated? Wistful? Hurt? Emotions were not her forte. Give her teeth any day.

This morning: the burned body. Tomorrow morning: the glacier skull. A full dance card. She entered the hospital and mentally inventoried the dental supplies in her crime kit: mirror, extraction forceps, tweezers, probe, toothbrush, lip retractor. What else? Her tiny light.

DI Katakana, dressed in a navy polo and neat tan pants, paced the anteroom of the autopsy suite, alone, when Alexa entered. "Good morning, Ms. Glock. Any luck with our skull?"

"I've got several dental records pending and some follow-ups to make."

The DI's dark hair, pulled back with a clasp, gleamed in the overhead light. "Get to it."

Alexa was confused. "Now?"

"When this fire mess is done. The request for your services was approved. You'll examine the teeth, right?"

"If possible. Sometimes with a burn victim the mouth is too stiff to pry open." Alexa peeked through the glass into the autopsy suite. A form, covered by a paper sheet, was on the dissection table, just like the skull had been Thursday afternoon. That poem again. "Fire and Ice."

If it had to perish twice...

DI Katakana followed her gaze. "We have no idea who it is. There have been no frantic calls to the station, no missing persons reported. That waitress you met said Graham Clark, the chef, and another server were still there when she left at ten. We're tracking them down."

"The owner said that they rent that apartment to guys who work the ski fields. Maybe someone hasn't shown up for their shift," Alexa offered.

"Aren't you here for a ski weekend? With DI Horne?"

She nodded. A slippery future stretched before her: Bruce skiing without her, a table set for one, an empty side of a bed. That's how life would be if she and Bruce joined forces and respected each other's erratic calls to duty.

"Checking in with the ski fields is a good idea," the DI continued. "Where is the DI skiing?"

"Coronet Peak."

"DI Horne won't mind making inquiries there, eh? We're stretched thin."

Alexa was reluctant to offer up Bruce. "He's with his daughters."

The DI ignored her comment. "I'm waiting for the FRIU report. Chances are the blaze originated in one of the wood-fired ovens. Escaped ember catches something, fire spreads."

Dr. McKenzie, a file in the crook of his arm, entered the suite with Sally, the police photographer.

"Good morning, ladies. Let me get you caught up." He tied on an apron. "A PMCT scan was completed when the decedent was brought in."

Postmortem computed tomography was routine prior to autopsies. The scans sometimes revealed the cause of death and spared the deceased a detailed dissection. "What did you find out?" Alexa asked.

"No foreign bodies. The genitals were damaged beyond recognition. But Dr. Pullen, the radiologist, said the abdominal wall preserved the prostate."

"A male, eh?" DI Katakana said.

Dr. McKenzie opened the file. "Sally was with me as I

performed the external exam." He glanced at the police photographer, who nodded grimly, and then stepped back so Alexa and DI Katakana could read it.

The first page listed the degree of carbonization: 70 percent.

The time-line flash cards she made to prepare for the odontology certification exam flickered in Alexa's mind. In a fire of 1100 degrees Fahrenheit or more, hair burns first, followed by fingertips. Arms carbonize in ten minutes. Facial bones take fifteen. The ribs carbonize in twenty minutes. It takes thirty-five minutes to carbonize the femurs.

She pictured Papa Penguin's, burning out of control in the dead of night.

Teeth, though, were tough cookies. She expected John Doe's teeth would show cracks and separation of the crown from the root. And color change. Teeth burned at high temperatures turned a bluish-gray. She crossed her fingers that she'd be able to pry the jaws open and take a look inside.

She studied the photographs. The body had been prone in photos taken at the scene. In the photos taken during the external examination, it was supine. The face was a blackened horror mask, the eyes and nose burned away, leathery lips parted to partially reveal the upper incisors. The single remaining limb, the right arm, bent at the elbow, the wrist level with the head. No chance of fingerprints: the hand was burned away.

Alexa checked to see how DI Katakana was coping with the pictures. Her coppery skin had a sheen, and she worked her jaw. "What can you tell us about the position the body was found in?" the DI asked Dr. McKenzie. "Was he trying to crawl away?"

"There's not a lot that can be said about a body's position after a fire, especially since we don't know whether he was alive or dead when the fire started. Heat causes the muscles to contract into a position that looks quite defensive. In this case, the muscles of the remaining arm contracted, so that is why it's bent at that angle."

An external examination form followed. Sex was filled in, but hair color, eye color, approximate age, and identifying features such as scars and tattoos were marked *Unknown*. The decedent's weight was listed at 36.19 kilograms, and height was ninety-one centimeters.

Alexa converted. The results made her stomach roil. John Doe weighed around eighty pounds and measured almost three feet. He was half a man.

"Have you run a tox screen?" DI Katakana asked.

"First thing I'll do when we start," he said.

Alexa kitted up, applied StinkBalm below her nostrils—this tube was lavender-scented—pulled her mask on, and followed the DI, Sally, and the doctor into the autopsy chamber. She sniffed, bracing for putrefaction, but no offensive odor penetrated her lavender barrier.

Dr. McKenzie removed the cover from the deceased without ceremony. "If you're wondering why he doesn't smell, charring tends to protect against major decomposition of the internal organs."

The expanse of skin covering the torso looked black and flaky, like the burned parts of barbecue chicken. The sight made Alexa gag. She lowered her head and sucked in air until her equilibrium was restored.

Then she peered at the decedent's teeth. Blue-gray upper incisors poked through the wizened lips, which were singed together at each corner, preventing more teeth from showing through.

Dr. McKenzie poked the upper lip. Then he gently probed the neck and jawline. "There's thermocoagulation of the facial muscles. Parting the maxilla and mandible will be hard. A dental autopsy might be necessary."

A dental autopsy entailed incision and dissection of the skin, muscle, and fascia in order to reveal the oral cavity. The victim had endured enough disfigurement. "Let me check the PMCT first," Alexa said. "Hopefully I can fill out the dental chart from it."

Dr. McKenzie nodded. "The extensive charring indicates a flame injury."

"As opposed to what?" Alexa asked.

"Electrical, chemical, radiation, scalding."

Alexa's back scars tightened.

DI Katakana's forehead was even shinier now. "Cause of death. That's what I need. And whether he was alive when the fire started. I don't have time to wait on lab results."

"Checking for signs of vitality during the fire and the precise cause of death are standard goals," the pathologist responded calmly. "But speed is dangerous."

Alexa knew the DI wanted to rule out foul play. If the victim was already dead, someone may have started a fire to cover their tracks.

"If the decedent died in the fire, and not prior to the fire starting, it's almost always from inhalation of products of combustion and not the thermal injuries," he said.

Alexa felt better for John Doe.

"Though a combination of both is possible. Where was the body found?"

"In the kitchen," DI Katakana said. "He might have smelled smoke—maybe from one of the pizza ovens gone kablooey—and come running."

"If he was alive, I'll see soot in the trachea, bronchi, and other passages. Perfect timing. Here's Ada now," he said.

Ada, his lab tech, greeted them with a sunny smile.

Dr. McKenzie removed a vial of blood from the heart area, surprising Alexa that there were any liquids left in the body. "Toxicology is important in cases like this, but it's actually the carboxyhemoglobin saturation that helps show whether someone was alive during a fire. We'll request a stat result."

"All good," the DI said.

Ada ran the sample to the hospital lab. When she returned, she and Dr. McKenzie got to work mapping the area, depth, and distribution of the burns. Every once in a while, Dr. McKenzie instructed Sally to take a photograph. The three of them were like a small dance troupe. Alexa sat on a bench, out of the way, listening to their talk about fixed flexion, subcutaneous fat loss, bone fragmentation, and muscle exposure. The DI paced along the back wall. When Dr. McKenzie moved to the skull, Alexa stepped up to watch. He palpated the cranium, announced it whole, and moved to the facial bones, probing with his fingers. "I feel some fractures. The CT will show bone damage."

DI Katakana was suddenly at Alexa's side. "Was he beaten?"

"I suspect the fractures are from heat damage."

DI Katakana leaned closer to the skull. "Can you look in his nostrils or trachea to see if there's soot?"

Dr. McKenzie's bushy eyebrows raised. "I'll do that after the internal organs and brain have been removed. I'll remove the trachea with the neck structures and then open it up along its length. Soot needs to be seen below the level of the vocal cords to be considered true inhalation of smoke."

The DI studied the wreckage of the body and then turned to Alexa. "Ms. Glock, this is wasting your time. Find that radiologist and identify our bloke by his teeth. Then find me."

Dr. McKenzie nodded his consent. "Go on then. Teeth are our best bet for identification. If the scans aren't sufficient, let me know."

Alexa was happy to leave. "I hope he has antemortem records somewhere."

"If he's a Kiwi, our country has free dental care from birth to age seventeen," Ada said. "Check with the NZ Health System."

"Right." She left the autopsy suite, threw the disposable apron and mask in the bin, and washed her hands. She saw through the glass that Dr. McKenzie was opening the chest.

The radiology department was on the second floor. Dr. Pullen's door was open. A gray-haired woman, feet on her desk, stared at the ceiling, a mug cradled to her stomach. "Dr. Pullen?"

She lowered her tennis shoes and set the mug on her desk. "I'm solving life's problems on the ceiling. How can I help you?"

Alexa liked her immediately and showed her badge. "I'm an odontologist. I need to see the burn victim's PMCT scans."

"Thermal amputation of three limbs. That's a first for me." Dr. Pullen used her feet to wheel over to a computer and pulled up the images. She zeroed in on jaw scans and backed up.

Alexa took over the mouse. She moved the two-dimensional image back and forth, up and down, and then enlarged the image of the teeth. The first thing she noticed was two bottom wisdom teeth. Wisdom teeth usually erupted in pairs between ages seventeen and twenty-five. The top two hadn't sprouted. "John Doe might be a teenager."

"Thought as much," Dr. Pullen said.

Alexa scanned the other teeth. "Two crowns are cracked. There's a composite restoration in the upper-right second molar." Alexa pushed away from the screen, relieved she had enough information to chart. She dug out a business card. "Would you email me the scan so I can complete the dental charting?"

Dr. Pullen took her card and fiddled at the computer. While she worked, Alexa called Dr. McKenzie and left a message that no dental autopsy was necessary. "I'll see you tomorrow morning for the glacier skull," she added.

Dr. Pullen flexed her fingers over the keyboard. "You should have the scans now."

Alexa wished her luck with the problem solving and left. She bought a "cappuccino" from a vending machine, sat heavily at a table in a waiting area, and opened her laptop. For the next forty minutes she charted the decedent's teeth and then sent the chart and the scans to local dentists to see if John Doe was a patient. She added *Needs Immediate Attn* to the subject line. She hoped diligent dentists checked email over the weekend. Then she called the NZ Health System. Being Saturday, she wasn't surprised no one answered. She left a message and made a note to call back Monday morning.

Next she checked her news feed. An update on the fire had been released one hour earlier:

RESTAURANT FIRE CLAIMS LIFE

A body was discovered inside the remains of Queenstown's popular Papa Penguin's Pizza Restaurant after crews extinguished a fire there in the early hours of Friday morning.

A police investigation is underway. It is unknown how the unidentified victim died. "This is currently being handled as a death investigation of an adult," Detective Inspector Pattie Katakana said. "If the public has any information to help us identify the victim, please call 111."

Alexa hoped the news brief would prompt someone to call in about a missing loved one.

She thought of her trip to Wanaka yesterday. A person had

been reported missing as she was leaving. She searched "missing climber Mount Aspiring" and found an update:

HUGS ALL AROUND

There were hugs all the way around when Alpine Cliff Rescue team volunteers arrived back in Wanaka from Mount Aspiring late last night having rescued Australian Army Lieutenant Barry Ehrman.

Lt. Ehrman, a solo climber, was flown to Dunedin Hospital to recover from his ordeal, which began when sudden bad weather pinned him near the top of Bonar Glacier. He set off his emergency beacon from a snow cave he constructed in a wind scoop. The signal was relayed to the Wanaka Rescue Centre.

Team leader Dan Wood and SAR rescuers Polly Fiore and Duane McClafferty reached Lt. Ehrman on Thursday evening and treated him for hypothermia and frostbite.

They were fortunate to get a clear patch of weather so they could get on to the mountain. "With a front moving in, it was touch and go," Wood said. He credited Lieutenant Ehrman for having a personal locator beacon and hunkering down. "Probably saved his life, though I don't recommend climbing alone."

Alexa was glad the army lieutenant was safe. It occurred to her that the glacier skull would be in the news, too. Her phone pinged, interrupting her new search.

DI Katakana texted: Papa Penguin's ASAP.

Something urgent must have pulled her away from the autopsy. Alexa dumped the horrid coffee and left the hospital. Car heater on high, she called Bruce to pass on DI Katakana's request. She hoped he wouldn't answer so she didn't have to sleet on his parade.

"Bruce Horne."

"You're not skiing right now, are you?"

He laughed. "Sammie and I are drinking cocoa in the lodge. We had some great runs. Now we're warming up before her snowboard lesson starts. Are you free to join us?"

"Not yet."

The tenor of his voice changed. "What's up?"

"We learned the fire victim is male, and we're working to identify him. DI Katakana would appreciate it if you would check in with the offices at Coronet Peak to see if any employee failed to show up. It would save her time. There's a chance the decedent worked at one of the ski fields. I think he's late teens, early twenties."

Pause again. "Let me get Zoi situated."

"Who?"

Sammie's voice blasted her eardrum. The kid must have grabbed Bruce's phone. "Zoi Sadowski-Synnott! She won a gold in boarding when she was twenty."

"Wow."

"And Cam from next door? He showed me how to strap in without sitting on my butt."

Bruce's voice returned. "We're taking the Coronet Express to where Sammie's class meets. Then I'll ski down and do your bidding."

Chapter Twenty

"Our victim was alive when the fire started," DI Katakana announced when Alexa arrived at Papa P's. "Doc McKenzie found soot in the trachea."

Incident Controller McBride and Constable Blume nodded gravely. Alexa wondered why she was summoned to the parking lot; the DI could have told her that by text.

IC McBride pointed past the caution tape. "Our investigators are in the kitchen area."

Three people in black pants and coats with shiny reflective markings worked in what was once the kitchen. One of them had a big yellow dog.

"Is it safe for them?" Constable Blume asked.

"Being open to the elements reduces exposure to smoke and toxins. We spent the bulk of yesterday removing debris to expose the floor where the fire originated."

Alexa took that as a "yes" but noted the workers wore masks.

A black Honda Accord pulled into the lot. DI Katakana frowned. "Another spectator?"

A man and woman got out; the man carried a video camera. "*Kia ora*. One News," the woman called. "I'm Nancy Capaccio. Have you identified the person who died?"

The man raised the video recorder.

"No, we haven't," DI Katakana said. "If you'd like to help, please appeal to the public for information."

Ms. Capaccio joined them. "We can do that. Is the victim male or female?"

"Male. Ms. Glock? Anything to add?"

"The decedent's teeth indicate he was likely sixteen to twenty-five years old," she said.

The reporter's on-the-hunt eyes gleamed. "Weight? Height?"

"No comment," Alexa responded.

"How did the fire start?" she asked.

"Our fire team haven't finished their investigation," DI Katakana snapped.

Another car drove up and parked. Two teenagers got out.

"People from far and wide keep stopping by." DI Katakana ducked under the caution tape. "I call it interference. Constable, please show our guests out and block entrance to the lot."

Constable Blume led the press toward their car as the reporter shouted questions. Alexa ducked under the tape and followed the DI and fire guy toward the rear of the burned restaurant. "We've discovered suspicious burn patterns," IC McBride said.

"Near where the body was located?" DI Katakana asked.

The incident controller nodded. The heavy stink in the air was like wet fireplace ash. Alexa studied the restaurant innards as they passed: scorched lumps that were once tables and chairs, a partial wall, twisted pipe. Most ash was black, but some was grayish white and piled in corners like plowed snow. Pieces of pottery and glass bottles were visible among the wreckage.

At the far corner, in the restaurant kitchen, a woman stood next to the dog. "This is Investigator Crow," the incident controller said. "What have you and Muffin found?"

The dog sat in the middle of the burned debris. To Alexa, she looked like an ordinary yellow Lab that should be fetching sticks in the backyard. Her kind brown eyes stared adoringly at her handler, and her pink nose was smudged with ash.

Investigator Crow held Muffin's leash and patted her broad head. "Good girl. That's a good, good girl, Muff." Muffin's tail wagged fiercely. It turned sootier with each sweep.

"She alerted me to the presence of an accelerant," Investigator Crow said. The protective suit she wore was like a firefighter's but thinner since it didn't have to protect her from heat. "I suspect from the burn pattern that a liquid was poured along the floor. Most likely by the smell, it's petrol. The trail starts at the kitchen door."

Alexa sniffed for the sweet pungent odor of gas through the burn smells, but *her* nose failed. She studied the kitchen area. The location where the body had been found was indicated by a placard. The area around it was strangely clear. The body had actually protected the concrete floor. A spasm of horror skittered up her spine.

Past the brick pizza ovens, an investigator shoveled ash into a sifting screen while a second shook it back and forth. She thought of John Doe's thermal amputations and wondered if they were finding bone fragments.

Investigator Crow guided Muffin around the debris and then pointed to a mottled black-brown-and-gray trail on the concrete floor, slightly different from the surrounding ash. "I believe the liquid was poured in that area. Samples will let us know if it's petrol."

"Bad news, that," Constable Blume said.

Alexa hadn't noticed he'd returned.

As if Investigator Crow's words hadn't registered, DI Katakana asked, "An accelerant was used to start the fire?"

"Yes," the woman said. "There was full-room involvement."

"What does that mean?" Alexa asked.

"The kitchen hit flashover. That's when all the oxygen in a room is consumed. The temperature would have reached over

500 degrees. Every combustible in this room would simultane-
ously ignite."

The image combusted in Alexa's mind.

"The door leading into the restaurant must have failed or
been open, and the fire, seeking oxygen, spread through it,
engulfing the rest of the restaurant," Investigator Crow added.

DI Katakana looked solemn. "Are you certain the fire was the
work of an arsonist instead of, say, a spark from those ovens?"

"Muffin detected an accelerant," Investigator Crow said.
"There shouldn't be ignitable liquids in this restaurant."

DI Katakana's hand went to the radio on her belt. "We have
ourselves a homicide."

Chapter Twenty-One

As soon as the DI passed on the information to her team, the dog handler said, "Petrol flashes in an instant. Our suspect may have suffered burns."

"Start a perimeter search for a container. And matches or a lighter," DI Katakana said.

"On it, senior," Constable Blume said.

Alexa stepped closer to the husk of a kitchen and stared at the spot where the body had been. "Can I enter?" she asked Incident Controller McBride.

"No need. My team is handling the evidence."

"You can sometimes recover fingerprints on charred surfaces under the char," she said.

"The damage is extensive," he replied.

"You can even discover writing on paper that has been charred if you use the right wavelengths of light," Alexa said.

IC McBride looked like his patience was charred. "Not when it's been burned to ash."

DI Katakana cut in. "Ms. Glock, go help the constable look for the container."

Class dismissed. Alexa turned her attention to the ground, but she was pessimistic. A couple inches of new snow had fallen since the fire. Even if they found a container or lighter, fingerprint recovery might be compromised.

"I'll take the woods," Constable Blume said. "You can check the lot."

She pulled her beanie out of her pocket, hair be damned. She retraced her steps to the parking lot, canvassing the ground. People and cars and trucks had churned it to a muddied mess. She kicked a clump of snow. Mud blotched her khakis. When she looked up, she spotted a thirtyish man with long black hair slouched against a rusting Subaru Impreza. It parked shy of the cones Constable Blume must have set up. "Can I help you?"

He straightened to a wiry six feet. The skin around his eyes was white, contrasting with his tanned face, probably a sunglasses tan. "Wanted to see the place for myself. Pay my respects. True that someone died?"

"Yes."

He frowned. "Who is it?"

"We don't know. What's your name?"

"What's yours?"

The cheekiness rankled, but Alexa showed her badge. "Forensics. I'm working the fire. What's your connection with Papa Penguin's?"

Ski Patrol was emblazoned on his dark parka. "Connection? Food. Been coming here for a feed ever since I moved to Queenie seven years ago. Devo, man, the fire. My name is Heath Weiner."

"When was the last time you were here?"

His dark blue eyes returned her gaze. "Thursday night, the night it burned."

It technically burned Friday morning. Alexa set her crime kit down and fished out a pad and pen. "I'll take your contact info. And a list of anyone else you know who was there."

"Half of them work with me at Coronet Peak. I run avalanche patrol. Started at four a.m. this morning."

Coronet Peak was where Bruce and the girls were skiing. "Is there a risk of avalanche?"

Heath smiled, his teeth white against his tanned skin. "It's impossible to eliminate the risk of avalanches. We mitigate it. I have a team of twelve, every morning, to open the slopes. New snow notches the risk up."

Her worry notched up. "How do you mitigate it?"

"Sometimes we trigger avalanches, you know, eh, to remove the riskier layers. This morning we did a little heli-bombing and closed Dirty Four and Sarah Sue. The snow is in good nick. The Avalanche Advisory put the risk at moderate."

Moderate? "But my friend is skiing there today." Alexa dropped the pad, which landed in slush, and whipped out her phone to warn Bruce.

Heath stared at the pad. "Aren't you going to take down my information?"

The phone went to voicemail. She left a text for Bruce to call ASAP and picked up the pad, wiping it on her pants. She was overreacting. "My friend is with his daughters. I just want to warn them."

"They'll be right."

She took a deep breath and refocused on the homicide. "What time did you leave the restaurant Thursday night?" Flakes landed on his dark hair. She looked up. It was snowing again.

"Eight, more or less. Waited over thirty minutes for my pizza. It was chockablock."

"Do you know who the victim might be?"

He studied the wreckage. The dog handler was leading Muffin to an SUV. "An unlucky bastard, that's who."

"You said some people you work with at Coronet Peak also work at Papa Penguin's. Was there anyone who didn't show up for work this morning?"

"Like they might be dead? That's heavy stuff." He opened his car door. "My team was accounted for. The mates who work at Papa P's are mostly lifties, come in as I'm leaving."

"Lefties?"

"Lifties. They work the lifts."

She ripped off a sheet of paper and handed it, and her pen, to him. "Their names, please."

He bent his head to write, his long hair hiding his face. He handed the paper back with three names and then opened his car door wider and yanked a vibrating phone out of the car's cup holder. "Yeah?" He swept his hair out of his face. His eyes went grave. "Call the team back. Patrol from other ski areas, too. And get the dogs."

Out of the corner of Alexa's eyes she saw DI Katakana jogging toward her patrol car, Constable Blume in pursuit.

"What's going on?" Alexa asked.

Heath slid into his car without answering and took off. She ran to DI Katakana's car. "What's going on?" she repeated.

"An avalanche at Coronet," Constable Blume huffed. "All hands on deck."

Chapter Twenty-Two

The flashing lights of the car disappeared around a bend, leaving Alexa to kick aside the two cones the DI had flattened. She ran to the Sorento, punching Bruce's number into her phone. As soon as his infernal voice message shut up, she shouted, "Are you okay? Call me."

Her hand trembled as she typed Coronet Peak Ski Resort into the GPS. Sixteen kilometers, State Highway 6, hazardous conditions. She squashed another cone leaving and obeyed commands to head northwest, merge, continue, turn.

Gorge Road was scraped until she crossed the Shotover River Bridge. On the far side, like a curtain, the flurries thickened to something wicked, and the narrow road became two rutted tire tracks through snow. A sign flashed that chains were advised. She let a steady stream of cars—probably leaving the ski resort—go by, and then for several miles, she passed no houses, no trees, no more cars.

Then the road steepened. There was a cliff to her left and a drop-off on the right. At a curve, she tapped the brakes. The SUV fishtailed. Jeez. The tires caught. She slowed to a crawl. A knob between the seats caught her attention: *Snow Mode.*

Idiot.

She turned the knob, activating four-wheel drive. She accelerated with more control.

The sound of honking made her yelp. A black pickup truck,

lights flashing, filled her rearview mirror. There was no safe place to pull over. Then a damn bus came barreling at her. She jerked left, toward the cliff. The bus slowed to pass, inches between them. "Coronet Peak Ski Bus" was emblazoned on its side. Glum passengers stared down at her. A Queenstown Snow Transport van followed the bus.

Skiers, leaving.

She let the pickup and another car go by. The chains on the car's tires churned up snow and ice. In ten minutes, a sign flashed: AVALANCHE HAZARD. CORONET PEAK CLOSED.

Her heart pumped double time. Was Bruce okay? She rounded a bend, relieved to see parking lots and buildings and, beyond, a wide bank of mountains with chairlifts. No skiers were on the slopes. She couldn't see signs of the avalanche. A large banner spanned the road: WELCOME SNOWBOARD JUNIOR NATIONAL CHAMPIONS.

A helicopter hovered over the mountains. Another one landed in a clearing near the cluster of buildings.

A man in a high-visibility vest blocked the parking lot entrance. His eyebrows were frosted with ice. Alexa rolled down her window. "I'm working with the police." She pointed to the crime kit on the seat.

He frowned. "What's that?"

"A crime kit. I'm a forensic investigator." She showed her badge.

"We're evacuating. The police are ordering everyone to leave."

Alexa fantasized mowing him over with her car. "I have room, if anyone needs a ride."

He considered that. "They're loading buses now. Might be stragglers. Check in the lobby staging area." He waved her through. In the first parking area, a line of people boarded another bus. She pulled over. No one in the line looked like Bruce or the girls.

A police SUV, lights flashing, came up behind her. She let it pass and then followed it to the almost-empty lot closer to the buildings, where it parked. One of the remaining cars was a black Subaru like Bruce's. She pulled next to it and watched the cop let a dog out of a crate and attach it to a leash. First fire dogs, now avalanche dogs. The two of them jogged toward a large two-winged building. An adjacent smaller building was marked with a red cross.

Wind whipped her hair as she got out. She peeked into the Subaru. Bruce's All Blacks beanie was on the dash.

He was here. The girls, too. If any of them were hurt, they might be in the first-aid building. She jogged there.

Three teens in green CC Boarder jackets and an older man huddled under its eaves. "I couldn't see anything," a girl said. "Just a cloud of powder."

Alexa made eye contact with the man. His badge said Christchurch/Canterbury Snowboard Team. "What happened?"

He looked bewildered. "Snow cracked off during the slope-style qualifiers. One of my girls is missing."

"She was running the course," a boy said.

"I hope they find her," Alexa said. She entered the building. A wall of benches was crammed with people, one stanching a bloody nose, another cradling her arm. No familiar faces.

An inner door opened. "Make way, make way," a man said.

Alexa backed into a table. The man and two other people bore a stretcher. Alexa craned to see who was on it. A young male, maybe fifteen, eyes closed. A woman walked alongside, holding his hand. They rushed him through the door, maybe to the helicopter that had landed. One of the CC Boarders asked if he was okay. The door closed before Alexa heard the answer.

The young woman behind the table cleared her throat. Alexa turned. "Are you in charge?"

"Doing my bit." She wore a Coronet Peak staff jacket. "Emma Thomas. How can I help you?"

"I'm with the police. Forensics. Have there been fatalities?"

Emma's eyes flickered. "Forensics? No fatalities have been reported. That boarder who just left was swept into a gully. At this point, three people are unaccounted for."

Bruce. Sammie. Denise. Alexa bit down on her lip, the pain a distraction. "Have they released names?"

Emma shook her head. "They're trying to notify next of kin."

Who would that be? Bruce's ex.

"The restaurant in the lodge is where you can wait if you're missing someone. Otherwise, the resort is closed. People have left in droves."

The door to the outside banged open. "We've found one," a man shouted. Alexa recognized Heath, the long-haired guy from the Papa Penguin's parking lot. He and another ski patrol guy supported a white-faced teen between them, though she appeared to be walking okay.

The CC Boarders crammed in behind them. "Zoe. Are you okay? What happened?" they clamored.

Zoe's helmet was askew. Her upper lip was split and bleeding. "I heard a crack. I could feel it coming." She grimaced. "I thought I could beat it, go diagonal, but it caught me."

"Make room," Heath ordered.

Alexa backed into the table again. Everyone on the bench jumped up. Heath and the other guy helped Zoe sit. She shook violently as they wrapped a blanket around her. "My board—I lost my board."

"They'll find it, Zoe," a CC Boarder said.

"Snow pushed down on me like a weighted blanket. I couldn't breathe."

"Where's a doctor?" Heath called.

An EMT appeared. He looked at the crowd and said, "If you aren't hurt, leave the clinic. In fact, leave the resort." Then he knelt by Zoe.

Alexa filed out behind Heath and the other rescuer. Heath said, "It's dodgy. Shouldn't have been a slip."

"Maybe we missed the signs," the other guy said.

"Not according to the data and the drones. I'll lose my job."

"Bollocks. You just saved that kid. This slip came out of nowhere."

Three snowmobiles careened around the corner. A dog rode piggyback on one. Heath and his coworker followed them. Alexa hustled to the lodge. The open lobby had a vaulted beamed ceiling and a wall of windows framing the expanse of ski mountains. Alexa held her breath as she canvassed the hillsides, but she was unable to see where the avalanche occurred.

An announcement blared over loudspeakers. "Group B. Your transport is ready. Group B."

Twenty or so people, faces anxious, a few wearing blue QAST jackets and hugging snowboards, hurried past Alexa toward the exit. Underneath QAST was QUEENSTOWN ALPINE SNOWBOARD TEAM. The locals. A girl was crying. "They found a body," she said.

Alexa's heart flipped. A young police officer walked by, talking into a radio. She waved to get his attention. "Has someone been killed? I can't find my friend."

His badge said Constable Tweed. "There haven't been any reported fatalities. You need to leave."

"I will," she said.

The rental shop to her left was strewn with helmets,

snowboards, boots, even snowsuits, as if skiers had shed their skin on the fly. It was empty of people. She followed signs to Heidi's Restaurant.

Large-screen TVs displayed the ski slopes, eerily empty. A snowmobile crossed the bottom of one and vanished offscreen. Only ten or so tables were full. She spotted the chaperone from Villa 5—Lance of the sideburns—pacing by a large stone fireplace, the flames dying behind him. The red-haired boy, Cam, and two girls sat at a table, eyes on their phones. Cam was the one who mistook her for Denise's mom.

She scanned the tables for Bruce. What color was his jacket? She couldn't remember. Two men in ski-patrol jumpsuits strode in, stripped gloves, and tossed them on a table. "Excuse me," she said. "What's the latest?"

The taller one unzipped his suit and rubbed his hands together. His chest was heaving as if he'd been running. "Rescue is on standby," he said.

"But what about the missing people?"

He stopped rubbing. "We can't risk more lives."

Past his shoulder she spotted Bruce, staring out the expanse of windows. Alone. Her heart lurched. She threaded through tables to reach him. Sammie sprang up from one and intercepted her.

"Denise is missing," she said.

Chapter Twenty-Three

Sammie's eyes were saucers. Before Alexa responded, she called, "Dad! She's here."

Alexa cringed.

Bruce swung around. When he saw it was her, hope drained from his face. He closed the distance between them in three strides and took her forearms. "Denise is missing. Two kids from the snowboard competition are, too, including that kid Tex."

"They just found a girl. Not Denise," she added quickly. "She's in the medical building."

Color leached from his skin.

"She's alive. She's talking."

"Maybe she saw Denise." Bruce let go of her and pulled Sammie to his chest. He said into the top of her mussy hair, "Alexa will stay with you." He caught Alexa's eye. His were frantic. She nodded emphatically.

"But Dad. What if Denise is buried?"

"Denise wasn't boarding where the avalanche happened, Sam. I just have to find her."

They followed him to the restaurant exit, as if he were magnetic, and watched him jog through the lobby, his parka flapping open. Alexa memorized its color: cobalt.

She was processing on the fly. Denise was missing, and Bruce was going to find her. Her job was to keep Sammie safe. "Are you hungry?" she asked.

"I already ate." Sammie led Alexa back to a table strewn with belongings. A backpack. Helmets and gloves. Boots under the table. A half-eaten burger, anemic fries.

An announcement blared from loudspeakers. "Coronet Peak is closed. The final shuttle is departing from the main parking lot." The message repeated.

Three thirtysomething men in Junior World Championship parkas rose from the next table. "A Mother Nature cluster-fuck," one said. "Let's go." A trio of teenagers wearing Taranaki Shredder jackets tailed them. Another snowboard team, Alexa guessed.

Sammie looked panicked. "Everyone is leaving."

"We're not leaving without your dad and Denise."

Sammie plopped on a chair, leaned on the table, and put her head on her arms. She didn't have shoes on. Her socks were purple.

Alexa located a trash can. She threw the burger away and stopped by the NZ SNO Z table. Lance was ordering the three teens to leave. "Last bus," he said. "Go."

"Not leaving without Tex," Cam said. "He'd do the same for me."

"I'm not bailing on him, Cambo," Lance said. "You lot head to the villa. I'll call as soon as I find the nutter." He noticed Alexa. She could see he was trying to place her.

"I'm Alexa Glock. From Villa 6. Denise Horne is missing, too."

"Who's that?" Lance asked.

What kind of chaperone was he? "She was at your villa last night. Were she and Tex together?"

"Might have been," Cam said. "Tex didn't make the cut. He left with Denise."

"Cam was in the start zone when it happened," a girl with

short black hair said. "He might have been buried if he hadn't veered off. This is some kinda messed-up trip."

"With Bui AWOL, he'd have won," the other girl said.

"Bui was killing it," Cam said.

"Time to go. Now," Lance said.

The teens grumbled and headed to the exit, their young faces conveying a mix of worry and fear: something big had happened in their lives. Something to blast on social media. Movement caught her eye: Sammie in her red parka running toward the lobby. Alexa flew after her and caught her arm.

"Dad forgot his gloves." Sammie shook them.

"He'll be okay," Alexa said.

"No, he won't." She jerked her arm free. "He needs them to find Denise."

"You don't have shoes on," Alexa said. "I'll take them." She tugged the gloves out of Sammie's hand. "Wait here."

Alexa jogged past the SNO Z team, her own coat flapping open, and out the door, dodging the people boarding the bus. She hurried down the walkway and reached the medical clinic door just as Bruce emerged.

She held the gloves out. "Sammie wanted you to have them." *I did, too.* "Did you find out anything?"

"I asked you to stay with her." He yanked the gloves from her hands and turned away.

A surge of anger bubbled up. Alexa tamped it. "Wait!" For a second she thought he would ignore her, but he stopped.

"Denise might have been with Tex, the boy from next door."

His eyebrow went up. "How do you know?"

She pointed to the SNO Z team in line for the bus. "One of the kids saw him leave with Denise."

Bruce headed in their direction.

She called his name again.

He swung around.

"Good luck."

His eyes were beseeching. "I've got to find her."

Sammie's face lit up when Alexa returned. "He said thank you. Put your shoes on, and let's sit by the fire."

Sammie stuffed her feet into the snow boots Bruce had tugged off her the day before. They huddled on the bench closest to the cavernous fireplace. Alexa started shivering and zipped up her coat. The logs, down to embers, only hinted at heat. Sammie clutched her phone. "I keep texting Denise, but she never texts back."

"When is the last time she texted you?"

"Last night." Sammie held out her phone for Alexa to see. Denise had texted at 9:45 p.m.: LMK A doing, followed by a wacky face emoji.

Alexa didn't know what it meant. "That was when we were watching *Shazam*. Did you text back?"

Sammie flushed and stuffed the phone in her pocket. The meaning dawned on Alexa. LMK = Let me know. A = Alexa. Denise had asked Sammie to keep tabs on her.

Lance and the ski patrollers were the only others left in Heidi's. She thought of asking Lance to join them, but he was jabbering into his phone. To Tex's parents, maybe? She spotted an urn on a counter and hot-chocolate packets next to it. She popped up and made two cups of steaming cocoa.

"Thanks," Sammie said.

The warmth through the flimsy cup stopped Alexa's hands from trembling. She blew on the cocoa and took a few sips. "Um, where were you when the avalanche happened?"

Sammie's lips were coated in chocolate froth when she began talking. "Dad and I were riding the big lift to the top. The Coronet Express. For my boarding lesson. I heard something like a gun. The ski lift stopped." She stuck her nose in the half-empty cup and inhaled. Now she had a dab of chocolate on the tip of her nose. "Daddy cussed. He was looking at a white wave over where the competition was. I thought it was cool, but then I saw a person skiing, or boarding, and the snow was catching up. I think, I mean, she was trying to ski away from it, to get ahead of it."

Alexa finished her cocoa and put her arm around Sammie's shoulder. She tensed for rejection, but Sammie leaned into her.

"Then it was like mist, like a cloud. I couldn't see anymore. We just hung in the air, in the ski lift, not moving. It was cold. Two boys were with us, and one of them started crying. Dad said he was a policeman and that we were safe. But we were so high. The wind kept rocking us."

"Then what?"

"The lift started moving. When we got to the top, the lift guy wouldn't let us off. He yelled to ride it back down. When we did, Daddy found the boys' parents—they were all, like crying and hugging. There could be more avalanches, but we can't leave, not without Denise." Tears pooled in her eyes. She wiped them with the back of her hand. "Do you think she's buried?"

"I don't think so," Alexa said. "I think your dad will find her."

"But where is she?"

A tinny voice came from Sammie's pocket. *Mum is calling. Pick it up. Mum is calling. Pick it up.* Sammie set her cup on the floor and pulled the phone out. "Mum! There was an avalanche. We can't find Denise!"

Oh, my God, Alexa thought. *Bruce's ex was calling.*

"It's true. I swear." After some silence Sammie repeated her story. There was no holding back the tears this time. Alexa jumped up and ran to the counter. She snatched napkins from a holder, one after another, four, five, six, postponing her return. She glanced out the windows. A snowmobile whizzed by.

She returned to the bench, to the inevitable.

"Everyone is gone," Sammie cried. She listened to Sharla's reply. "I don't know *where* he is." She wiped her nose with the back of her hand. "In Heidi's, all by myself."

Alexa thrust the napkins into her hand to remind Sammie that she wasn't alone.

Sammie sniffled. "Dad's friend is here." She listened, paused. "*You know.* The tooth lady." She listened, nodded, and then held the phone toward Alexa. "It's my mum."

The inevitable had arrived. Alexa took the phone. "Sharla? This is Alexa Glock. I'm a forensic investigator."

"Forensics?" Bruce's ex-wife's voice teetered on the edge of a cliff. "Are you Bruce's girlfriend?"

"Um, yes. Bruce asked me to stay with Sammie. She's safe."

"Where's Denise? Have they found her?"

"Not yet. Bruce is looking for her."

"Her phone goes directly to voicemail, and Bruce doesn't answer his."

"He'll call you as soon as he finds her."

"The news said a survivor was buried to her waist."

"I saw the girl. It wasn't Denise."

"The reporter said the avalanche happened on Greengates while it was closed for the snowboard competition. So Denise couldn't have been there."

Sharla knew more than she did. "You're probably right. They've got dogs and helicopters."

"The news said the search was suspended."

"I don't know," Alexa lied. "Even if it is, it won't stop Bruce."

Sharla's voice sharpened. "I'm on my way."

Chapter Twenty-Four

Alexa walked to a large, color-coded map of Coronet Peak ski runs to give Sammie privacy with her mom. *Jeez.* She had just survived a conversation with Bruce's ex-wife. She had sounded sane and concerned.

She studied the map to get a sense of where the avalanche had occurred. The ski area had three chairlifts: Meadows Run to the right, Coronet Express in the middle—the one Sammie and Bruce had been riding—and Greengates to the left, where Sharla said the avalanche occurred.

Past Meadow's Run there was Kiwi T-bar to Easy Rider. *The bunny slope,* she thought dismissively.

Greengates Express led to several runs. Black Bowl and Sarah Sue were expert slopes. Greengates—halfway down Black Bowl—was the advanced slope where the competition had been taking place. Two other runs were classified as intermediate slopes. Alexa peered left out the windows. The Greengates chairlift wasn't visible. The loudspeaker made her jump. "The final bus has left the resort. Coronet Peaks is closed."

Alexa buried her hands in her pockets and felt a slip of paper in one. She pulled it out and examined three scrawled names. She almost crumpled it before she remembered they were names of Papa Penguin's employees by night and the ski slope employees by day. The avalanche patrol guy Heath had written them.

The burned body flickered in her mind and then faded away. Denise was her focus.

The cop she'd seen earlier—Constable Tweed—stalked over. "You're still here? You need to leave."

"My friend—DI Bruce Horne, Auckland Serious Crime Unit—his daughter Denise is missing." She pointed at Sammie. "That's his other daughter. We're waiting for news. Has the search been resumed?"

"Not yet. Heaps of people are waiting for the go-ahead. But you and the girl need to leave the ski resort. Safety reasons." He lowered his voice. "Could be another one."

"Another one what?"

His eyes darted to the expanse of glass. "Avalanche." A drum circle started in her eardrums as she followed his gaze. The mountains looked sinister.

Sammie ran over. "Have you found Denise?"

The constable stepped back.

"They haven't found her yet," Alexa said.

Sammie persisted. "You'll find her, right?"

Constable Tweed's eyes jumped back to the windows. The Coronet Express chairlifts rocked in gusts of wind. "We're under evacuation orders," he said. "No exceptions except for law enforcement and rescue workers."

"I'm not leaving," Sammie said.

It was Alexa's sole job to keep the kid safe. "We'd better go, Sammie." Her eyes widened.

Constable Tweed chimed in. "You'll be safer to wait off the mountain, eh?"

"No." Tears streamed down Sammie's face.

"I'll call your dad and tell him," Alexa said desperately. She pressed Bruce's number, surprised he picked up right away. "Any luck?" she asked, her eyes on Sammie.

"One of the SNO Z girls saw Denise and Tex on Greengates right before the avalanche. They won't let me up there."

On Greengates. That was not good news. "Where are you?"

"Waiting in the lift hut for the search to resume."

In the path of another avalanche. "The police are ordering us to evacuate." She didn't want to alarm Sammie. "As a precaution."

"Do it," Bruce said.

An image of wrestling Sammie out the door popped into her head. "Sammie doesn't want to leave."

"Put her on."

Sammie grabbed her phone. "Dad. Where are you? Do you have Denise?"

Alexa couldn't hear what he said. Sammie's chin quivered. "But I want to wait here."

She listened some more, studied her boots, sniffed, and finally thrust the phone at Alexa without saying goodbye.

"Bruce?"

The line was dead.

Sammie spoke to the constable. "My dad said my mum is coming, and I have to meet her at the villa."

"Good plan," Constable Tweed said.

Alexa tamped a spark of jealousy. It figured that Bruce and Sharla would have communicated. She and Sammie stuffed everything on the table into a backpack except the two helmets. "Why don't you wear yours to the car?" Alexa suggested.

Sammie tugged it on. Alexa was tempted to wear Bruce's but carried it by the strap and hefted the backpack. The lobby was eerily empty. Constable Tweed escorted them to the parking lot. The Sorento was covered with two inches of fresh snow. Bruce's car had even more on it. Sammie drew a big heart on its windshield. It broke Alexa's heart to watch. When would Bruce unlock it? Would Denise be with him?

The constable cleared the Sorento's back window as Alexa

swept the front clean with bare hands. "Do you have chains?" he asked.

"I have Snow Mode." She unlocked the doors and set their stuff in the back seat. Sammie sat in the front. A dog and handler passed by, the dog straining at its lead.

"Drive slow. Keep to the middle," Constable Tweed said. "You won't meet traffic; the road at the bottom is barricaded." He pulled up his collar and headed back to the lodge like a good soldier. All the police and rescue workers were in peril. Alexa turned the heat on full blast. She felt ill-equipped and was facing peril, too.

What had she gotten herself into? Having responsibility for Sammie was terrifying. How did parents do it? Caring was too scary.

Let me keep this child safe.

Sammie pulled the helmet off and studied her.

Alexa smiled wanly. "Buckle up."

Snow fell lightly. She turned the wipers on low and edged the SUV around the cones blocking the parking lot entrance and banked the first curve. Then the windshield fogged up. Sammie cleared a circle with her hand. Alexa fumbled for the defroster and inched along until she could see again. She focused on the missing-Denise puzzle.

First: a time line. It was currently one o'clock. The avalanche had occurred at eleven. Denise and Tex had been missing for two hours. Where were they? Buried?

The information she possessed was bare-boned. Greengates had been closed to the public. Denise should not have been in the path of the avalanche. Also, Tex and Denise might be together. She didn't know if that was a positive or negative.

Sharla photobombed her thoughts. Bruce's ex-wife was on her way.

Holy crap.

She did the math. Sharla was on the North Island, and Queenstown was on the South Island. Sharla would have to get to an airport, wait for a flight, fly two hours, rent a car.

Alexa exhaled. She focused on her quiet passenger. "There's a frozen pizza at the villa. We'll heat it up when we get back. How does that sound?"

"It's Denise's birthday. We're going out for dinner."

Holy crap again. What if—no—she wouldn't go there. Denise had to be okay. "The pizza will tide us over."

She kept to the middle of the road, as Constable Tweed suggested. Tracks left by departing vehicles were quickly disappearing. The road began descending. Past Sammie's shoulder, beyond the precipitous drop-off, a pearly landscape stretched into the distance. She double-checked that the 4WD was in Snow Mode and hunched forward. A blast of wind juddered them. She squeezed the steering wheel and slowed. "We don't get much snow where I'm from," she told Sammie.

"We don't, either. That's why Nana and Granddad have a villa. So we can see snow."

Alexa wondered if the grandparents knew what was happening. She pushed her glasses up her nose and glanced at Sammie. She clutched her phone. She must have felt Alexa's gaze, because she said, "No service. Denise can't call me."

Alexa hated being cut off from civilization. It happened all the time in New Zealand. In her nervousness she steered too close to the snowbank out her window. It scraped the side-view mirror. She jerked toward the middle. Her greenstone pendant, burrowed under puffy coat and fleece, heated up against her chest. Its carver spoke in her ear: *accelerate*. She pressed the gas not knowing why.

A loud thump sounded out of nowhere. Something hit the

car. The interior dimmed. The car slid sideways as if shoved by hulking hands. Toward the drop-off. Alexa tapped the brakes and wrenched the steering wheel, but the car was no longer under her control.

Chapter Twenty-Five

When the car stilled, Alexa tried to make sense of it.

Someone had thrown a bucket of white paint over the windshield. Or someone had dropped a snow bomb. Was there such a thing?

Sammie yanked her door handle. The door wouldn't open. She used her shoulder and shoved. The door opened halfway, the bottom scraping against snow. They were close to the drop-off.

Holy shit. "Close your door, Sammie. Don't move," she ordered.

Sammie froze but left the door open.

Alexa yanked at her door handle and pushed. The door wouldn't budge. She lowered her window and punched through a wall of snow. Her fist left a hole, but there was no light at the end of the tunnel. She raised the window, her hand freezing.

"What happened?" Sammie asked.

Alexa fought panic. "I'm not sure." She unbuckled her seat belt and pulled back the sunroof cover to reveal a mantle of white. The view out the rear window was also grayish white. Through Sammie's open door was the way to see out, and Alexa didn't like the view.

"What's the noise?" Sammie asked.

The motor. The car was still in drive. Alexa put it in neutral. Could she back up? Push the snow? Too risky. She tried the windshield wipers. They struggled futilely.

She thought of the tailpipe—clogged. Exhaust fumes would build inside and asphyxiate them. She quickly turned the car off. Then she laughed. Sammie's door was open, so asphyxiation was one peril she could banish.

"What's funny?" Sammie asked.

"Nothing." The open door was their escape. "I need you to change seats with me."

"No." Sammie pushed the door open another inch and leaned out.

Alexa grabbed her by the sleeve. "Change seats with me. Or climb into the back."

Sammie looked incredulous. "Why? What even happened?"

"I think a tiny avalanche."

"But it pushed the car." Sammie's voice was high-pitched. "How is that even tiny?"

"We're okay," Alexa said. Whether that was true or not she didn't know. "I want to be the first one out, to see if it's safe, and my door is stuck." She lowered her voice, tried for a gentle tone. "That's why I want you to hop in the back."

Sammie wriggled over the armrest, squeezed between the bucket seats, and flopped into the back seat. Alexa struggled across the gear shift, her coat catching, and plopped in the passenger seat. "We did it," she panted.

"Now what?" Sammie demanded.

Alexa stuck her head out. The view sucked the air out of her lungs. They were three feet from the edge. What if Sammie had bolted from the car and slipped? She closed her eyes and conjured Bruce's face. He trusted her, trusted that Sammie was safe so he could concentrate on Denise. Alexa pushed the door open farther. A clod of snow fell from the roof, but other than that, nothing happened. She craned her neck toward the resort, but the road was blocked by mounded snow. She checked the other way. The road to Queenstown was fine.

She tested the ground. Her boot sank in crusty snow. "We can get out this way, but we have to be careful. Put on your warmest clothes. We might have a long walk."

Sammie yanked things out of the backpack and pulled on various items. "Should I wear my helmet?"

Alexa nodded. Her medium-twill khaki pants concerned her. She had dressed for an autopsy, not an avalanche. At least she wore boots and had a hat, gloves, and her puffer jacket, which came down to her waist. She wondered about lugging the crime kit with her but decided against it.

Burning buildings or avalanches. Only take what's necessary.

She called 111. There was still no service. "Let me go first and make sure it's safe." She pulled on her gloves. "Wait for me to say it's okay to get out."

She stepped out, keeping her hands on the car door. One foot slipped. She scrambled to catch her balance and then, keeping one hand on the car, walked the narrow shoulder. She made herself look down the cliff; an icy ledge was ten feet below, and after that, a void. A blur of movement caught her eye, and then Sammie was out of the car behind her.

"I wasn't staying in there."

The kid reminded her of herself. "Keep your hands on the car."

They trudged the length of the SUV to the road. When they were a few yards past, they turned to look. A fifteen-foot-high heap of snow—embedded with roots, rocks, and ice—blocked the entire road. Alexa could see its merciless path down the hillside. She backed up farther and stood on her tiptoes. The slide was too jumbled to climb over. If she hadn't accelerated when she did, they'd have been buried on all four sides. Her knee joints liquefied.

"Wicked," Sammie said.

The road leading back to the ski resort was blocked. Until earthmovers arrived, the people there—Bruce, Denise—would be trapped. Alexa tried her phone again. No bars.

"Let's start walking," she said.

"Where to?" Sammie asked.

"Queenstown." Constable Tweed had said the resort road was barricaded, so chances were as slim as two daughters in two separate avalanches that they'd meet a car.

A helicopter swooped overhead. Black with red lettering on its belly. Alexa waved until it dipped out of sight. It couldn't land where they were, but the pilot would have seen the slide. She felt hope as they walked away from the mess. For five minutes Sammie was quiet, but then she asked, "Do you think Dad has found Denise yet?"

"I hope so."

"Denise is in love with Tex."

Alexa skirted an icy spot. "She is?"

"Tex's luck ran out."

"What do you mean?"

"He went to a party at Papa Penguin's the night it burned down." Sammie wandered close to the drop-off and then veered back to Alexa's side. "A secret party, after the restaurant closed. He was lucky the party was over before the fire, but today he isn't lucky."

The hairs on the back of Alexa's neck stood. "How do you know about this party?"

"He told Denise, and she told me. All the kids from Villa 5 went."

Alexa's mind ricocheted. If the decedent was a snowboarder, surely some parents would be frantic. Maybe they had called the police by now. But what about the arson aspect? Did one of the kids set the fire?

Her mind explored possibilities, like a wolf slinking through the woods scenting prey.

"Why is snow quiet when it falls but crunches when you walk in it?" Sammie asked.

Alexa searched the hillside, alert for another avalanche. The wind cut through the fabric of her pants. She could see her breath. "Friction maybe?"

They rounded a bend, and the road straightened. "Tell me another tooth story," Sammie said.

Alexa searched her data bank. A sliver of blue breaking through the gray clouds reminded her of the Blue Nun. "Do you know what plaque is?"

"That's why we brush our teeth. To get rid of plaque."

"If you don't brush your teeth, things can get trapped in the plaque."

"Like what?"

"All sorts of weird things. Food particles, bacteria, fibers, even insect wings." She eyed her phone: still no bars.

"Bug wings. Gross."

"Right? Archaeologists found an old, old skeleton of a nun in Germany. When they looked at the nun's teeth, they saw bright blue stuck in the plaque."

Sammie's nose ran. She swiped at it with her mitten.

"The blue was the same color as your eyes. And your dad's." Bruce. She hoped he was okay, safe. "They did tests to see what the blue was."

"Was it ink?"

The kid was smart. "It was particles of lapis lazuli, a stone ground down as a paint pigment. The nun was probably a painter."

"Cool," Sammie said. "How did the blue stuff get in her mouth?"

"They think she wet her paintbrush to get the tip right. It's cooler than cool because it proves women were painters back when everyone thought only men were trusted to be painters."

"Look," Sammie yelled.

A bright-orange dump truck approached, its front plow suspended above the road. The driver stopped ten feet away and stuck his head out the window.

Alexa smiled. "My car is stuck half a mile up the road. Can you get it out?"

"There's been another avalanche," he said. "That have anything to do with it?"

"Everything," Alexa said.

Chapter Twenty-Six

Alexa brushed a candy-bar wrapper from the bench seat and scooched over so Sammie could sit by the window. The cab was warm and sat high.

Their savior, Ted, situated his bulk next to her. "Chopper pilot reported the Coronet Peak egress was blocked. Trouble follows trouble, eh?"

"Story of my life," Alexa said.

"Our car was buried," Sammie said. "We almost died."

Sammie's words were close to true.

"My sister might be buried," Sammie added.

Ted caught Alexa's eye.

"Her sister and a boy are missing. You know. The avalanche that closed the slopes." Alexa put an arm around Sammie, and she didn't pull away.

The dump truck retraced their trek, and minutes later they arrived back. Ted whistled when he saw the Sorento. "Pushed you close to the edge, eh?" He checked his phone for service, tossed it on the dash, and picked up a radio. "Fanny?"

"Eh, boss."

"Send more plows to clear the road. And a tow truck."

"I'll see who I can rustle up," the Fanny person said.

Ted put the truck in park and left the motor running. "No worries you'll freeze," he said.

He pulled on gloves, grabbed a shovel from the back, and

attacked the mound a nibble at a time. When a second truck arrived, he jumped in the cab with the driver. They lowered the plow and started tunneling and clearing. Then a tow truck arrived and pulled the Sorento out. The driver's door was dented. Alexa exchanged payment information and asked Ted how long it would take to clear the road.

"Couple hours. You get your lass home."

My lass.

A sandbag weighed on her shoulders as she crawled down the mountain—twice squeezing past snowplow trucks.

Denise was missing. Maybe dead. Time to face the facts.

She glanced at Sammie. The kid was nodding off. Her dark hair curled around her face, her long eyelashes brushed her cheeks. Alexa knew the concept of "maternal instincts" was rooted in sexist ideology and not biology, but the sight of Bruce's younger daughter poked and prodded at motherly feelings deep in her heart.

Her phone buzzed. She patted her pockets and couldn't find it. She jerked the Sorento to the side of the road. A slab of snow slid off the roof, smothering the windshield. *Jeez.* The phone was in the cup holder. Bruce's name flashed. "Hello?"

"They found her."

Her heart stopped.

"Search drones spotted them on Sarah Sue, a slope that was closed. They've been flown to hospital. Denise is early stages hypothermic, but they're warming her up. A second avalanche blocked the road. I can't get to her."

"Oh, Bruce."

Sammie woke with a start. "Is it Dad?"

Alexa put the phone on speaker.

"Daddy? Did you find Denise?"

"She's okay, Sam. Denise and Tex were helicoptered to

hospital to get warm and be checked out. We'll see you soon, okay?"

"Okay. But when?"

Alexa yelled, "We'll be waiting at the villa," and hung up. She didn't want Sammie to worry Bruce about how they'd almost been buried themselves. He had enough to deal with.

The sandbag lifted from her shoulders. She high-fived with Sammie. In town the roads had been cleared and the snow had stopped falling. When they reached the villa, she parked right in front instead of in the guest spot.

Sammie punched in the code, and they were inside. After ditching her coat, Alexa scurried straight to the kitchen to pre-heat the oven.

Calories. She was desperate.

Sammie ran to her bedroom.

Alexa heard a thump from the snowboard team's villa. The kids were probably alone while their chaperone—Lance—was stuck at Coronet Peak with Bruce. They might not know Tex was okay. She wanted to eat something hot and gooey and then curl up in bed and let the adrenaline drain from her body. But the kids deserved to know their teammate was alive.

Sammie sat on the edge of her bed, phone in one hand and stuffed tiger in the other. She tossed the tiger on the floor when she saw Alexa. "Mum doesn't answer."

The thought of Sharla showing up made Alexa's knees buckle. "Your mom is probably in the air, you know, flying here. She'll call you as soon as she lands." Alexa sat on the bed across from Sammie, who obviously felt abandoned by her family, and picked up the tiger. "Sometimes I feel all alone in New Zealand." She petted the tiger's soft head. "Does he have a name?"

"No. That's stupid. Why do you feel alone?"

Alexa hugged the tiger to her chest. "I might get one of these for Benny. I mean Ben. My nephew. That's what he wants to be called now. I keep forgetting." She rambled. Maybe parenting was rambling. And stumbling. "I feel alone because, well, I'm not good at making friends." Or making commitments.

Sammie didn't look up. "How come you don't have kids?"

"Well, not everyone wants to have them." Why would she say that to a kid? "I work too much. I'd never be home to take care of one. But if I had a kid, I'd want her to be like you. You're brave and smart and like tooth stories."

"Dad is never home." Her Bruce-clone eyes met Alexa's. "Denise says I'm too old for stuffed animals."

Alexa snorted.

"Charlie," Sammie said. "My tiger is Charlie."

"That's a great name. That's my brother's name."

They sat in comfortable silence. Then Alexa struggled to her feet and put Charlie in Sammie's lap. "I'm going to put the pizza in. While it's baking, I'll pop next door to check on the snowboard team. They might not know Tex is safe."

Plus she could ask about the Papa Penguin's party.

Chapter Twenty-Seven

Cam answered the door.

"I'm Alexa from Villa 6. Did you hear they found Tex?"

The girl with short black hair popped up behind him. She was petite and of Asian descent. "Is he okay?"

Poor kids. No one told them. "He's okay. Denise Horne is, too." She stepped into the foyer, forcing the kids to back up, and pulled the door shut. "What's your name?" she asked.

"Kool."

"Cool name."

The girl rolled her eyes. "Spelled with a K."

Alexa regretted the name comment. She got them all the time. *Alexa, what's the weather? Glock? Like the gun?* "Are any adults here?"

"Lance is stuck at Coronet Peak," Kool said.

"Denise's dad, the police detective, called me. He said Denise and Tex are at the hospital. They're okay."

"Where were they?" Cam asked.

"On Sarah something. A slope that was closed."

Cam and Kool looked at each other. "Tex is always hooning around," Kool said.

"I saw Tex on top of Greengates," another girl called. She slid around the corner in socks. Her frizzy brown hair was parted in the middle and hung to her shoulders. She was taller and heavier than Kool and Cam. "Right before the avalanche."

Alexa stepped over strewn coats. "What's your name?"

"Breezy. Tex is okay?"

Could Kool and Breezy be real names? Maybe snowboarders had stage names. "Yes. He's being checked out at the hospital."

"Sweet as," Breezy said.

To catch them off guard, Alexa asked, "Were you guys with him Thursday night? At the Papa Penguin's party?"

Kool bit her lip. Breezy rolled her shoulders. Cam paled.

Alexa tried a different approach. "Someone died in the fire. I'm working with the police, and we don't know who he is." She scanned their young faces and worried eyes. Could one of them have set the fire?

Breezy's eyes widened so much that the white above her irises was visible. "Who is he?"

These kids were barely older than Sammie. "We haven't identified him yet," she repeated. "He's in his teens or early twenties."

"He wasn't at the party, was he?" Breezy asked.

"Maybe. That's why I need your help. Who all was there?"

Kool raised her pointy chin toward Breezy. "Maybe it's one of your QAST *friends*."

"Up yours." Breezy's face reddened. "It was us, some Papa P servers, and a few other boarders. A couple of kids got crunk. They tried to cook a pizza."

"Drunk?" Alexa asked.

"Crazy drunk," Breezy clarified.

"Was your chaperone at the party?"

Breezy pantomimed putting on headphones. "Not even. Lance was deaf to the world."

Alexa would order Bruce to never let his girls go on a chaperoned trip. She walked to the dining table. It was littered with soda cans, dirty plates, and three ski helmets, one pink, one blue, and one black. She removed a backpack from a chair and sat. "How many people were there?"

Cam slumped in a chair. Kool and Breezy leaned against the kitchen counter. "Twenty, maybe," Breezy said.

Kool elbowed her.

Breezy elbowed Kool back. "A guy who works there let us in. He had permission from his boss."

"What's his name?"

Cam swallowed. "Are we in trouble?"

Let me count the ways. "You'll be in less trouble if you help us."

"Graham," Breezy said. "That's his name. I used to watch him ride the rodeo."

"Rodeo?" Alexa asked.

"Tricks. Front flip with a twist. He did the backside rodeo, too. Or could. He invited us when we were eating at Papa's earlier that night. We didn't know anything about the fire until the morning."

Alexa paused. "After I came over Thursday night to ask you to turn the music down, you all went out?"

Kool looked sheepish. "We walked. But Papa's was fine when we left."

"What's Graham's last name?"

"He won Junior Champs a couple years ago." Breezy searched on her phone. "Graham Clark. FreeSki Big Air."

"He was dope," Kool said.

Maybe John Doe was this Graham person. Alexa stood up. "A police officer will need to speak with you. Try to remember more details." She didn't want to leave them alone to concoct a story. "Want to come next door for megameat pizza?"

Kool cringed. "I don't eat animals."

The other two followed her.

Chapter Twenty-Eight

"Sammie? We have company."

Sammie waved an oven mitt. "I took the pizza out."

Crap. The kid could have burned herself. Keeping Sammie safe was fraught with peril.

Breezy and Cam stood behind her. "I've seen you at school," Cam said. "Isn't Lindsey in your class?"

Sammie's eyes lit up. She nodded.

"This is Breezy," Alexa said. "They're ready for pizza."

The teens followed her into the kitchen. Alexa sliced the large pie. The melted cheese, sausage, pepperoni, and Canadian bacon smelled divine. Her stomach rumbled as she handed out plates. She studied Breezy's and Cam's fingertips as they accepted them. Nothing bright red or blistered.

Even though she was starved, she let the kids go first. Cam piled three slices on his plate. Breezy did the same, and Sammie scarfed the last two. She watched as every bite disappeared down the gullet of these giant baby birds. How was that possible?

Alexa petulantly ate a banana. The kids took over the sofa, seeming to take comfort in the others' proximity, Sammie looking small next to Breezy, who waved her phone at Cam. "Tex doesn't answer."

"He lost his phone," Cam said.

Alexa's phone was almost dead. She went into her bedroom and plugged it in to call DI Katakana, who, she remembered, was stuck at Coronet Peak, too, unless the snowplow had liberated everyone. The DI didn't answer. Alexa left a message and called the police station's general number. She told the desk clerk she had information about the Papa Penguin's fire. "Someone needs to call me as soon as possible."

Her khakis were muddy. Before tossing them aside for clean jeans, she checked the pockets, finding a note with three scrawled names: Graham Clark, Dane Bui, Mutt Stanford.

The avalanche patrol guy had written the names of the lifties who also worked at Papa Penguin's. She had asked Bruce to check whether they had showed up for work at Coronet Peak; he'd been diverted. Breezy said it was Graham Clark who had invited them to the party. Alexa pressed out the creases, photographed the slip, and sent it to the DI.

She was tethered to the charger and couldn't sprawl on the bed. She sat at the edge and checked her email. Three dental practices had responded regarding the glacier skull. The results were discouraging: "No such patient," times three.

The skull made her think of her nightmare on the glacier. A quick search took her to an article:

HUMAN REMAINS ON MOUNT ASPIRING

A human skull and foot found on Mount Aspiring are thought to have been on the mountain for more than 40 years.

The remains were found by ice climbers on the "toe end" of Blue Peak Glacier on August 19.

The ice climbers contacted police, who alerted Wanaka Search and Rescue. An alpine rescue team accompanied by DI Pattie Katakana and a forensic odontologist retrieved the remains. "We're working as swiftly as possible to confirm the identity of the decedent before contacting relatives," DI

Katakana said. "Additional remains were discovered in a crevasse. We hope to retrieve them soon."

A pelvis in a Speedo, embedded in ice. Alexa had nearly been embedded, too. A bang made her drop her phone. Voices filled the hallway.

"Denise," Sammie screamed.

Alexa dropped the phone and raced into the hallway.

Sammie flung her arms around Denise. Bruce, holding Denise's new snowboard, watched his girls embrace, the relief in his eyes large as a billboard. The thought of losing one of his daughters, of never seeing the sisters together again, must have been excruciating.

Bruce broke his reverie, leaned the board against the wall, and caught Alexa's gaze. He held them like they were alone. Warmth flooded her chest. "Denise. I'm so glad you're okay," she said.

Cam and Breezy crowded the foyer. Denise broke free from her sister, ignored Alexa, and struggled out of her coat.

"I invited the SNO Z kids over since they were alone," Alexa said.

"Are Tex and Lance back?" Breezy asked.

"Lance is waiting for Tex's mother to arrive," Bruce told her. "They're still at hospital."

"Tex's Mum is coming?" Breezy asked.

Bruce nodded.

Sharla was probably on the same plane as Tex's mom. Alexa looked toward the front door, planning an escape route.

"Is Tex hurt?" Cam asked.

"His body temperature is a little low," Bruce said. "They're warming him up."

"What happened during the avalanche?" Cam asked Denise. "Everyone thought you guys got buried."

Denise glanced at Bruce and then away. "After Tex was eliminated, which was like so close, like less than a second…"

"Not that close," Breezy said.

"He thought it would be fun to board Sarah Sue, the slope that was closed. Like have it all to ourselves. We were heading there. Tex was cutting back and forth, showering me with powder."

"Snow bath," Breezy said.

"I heard a crack and a whumpf, and then everything below us was a dust cloud." Her voice broke. "I didn't know what it was at first. I didn't know if people were dead."

"Dad and me were in the chairlift," Sammie said.

Bruce's face stayed neutral, but his eyes were barometers. Alexa recognized a storm brewing in them as Denise's story clarified in her brain. The kids had been above the avalanche—in a closed area—not in the avalanche's path.

"I was in the start zone. It almost mowed me over," Cam said.

"We were in an avalanche, too," Sammie said.

Everyone ignored her. Alexa was relieved.

Denise focused on shedding her boots. "We tried to board down Sarah Sue, but it was blocked off. Avalanche netting or something." Her voice quickened. "I didn't know what to do."

Cam edged past, toward the door. "Better check on Kool," he said. "Give her a report."

Miss "I Don't Eat Animals." She was alone in Villa 5.

"You're welcome to stay," Bruce said, but Cam waved and left. Bruce hung his coat and sniffed the air. "Do I smell pizza?"

A man after her own stomach. "The kids ate it all," Alexa said. "I'll run get another one." She grabbed her tote and bumped into Bruce in the hallway. She pulled him into a hug, the solidness and scent of him evidence that he, and his girls, were safe.

His neck and back muscles were taut. "I was so damn scared," he said.

She would tell him about the second avalanche later. And what she'd found out from the NZ SNO Z kids. He was Mr. Dad now, not a police officer. "Your wife, I mean ex-wife, is on her way."

He pushed back and stared at her. "You talked to Sharla?"

"She called Sammie when Denise was missing, and we spoke. I told her you'd find Denise."

"I haven't been able to reach her. She's probably in the air."

Alexa looked toward her bedroom. "I can find another place to stay."

"Why? You're staying here."

A smile tugged at her lips as she drove off but evaporated when she passed Papa Penguin's. The ruins were ethereal in a coat of fresh snow. Her *pounamu* pendant pulsed beneath her layers of clothes. What was it telling her?

Ugliness hides beneath beauty.

Her body ached as she drove. She felt like Gumby, the stretchy retro toy. Bruce tugged one leg. The arson case tugged on the other. The glacier skull pulled one arm. Her need for autonomy stretched the other arm.

In the middle, being tugged, too, was her heart. Like her stomach, it had a life of its own.

She bought two extra large pizzas, one meat and one veggie, in case Kool needed nourishment. She added a family-sized bag of sour-cream-and-chive potato chips and a box of donuts. She ate one on her way back to the villa.

The spot in front of Villa 5 was still vacant. No Lance or Tex yet. The three girls, cuddled under a blanket, watched TV. Alexa dangled the potato chips above them. Breezy grabbed the bag. The scent of salt, oil, and chives as she tore it open made Alexa salivate. She put the pizzas in the still-hot oven—damn, she had forgotten to turn it off. Competent homemaker she was not. She found Bruce, eyes shut, stretched on the king bed in the primary bedroom. She sat on the edge. He opened his eyes and smiled.

The smile would vanish. "Right before the avalanche, fire investigators discovered evidence of arson at Papa Penguin's. Someone used a liquid ignitable. Gas, probably."

He sat up.

"It gets worse. Tex and the Villa 5 kids went to a party there the night it burned. An after-hours party."

"How do you know?"

It would sound like the whisper game, but she plunged ahead. "Tex told Denise who told Sammie who told me. I talked with the kids before you got back, and they admitted it."

He swung his legs around and sat next to her. Her phone buzzed. She pulled it out and showed Bruce the name on the screen: DI Katakana. She answered.

"Ms. Glock. I trust DI Horne's daughter is rescued?"

"She's safe and back at the villa. I'm here with Bruce."

"*Tino pai.* That's great. You left a message?"

She repeated what she had told Bruce.

"Bloody hell. That makes them suspects."

"A few of them are staying in the villa next door. Their chaperone is still at the hospital with the boy Denise Horne was with."

"Constable Blume and I will be there in thirty. Get over there. I don't want them alone."

Chapter Twenty-Nine

Alexa glanced longingly at the meat pizza, slid the veggie pizza on a tray, and hoisted it. "Let's go, Breezy. The police are on their way."

Denise's mouth dropped. "Why?"

Bruce frowned down at his elder daughter. "I think you know why."

Sammie looked clueless.

Next door, Kool eyed the pizza like it was first prize, even after Breezy said the police were on their way. "I'll get plates," she said.

The donut she'd scarfed in the car had only stoked Alexa's appetite. The pizza tasted decent once she pulled off the mushrooms, and the calories stoked her energy level.

Breezy demolished a slice, even though she had already eaten three next door. "Where is Cam?" she said.

Kool pointed toward the bedrooms.

"Cam," they screamed in unison.

A rapping at the door shut them up. DI Katakana peered through the glass. Alexa jumped up to let her and Constable Blume in.

Hair had escaped from the clasp at the DI's neck. Her pants, which had been freshly pressed when they'd attended the autopsy early this morning, were wrinkled and marred by avalanche or ash. "What's the screaming about?"

"The girls are rallying the troops."

The constable removed his cap and looked suspiciously beyond Alexa.

The three boarders slunk into the foyer like delinquents. Alexa took a fresh look at them. Breezy, tall and muscular, rolled her shoulders. Her deep-set brown eyes were wary. Cam ran a hand through his red hair, leaving it sticking up in places. He wore socks with flip-flops. Kool held her chin up. Alexa sensed people underestimated her because of her petite stature.

The DI nodded at them. "*Kia ora.* I'm Detective Inspector Katakana, and this is Constable Blume. All three of you went to this Papa Penguin's party Thursday night?"

They nodded in unison.

"Is your chaperone here?"

"No," said Breezy.

"What's Mr. Brown's number?"

Breezy found it on her phone and read it aloud.

"I'll let him know what's going on." The DI stepped past the teens and into one of the bedrooms.

"Let's move to the table," Constable Blume said. "I'll take down your names and ages." His boyish freckles and gentle voice swayed the girls. They sat obediently. Cam sank on the sofa a few feet away, his back to them.

Breezy pushed the leftover pizza out of the way. "I'm Breezy O'Brien, sixteen. My mother is a lawyer."

"Like how is that relevant?" Kool asked.

Breezy rolled her shoulders. "How is it not?"

"All good." Constable Blume sat across from the girls. "Is Breezy your real name?"

"It's what everyone calls me."

"Eh, is it officially your name?"

"Elizabeth is on my birth certificate."

Alexa leaned against the counter, glad to let the constable do the questioning.

Kool fidgeted with a bracelet of braided colored threads on her wrist. "I'm Kool Shima, fifteen. Are the Junior Championship qualifiers canceled?"

"I don't know. Is Kool your given name?"

"It's Katelyn." Her eyes hid behind her shiny black bangs. "Ms. Glock said you don't know who died in the fire?"

"That's right," Constable Blume said.

Cam turned to face them. "The competition doesn't matter. We're in heaps of trouble."

Kool peeked out from under her bangs. "We just partied. We didn't burn the place down."

"What's your name?" Constable Blume asked the boy.

"Cam Keeline."

"Cambo, " Breezy said.

"Might like my own nickname," Constable Blume said.

"I can hook you up," Breezy said. "How about Boom Boom?"

He flushed. "Just so you know, you have special rights because of your ages."

"Like we can have a lawyer?" Kool asked.

"That's right," Constable Blume said. "You don't have to speak to us." He smiled as if *that* were a dumb idea. "You can remain silent, or you can wait until your parents are here or pick an adult of your choice as a support person. Like your chaperone."

"Lance is a dag," Breezy said. "I'm calling my mother. I'll do what she says."

"I don't want to bother my dad." Cam pointed at Alexa. "I'll take her as my support person."

Alexa snapped to. "Um, I'm kind of busy. Plus, I don't know what a support person does."

"Make sure he understands his rights, that's all," Constable Blume said.

DI Katakana returned to the dining area. "Mr. Brown has contacted each of your parents with updates and has assured them you're safe. He has been notified by the qualifying committee that the competition will continue. The location is to be announced."

Kool clapped her hands like a kid, *which she was,* Alexa reminded herself.

DI Katakana did not look amused. "Mr. Brown asked if one of you would pack up Tex's things."

"He's leaving?" Cam asked.

"His mother is assuming responsibility for him," DI Katakana said.

Cam slid off the couch with the agility of an otter. "I will."

"Wait," Constable Blume said. "DI Katakana will talk with you first, then you can."

"I'll just follow you, eh?" the DI said.

"He wants Ms. Glock as his support person," Constable Blume called.

The DI looked at Cam, who shrank under her gaze but nodded.

In the bedroom, Cam leaned against the dresser, staring at his feet. DI Katakana stepped over discarded clothing and sat on the edge of one of the unmade beds. Alexa stood in the doorway. The room smelled fecund and sweaty. Teen-boy chemicals, she deduced.

The DI used her phone as a recording device. "I'm not reading you your rights because you haven't been arrested. I just want to hear about the party. You don't have to speak. Do you understand?"

"Yeah," he said. "The other cop said the same thing."

"And you want Ms. Glock, a forensic investigator, as your support person?"

"I guess."

"Tell me about your family," DI Katakana said. "Who's your mum and dad? Where do you live? Go to school?"

"Rotorua Lakes High School, same as Tex. Well, Tex transferred to ACG Tauranga." He looked at Alexa. "Denise Horne goes to Rotorua Lakes, too."

"You're what year?" DI Katakana asked.

"Form six." Cam let out a long breath. His tannin-colored eyes filled with tears. "I live with my dad and sister, Lindsey. She's twelve."

Why was he tearing up? Alexa wanted to protect her support kid.

"What about your mother?" DI Katakana asked.

His voice was barely audible. "She died a couple years ago."

The DI's face softened. "*Ka aroha hoki.* Does your father know about the party?"

"Which one?"

"There was more than one?"

Cam's voice was shaky. "Wednesday night at Nomads and Thursday night at Papa Penguin's."

This was news to Alexa. Were snowboarders big partyers? Was it the culture?

"I'm interested in the Papa Penguin's party," the DI said.

He stared at his socks, yellow and gray stripes. His nose dripped. Alexa looked for tissues. The dresser top was a jumble of sunscreen, ChapStick, deodorant, receipts, sunglasses, a glove, chargers, water bottles, and a vape device. The vape device stopped her for a second, but she didn't think e-cigarettes needed a lighter to work. She popped into the Jack-and-Jill bathroom—a bigger jumble—and grabbed tissues.

"Someone died in the fire, so you understand why I ask," DI Katakana said gently. "The fact that you were at the restaurant earlier in the night is important to our investigation."

Alexa handed him the tissues. He balled them in his fist and answered the DI's questions. They left the villa at 10:45 p.m. and walked to the restaurant. The server Graham let them in. The party was in the kitchen and dining area. Maybe twenty people showed up.

"Was the party for a specific reason?" DI Katakana asked. "A birthday or graduation?"

"I didn't know we weren't supposed to be there. It was just a party."

"Alcohol was stolen from the bar. Do you know anything about that?"

Cam didn't answer, and Alexa wondered how the DI could know that, since everything burned up.

DI Katakana continued. "Did any fights or arguments break out?"

He finally wiped his eyes. "Everyone had a good time, just chilled."

The softness was gone. DI Katakana leaned forward. "A young man died in the fire. Imagine his parents. Who do you think he is?"

Cam lifted and dropped his shoulders.

"How do you think the fire started?" the DI asked.

"I don't know. Maybe from the pizza oven? But there was no fire when we left."

"What time did you leave?"

He surveyed the bedroom. "We were back here at like one a.m."

Alexa remembered Cam and Tex showed up at the restaurant the next morning. She wanted to ask why but figured the support person shouldn't butt in.

The DI narrowed her eyes. "Who was in the restaurant when you left?"

His fists balled up. "I think Graham, another server, the QAST kids. Their Uber drove up as we left. A Jeep, I think."

The DI stood from the bed. She scanned the room, her eyes landing on various items: the piles of clothes, the mess on the dresser, the phone in a charger on the nightstand. Then she motioned for Alexa to follow her into the hallway. "What do you think?"

"He's scared."

"I doubt a kid set the fire, but they're all under suspicion until we know otherwise."

Alexa was jolted by a memory. "The owners—the Parrs—drive a Jeep. Maybe it wasn't an Uber."

The DI frowned. "Fancy that. Go visit them with Constable Blume while I finish up here. Do a home visit. Check for burns. Get their fingerprints."

If Alexa were an English setter, she would have lifted her paw.

Chapter Thirty

"Better if we take your ute," Constable Blume said. "So as not to leave the DI stranded."

Alexa pointed to the Sorento, and he followed her. "Is it far to their house?" she asked.

"Ten minutes. City center." He took his police cap off in the car. His light-brown hair was conservatively cut.

Alexa steered them onto Queenstown Road and followed his directions. Fine-grained snow peppered the windshield. "Turn here," Constable Blume instructed.

The house was five blocks up a steep plowed hill. "Nice view," the constable said.

When Alexa got out, she saw Lake Wakatipu—battleship gray—past suburban rooftops. *Was its heart beating?*

Houses crowded either side of the Parrs' single-story ranch. A picture window capitalized on the lake view. A black Audi sedan was parked in the driveway. Alexa wondered where the Jeep was. She slung the crime kit over her shoulder and followed the constable to the front stoop.

After he rang twice, Mattie Parr opened the door. Her dark thick hair hung over her right shoulder like a horse tail. Her yoga pants and clingy T-shirt showed off her toned physique. Her eyes darted back and forth between them.

"G'day, Mrs. Parr. I'm Constable Blume. We met at the scene of the fire. DI Katakana sent us to share some updates with you and Mr. Parr. Is he in?"

"Kip is meeting with our insurance agent at the restaurant. Who are you?" she asked Alexa.

"I'm with forensics. I was at the scene when you showed up Friday morning."

"If you say so. I was in shock. Still am." Her brown eyes widened to emphasize the fact.

"I'm sorry for your loss," Alexa said. That sounded weird. The restaurant wasn't a person.

Mrs. Parr backed up. Alexa and Constable Blume dutifully wiped their feet and followed her into the sitting room. A built-in bench, the length of the picture window, was covered by a seat cushion and furry pillows. "It's a beautiful view," Alexa said. She settled on the bench, the crime kit at her feet.

"I never tire of it." Mrs. Parr took a seat on the edge of the sofa, hands clasped in her lap. Her skin, etched with fine lines, sagged slightly at her jawline. "Do you know who died in the fire? Is that why you're here?"

"We haven't identified the body yet, but we know the deceased is male and sixteen to mid-twenties," Alexa said.

She covered her mouth and looked toward a hallway. Alexa followed her gaze, but the hallway was empty.

"The decedent hasn't been reported missing by family or friends. Odd, that." Constable Blume sat opposite her in a recliner, notepad ready. "Have you compiled the list of employees?"

"That our staff used the restaurant after hours, to have a party, kills me," she said. "Where's the trust? We leave for two frickin' nights, and they burn the place down?"

"The list?"

"I emailed it to your boss."

"Brilliant." Constable Blume shifted. "Mr. Parr and the

insurance adjusters will need to hear this. The FRIU team discovered that the fire was deliberately set."

Mrs. Parr's eyes twitched. Her lips pursed. "Son of a bitch."

"Who would want to burn Papa Penguin's down?" Constable Blume asked.

"Why would someone do that?" Mrs. Parr responded.

"Lots of different reasons," he said. "Have you fired anyone recently?"

Mrs. Parr laughed. "We're so desperate for servers and cooks that unless they steal or come to work drunk, they call the shots."

Alexa heard footsteps. A young man gazed at them from the hallway. "Mum?"

Mrs. Parr stood but then sat again. "This is Dylan, our son."

"Hi ya," Constable Blume said.

Dylan wore athletic shorts only. What hair he had on his chest and cheeks was downy. His dark brown eyes looked worried. "Have you found out who died?"

"They haven't. Go put a shirt on," his mom said. She turned back to Constable Blume. "We were at Dylan's commencement. That's why we were out of town. A once-in-a-blue-moon occurrence, getting out of town."

"I'm sure running a popular restaurant is a lot of work," Constable Blume said.

Dylan returned in a long-sleeved T-shirt, slip-on shoes in his hand. He sat next to his mother and worked his bony feet into them. Checkerboard Vans, Alexa noticed.

Constable Blume introduced himself and Alexa. "Congrats on your commencement. What did you study?"

"Data science." He glanced at Alexa. She smiled.

"What are your plans?" she asked.

"Mum and Dad need me to work at Papa P's. Payroll, scheduling, dishes." He nudged his mom. "Guess I'm free after all."

"Someone set Papa's on fire," she said. "They just told me."

His mouth dropped. "No way. Who would do that?"

"That's what we want to know," Constable Blume said.

He stared into space. "That means, because of the body, holy hell. Is that murder?"

"It could be that whoever started the fire thought the building was unoccupied," Constable Blume replied. He repeated his question to Mrs. Parr. "Who would want to burn the restaurant down?"

"I don't know," Mrs. Parr said. "I can't think."

"Do you keep spare petrol at Papa Penguin's?" Constable Blume asked.

"I can't think why," she nonanswered.

Alexa was impatient. They weren't getting anywhere. "Petrol was used to start the fire. If we're able to find the container, there might be fingerprints on it. That's why I need to take yours. For elimination."

"Fingerprints?" Mrs. Parr's brows furrowed. "But we were in Dunedin."

Constable Blume referred to his notes. "But you weren't, eh? The commencement was Wednesday evening. Mr. Parr said you came home Thursday."

"Well, yes, but late," she said.

"Half-past eleven," Dylan said. His hair, dark like his mother's, was finer and straight. "An accident slowed us down. Then the snow. We were knackered. Went straight to bed."

"Anyone confirm that?" Constable Blume asked.

"What are you insinuating?" Mrs. Parr asked.

Dylan slipped a key fob out of his pocket. "Dad, me, and mum confirm it."

Constable Blume diffused the tenseness with a shy smile. "The FRIU crew determined that the fire had burned at least thirty minutes when they arrived at two a.m."

"Are you accusing one of us of setting the fire?" Mrs. Parr asked.

"Chill, Mum." Dylan stood, tossing the key fob from hand to hand.

Constable Blume looked at Alexa. She got out her mobile fingerprint device, switched it on, and made sure the scanner plate was clean. "I'll just take your prints now."

She pressed Mrs. Parr's fingers, one by one, on the screen as directed. Her fingers were calloused and strong. Before she finished, Dylan opened and slipped out the front door.

Constable Blume lunged after him. "Wait," he called.

"Leave him alone," Mrs. Parr said.

But Dylan froze. He stood by the Audi, no coat, snow melting into his Vans, and allowed Alexa to take his prints as his mother watched from the stoop.

"What's the rush?" Constable Blume asked him.

"Dad needs to know what's going on."

Alexa doubted he was speaking the truth.

Chapter Thirty-One

"Dodgy, him running off like that," Constable Blume said. "Maybe he burned Papa P's down, so he wouldn't have to work there."

"That would be overkill." Alexa checked the results of Mrs. Parr's prints as the car warmed up. She was a convert now, fond of the gadget's speed and accuracy compared with taking prints with paper and ink. She just had to remember to keep it charged. "Mattie Parr isn't in the criminal system." She checked Dylan Parr next. "No hits for Dylan, either. But if we find that gas can, we're ready. Where do you want me to drop you?"

"Nah, yeah. The station. The team meeting is at seven thirty. Aren't you coming?"

It was six p.m. "I have a few things to do beforehand."

She wanted to check on Bruce and the girls. She dropped the constable off at the Queenstown Police Station and drove through pelting snow to Alpine Villas. It was time to tell Bruce about the second avalanche. As she parked in a guest spot, she noted Lance's big SUV was in front of Villa 5. The chaperone had returned to his scared flock. He'd be in almost as much trouble as they were when parents found out about the late-night party and horrific results.

Bruce's voice stopped her cold in the villa threshold.

"I pay that bill every month, so I can get in touch with you," he bellowed. "If you had had it charged, I would have known where you were."

Alexa hadn't ever heard him lose his temper, even when interrogating people who had committed heinous crimes.

"It's not my fault. I forgot," Denise yelled back.

"And Mr. Zafiro? Why didn't you use his phone?"

"His name is Tex. He lost his phone. I told you that."

Alexa hung up her coat. She understood why Bruce was venting, but it was jarring.

"What were you doing in a closed area? What have you got to say about that?"

"Dad! I almost died."

"Why were you there?"

"Mum wouldn't yell at me. It's my birthday."

"As soon as you knew about the Papa Penguin's fire, and Mr. Zafiro's involvement, you should have told me."

"Sammie," Denise screamed. "I'll kill you."

"Leave Sam out of it. You've put her through hell today."

"It was just a party. Tex said he and the others left way before that fire started."

Alexa tiptoed into the bedroom hallway, bumping into Sammie, who must have been spying. "Hey," she whispered.

"Alexa is back," Sammie shouted.

Silence. Then Denise shouted, "Tell her to go away."

"That is enough." Bruce's voice was steely.

Heat bloomed in Alexa's chest. She brushed past Sammie and shut her door. She tossed her suitcase on the bed and threw her pajamas and dirty khakis into it. She was not cut out for drama. That's why she devoted her life to science. Science was certainty. Families were fraught. Science was detached. Love was sticky. Science was objective. Her feelings for Bruce anything but. She threw her brush into the suitcase along with her forensics journal.

No.

She wouldn't run away. She wouldn't let Denise scare her off. She pushed the suitcase aside and flopped on the bed, listening to

Denise and Bruce, their words indistinguishable. She closed her eyes and breathed deeply. It had been a hell of a day. A hell of *two* days. Tears pushed their way down her cheeks, onto the pillow. Stress hormones and chemicals: she gave herself permission to let them flow for five hot, wet minutes. A crying sesh. Then she rolled off the bed to find a tissue and actually felt better. She blew her nose, drank a glass of water, and opened her laptop.

An email response from her missing-hikers inquiry sent a frisson through her body.

Ms. Glock:

I am a retired dentist from Wellington, where I practiced for forty years. I have attached AM radiographs of a patient of mine, William (Bill) Gilroy, taken in 1980.

Your note sparked my memory. Mr. Gilroy lost his lateral incisor due to trauma from a car accident. I performed a two-stage threaded titanium implant, a fairly new product and procedure at the time. (I have attached the specifics.) The prosthetic had integrated well by Mr. Gilroy's six-month check-up. I never saw him again and later learned he went missing on Mt. Aspiring.

Mr. Gilroy was an only child. His mother and father were also my patients. (William Gilroy, senior, is deceased.) They mentioned their desire to find their son on every visit through the years. I prayed that the implant might someday be the key to identifying his remains.

It is my hope that the implant matches, and Mr. Gilroy's remaining whānau find peace.

Noho ora mai rā,
Stephen Valdez, DDS

Tears pushed out of her eyes again. The glacier skull most likely belonged to Bill Gilroy. What were the odds that it was someone else? The "autopsy" of the skull and boot was scheduled for the morning. The big thaw was over. She smiled with anticipation.

She locked the bathroom door, so Denise couldn't barge in. She splashed her blotchy face and checked her hair: haywire. She couldn't find her brush—not that it would tame her curls, anyway. She coaxed her mane into a ponytail. The gash on her forehead was scabbing. Her lip gloss was AWOL.

Boldly, she entered the den. Bruce and Denise stared at her. "I'm off again." She caught and held Bruce's eyes. "There's a meeting at the police station. About the fire."

"I'll walk you out." He jumped up from the couch. His hand at the small of her back was comforting. "I'm sorry," he said. "This ski trip…"

The door burst open. A woman ran in.

"Mum!" Denise shouted.

Chapter Thirty-Two

Sharla flew past Alexa and Bruce and pulled Denise into her arms. "Oh, baby, I was so worried."

Denise's cheek pressed against Sharla's suede coat. "I was scared and cold and didn't know what to do. We got rescued in a helicopter."

Alexa reached for the door. Bruce took her arm. "Wait. Let's get this behind us."

The *us* gave her courage to stay.

Sharla didn't match her glamorous real-estate photo. Her big hair was flat, her skin pasty, a constellation of pimples marred her chin. Her jeans were too long—maybe she usually wore heels instead of tennis shoes—and the cuffs were wet. "Tell me what happened." Her eyes flickered to Alexa's and settled on Bruce.

"She's okay," Bruce said. "Right, Denise?"

Sammie barged into Denise and Sharla's huddle, and they readily accepted her. A lump mushroomed in Alexa's throat. The girls needed their mom, and Sharla must have been so scared. Sammie extended an arm toward Bruce. "Group hug, Daddy. Come on."

Alexa bumped into the wall.

"Let's sit down," Bruce said.

Denise pulled her mother to the couch. "You're going to stay in the villa, right? With us?"

"She's not staying here," Bruce said.

Denise shot daggers at her father.

When Sharla was situated between the girls, Bruce led Alexa into the lounge. "Sharla, this is Alexa." He squeezed Alexa's hand.

"She's the tooth lady," Sammie said. "We were in an avalanche, too."

Alexa's heart pounded like a drum. It hurt her ears. "Pleased to meet you," she said over the din. "We spoke on the phone."

Sharla ignored her. "What is Sammie talking about?"

"She's going through a phase, copying everything I do," Denise said. "I got a snowboard, she wants to snowboard. I got caught in an avalanche, she lies and says she did, too."

"I'm not lying," Sammie said vehemently.

"And you didn't get caught in an avalanche," Bruce said to Denise. "You were above it." He sat on the ottoman in front of Sammie, leaving Alexa's side. "What are you talking about?"

Crap, Alexa thought.

Sammie buried her hands under her thighs and leaned forward excitedly. "When she and me drove away from Coronet Peak, you know, when you were looking for Denise, an avalanche shoved us over the cliff, well almost over, right, Alexa? We had to walk and get a tow truck."

Alexa felt so alone. "She's right."

Bruce's eyebrows skyrocketed.

"I didn't have a chance to tell you, what with everything," Alexa said. "But we're okay. The car is fine."

"*I* told you," Sammie said to her dad, "but you didn't listen. No one listened."

"The slip that closed the road?" Bruce asked.

Alexa nodded.

"We had to climb out my door," Sammie said, "and hold on to the car to get around it."

Sharla glared at Bruce. "Why did you let her out of your sight?"

His eyes darkened. "Did you want me to find Denise?"

No more family drama for Alexa. She edged toward the front door and escaped.

Chapter Thirty-Three

The clammy smell of sweat competed with the coffee aroma; the people gathered in the incident room had already had a long day. DI Katakana rapped her knuckles on the table. "Let's get started."

Alexa poured a cup of coffee from a side table to settle her jangling Sharla-nerves and sat at the rectangular table, across from Constable Blume and the police photographer, Sally. Incident Controller McBride from the Fire Research and Investigation Unit sat on her left. Next to him was the cop who had escorted her and Sammie to the Coronet Peak parking lot, Constable Tweed. At the far end of the table, a man in civvies looked familiar.

DI Katakana squared her broad shoulders. "My team know everyone except Ms. Glock, a forensic investigator with a specialty in teeth." The DI nodded at her. "You've met our photographer?"

Alexa smiled at Sally.

"And this is our Constable Nick Tweed."

He waved at her. "We've had the pleasure," he said.

"Remember Senior Sergeant Fielding? You worked together before, eh? When the Arrowtown principal disappeared."

The cleft between the senior sergeant's eyebrows deepened, jiggling her memory. He'd been a jerk. "Nice to see you again," Alexa lied.

Recognition dawned in his eyes. And begrudging respect. It was her forensic analysis that had solved the principal's murder.

"Incident Controller McBride will start things off," the DI said.

Alexa leaned back. Here in this room was order, whereas at the villa was chaos.

Sally projected a photo onto the screen behind the DI: an aerial view of Papa Penguin's, or what was left of it. "The degree of destruction is 80 percent," IC McBride said. "The fire was a rampaging beast."

Fire as a beast, something alive, distracted Alexa. *Was fire alive? It grows, needs air to breathe, needs nourishment, can kill, can be killed.* These thoughts made her jumpy, as if she were being stalked.

"The water-suppression system was inadequate for the size and volume of the fire," the IC continued.

"Is that a violation?" DI Katakana asked.

"The flow rate could not contain spread; it was overwhelmed, but that's not a violation."

Fire is a chemical reaction, Alexa reminded herself. *It can't think or make choices.*

The next images were interior. Ash, soot, destruction, and a few remnants: a chair, a glass bottle, the shape of a commode. The final images were of the kitchen with the body in situ. The air felt sucked from the incident room.

"Still no ID. Ms. Glock, Sally, and I attended John Doe's autopsy this morning," the DI said. "Dr. McKenzie determined our decedent is male and was alive when the fire started. Ms. Glock, what can you add?"

"His teeth indicate he was sixteen to mid-twenties."

IC McBride pointed out the burn pattern on the floor. "This is our point of origin," he said. He explained about fuel, oxygen, temperatures, and chemical chain reactions as the fire spread throughout the restaurant. "Tests confirmed that it was petrol used to start the fire."

A treat for the arson dog. "Did you uncover any other forensic evidence?" Alexa asked.

"The fire burned uncontrolled for more than thirty minutes before we arrived. All evidence was destroyed."

Alexa's heart sank. She might be out of a job.

"Any progress on finding the container, matches, or a lighter?" DI Katakana asked.

"Muffin searched the parking lot and woods behind and to either side of the restaurant. Nothing was recovered."

"Were there security cameras on the premises?" the DI asked.

"No security cameras. Motion-detector lights melted."

"There's a traffic camera half a kilometer up the road toward town," DI Katakana said. "Infrared for nighttime. Who's on it?"

"I'll take it," the senior sergeant said.

IC McBride sat heavily. "Scrutinize the owner's insurance policy. Whoever stands to gain financially should be a suspect."

"Ta. Time to look into this blasted party and who was last to leave it." The DI retracted the pull-down screen to expose a list of names on the whiteboard. It was divided into two columns. Snowboard kids were on the right. On the left were the Parrs and Papa Penguin's employees, including Graham Clark, the party host.

DI Katakana tapped the left side. "We've had initial conversations with half of the wait staff."

One of them must be the waitress Alexa met in the parking lot. Stringy blond hair, skinny.

"On the right are nine confirmed snowboarders who attended the party. We may be missing a few."

Alexa located Breezy, Kool, Cam, and Tex.

"Their futures will be kicked in the arse when the press finds out what the little darlings have been up to," the DI said. "I just checked with the competition officials. The Junior Championship qualifiers will continue. The Avalanche Advisory board have analyzed the slip from the air. They called it a 1.5 on the danger scale and unlikely to pose additional threat."

"What about the second avalanche?" Alexa asked.

The DI checked her notes. "It's been labeled an isolated snow slab, not an avalanche."

Alexa was insulted.

"I am withholding information about the after-hours party from the press until tomorrow afternoon," the DI said. "Otherwise, the competition might shut down and our snow bunnies will hop away. Our digital forensics team are snooping on Snapchat, TikTok, and Instagram for pics of the party. Kids are keen to share."

"My bet is a disgruntled employee, someone who was fired," Senior Sergeant Fielding said.

"Look into that," the DI said. "Other ideas?"

"A pyromaniac," Constable Tweed offered.

IC McBride cleared his throat. "Fifty percent of arson cases are caused by males under the age of eighteen."

"Like our snowboarders," Constable Tweed said.

"The typical arsonist is a loner and minimally educated, someone who struggles with anger issues, maybe pain or trauma. Probably lives close to the scene, too, statistically speaking."

"Is it true arsonists like to return to the scene?" Constable Blume asked.

"It happens," IC McBride said.

"We're poring over scene photos," Sally said.

Constable Blume waved a hand. "When Ms. Glock and I

visited Mrs. Parr this afternoon, the son, Dylan Parr, basically did a runner, but we stopped him. Ms. Glock searched his fingerprints, though. His record is clean."

DI Katakana added Dylan Parr to the list and then underlined Graham Clark's name. "An officer is bringing in Mr. Clark as we speak. From accounts, he initiated the party."

"I wondered if he was our John Doe," Alexa said. "He works at Coronet Peak. None of the NZ SNO Z boarders saw him on the slopes today."

"Lucky for Mr. Clark, he's alive and well." The DI underlined the names Dane Bui and Mutt Stanford. "These are also Papa Penguin's employees who work at Coronet Peak. Could be our John Doe is one of them."

Alexa had asked Bruce to check if they'd shown up for work. The avalanche had sideswiped that task. This morning felt a week ago.

"We don't know if we have a case of intentional homicide," the DI said. "Did the person who lit the fire act to end another person's life, or was the death an unintended consequence?"

The question hung in the air like smoke on the horizon.

Chapter Thirty-Four

Graham Clark, his black ball cap on backward, was cooperative as Alexa pressed each of his fingers onto the scanner pad. His blond hair spilled out either side of the cap, brushing his shoulders. His mustache and sparse beard hinted at red, and his troubled eyes were sea green.

As soon as he was led away, Alexa caught up with DI Katakana outside the interview room. "No priors. Can I watch?"

"Fine by me."

Alexa was stalling her return to the villa. *What if Sharla was still there?* She watched through two-way glass as DI Katakana settled at the rectangular table and informed Graham that she was recording their "little talk." She asked his name and age.

He pushed up the sleeves of his brown fisherman's sweater and leaned toward the table. "Graham Clark, twenty-two."

"I have a list of charges here, Mr. Clark. Breaking and entering. Theft of alcohol. Endangering the lives of minors. Arson. Murder."

"Murder?" Graham looked sick.

"Someone set that fire, and a bloke died. Who is he?"

"I don't know who he is. My solicitor is on her way."

DI Katakana huffed and terminated the recording. As she stood, the door opened, and a young woman strode in. She had dark hair, eyebrows, eyes. "Ella Cordis, solicitor. I'd like a word with my client before we begin."

"Ten minutes," DI Katakana said.

Alexa found DI Katakana in the hallway. "It didn't seem appropriate to tell you earlier, but I have a lead on our glacier skull, from a retired dentist. He had a patient with a single-tooth implant who went missing on Aspiring in 1984. Tomorrow I'll take proper X-rays and see if the implants match."

"That is hopeful news. Wanaka Search and Rescue is heading to Mount Aspiring tomorrow to try and retrieve that pelvis," the DI said. "They've a narrow weather window."

The pelvis in a Speedo.

Alexa's imagination trekked back to Mount Aspiring, to the crevasse that she shared with the pelvis. The terror had receded, and the cold beauty, the silence, and the blueness were etched in her mind.

DI Katakana snapped her fingers, jarring Alexa back to the present. "Before you head to the hospital tomorrow, fingerprint every single person who was at that party. All good?"

Alexa nodded. She returned to her position behind the glass and readied her notepad.

As soon as the DI entered the interview room, Ms. Cordis, who sat next to Graham, asked, "Have you charged my client with a crime?"

DI Katakana unbuttoned her blazer and took a seat. "Mr. Clark is here for questioning."

"He indicated you threatened him with all sorts of charges. Arson and murder?"

Graham's ball cap was on the table in front of him. Maybe his solicitor had encouraged him to remove it. He kneaded the brim with his slender fingers.

"I mentioned those charges as possibilities. Your client is up a creek, no waka. Multiple witnesses claim Mr. Clark invited them to the after-hours party at his place of employment. But let's start with the simple questions, eh? Mr. Clark, where do you currently reside?"

"I share a house in Frankton with some mates."

Alexa strained to hear him through the speaker.

"Who are these mates?"

"Dane Bui, Mutt Stanford, Pāora Henny." He provided the address.

"What do you do for a living, Mr. Clark?"

He continued kneading the brim. "Up until last year I was an NZ free ski snowboard champ. Then I broke my foot skateboarding. Now I work lifts and wait tables."

The DI opened her file and tapped the top paper. "The owners of Papa Penguin's, Mr. and Mrs. Parr, said you rented the flat above the restaurant. Is that true?"

"At the beginning of the season."

"Why did you move out?"

Graham looked at Ms. Cordis. "Do I have to answer?"

Her blunt black hair swayed back and forth. "You do not."

"Why wouldn't you if it mitigates the mess you're in?" DI Katakana replied.

Graham stayed quiet.

"Let me guess. The noise in the apartment was too loud? Smelled like pizza? Not enough privacy?"

Graham shifted in his chair.

DI Katakana leaned across the table. "Did you have a run-in with the bosses?"

"Next question," Ms. Cordis said.

"Do you know of any Papa Penguin's employees who have a beef with the Parrs?"

His fingers stilled on the cap. Without looking up he said, "Autumn Ware. A server."

"What makes you say that?" DI Katakana asked.

"She was at the party. Going off about this and that. She can speak for herself."

"And I'll listen to what she has to say. When did you get the idea for the party?"

He sighed. "I don't know. Spur of the moment, I guess."

"You took advantage of the Parrs being out of town?"

"I thought it would be cool to shoot the breeze with some boarders. Afterward, I cleaned up and locked up. Papa's was fine. I didn't know about the fire until the next day."

"How did you decide who to invite?"

"Serendipitous like. Just made the rounds earlier in the night to whatever boarders were eating at Papa's."

"Bad luck for them, eh? Did any of them use your old apartment during the party?"

"I don't know."

"Did you check it before you left?"

"No."

"What time was the party over?"

He pushed his hair behind his ears and pulled the cap on, backward again. "One o'clock, maybe one fifteen." He looked at his solicitor. "I was last to leave. A friend picked me up."

The DI leaned toward him. "What friend?"

"No comment. But the restaurant was empty."

"But it wasn't empty, was it? A young man was killed in the inferno. Burned to a crisp. Terrible, terrible way to die." The DI pushed paper and a pen toward him. "Names of every single person at the party and a minute-by-minute account of it."

Her chair screeched as she stood.

Chapter Thirty-Five

It was nine thirty when Alexa pulled into the guest spot at Alpine Villas. Bruce's rental car was out front. So was Lance's big SUV. Light shone forth from both villas, as well as a few others. Alexa turned off the engine and surveyed the two other cars in visitors' spots. She had no idea what Sharla had been driving. Maybe one was hers. It was Denise's birthday. The family might be sitting around the dining table, eating cake, reminiscing, laughing.

She thought of that family photo in the master bedroom as she groped through her pockets for her phone. Maybe Bruce had called or texted: Better if you stay somewhere else. Sharla and I are back together.

Stop it.

Her pockets were empty. Her phone was missing. It was still charging in the bedroom.

She locked the car and crunched slowly toward the villa. Something was different. She froze in the dark, alert, trying to figure out what. The air was crisp, dry, spiced by Antarctica and cold lake water. She looked up.

It had stopped snowing.

The moonless sky was a cluster of red, silver, and blue jewels. She'd been in the Southern Hemisphere long enough now to realize everything astronomical was upside down and inside out, including her heart. A ghostly green light pulsed and flashed. Lightning?

She hurried to the front door and found it unlocked. She stepped into quiet. Low light seeped from the den area. The dining table, in her line of sight, was empty. Her heart sank. The Horne family had gone out to celebrate. "It's me," she called anyway.

Bruce, in a robe, appeared from the hallway. He smiled. "It's about time."

A robe? Her insides tingled. "Where are the girls?"

The happy look on his face dimmed, but only for a second. "They clamored to spend the night with Sharla at her hotel. They'll be back in the morning."

Was this the answer to a prayer she hadn't known she'd prayed? She set her crime kit down and slid out of her coat. "Guess what."

He cocked an eyebrow.

"It stopped snowing. There are a million stars in the sky."

"We're going to view them from the hot tub."

The scars on her back protested. "Um, well, I don't have a…"

"You don't need one."

He disappeared down the hallway and reappeared with a robe for her. By the time she stepped onto the deck, her bare feet screaming in the snow, he'd set the jets to hot and bubbly and climbed in. She disrobed and eased in next to him. The meeting of freezing air and hot water on different parts of her skin reminded her of her first friend in New Zealand, Mary, describing the sacred place on the tip of the North Island where the Tasman Sea meets the Pacific.

When the male sea Te Moana Tāpokopoko a Tāwhaki meets the female sea, Te Taio Whitirela, whirlpools and currents collide.

Mary had been killed in a car wreck, but tonight, right now, Alexa heard her voice: "It won't be easy merging seas, but your paddle is strong, your waka is seaworthy."

Bruce's thigh was solid next to hers. His face was obscured by steam. "Look up," he said.

Pulsing light danced in the sky. Above the lime green, a throbbing layer of pink and purple ebbed and flowed, warped and weft, waxed and waned, disbanded and joined forces, rode invisible and otherworldly waves. Her mouth dropped.

"The Aurora Australis." Bruce's submerged hand found hers, and their fingers entwined. The show shifted, stars peeked through, new colors collided, bounced off snowy mountains, shape-shifted, showed off.

No poet could ever describe the southern lights over Lake Wakatipu, Bruce by her side, on an August winter's night. Not even that "Fire and Ice" Frost guy.

Bruce whispered in her ear, his words barely audible over the bubbles, "I love you."

Her vision blurred. She blinked to clear it, and her panic passed. But still no words formed. All she could manage was to squeeze his hand.

The light show lasted ten minutes. When it was over she led half-hot, half-cold Bruce to the king-sized bed. When they were through colliding and whirlpooling, joining and disbanding, Alexa closed her eyes and reviewed the day's events of arson, autopsy, and avalanche, each a warring color vying for her attention.

Bruce had been through hell today. Both his daughters were safe, and she would wait until the morning to update him.

His bare back was turned to her. She whispered "I love you" into his shoulder and drifted into a deep and dreamless sleep.

DAY THREE

14 NOVEMBER 1984

Christian shook me awake at one a.m. The zipper on my parka stuck, and my equipment clanked against my pack.

I downed tepid tea and swallowed two muesli bars. Cold slapped me awake. We crunched through snow, sometimes thigh-deep. My headlamp illuminated snow falling from a moonless sky and, up ahead, C leading the way.

Summit day. I felt the pressure and spirit of Tititea/Aspiring calling my name. From the hut it was two hours of uphill silence except breath and squelch and squeak to Quarterdeck Pass. Then a nice flat section. We roped up and headed sideways, crossing through a couple seracs, pressing against massive ice blocks to skirt that crevasse the ranger warned us about.

Hello, Bonar Glacier. The world became crunch and wind and bobbles of light.

Just like that, C's bobble extinguished. "Christian?" I screamed.

No answer. But no pull on the rope, either. I slithered to the rim, found him three feet below the ice standing on a ledge, his headlamp illuminating a slick blue tube inches from his boots. "You okay?"

"Yeah, man. Wanted to see what it was like."

I worried the ledge might collapse. "Climb out of there."

My friend emerged in a roar. I felt vibrations under my belly. Fuck, fuck, fuck. Avalanche. I crouched, hands over my head, pulled in air.

It thundered from the other side of the ridge.

C said, "If I had fallen in that crevasse, I would have corked."

The image dangled in my head: Christian wedged into a fissure like a cork in a wine bottle.

We made a long descent under icy bluffs toward the base of the southwest ridge, passing the helter-skelter remains of another avalanche.

I heard voices in the dark and stopped to listen, forcing C to stop, too. Other climbers, taking a different route. C jerked the rope. "Let's go." We aimed for the western flank. At five a.m. we crouched between two boulders, out of the wind. C couldn't find his scroggin. I gave him jerky. The coffee was warm. Caffeine courage. We reloaded.

The merest pearly light separated ground from mountain from sky. As the sun rose, I stared at Aspiring. She was a pink arrow pointing straight up.

"Bastards," C said.

Two tiny figures, one yellow, one green, crossed a steep rocky ridge at a steady gait. I recognized the colors of Zittydog's and Bill's parkas. "Who cares?" I asked.

C said we'd climb directly up the face so we could overtake them and reach the gully first. There was no arguing with him, and besides, it was perfect for ice tools. We switched from ice to rock to ice, most of it face-in. Dead vertical for a four-meter stretch. C, breathing hard, led the way.

I caught a crampon crossing jumbled ice and fell on my face. Bloody nose dripped on the snow. The Wellies caught up with us on the ridge crest, all cheery. C gave me a look. What's his deal? I concentrated on ridges and grooves.

Clouds cleared. She preened: Tititea, the enchantress, surrounded by her admirers: Bonar Glacier, Volta Glacier, Mount

Avalanche, Blue Peak, Mount Tutoko, Mount Earnslaw. Then she was gone again.

We leapfrogged the Wellies on ice—anchors, warthogs, ropes—they passed us on snow—ice pick, crampons, neve. Time slowed. We were in the clouds. Snow blew in swirls, confused as to what was up and what was down.

Then we reached the infamous ice couloir.

C double-checked our ropes and led.

Not so bad at first, but as I wrapped around, the pitch and the wind increased, my pack got heavier, and the snow turned to blue ice. I freaked.

I forced myself to take deep breaths and assessed my situation. I tunnel-visioned. From here—get to the next notch. Repeat. Crampons placed firmly in the ice, ice axe and snow stake in hand, I followed C up.

We unroped on the ridge below the summit. Cliffs dropped away on either side. My hands shook, and my fingers tingled. Onward.

The Wellies passed us when the summit was one hundred yards away.

Fifty yards later, C passed the Wellies.

I didn't see who got there first, didn't care. I trudged those final steps to the top of the world. Tititea tumbled away on all sides. The clouds parted. I tossed a snowball—or rather a fist-sized ball of ice—for Mum.

C and Bill clapped me on the back.

Zittydog offered us scroggin.

"That's my fucking stash," C said.

Zittydog looked horrified. "You left it at the hut, man."

C grabbed the bag, and it ripped. M&M'S and nuts and sultanas disappeared in the snow.

Chapter Thirty-Six

SUNDAY

When Alexa turned on the bedroom lamp in the morning, Bruce's side of the bed was empty, and the family-foursome photo was gone from the wall. Around the bare spot Bruce's parents and siblings grinned at her from different ski slopes. She blushed in her nakedness. She donned the slightly damp robe, smelling of chlorine, and quickly checked for updates from the DI. Still no ID on the body.

She followed the aroma of coffee to Bruce, dressed in jeans and an All Blacks pullover, standing at the Nespresso machine.

"You're up early," she said, "and doing my second-favorite thing."

His blue eyes bore into hers as a smiled tugged at his lips. Had he heard her whisper "I love you" last night? She went to him. He pulled her close, but their kiss was all too brief. Bruce stepped back and handed her the mug of coffee. With her free hand she pulled the robe tighter.

He put another pod into the machine. As it hissed and gurgled out the inadequate amount of brew, he said, "I just checked with the hospital. The two kids injured in the avalanche are in good condition. The girl was released last night, and the boy is due to be released this morning."

The girl, Zoe, had been rushed into the ski resort first-aid clinic. She had tried to outski the avalanche. Alexa added milk to her mug and sat at the table. "That's good news."

"The bad news is that Denise could be charged with reckless endangerment." He joined her at the table. "One of the spectators caught the avalanche on video and sent it to the snow-safety investigators. They claim it clearly shows Tex and Denise above the avalanche."

"How is that reckless endangerment?"

"In the video, Denise is standing behind Tex, to the side, watching him. Apparently, he's boarding in a way that could have triggered the avalanche."

"Even if that's true, it wasn't Denise," Alexa said.

"What if someone had been killed?"

"No one was."

"Denise and that idiot were in a closed area, and thirty people risked their lives searching for them. If there's evidence Tex's boarding triggered the avalanche, the police will press charges. Denise will have to face up to her part."

No wonder he was all-biz this morning.

"Sharla will want me and my father to rescue her."

His father the barrister. Alexa spotted their reflections in the window glass: They could be any middle-aged couple discussing the day's events. If only the day's events weren't so serious. She updated Bruce on the Papa Penguin's arson-cum-homicide. "The kids who attended the party are on the suspect list. The DI wants me to fingerprint them."

"Thank God Denise wasn't at the party."

"The DI is keeping the details from the press, so the qualifiers aren't canceled. She doesn't want the snowboarders to scatter." She took a breath. "She's going to request your help."

A twitch and a spark lit his eyes. He was interested in helping. But the spark died.

"Denise is my priority," he said.

———

Lance failed to place her again.

"Alexa Glock from Villa 6. I'm glad Tex was found safely."

"We're getting ready to leave," he replied.

Breezy appeared behind him. Her purple T-shirt said "Girl Get After It" in swirls, and she wore three-quarter-length leggings with socks.

"May I come in? I'm working with the police."

Lance backed up reluctantly, and Alexa stepped into the foyer.

"She was here yesterday," Breezy said, "when you were at hospital with Tex."

"Not sure that's kosher." Lance scratched at a sideburn. "These kids are underage."

"Detective Inspector Katakana and I respected that." *If you had kept them under wraps, they wouldn't be in trouble.* "How's Tex?"

"His mum dragged him to some lodge," Breezy said. "At least she showed up."

"Are Cam and Kool around? The DI sent me to take your fingerprints."

Kool, brush in hand, zoomed around the corner. "Fingerprints? Why?"

"Have you read the latest news?"

"Nah, yeah." She waved her phone. "The qualifiers are a go."

"That's not what I meant. The Papa Penguin's fire has been declared arson."

Blank faces, and then dropped mouths in synchronicity. Lance, Kool, and Breezy were speechless.

"Since you kids were there, I need permission from your parents to take your fingerprints. They'll want you to cooperate so we can eliminate you from the suspect list."

Breezy's face drained of color. "Suspect list?"

"Whoa now," Lance said. "I need to inform the director." He twirled around and disappeared toward a bedroom, leaving the kids unchaperoned again.

"Do they know who died?" Kool asked.

"Not yet," Alexa said.

Cam's voice called from the kitchen. "Papa Penguin's was fine when we left."

Alexa walked to the dining table, cleared a spot, and told him to join them. She readied the portable scanner. "Get your parents on the phone."

The girls grumbled but obeyed.

Breezy's mother introduced herself as Michelle O'Brien, CEO of Queen City Law. "I refuse to give permission. I don't trust the police with my daughter's biometric data."

"Fine," Alexa said. "We'll still be looking into her involvement."

"I've advised Breezy not to answer questions."

Lawyer Mom knew her kid was in trouble.

"What about Lance Brown? I hold him responsible," Ms. O'Brien added.

"You'll have to talk with Mr. Brown directly or with the program director."

Kool's father was cooperative. "She's grounded until uni. Will the owners of the restaurant press charges? Do we need a lawyer?"

"That's a good idea," Alexa said.

"Take my daughter's fingerprints, if it will be of help."

Only if Kool didn't start the fire, Alexa thought. "I'll need that in writing." She gave Mr. Shima her email before hanging up. Kool's slim fingers trembled as Alexa took her prints.

Lance reappeared. "The director wants your phone number."

Alexa gave him DI Katakana's contact info. "I'm just the messenger. I want your prints, as well."

He had a deep cut on his right middle finger. "Dropped a glass," he explained.

Cam fidgeted. "You're my support person. Can you give permission?"

"No." She remembered his mom had died. "Call your dad."

He reached his father, explaining and apologizing. His Adam's apple slid up and down, and his shoulders sagged. He finally handed her his phone. "It's him."

Alexa introduced herself and patiently answered Mr. Keeline's questions: How did the kids get there? How did they get in? Where was the chaperone? Who died? Who is in charge of the investigation? Eventually he granted permission for "Cameron" to be fingerprinted and promised he would confirm his permission via email.

Before leaving, Alexa asked Lance for the name of the lodge where Tex was staying. He sent her a link.

"Do you have his phone number?"

"He lost his phone," Kool said. "Probably doing backflips."

It was a reminder that these kids were trained athletes.

Outside, Alexa blinked in the sunshine. A candy wrapper blowing across the drive sparked a memory from two mornings ago when the scent of smoke had lured her to Papa Penguin's. There had been trash along the road. What if it had been a piece of evidence? A lighter or matches discarded by whoever set the fire?

It was only eight o'clock. Her date with the glacier skull was nine a.m. She grabbed some evidence bags and the camera, locked the kit in the trunk instead of in the villa—giving Bruce space—and went in search.

The sunshine was deceptive. The temperature was below freezing. The climb up the steep drive to the road wasn't long enough to warm her up. She zipped her parka to her chin, itched to jog—but knew that wasn't wise—yet felt happy nonetheless to stretch her legs.

She considered the snowboarders but couldn't believe one of them set the fire.

If not, who did? That waitress with the long blond hair? Graham Clark? Why had he moved out of that apartment? And whose marred body lay on a slab at the morgue?

No cars were coming. She walked on the road, her eyes scanning the snowy shoulder. How many inches had fallen since Friday morning? Six, she guessed. This was a fool's errand. Still, she traipsed onward, looking for a lump or glint, a blur of color. Where had she seen the trash? She climbed down the verge and kicked clumps of snow. The blanketed ground guarded its secrets.

She continued to Papa Penguin's, the pungent smell of wet ash still heavy in the air.

A silver Jeep Wrangler idled in the lot. She saw the bearded owner Kipper Parr in the driver's seat. His head almost touched the roof. He stared at Papa Penguin's even as Alexa approached the window. She rapped on it.

He lowered the window, his eyes doleful.

"Good morning. I'm working the arson case." Alexa faltered when he didn't respond. What was wrong with him? "Are you okay?"

He lowered his forehead to the steering wheel.

Alexa shifted closer. "Can I call someone?"

He lifted his head and raised the window. Alexa stepped back, worried he was going to peel away. Instead, he cut the engine and got out, stretching to a lumberjack height of six feet, three or four inches. The shiver of fear she felt dissipated when she saw his stricken face. He walked to the passenger door and pointed.

Had he been in an accident? She searched for dents.

"It's gone," Mr. Parr said.

"What is?"

He tapped a black contraption mounted on the panel between the hood and door. "The jerry can."

Chapter Thirty-Seven

It hit her like a bolt: Fuel from the extra gas can could have been used to start the fire. Pieces of the puzzle sifted into place.

That would mean one of the Parrs had been to Papa Penguin's the night of the fire. The snowboard kids mentioned seeing a Jeep as they were leaving. She appraised Mr. Parr with a sideways glance before turning her back and calling DI Katakana.

"Give me ten minutes," the DI said. "Keep Mr. Parr there."

Alexa stomped her feet to keep the blood circulating and told Mr. Parr that the DI was on her way. "Um, when did you last see the jerry can?"

"When we drove to Dunedin. Ergo, it was on when we returned."

Just because the jerry can was on the Jeep on the way to Dunedin did not mean it was on the Jeep on the way home, but Alexa let it slide. "When you drove up Friday morning to see the fire damage, was the container still there?"

"I don't bloody well know."

"When did you discover it was missing?"

"Just now. I'm waiting for the insurance agent to assess the damage."

Alexa stuffed her gloves in her pockets and photographed the empty mount. *Why did jeeps carry extra fuel, anyway?* Probably for the cool factor. "How do you pop the container in and out?"

"Undo the strap and rotate the handle." He brushed past

her and got back in the Jeep. He closed the door and started the engine. Again, she thought he might drive away, but he just idled. She tried the passenger door. It opened. "Cold out here," she said.

"Be my guest," Mr. Parr said.

She climbed in and at once regretted her decision. What if he took off? She surreptitiously set her hand on the door handle.

"Do you know who died in the fire?" he asked.

"Not yet."

The minutes dragged in uncomfortable silence. Alexa hopped out the second DI Katakana drove into the lot.

Mr. Parr retold his story through his open window. "I don't know if it was on the Jeep Friday morning. I had other things on my mind. Someone must have nicked it."

"What does the jerry can look like?" the DI asked.

He found a photo on his phone. "Ten-liter Rotoplax. Mounted it myself."

Alexa looked over the DI's shoulder. Red molded plastic with a handle, black cap on the spout. A shock went through her. "I took a photo of your Jeep Friday morning." She scrolled through on her phone and found it. "The container was missing."

"See? Someone nicked it," he repeated.

"Let's head into the station to talk," DI Katakana said.

Mr. Parr drummed his fingers on the steering wheel. "I have an appointment."

The DI smiled. "Come afterward."

Mr. Parr raised his window.

Alexa wondered why she was being so accommodating, but then DI Katakana rapped on his window. He lowered it with a look of exasperation. "We spoke with the bloke who rented your flat at Papa Penguin's. Graham Clark. He instigated the after-hours party."

"Bloody bastard."

The DI leaned closer. "Why did Mr. Clark move out of the flat?"

Air escaped through his lips in a hiss. He didn't answer.

"Mr. Clark wouldn't say why, either," the DI said. "He mentioned one of your employees, Autumn Ware, has reason to be disgruntled. What's that about?"

"I'm through answering questions." He raised his window and grabbed his phone. The DI backed off and beckoned Alexa to follow. "Fruitful, eh?" She looked around the parking lot. "How did you get here?"

"I walked from Alpine Villas."

"I'll give you a lift back." The patrol car was blissfully warm. The DI waved to Mr. Parr and pulled out of the lot. Alexa wrapped her arms around her torso. She was shivering.

"The Jeep your NZ SNO Z kids saw as they left that party?" DI Katakana said. "It wasn't an Uber. We checked. One of their drivers picked up two riders at 12:55 a.m. and drove them to two different addresses in town. In a sedan."

"It's looking bad for the Parrs."

But which Parr? Alexa pictured meeting Dylan and Mattie Parr yesterday afternoon. "The three of them arrived home around eleven thirty Thursday night. Dylan said they went straight to bed. Maybe just Mom and Dad went to sleep and Dylan took the Jeep. Maybe he was invited to the party."

DI Katakana tailed a slow driver, who then slowed down even more. "The Parrs had a total loss endorsement, so their insurance payout should be equal to the value of the property. It's a motive, eh, if they wanted to escape the restaurant biz. The insurance company does their own investigation, though."

"Maybe the day-in, day-out work wore them down," Alexa said.

The DI turned down the steep drive. "Which villa?"

"Six."

She parked in the SNO Z team's empty spot. Alexa listened as she called Constable Blume and told him to bring Dylan Parr and Autumn Ware to the station. "Hold them until I get there."

Then she turned to Alexa. "DI Horne hasn't returned my call." She got out without waiting for a response and knocked on Villa 6's door.

When he opened it, Bruce looked surprised.

"I found your Ms. Glock wandering the streets," DI Katakana said.

Bruce studied Alexa. "I wondered where you were."

"I'm happy to hear your daughter is safe," DI Katakana said.

"Thank you, Pattie. She may be in some trouble." Bruce led them to the den but remained standing. "You have a lot on your plate. How can I help you?"

The DI stepped to the glass doors and gazed at the snow-crusted deck. Footprints led to and fro. "Hot tub, eh? Under the stars?" She turned around. "*Tahu-nui-ā-Rangi,* the Māori name for the Aurora Australis. Did you see them last night? The flaming colors are the campfires of our ancestors, our connection to the past, our ancestors' way to watch over us."

Alexa's *pounamu* pendant pulsed against her chest. She and Bruce exchanged a look that warmed her toes.

The DI launched into specifics, including Mr. Parr and the missing petrol container.

As the DI reeled Bruce in, Alexa's phone pinged. She stepped into the kitchen and played a voicemail from the NZ Health System. She listened twice to make sure she had it right and then called, "I think we have a name for our fire victim."

The DI went still. "Did someone report a missing person?"

"It's a dental match. His name is Dane Bui."

Bruce cocked an eyebrow. "That's one of the lift workers you texted to me, just before the avalanche."

Alexa corralled her thoughts. "He works—or worked—at Papa Penguin's and at Coronet Peak. That's according to the avalanche patrol guy."

An ID meant they were closer to knowing what happened and who'd killed him. The decedent was the sun, and his friends, relatives, and enemies were the orbiting planets to explore.

There was something else. Alexa retrieved her notepad and flipped through it. "He's one of Graham Clark's roommates."

"Mr. Clark didn't mention his flatmate was missing," DI Katakana said.

"I'll pull the report up, just to confirm it's a match." Alexa hurried to her bedroom and opened her laptop. The dentist's report was in her mailbox. Dane Bui had last been to Dunedin Smiles when he was seventeen. According to his birth date, he would turn nineteen next month.

She froze. Dane Bui would never turn nineteen. He was young to be out of the nest, living with roommates, and working two jobs. What was the story?

She kept reading. Dane Bui's parents were listed as Delphine and Dave Bui of Angler's Avenue, Seacliff. He had checked *Yes* to International Travel Within Last Thirty Days. Switzerland was scrawled to the side. Bui had no medical issues and wasn't taking any prescriptions. No head or neck pain. No dental implants, dry mouth, or gum disease. The dentist had one concern: bruxism.

What had caused the seventeen-year-old Dane Bui to grind or clench his teeth?

She pulled up the X-rays and opened another screen so she could view them side by side with the postmortem CT scan. Only the bottom two wisdom teeth were erupted in both. The top two lurked below the gum line, impacted. The composite restoration in the upper-right second molar matched, as did a minor filled cavity. The two crowns that were cracked in the postmortem CT scan were not cracked in the antemortem X-ray. Thank 500-plus degrees Fahrenheit for that.

Alexa's heart cracked open for Bui's parents. Their grief, she imagined, would be insurmountable.

She did an internet search to see if she could find a picture of Dane Bui and was surprised that several snowboarding articles popped up. She read one dated a year ago.

BUI BUSHWHACKS AT CORONET COMPETITION

Young Kiwi Dane Bui (QAST), 17, started strong with super technical 360s but ended up in third place after he launched over an avalanche barrier and never looked back. Less than four points separated Bui and rivals Tex Zafiro (NZ SNO Z), 16, first place, and Tony Krammer (CC), 18, finishing second.

Bui said, "Coronet Peak is insane. Resorted to some improv that my coach didn't like when I went over some barriers. What can I say?"

So Bui was a snowboarder. She shouldn't have been surprised.

The photo from the article showed the three boys, ski goggles pushed up on their foreheads and holding snowboards. Dane Bui stood on Tex Zafiro's right, impish grin, chin high, thick neck. Tex and the other boy also smiled, radiating youth and verve.

She carried her laptop to the den. "The dental images are compatible. Our decedent is Dane Bui. I've got his parents' names, address, and a phone number." She held the laptop for the DIs to see. "He's also a snowboarder. Here he is competing last year." She showed the photo from the article. "That probably means he was competing this year, too."

"Easy to find out," DI Katakana said.

Bruce pointed to Tex. "He's the one that was with my daughter yesterday."

"A rival of Bui's," DI Katakana said. "Where is he now?"

"At a lodge with his mother," Alexa said.

"How did Bui get to the party? Where's his car? If he rode with someone, why didn't they report he was missing?" DI Katakana demanded.

Before they could discuss it, the villa door banged open and Sammie burst in, followed by Denise and Sharla. Denise stopped short at the sight of DI Katakana.

Sharla looked refreshed, and her makeup was artfully applied. Her expression, landing on DI Katakana, was fierce. "That boy talked her into it," she said.

The DI's brow furrowed.

Bruce stepped forward. "DI Katakana, this is my ex-wife, Sharla Horne, and our daughters, Sammie and Denise. Sharla is referring to Denise's misadventure yesterday."

"Are you here to arrest me?" Denise asked.

"Do I need to?" the DI asked.

Denise looked down at her UGGs. "Dad said I might be in trouble."

"My daughter knows she was wrong to be in a closed area, but she had nothing to do with starting an avalanche," Sharla said.

DI Katakana buttoned her jacket. "I have a team meeting. It was nice to meet you all. May I have a word outside?" she asked Bruce and Alexa.

Bruce followed her. Alexa dashed past Sharla, into her bedroom, and grabbed her tote. Her crime kit was already in the trunk. She had no intention of lingering. She waved at Sammie and joined the DIs in the cold.

"Ms. Glock," DI Katakana said, "I intend to find that jerry can. When I do, we'll need fingerprints for comparison. Start with our lad Tex Zafiro, and then finish collecting them from everyone on our suspect list." She softened her tone. "DI Horne? I'd love to have you on board."

Bruce's eyes settled on Alexa's. "I'll wrap up some family issues and accompany Ms. Glock."

The DI looked surprised. "When you're finished with the boy, come to the station, both of you."

Chapter Thirty-Eight

Alexa called Dr. McKenzie from the car. "The arson/homicide case has heated up. I'm not going to be able to join you this morning to examine the skull."

"A pity," he said. "There's something embedded in the teeth I want you to see."

He had her at *teeth*. "What is it?"

"That's what I need you to determine."

"I'll get there as soon as I can," she promised.

Bruce slid into the passenger seat ten minutes later. "The girls did not need a repeat of why Sharla couldn't live with me, but they just heard one."

Alexa imagined the litany included how he put work over family. "I'm surprised you're coming with me."

"I'd like to hear what Mr. Zafiro has to say."

Alexa figured his mind was on Denise and the avalanche, not murder. She had already programmed the address of the lodge into the GPS and followed the directions toward the city center.

"I promised the girls I'd meet them at Coronet Peak later. It's our last night here," Bruce said.

Family pull was not something that Alexa wrestled with. She was free to work late, work weekends, work holidays. She liked it that way. "I wish we could call ahead, but Tex lost his phone, and I don't have the mother's number."

"Yesterday Denise's phone was out of juice, and Tex didn't

have one. Meanwhile the rest of us thought they'd been buried by an avalanche."

He had been through Father Hell. She squeezed his hand, the feel of his skin igniting replays of last night in her head. They rode in silence, each with separate thought bubbles.

Manata Lodge was on the other side of Queenstown and down a scraped road lined with snow-draped evergreens. The lodge was a large brown colonial. Bruce rang the doorbell and pushed open the door. They stood in a paneled lobby until a woman backed a cart out of a small elevator. "*Kia ora*," she said. "Be right with you."

She zipped the cart, laden with breakfast dishes, through swinging doors. Alexa smelled baked goods and coffee. The woman returned. "Welcome. I'm Lucy Walker, the owner. We're fully booked if you're inquiring."

"Thank you, no." Bruce showed his badge and introduced Alexa. "I'd like to speak to some of your guests. Where can I find the Zafiros?"

"Oh," Lucy said. "I wouldn't want to bother them."

"I need you to."

Lucy thought a moment. "Why don't I give Mrs. Zafiro a buzz? See if she's amenable? What shall I say it's about?"

"Please inform Mrs. Zafiro the police are here to talk with her. And her son."

"Very well. Help yourself to coffee or tea." She pointed to a buffet spread out in an adjoining dining area.

Bruce headed for the room's windows. Alexa set the crime kit on a chair and gazed at a platter of currant scones and the cream and jam next to it. There had been no "help yourself to pastries," so she poured half a cup of coffee and added a dollop of cream. She watched it whirl and blend into the coffee. Could she whirl and blend with Bruce? At the moment he was a stranger, and she was unsure of his motives.

She sipped the rich strong coffee and reflected on the fact that Bruce had cheated on Sharla. When she confronted him—even though Charlie said it wasn't any of her business—he had not denied it.

The thought of his infidelity had almost sent her packing to Scotland. Instead of running away, though, she had probed her feelings—that had been worse than pulling teeth—and concluded that Bruce hadn't hurt *her*, and he didn't need her forgiveness.

They had to accept each other's pasts if they were to have a future. She studied his straight back and worried he was using the arson homicide to gain information about Tex and Denise's escapade. Maybe even to save his daughter from prosecution.

Lucy returned. "Mrs. Zafiro is expecting you. Straight down the path. It's been cleared. The Wakatipu is the larger of the two cottages on the right."

The grounds were winter-wonderland stunning. As they made their way, Alexa wondered how Mrs. Zafiro had snagged a cottage. Her trip, like Sharla's, had been spur of the moment.

Tex answered the door in a T-shirt and sweatpants, his mop of hair damp and curly. "Hello, sir, Mr. Horne. Where's Denise?"

Bruce's eyes narrowed. "She's with her mother. I'd like to speak with yours."

"My mother is in the kitchen." He led the way to an open lounge room. The Remarkables were visible through French doors.

A woman bustled out of the kitchen area, a phone in her hand, her nails polished red, her leopard-print blouse, camel sweater, and ankle-hugging jeans very stylish. She addressed Bruce. "I'm Stefanie Zafiro. Tex told me you are the girl's father. He tried hard to protect her."

Bruce held out a hand. "DI Bruce Horne, Auckland Serious

Crime, and this is Alexa Glock, forensic investigator. You flew in yesterday?"

She huffed and ignored his hand. "Straight from an important meeting. I own Healthy Alternatives in Rotorua and Dunedin." She gestured to the sofa. Her dark, thin eyebrows appeared painted on. "Sit, sit. We have important matters to discuss, and I don't have much time. I expect you're here about the complaint from the Snow Safety Board? Utter nonsense. Tex and Debbie…"

"Denise," Bruce corrected.

"Tex and Denise did not cause that slip. It's a ridiculous idea." Her eyes darted to her phone, checking the screen. "I was just speaking with my lawyers."

Alexa sat next to Bruce and put the crime kit between them.

Tex padded into the kitchen and rummaged through a plate of pastries, snagging a sticky bun. "It's all bollocks," he said.

Mrs. Zafiro ignored him. "We need a copy of that video of the avalanche that someone took. And quickly. I've a plane to catch this afternoon."

"We can discuss the Snow Safety Investigation at a later time." Bruce eyed Tex. "Ms. Glock needs to take your fingerprints. You were at the Papa Penguin's party Thursday night. I'm assisting DI Katakana with the investigation."

A sigh of relief escaped Alexa's lips. Bruce was on the case.

"You do know the helicopter was a necessity," Mrs. Zafiro continued. "Tex needed immediate medical attention. Frostbite. Another avalanche blocked the road. Do they think he caused that one by psychokinesis?"

A tiger mother, Alexa thought.

Bruce's voice was modulated. "Did you know Tex was at the after-hours party the night Papa Penguin's restaurant burned down?"

"Tex and his teammates were invited to a gathering." She looked at Tex. "A birthday party, was it?"

He licked a finger. "A graduation party."

Dylan Parr's face floated into Alexa's head. "Who was the graduate?"

Tex popped another chunk of pastry in his mouth. With a bulge in one cheek, he added, "I don't know. He never showed up."

"Investigators discovered evidence of arson," Bruce said.

Tex stopped mid-chew.

"A young man died in the fire, so that makes it a possible homicide," Bruce said. "We aren't releasing his name until his family has been notified."

"You know who he is?" Tex asked.

His mother talked over him. "What have you gotten yourself into this time?"

Anger flashed in Tex's eyes. "The restaurant was fine when we left."

Bruce nodded. "Ms. Glock still needs to take your fingerprints."

"For process of elimination." Alexa took the scanner out of the kit. "In case we find evidence of who set the fire."

Mrs. Zafiro glared at her son.

He flashed a high-voltage smile. "No worries, Mummy." The smile didn't work. Mrs. Zafiro's glare continued until her phone buzzed. She glanced down. "A client. Excuse me." She stalked past, into the hallway.

Alexa carried the scanner to the counter but recoiled at the sight of Tex's sticky fingers. She didn't want his loops or whorls compromised by caramel. "Wash your hands."

Tex soaped up and scrubbed under the faucet. His hands were cold and damp when she took them. "Still wet," she said. He dried them more thoroughly on a towel.

Alexa set the scanner on the counter, took his left hand, and examined it. His fingertips were bluish-white. "What's wrong with them?"

"Frostbite."

"Do they hurt?"

He glanced toward Bruce. "My new gloves are shite."

She guided his fingers one by one. "Are you leaving with your mom this afternoon?"

He hesitated. Something crossed in his eyes Alexa couldn't decipher. A yearning? "Nah. I'll get up with the SNO Zs."

"You must be worried about the fire and all," she said. "How many people were still at the party when you left?"

"A few. The waitstaff."

Mrs. Zafiro's voice rose in decibel. "My supplements are impeccable. You'll hear from my solicitor if you print that."

Tex flinched.

"Were there any arguments at the party?" Alexa asked softly. "It might help us figure out why someone died."

He blinked, then shrugged. "Just the usual riffing about tricks and scores."

"Did you see who was driving that Jeep when you left the party?"

"What Jeep?"

Bruce stood. "Did you leave the party with your teammates? Together?"

"Yes, sir."

———

Alexa's glacier sunglasses offered protection from the rays bouncing off the snow. As they walked to the car, she asked, "What do you think of Mrs. Zafiro?"

"The avalanche business is her priority, not the fact that her son is a person of interest in a homicide arson investigation. Is Tex's record clean?"

Alexa thought Mrs. Zafiro's priority was more business than son. "No hits. We learned the party was a graduation celebration, and the guest of honor never showed. Or at least not while the SNO Z kids were there. That had to be Dylan Parr driving up in the Jeep as they were leaving." Tex hadn't seen the Jeep, but the other three kids had.

Bruce called the DI and relayed the graduation-party information. He paused, listening, his face grave. "The pathologist will help you answer their questions." He listened some more, then terminated the call. "The DI is on her way to meet Dane Bui's aunt and uncle at the morgue. A Mr. and Mrs. Katz."

"Aunt and uncle? Why not his parents?"

"Bui's parents moved to Melbourne a year ago. Bui talked them into letting him stay in Queenstown. He's been living on his own, training with QAST, trying for a last chance to go on to World Championships. Working two jobs, too. He must have been a driven kid." Bruce shook his head.

"That explains why they didn't report him missing." Something niggled Alexa's brain. She couldn't remember what.

"Since Pattie is meeting Bui's relatives, she asked me to question Dylan Parr," Bruce said.

"I wonder if there was bad blood between him and Bui?" Alexa commented.

"Pattie also said Senior Sergeant Fielding is waiting to question Autumn Ware. Do you know anything about her?"

She sifted through her mental notes and arranged them in order. "She's American, worked as a server, and was at the party. She showed up at Papa Penguin's Friday morning. Arsonists sometimes return to view their destruction," she added.

"Graham Clark—the party host—said she had a beef with the owners."

Alexa smiled. There were finally some suspects they could sink their teeth into.

Chapter Thirty-Nine

Mattie Parr sprang from a bench when Bruce and Alexa entered the police station. She grabbed Alexa's arm. "What's happening to Dylan? They won't let me see him."

Alexa withdrew her arm. Bruce cleared his throat.

"Mrs. Parr, this is DI Bruce Horne," Alexa said. "He's helping with the case."

"I can find someone to explain the situation to you," he said kindly. "What charges are you and your husband planning to bring against the individuals who attended the party Thursday night?"

Mrs. Parr buried her hands in the pockets of her faux-fur vest. She opened her mouth. A blotch of coral lipstick stained her bottom incisor. "What charges do I have available?"

"Trespassing, underage drinking if that can be substantiated, theft of alcohol."

"Whoever burned our restaurant down needs to be punished. I'm laying off our entire staff. It's dire for them. They depend on Papa Penguin's."

She didn't answer the question, but Bruce let it go. "Ms. Glock will keep you company until I locate a liaison to assist you." Bruce nodded and left. Alexa felt thrown to the wolves. But she could troll for information. "Can I get you a water or some coffee?" she asked.

"Just get me my son."

Alexa sat next to her.

"Why did they pick Dylan up in a police car? He hasn't done anything."

"I ran into your husband at the restaurant this morning. He had just discovered the spare gas container on your Jeep is missing."

Mrs. Parr twitched. "That doesn't mean anything."

"Maybe it was used to start the fire," Alexa suggested. "Is there a chance Dylan drove the Jeep to that party Thursday night?"

"We all went straight to bed," she snapped.

"Is Dylan friends with some of the staff?"

"I wouldn't say friends, but he's worked there on and off for years."

"Anyone in particular? Graham Clark?"

Her mouth dropped. "Oh, here's Autumn."

Alexa followed her eyes. The woman she had spoken to in the restaurant parking lot opened the door and entered. A fellow American. Blond and thin.

When Autumn strode by, Mrs. Parr stood. "What are you doing here?"

It wasn't the greeting Alexa expected.

Autumn stopped. Her eyes were smoky gray. "The police requested I come. It's probably about the complaint I asked you to file."

Mrs. Parr sank onto the bench.

Autumn looked down at her. "I got your message that I'm laid off. What about my paycheck? When will I get my wages?"

Mrs. Parr pasted a concerned look on her face. "We'll do what we can. Our assets are frozen. Insurance and all. Once that's sorted, you'll receive redundancy compensation."

Autumn crossed her arms across her chest. "My rent is due."

Mrs. Parr bristled. "You'll find another job easy. I'm concerned about Dylan now."

"What wrong with Dylan?"

"It's that blasted party. You weren't there, were you?"

Autumn shook her head and turned away. They watched her check in with the desk clerk.

Mrs. Parr narrowed her eyes. "Obviously, she was there. I don't trust her."

Alexa was starting not to trust Mrs. Parr. "What complaint was she talking about?"

"A harassment complaint against one of our customers. It's common."

"Common for a server to file a complaint?"

"Common for customers to flirt with the staff. I mean— it's part of the biz. No biggie. We took care of it."

No big deal unless it's happening to you.

"How long has she worked at Papa Penguin's?"

"I can't keep track. Servers come and go. Six months, maybe?"

When the liaison showed up, Alexa hastily retreated.

Chapter Forty

Alexa told the desk sergeant that she would walk Autumn to the interview room. "We met Friday morning," she reminded Autumn. "When you stopped by the restaurant."

"I can't believe I'm jobless. Have they identified who died?"

Alexa pointed to the stairwell. "Yes, but the name won't be released until his family has been notified."

"Well, who is it?"

"I can't say."

Autumn followed her up the stairs and into the hallway. "I'm here because of the party, right?" she whispered.

So she had been playing Mrs. Parr. "The police are talking to everyone who was there."

"It was just for fun, you know? Few drinks, hang out with the baby boarders." Her voice sobered. "Oh, shit. They'll kick me out of the country."

They passed the incident room. Alexa stuck her head in. Senior Sergeant Fielding looked up from his computer. "Autumn Ware is here."

"Interview room two," he said.

The room was small and cold. Autumn looked at the colorless walls, her eyes growing bigger. She set her large pocketbook on the table and sat. "Can't you stay with me? I don't want to be alone."

First the kid Cam wanted her, and now this. Alexa felt like a support dog. She took the chair next to Autumn. "Just until the senior sergeant shows up." No way he'd let her sit in. "Where are you from?"

"Outside Chicago. What happened to your forehead?"

Alexa touched the scab she thought her bangs hid. "I bumped into some ice. I'm from North Carolina. Ever been there?"

"No."

"We're even. I haven't been to Chicago. How long have you been in New Zealand?"

"Three years?" A dangling thread at the seam of her puffer coat caught her attention. She pulled and tugged, consequences be damned. "I started by WOOFing."

"Woofing?"

"Worldwide Opportunities on Organic Farms. Work for experience, food, and accommodation. I had a go on a veggie farm. In Waikato. Then I got a restaurant job in Lincoln. Met a Kiwi guy—a skier—and followed him here. He's gone, and I'm not. You know."

"Sounds adventurous. How long have you worked at Papa Penguin's?"

She considered. "Eight, nine months? Long enough that they owe me loyalty. I can't believe Mattie turning her back on me."

"It must be devastating for the Parrs to lose their restaurant. I'll take your fingerprints while we wait for Senior Sergeant Fielding. We're fingerprinting everyone who was at the party."

Autumn stiffened. "No need. I'm in the system. In the States, anyway." She gathered her long blond hair over one shoulder and studied the ends. "Possession. Years ago. Follows me around like a little dog."

"I'll take them anyway, just to be sure. How did you get to the party?"

"Drove my clunker."

Autumn was docile as Alexa pressed each of her fingers to the touch screen. Her fingertips and palms were not singed. They didn't speak as the computer searched the national and international data banks. In a few minutes, the prints registered compatible with Autumn Jessica Ware from Long Grove, Illinois, now twenty-six, possession of a controlled substance with intent to deliver or manufacture, dated five years earlier.

"That's more than possession," Alexa blurted. "Did you, um, serve time?"

Autumn scoffed. "Probation. But it was a long time ago. Like I said, it hounds me."

"Were people doing drugs at the Papa Penguin's party?"

"Not that I know of."

Alexa put the scanner away and took out her notepad and pen. "You mentioned a harassment complaint to Mrs. Parr. What was that about?"

She picked at the ends of her hair. "It's hard to figure out what my rights are, you know, as a foreigner. Like pay for being laid off? I don't know if I qualify."

"That complaint?"

"This dude came into Papa's like every night for a week, sometimes with a group and sometimes alone. Old. Maybe thirty-five."

Old? "What's his name?"

"Jay Pierce. He always asked for me. He was okay at first. He tipped, even though no one in New Zealand tips. Said he liked my accent. He bragged about the place he was staying. Some fancy lodge. Invited me to see it. I stupidly gave him my number." She studied Alexa, gauging her response.

Alexa kept her face neutral.

"So natch, he sends lewd texts. Photos, too. Like he's God's gift. That was it. I refused to wait on him or meet him. He was in the parking lot when I got off one night. I made big Mutt—he's the cook—walk me to my car. I was afraid he'd follow me home, you know? I told Mattie, and she said he'd be leaving soon, to let it go, but I wrote," she used air quotes, "an 'official letter' to my employer, like the website said. I didn't feel safe."

"You did the right thing. What happened after that?"

"Nothing. He left, I guess. No one has my back but me. But the freaky thing?"

Alexa waited, pen poised.

Her eyes glinted. "He was at that party."

"Do you have your phone? Can you show me the photos he sent?"

Autumn laughed. "I can show you his dick."

Alexa ushered Senior Sergeant Fielding into the hall when he opened the door and shared the information. "Look into this Jay Pierce guy."

Instead of thanking her, he said, "Leave the policing to the police."

Chapter Forty-One

Alexa and Constable Blume stood at the one-way glass, waiting for Bruce to interview Dylan Parr. Maybe the young constable would be more grateful for the information she gained. "I talked to the server Autumn Ware. She mentioned some guy—Jay Pierce—was at the party. An older guy."

"Jay Pierce? Not heard that name before," Constable Blume said.

She was about to share that Autumn Ware had a record, but Bruce and Dylan Parr entered the interview room. Dylan didn't sit when Bruce told him to. He stared into the glass as if he could see them. Or maybe he was checking his appearance. Today his dark fine hair stood in tufts, gelled.

"Please sit," Bruce repeated. "Our conversation is being recorded. You are not under arrest. You're just here for questioning. Do you understand?"

Dylan turned from the glass and slipped onto the chair. "I get it. My dad will be here any minute."

Bruce took a seat across from him. His voice was clear through the speaker. "Your father will be questioned in another room."

"Why did they take my phone?" Dylan asked.

"The police have the right to seize your mobile. It will be returned when they're finished checking it out. Would you like a solicitor present?"

Dylan didn't answer.

"Answer for the recording. We can reconvene later if you desire counsel."

"Just ask me whatever so I can get out of here."

"Do you know why you're here?"

Dylan shrugged. "You want to ask about the fire. Do you know who it was? Who died?"

"We do," Bruce said somberly. "We aren't releasing his name until we notify his family."

"It's such a nightmare," Dylan said.

Bruce opened a file and studied it. "Congratulations on your graduation. Otago University is where I studied. Bachelor of Laws with Honors."

A law degree? Alexa hadn't known this. So much about Bruce she didn't know.

"Why aren't you a lawyer?" Dylan asked.

"Couldn't bear the thought, though it disappointed my father." He paused, his bright blue eyes trained on Dylan. "Tell me about your degree. What are your goals?"

Dylan's right fingers, splayed on the table, tapped nervously. "Data science. Programming, analysis. I'll probably move to Dunedin or maybe Christchurch, well, since Mum and Dad don't need my help anymore. You know, because of the fire."

"How does that feel?"

"Graduating?"

"How does it feel that you won't be needed at the restaurant?"

His fingers tapped out a rhythm. "Truthfully? Papa Penguin's is a ball and chain, especially for Mum. She wants to travel. Gives Dad a hard time. We never go anywhere."

Constable Blume nudged Alexa. "The insurance payout will set the mum free."

"Shh," Alexa said. "I want to hear."

"You went off to uni," Bruce pointed out.

"I came home every break. I'm the finger in the dike. Only child. Fill in here and there. I don't mind, didn't mind. Hard to get used to the idea that Papa's is gone."

"Did you grow up skiing or boarding?" Bruce asked.

"Not my thing. Dad wishes I was like the staff at the restaurant, the lifties. He always tried for male-bonding opportunities."

"Are you friends with the staff?"

Dylan crossed his feet at the ankle. Alexa could see his checkerboard Vans. "Some of them."

"Who in particular? We're looking into the staff. Anyone with a grudge or who was fired."

"I don't know anyone who would burn Papa's down."

Bruce opened a folder and ran a finger across a sheet of paper until he found what he was looking for. "Papa Penguin's employees Autumn Ware, Mutt Stanford, and Graham Clark were at the party. Chummy with any of them?"

"Mutt's a local, a good guy, but we're not mates," Dylan said. "Autumn? Not mates, either."

"What about Graham Clark? Mr. Clark is the one who invited people to the after-hours party."

Dylan's downy cheeks flushed to match the red of his flannel shirt. "I know Graham."

"He used to rent the flat over the restaurant, right? Why did Graham move out?"

Dylan had no poker face. He looked stricken. "Ask my father."

"DI Katakana did. Your father wouldn't answer."

"He's bloody embarrassed, that's why."

Bruce's left eyebrow raised. "About what?"

Dylan wrapped his arms around his torso and pressed his lips together.

Bruce opened the folder again and removed a paper, which he slid—police fashion—across the table.

Dylan stared.

"That's a CCTV infrared photo, taken at Jack's Point, Queenstown Road, at 12:55 a.m. Friday morning. Half a kilometer from Papa Penguin's. Isn't that your Jeep Wrangler?"

"It's blurry."

Bruce slid another photo across. "Close up of the license plate. Not blurry. PG9060 is it?"

Dylan shrank into his shirt until his chin was buried in soft plaid. "It's my father's Jeep."

Alexa nudged Constable Blume. "Is the jerry can on the side?"

"I don't know," he whispered.

"Were you driving?" Bruce asked.

Dylan shook his head no.

"Your mother then?" Bruce's voice took an edge. "Was she tired of owning a restaurant and burned it down? Maybe she didn't know someone was in the building."

"It was me. I was driving." His voice trembled. "I went to the party after Mum and Dad went to bed. They didn't know."

Bruce leaned back. "You're an adult. Why the secrecy?"

Dylan stacked one fist on top of the other on the table and rested his forehead on them. Alexa saw the whorl of fine dark hair at the crown of his head. It traveled counterclockwise.

"Did you set the fire?" Bruce asked.

"As if." He raised his head. "The restaurant was fine when we left."

"We?"

"Okay. Nah, yeah, Graham Clark is my, was my boyfriend. My father caught us in the flat. In the bed. He was disgusted." His pale Adam's apple raised and lowered. "I never felt shame until then. That moment. That's why Graham moved out, pissed at Dad for making us feel that way. Or me."

Alexa and Constable Blume eyed each other.

"Mr. Clark must resent your father," Bruce said softly.

"Graham doesn't care. He's not cowed by Dad. He still works there. Or did. Dad doesn't have the balls to fire him or to talk with me about what he saw, barging in. It's as if it never happened."

"And your mother?"

He shrugged. "I don't know if he told her."

Bruce tucked the photos into the folder. "Where did you go when you and Mr. Clark left?"

Dylan's shoulders sank. "I guess I need a solicitor."

Bruce ended the tape. "We'll reconvene when your representative joins you. I'll make sure you have access to a phone to make your call."

"I can't leave?" Dylan said.

"Not at this time," Bruce said.

Chapter Forty-Two

Alexa called Incident Controller McBride before finding Bruce. She wanted to hear what evidence the forensic fire team had found, if any.

"The length of time the structure burned uncontrolled, the resulting flashover, and the subsequent water and chemical damage during the containment period destroyed anything of value," IC McBride said. "Some bone and teeth fragments were retrieved."

Bone and teeth. Just like Dan's Aunt Phyllis.

"Gas chromatography and infrared spectrometry confirm the accelerant was petrol."

She thanked him and found Bruce and Senior Sergeant Fielding in the incident room, examining a document at the table. Constable Tweed worked on a laptop. No sign of DI Katakana.

"Alexa," Bruce said. He colored. "Ms. Glock."

Alexa was usually the one blurting "Bruce" when "DI Horne" was more appropriate. "I watched you interview Dylan Parr." She ignored Senior Sergeant Fielding. "Can I see the photos of the Jeep?"

Bruce slid the folder to her. The image of the Jeep Wrangler was blurry, the driver just a dark head hunched forward, but a splash of red stood out on the side panel. "That's the jerry can. Is the Jeep heading to the restaurant or leaving?"

"It's heading south, toward the restaurant," Bruce said. "The time stamp is 12:50 a.m. It doesn't prove Dylan set the fire. Someone from the party could have grabbed the jerry can."

"Did Senior Sergeant Fielding inform you that a Jay Pierce was at the party?" Alexa asked.

Bruce nodded. "We've tracked down Mr. Pierce's address in Auckland, but not a local one."

"You'll want to hear this," Constable Tweed interrupted. "Dane Bui didn't have an arrest record until a few days ago. One of our constables charged him with intoxication and vandalism last Wednesday night. He pulled a fire alarm at Nomads."

"What's that?" Bruce asked.

"A Queenstown hotel. It's where the Canterbury Christchurch snowboard team are staying. The CCs."

"Was he arrested?" Bruce asked.

"Formal warning and court date," Constable Tweed said. "He was back to partying the next night at Papa P's."

Alexa thought of the article about Bui careening over a barrier on his snowboard. *He had careened out of control in other settings, too.*

Bruce pulled out his ringing phone and answered. "DI Katakana?" He listened and nodded for a while. "Not surprising. We just learned Bui was charged with intoxication and vandalism Wednesday night. At Nomads." He frowned, listened a bit longer. "I'll let the team know." He terminated.

"What's up?" Senior Sergeant Fielding asked.

"DI Katakana got Bui's toxicology report. His alcohol consumption was over the limit and likely to have caused, prior to death, slurred speech, even staggering."

Constable Tweed whistled. "Would have been hard to gap it or put out the fire in that condition."

Bruce nodded. "Ms. Glock, the DI wants you and Constable

Tweed to head to Coronet Peak and finish collecting finger-prints before the qualifiers are over."

Constable Tweed thrust a list at her. "Here's the list of board-ers and Coronet Peak staff who were at the party."

Alexa skimmed it. She took out her Pilot G-2 and crossed out names of people she already had fingerprinted. She wrote *deceased* by Dane Bui's.

Breezy O'Brien, 16, NZ SNO Z
~~Kool Shima, 15, NZ SNO Z~~
~~Cameron Keeline, 16, NZ SNO Z~~
~~Tex Zafiro, 17, NZ SNO Z~~
Ally Radtke, 16, QAST
Rickie Collins, 17, QAST
Dane Bui, 18, QAST—*deceased*
Hannah Larrew, 18, CC
Wing Ozborn, 15, CC
~~Autumn Ware, 26, server~~
~~Graham Clark, 21, server, lift operator~~
Mutt Stanford, 25, server, lift operator

Senior Sergeant Fielding, peering over her shoulder, poked Breezy's name with a finger. "There's some social media posts of Miss O'Brien and our victim having a snog at Papa Penguin's. Did Bui do Miss O'Brien wrong? Get up with another girl later? Miss O'Brien doesn't like it and torches the place?"

In Raleigh, Alexa had worked a case where a jilted fifteen-year-old girl was charged with stabbing another girl over a boy. Her fingerprints had been on the knife handle. "Breezy's mother is a lawyer. She refused to let Breezy be fingerprinted or to answer questions."

"Miss O'Brien is a person of interest," Bruce said. "If she refuses again, bring her to the station."

Hardball time. "Do the social media posts show an older guy?" Alexa asked. "The one Autumn Ware mentioned?"

Senior Sergeant Fielding pushed a pile at her. "Printouts. Dane Bui is in a lot of them."

Alexa flipped through them. Someone with the username TakeWing had posted a picture of Bui's arm around Breezy, their faces mashed together.

"Srumpy," someone had commented. Someone else posted a row of lip emojis.

One image showed Tex Zafiro guzzling a beer. It was posted by ally_rad, and captioned "Absolutely hell yeah." It had thirty-eight likes and a few comments: "form looks great," "chasing the stubbies," and "wait until tomorrow, dude."

Three faces crammed in at different angles in a selfie. Alexa recognized Kool Shima and Breezy O'Brien. She pointed to the third girl. "Who is this?"

"Hannah Larrew, Christchurch," the senior sergeant said.

Lots of clap-hands and ski emojis and one comment: "kool fab sisters."

In a post by Rickie Collins, Graham held a pizza aloft. In the foreground, Breezy sat on Bui's lap. His arms encircled her, but his eyes were on the pizza. The two comments were: "She be dreamin" from readyornot and "ewww" from KoolShima.

"Look at this one," Bruce said.

KoolShima posted one of Tex Zafiro, mouth open, in Dane Bui's face. They looked angry. There were four comments: "Face Off" from the_chug, "talkin trash" from everybody_twerk, "bad dawgs" from heavennz, and "homies going at it," followed by multiple fire emojis.

"What's with the fire emojis?" Alexa asked.

Constable Tweed laughed. "Fire emojis mean something is cool, awesome. It might also mean someone is, well, hot. Good looking."

"We've created an account to interact with some of the posters, but no response yet," Senior Sergeant Fielding said.

Autumn Ware was in one image posted by ski#night. She held a beer and kissed a delighted-looking Dane Bui's cheek. No Breezy now. Three comments: "bad bad Bui," "swag man," and "cougar."

Cougar? Autumn was twenty-six, and Dane was eighteen. Eight years was probably a bigger deal the younger you were. Alexa searched the printouts for an "older" guy, but he didn't appear. It was kids having fun somewhere they shouldn't have been.

Bruce cleared his throat. "Take the fingerprints in a public place. Don't be alone with anyone on the list."

The warning gave her pause.

He cleared his throat again. "Once you've collected the prints, DI Katakana is releasing you from the arson case. There's not enough physical evidence to justify the expense of a travel forensic."

Alexa opened her mouth to protest, but Bruce had turned away.

Chapter Forty-Three

Alexa popped into a restroom and splashed water on her face. Being told she was not needed ignited the fighting instincts that occasionally landed her in trouble. And Bruce saying it in front of the senior sergeant and then turning his back?

The cool water dampened her temper. She had known this was coming.

The act of arson destroyed the bits and bobs—a Kiwi phrase she had adopted—needed to help solve cases. Everything up in smoke.

She cheered up by thinking of the skull from the glacier. Dr. McKenzie said something odd was in its teeth. And maybe the Search and Rescue crew would extract the pelvis today. A dangerous mission. She met Constable Tweed in the parking lot and asked if he had dug up anything else about Bui.

The constable blinked rapidly, probably debating whether to share information with someone who had been dismissed from the case. "Yeah, he should be on the mountain today, not in the morgue. Here's an article from last Thursday, first day of the qualifiers. Check out the third paragraph."

Alexa took his phone. The first paragraph was women's freestyle results. The second was women's parallel slalom results. Alexa read the third paragraph.

In the men's side of the national qualifiers at Coronet Peak, it was 18-year-old Dane Bui (QAST) who raced the fastest performance of his career in the parallel slalom, ousting teammate Rickie Collins and rival Tex Zafiro (NZ SNO Z). Cam Keeline (NZ SNO Z) and Wing Ozburne (CC) hope to beat his performance Friday morning as the showdown continues.

The final *day* of Bui's life had been good, but the showdown had not continued for him, thus nudging up the rankings of his competitors. Did Tex, Cam, or Wing go homicidal to win? She handed the phone back. "Do you have the latest on avalanche conditions?"

Constable Tweed searched on his phone. "Generally safe avalanche conditions at Coronet Peak. All slopes clear and open. Unstable snow in isolated spots."

Watch for homicidal arsonists in isolated spots, too. As Alexa tailed the constable's patrol car through the busy streets of Queenstown, she flipped through scenarios.

Mr. or Mrs. Parr torched Papa Penguin's to escape its never-ending drudgery and unwittingly killed Bui.

A homophobic Mr. Parr thought Graham Clark was still in the apartment and set the blaze.

Breezy set the fire over being jilted by Bui.

Dylan burned the restaurant to gain his freedom, or to punish his dad.

Autumn set the fire because her harassment complaint was ignored.

A Junior Championship participant killed Bui to gain ranking in the qualifiers.

And then there was the unknown. The wild card. A motive or suspect off her radar.

The roads were clear, and Lake Wakatipu was a chameleon this morning, blue and smooth as glacier ice.

There were no chameleons in New Zealand, but people changed color under different light. Under police scrutiny. Under the southern lights. In front of friends. Away from parents. She was sad for Bui; he'd never mature and use his energy for good. She thought of her sun-and-planets metaphor and decided Bui's death was intentional murder.

That meant she needed to look harder at his orbit, including the snowboarders.

She slowed on curvy Gorge Road, and Constable Tweed's police car vanished around a bend. The debris from "her" avalanche was visible as mounds on either side of the road, just wide enough to pass through. Her pendant throbbed. She felt its shape through her fleece. *Thank you for protecting me. And Sammie.*

The Junior World Championship banner flapped above as she searched for Constable Tweed's patrol car. The lot closest to the lodge was full, so she circled back to the first lot and found a space. Her phone buzzed, and Bruce's name flashed on her caller ID.

"Hello?"

"Checking in to make sure you're okay about DI Katakana's decision."

"Not really. What if she needs me and I'm off the case?"

"The DI is capable. You can't control everything."

"Is that what you think I do? Control things?"

"You can control me," he said lightly. Then his tone changed. "Kipper Parr is here. He admitted kicking Graham Clark out of the apartment after seeing him and Dylan together. 'No son of mine could be queer,' is what he said. He's angry. And devastated. I'd be suspicious of him if Dylan hadn't been the one driving the Jeep that night."

She hoped Mr. Parr could work through his hang-ups and

support his son. Her mind jumped to the list folded in her pocket. "The kids are going to ask if we know who died in the fire. Is it okay to tell them?"

"Constable Tweed should answer questions."

A group of teen girls in ski jackets of different bright colors ran through the parking lot, drawing her eyes. "Is it okay for Constable Tweed to tell them?"

"Bui's family has been notified, and the media has been informed, so yes." He hesitated. "Pattie knows I'm leaving early this afternoon to meet the girls at Coronet Peak. Sharla is dropping them off at one. Ready to ski?"

Through the windshield, the Coronet Peak mountains stared down at her. They were higher than the ones in North Carolina. Bigger. Steeper. "You're going down," she told him.

He laughed.

She pulled on her hat and gloves, zipped her puffer, extracted the scanner from her kit, and found Constable Tweed waiting by the lodge entrance. "Let's head to the viewing platform and round up the snowboarders," she told him.

He straightened to his full six feet. "Better we go to the management office and have them contact the team coaches."

His was the better approach.

The lobby bustled. The ski shop had a line at the counter. The scent of pizza and french fries wafted from Heidi's. They went downstairs and filed past long benches of animated people zipping and clipping into snowsuits and ski boots.

Constable Tweed gestured for her to follow him down a hallway. He knocked on a door marked *Operations* and opened it. A woman stood by a sprawling desk, speaking to a heavy man seated behind it. They frowned at the interruption.

"Constable Nick Tweed. May we come in?"

The man stood. "Robert Johnson. Operations manager."

His face was ruddy, his hair thick and curly. "What's the problem?"

"I need a private spot where I can speak with the snowboard team members. Immediately." He gestured toward Alexa. "A place where our forensic investigator can take their fingerprints."

Alexa lifted the scanner.

The woman straightened her blazer. "I'm Ashley Pitt, Junior Snowboard Championship director. Why do you need to fingerprint our athletes?" Her eyes jumped to a wall of TVs, each with a live view of action on the slopes. "It's final rounds. We're behind because of yesterday's delay. Pulling the boarders will be detrimental to their concentration."

Did she not know what was happening with the kids?

Constable Tweed glanced at the TVs. "You've heard about the Papa Penguin's fire?"

Mr. Johnson nodded. "Have the police found out who died?"

"His name has just been released," Constable Tweed said. "It's one of the boarders. Dane Bui."

Ms. Pitt gasped. "Our Bui? He was the men's leader. He never showed up yesterday morning."

"Shocking, shocking." Mr. Johnson sat heavily, his chair protesting. "Bui is one of our snowboard instructors. After a couple hours with the wee ones, they're off together on the lifts."

Alexa imagined Bui riding a chairlift with some kid, probably joking and calming her fears.

Mr. Johnson clicked and clacked at his computer. "Here we go. Bui worked here half days at the weekends and Monday nights. He took three days leave so he could compete." His eyes widened. "I remember now. He also works at Papa Penguin's." He paused. "But why the fingerprints?"

Constable Tweed turned from the TVs. "There was an illegal party at the restaurant Thursday night. Lots of the junior snowboarders attended. The owners might file charges. We need to print them before they head home."

Ms. Pitt's expression hardened. "I assume alcohol was involved?"

"The toxicology report showed Bui was intoxicated," Alexa said. "Social media posts show some of the other kids were also drinking."

"That's a code of conduct violation." The director clenched her hands. "No consumption of alcohol is permitted for those individuals under the age of eighteen. Members under twenty-one are forbidden to participate in gatherings involving consumption of alcohol." She pulled out a chair and sat. "The athletes who attended the party will be disqualified. The press will splash it all over. First an avalanche, now this."

"Can you find us a room and get the teams in here?" Constable Tweed asked.

"Our employees have radios," Mr. Johnson said. "I'll call to the platform and dispatch a snowmobile to pick them up."

Alexa had a sudden thought. It had been freezing early Friday morning. Perhaps the perpetrator wore gloves. If they found the jerry can, it might be possible that the weave of a ski glove—instead of a fingerprint—transferred a pattern onto its surface. The fabric might have soaked up gas, too. "Tell them to bring their gloves."

Chapter Forty-Four

They were given an employee break room that smelled of greasy food. "I'm going to spread a little misinformation," Constable Tweed told her as they waited. "The ripple effects could be useful."

Before Alexa could ask what misinformation he planned to sow, two boarders in blue QAST jackets raced in, both dangling helmets and goggles from their wrists. "Coach said you wanted us. I need to be back in ten minutes," the boy said.

"Name?" Constable Tweed asked.

"Rickie Collins." He had an almost-mustache. "This is Ally Radtke. What's up?"

These were the local kids, and Dane Bui had been their teammate, Alexa realized.

From under flattened green bangs, Ally's eyes were fearful. "Is this about the party?"

"That's right. We know you were there," Constable Tweed said. "Papa Penguin's burned down that night *and* a young man died in the fire."

"Who is he?" Ally asked.

He didn't soften the blow. "Dane Bui."

Ally covered her mouth with her hands and emitted a squeak.

As the news sank in, Rickie's forehead beaded with sweat. "We Ubered together to the party, but he wouldn't leave Papa's with us. He was, well, you know."

"Crunk?" Alexa asked.

Rickie nodded.

That answered DI Katakana's question about how Dane got to the party. "Did you notice Bui arguing with anyone?" Alexa asked. Constable Tweed frowned at her. She ignored him.

The kids shook their heads. "We never should have left him," Ally said.

"Why didn't you or your coach report him missing when he didn't show up Friday?" Constable Tweed asked.

Ally's chin trembled. "Bui got in trouble the night before the Papa's party. At Nomads. Coach kicked him off the team. He got messed up Thursday night like he didn't care."

"Shut up, Al," Rickie said. "Give him respect. He did care."

"Who did he hang with?" Constable Tweed asked.

"He bounced around," Rickie said.

Ally wrinkled her nose. "Yeah. From Breezy O'Brien to that waitress."

"Did that cause trouble?" Constable Tweed asked.

"Dunno," Rickie said.

"Was there an older guy—Jay Pierce—at the party?" Alexa asked. "Over thirty?"

"No old dudes," Ally said.

A middle-aged couple barged in. "Rickie? Coach Van Kirk sent us to find you. What's happening?" the man said.

Rickie's face turned crimson.

Constable Tweed said, "Are you Rickie's parents?"

They nodded. "Ben and Natalia Collins," the man said. "What's going on?"

"Rickie is in a spot of trouble," Constable Tweed said. "There was a party at Papa Penguin's the night it burned down. The fire was deliberately set. Your son was there. We need to fingerprint him."

"I didn't have anything to do with the fire," Rickie said.

"But you had a team meeting Thursday night," Mrs. Collins said.

Rickie stared at his feet. "We went afterward. For a little while."

"There's evidence from the debris, so this is a way to eliminate your son from the suspect list," Constable Tweed added.

There was no evidence from the debris. Suspects expected the police to be truthful, so this made Alexa uncomfortable.

His parents stared at Rickie until he looked away.

Alexa retrieved the mobile scanner. She asked the kids casually, "Did you wear gloves to the party that night?"

Rickie let her take his fingerprints. "My gloves? Yeah. It was freezing waiting for the Uber."

Alexa reached for them, and he handed them over.

She smelled them and photographed them as everyone watched. Alexa scanned Ally's fingertips, too, and smell-tested her mittens.

Chapter Forty-Five

"Strange they didn't see this Jay Pierce person," Alexa commented after they left. Had he hidden? Lurked in the recesses to spy on Autumn?

Round two started when the Canterbury Christchurch coach, Mason Kennedy, ushered her team into the room. The coach—mid-thirties and fit—glowed with vitality. Her three progeny stood in descending height order in matching green CC snow bibs. "This is Hannah Larrew, Wing Ozborn, and Luke Burton."

Luke looked ten. "How old are you?" Alexa asked.

He scowled. "Thirteen."

"Squees like a girl, but he's fast as hell," Wing said. He was square-jawed, with short sandy hair and a stump of a neck.

"One of my team got caught in the avalanche," Mason said. "Zoe Izzard."

The girl from the first-aid building. "How is she?" Alexa asked.

"You can't outski an avalanche. Within five seconds it's traveling over a hundred kilometers an hour. Zoe is okay physically. Don't know about mentally. Her parents flew her home."

Hannah rubbed her eyes as if to wake from a bad dream. Her cheeks were sunburned, and her dark hair hung in a single braid.

"We're investigating the after-hours party at Papa Penguin's Thursday night," Constable Tweed said. "You've heard about the fire, eh, and that someone died? Lots of snowboarders were there."

"Not my team," Mason said. "We ate there earlier but were back at Nomads by nine o'clock."

"The deceased is Dane Bui. He was a member of the Queenstown team."

Mason's mouth dropped. "Bui? He's the kid who made trouble at our hotel."

"The fire alarm dude," Luke said.

Hannah's shoulders slumped. "Dane Bui? Dead?"

Wing looked whipped but then straightened. "Bui got into it with Rickie Collins Wednesday night, over some girl."

Constable Tweed and Alexa exchanged glances. Rickie hadn't mentioned a squabble. "What girl?" Alexa asked.

"Breezy O'Brien. SNO Z," Wing said. "But it was, like, okay in the end."

"Why do you want my boarders?" Mason asked. "We're in a hurry."

Hannah's eyes darted around the room.

"Mr. Ozborn, Miss Larrew, were you at Papa Penguin's after it closed?" the constable asked.

Hannah stubbed the tip of her boot into the concrete floor. "I was."

Mason's mouth dropped. "Are you freaking kidding me? You went back out?"

"Luke didn't go," Hannah said.

Mason stared at Wing. He cowered. "Nah, yeah, I went."

The coach's face crumpled. "Guys. You've worked so hard. *We've* worked so hard. Why would you jeopardize that?" She put an arm around Luke. "Good on you for obeying curfew."

Constable Tweed told Luke he didn't have to stay.

Luke frowned at Hannah and Wing on his way out. "Can't believe you didn't take me."

"Ms. Kennedy, you and Hannah wait in the hall," Constable Tweed said. "I'll start with Mr. Ozborn."

A divide-and-conquer approach, Alexa noticed.

"Wing's a minor," Mason said. "I'll stay. Stupid of me to ask, but was there drinking?"

"Yes." Constable Tweed told Hannah to wait in the hall. He closed the door and turned to Wing. "How did you hear about the party?"

Wing shrugged. "Graham Clark invited us when we ate there earlier. We thought, why not?"

Alexa cleaned the screen of the scanner and took his hand. He jerked it back.

"You need to cooperate," Constable Tweed said, "or I'll escort you to the station."

This time he didn't resist. His fingertips were thick. She asked for his gloves.

"Why? I didn't wear them to the party."

"For elimination." His comment made her second-guess her glove theory. It was probably a waste of time. He dug them out of his coat and handed them over. She brought them to her nose. No odor of gas. She photographed the palms and tips.

"How did you get to the party?" the constable asked.

"Hannah drove. She didn't drink, I swear." He raked his short hair. "Everyone just wanted to be together, talk tricks, and brag and speculate about what the fresh dump was doing to the course. There was lots of good energy."

"Lots of drinking and drugs, too?" the constable asked.

He shrugged.

Mason punched his shoulder. "Answer him."

"Some drinking, a little weed."

Constable Tweed nodded. "Who did Dane Bui hang out with?"

Wing's face colored. "Breezy from SNO Z. Some older girl got her claws into him, too."

Hell hath no fury popped into Alexa's head. "Was an older guy there? Maybe thirty or thirty-five?"

"Nah."

"What time did you leave?" Constable Tweed asked.

"One a.m.?"

"Did you see any cars arrive as you left?"

"A Jeep, maybe. Is that important? I couldn't see who was driving."

When Constable Tweed opened the door for Hannah, she was gone.

Chapter Forty-Six

"What the hell?" Mason said.

Lance and the four NZ SNO Zs walked toward them in matching white jackets and zebra-print ski pants. "Did you see Hannah Larrew leave?" Constable Tweed asked.

"Hannah Banana from Christchurch?" Tex asked.

Kool and Breezy shook their heads. Cam looked blank.

"What's this all about? We're up the guts if we don't get back," Lance said. "Cambo is tied for first."

Constable Tweed told Alexa to stay while he searched for the CC escapee. She beckoned the team to enter. She knew her news would be shocking. "We've identified the fire victim."

"Dane Bui," Lance said. "A QAST told us. Everyone is freaking out."

Alexa debated whether to pass on Constable Tweed's "misinformation." Maybe it would shake things loose. "We discovered key evidence that survived the fire. I have your fingerprints—except for Breezy's. Now I need to examine your gloves."

Kool swiped her beanie off. Her hair stood at attention. "Why?"

"I can't say."

Breezy stepped back. Alexa hoped she wouldn't bolt. She smelled and photographed Kool's gloves, then the boys'. Tex's didn't match; he had one Swiss Alpine and one Burton Gore-Tex.

He flashed his charming smile. "Like mismatched socks. For cool factor."

"Gotta go," Lance said.

She stared him down. "The night the kids sneaked out, did you hear them leave or return?"

"Noise cancellation headphones. Didn't hear a thing. Know I shoulda been more—what—aware?"

Ya think? She told the team they could leave. "Not you, Breezy. I need your fingerprints."

Lance and the others rushed out.

Breezy rolled her shoulders, maybe feeling abandoned. "My mum said not to."

"Constable Tweed will have to take you to the station then."

"But I have another event." She seemed to deliberate, looking down at Alexa, but only for a second. "Whatever."

Alexa took her prints and asked for her gloves.

"Mittens." They dangled from her pocket by a little leash. She unhooked them. "Warmer than gloves."

They were white Hestra Heli mittens. The palms, marred by stains, were a soft leather. There was no odor of gas. As Alexa photographed them, she said, "You hung out with Dane Bui Wednesday and Thursday night. Was he your boyfriend?"

Blotches of red broke out on her cheeks. "So what?"

Alexa gave her the mittens. "Burning up in that fire was horrific. Did someone want to hurt Bui? Was someone jealous because he was with you? Or the other way around. Did Bui taking up with Autumn make you jealous?"

Breezy's face hardened. Fear scampered up Alexa's spine.

"They're looking at me weird," she said. "Tex, Kool. Even Cam, like it's my fault Bui burned up. He's dead, so how can I trash him?"

"Telling the truth will help us find out what happened."

She rolled her shoulders and took a deep breath, as if launching from the starting platform. "I saw him going up those apartment stairs at Papa Penguin's with that American girl. Right in front of me." Her voice caught. "We knew each other from all the comps. Cyber Slopestyle, Cardrona Park Attack, Mt. Hutt, Coronet Peak last year. He acted all pumped to see me Wednesday night—we got together—and then Thursday, we kissed and all, then he's hopping around." Tears welled in her eyes. "It was mortifying. I wished he was dead and now he is."

Alexa felt humiliated on Breezy's behalf. Being a teenager was so hard.

Constable Tweed rushed in. "Couldn't find the girl. Everything good here?"

Alexa updated the constable in the hall, gathered her things, and left with a mission. The AWOL Hannah was the final snowboarder on the list.

Chapter Forty-Seven

Alexa speculated that Hannah had either left the ski resort in her car, in which case she'd be rounded up later, or had returned to the competition. She stopped a Coronet Peak employee and asked how to view the qualifiers.

"Ride the Greengates Express to the viewing platform. Or you can watch it from Gully T-Bar or Heidi's."

The aroma of fried food lured her to Heidi's. She stood in line for a Thai sandwich wrap and ate it as she studied the big screen TVs. Dane Bui's handsome and slightly defiant face filled the right one, stopping her mid-chew. The volume was off. A crawl read "Dane Bui, Queenstown Alpine Snowboard Team contender for Junior Championship, identified as fire victim. Distraught parents en route from Melbourne."

The news moved on to New Zealand hop growers.

She scanned the diners for reactions. A few people looked shocked, but most everyone's attention was on the second screen showing live footage of the competition. Alexa finished her wrap and moved closer. "What's happening?" she asked two intent teens.

Without turning, the guy said, "Slope-style men's finals. Two rails, four jumps."

On the snowy course, a competitor skidded down a rail on his snowboard and somersaulted off it. "Lovely front flip nose grab," the announcer said.

"So sick," the girl murmured.

The boarder did something fancy on a second rail and then flew up a steep ramp, launched from the lip, and took flight. He crouched and held the board as he spun, a blue blur.

"Steazy," the guy said.

Alexa was awestruck as the boarder rode the dizzy sky like a magic trick. But as he touched down, he fell back and was sliding on his butt.

"Ah. Not what he was hoping for," the announcer said. "Collins is down."

"Is that Rickie Collins?" she asked the teens.

They nodded.

The camera zoomed in on Rickie's face at the bottom of the course. With goggles, helmet, and a chin guard, he could be anyone. His breath came hard, and his mirrored goggles hid his reaction.

"Rickie Collins usually delivers under pressure, so this is a major disappointment," the announcer said. "He's got a final chance next year."

Alexa wondered if the news about his teammate had interfered with his performance.

"Up next is NZ SNO Z's Cam Keeline, who has absolutely smashed it during practice, avalanche and all," the announcer said. "If he has a clean run, he'll take the prize."

Cam, a flash of red hair peeking from his helmet, sporting zebra-patterned ski pants, separated from a crowd of people. Her support kid bent over to clip into his snowboard. Alexa puffed her chest with pride. She considered with fresh eyes what athletes these kids were. Fearless and driven, acrobatic and artistic. Until now they'd just been a bunch of teenagers who had made a poor decision.

People in Heidi's yelled, "Let's go, Cambo, let's go, Cambo."

Alexa checked to see who his fans were. Mostly teens, a smattering of adults, a server in the cafeteria line. She turned back to watch.

Cam adjusted his goggles, then swiveled his hips so that the board was more like a ski now, pointing down the course. He was off, leaping onto and riding the first rail. "Perfect pretzel flip," the announcer yelled.

Cam touched down on the second rail with a clack and dismounted backward.

"He's an all-terrain vehicle, can ride anything," the announcer shouted.

Then Cam was in the air, crouching and spinning, "a really nice ten there," the announcer said, then he hit another jump, spread his wings like a black-and-white bird, landed, boarded down a steep hill, gained elevation and flew up again.

Alexa marveled at airborne Cam. He was facing his fears head on, with avian athleticism. His flight was daring, inspirational, and courageous, all at dizzying speed. Alexa decided she could do likewise. Face cliffs, sharks, gaffs, Māori war clubs, swinging bridges over roaring rivers, helicopters. She'd done all this in the past year. She had spread her wings and flown.

Cam landed with a flourish.

The camera showed a slo-mo of Cam in the air.

"One, two, and…three," people shouted.

"A Cambo triple," the announcer said. "That's how it's done!"

A crowd amassed behind Alexa, clapping.

"And he kicks up a cloud burst to end it," the announcer said as Cam swirled to a stop at the bottom of the course and gave thumbs-up to the crowd.

"This run does it!" the announcer said. "World Junior Championship-nominated athletes will be announced at two p.m., and you can bet Cam Keeline will top the list."

The run of his life.

The camera panned the viewing platform crowd. There was Hannah, threading through.

Chapter Forty-Eight

An oversight: she didn't have Constable Tweed's contact info. Alexa stepped back from the crowd and called DI Katakana instead, who answered on the first ring. "Ms. Glock?"

"Did Constable Tweed tell you that Hannah Larrew disappeared?"

"Yes, and while I've appreciated your contribution, if you've finished with fingerprints, you need to step away from the case."

"But I just saw her. On the viewing platform. On Greengates."

"I'll let Constable Tweed know."

"None of the kids saw the older guy at the Papa P's party— Jay Pierce—that the server Autumn mentioned," Alexa said. "And Autumn was with Dane Bui. They went into the apartment together."

"Noted."

Phones didn't click anymore when people hung up, but the DI had. Alexa stuffed hers in her pocket, disheartened and dejected. She turned back to the live view. A QAST girl was on the same course Cam had just nailed. She rode the rail like a surfer, then twirled.

"Ally dismounts backward," the announcer said.

Ally, skyrocketing into the air, was the one with dyed green hair.

"She vaults," the announcer yelled. "Look at that. A double cork!"

Alexa turned her back on Ally and took out the list. Not a single snowboard kid had a police record, unless Hannah did. That would change if the Parrs pressed charges.

Another name besides Hannah's wasn't crossed out: Mutt Stanford.

He worked the lifts and was a cook at Papa's. Autumn had mentioned him. Alexa smiled; she wasn't off the case until she found him.

She checked the Coronet Peak map. There were six lift huts, one each at the bottom and top of the three chairlifts. She jogged back to the management office to see if Mutt was working today.

Mr. Johnson had his phone squashed to his ear. He frowned and held up a hand. Alexa eavesdropped as she waited.

"How many?" Mr. Johnson asked whomever he was speaking to. He paused, looking pained, then checked a wall clock. "The ceremony is at two o'clock. I vote for afterward."

Alexa moved to the live-view screens, which played on mute. A boarder in a white jacket and zebra pants flew off the ramp, rotated multiple times while squatting and grabbing the board, and crashed on her landing. The banner flashed KOOL SHIMA DOWN.

Alexa held her breath, but Kool was up and over a final jump. She couldn't watch the rest.

Mr. Johnson put down his phone. "Police, right? The debate is whether to announce the boarders' involvement before or after the ceremony. If the NZ Junior National Championship committee disqualifies the kids who were at the party, a lot of our second- and third-place contenders will suddenly be first." He rubbed his eyes. "Not to mention a development in yesterday's avalanche."

Alexa thought about Denise being charged with reckless endangerment. "What's that about?"

He looked tired. "An initial report has been compiled based on a video of the incident. Bad news, but how can I help you?"

"I need to see one of your lift operators. Mutt Stanford. He was at the party, too."

"Bloody hell." He swirled to his computer screen, opened a window, and scanned. "He's off at five o'clock."

"Where is he now?"

"Top of Coronet Express."

Chapter Forty-Nine

Alexa hurried to the rental shop and found out she needed to purchase a pass and lift ticket first. She ran back. The ticket agent said, "That will be one hundred and fifty-nine dollars. Credit card?"

Alexa showed her forensics badge. "This is police business."

"I guess it's okay then," the agent said uncertainly.

She snatched the pass and ran back to the rental shop.

"What kind of skier are you?" the guy asked.

Three times at Appalachian Ski Mountain. All good. "Intermediate."

"What type skis do you want?"

"The downhill kind."

"Ha ha," the guy said. "We've got slalom, all-mountain, twin tip, and off-piste."

Jitters ambushed her. What the heck was off-piste? "All-mountain."

He asked her weight and shoe size, disappeared into an equipment room, and came back with the goods.

Liberated but encumbered with boots, helmet, bibs, goggles, skis, and poles, she clomped to a bench and suited up. Buckling the boots, she flashed back to the glacier and her sudden slide toward the lip of Gloomy Gorge. That big guy Rongo had hurled himself on top of her. He had risked his life to save hers. To what did she owe that honor?

Pay it forward, she decided.

"There's always next year," a familiar voice said. Two benches away, Breezy comforted Kool. They didn't notice her.

She squashed her hair with the helmet. Outside, she leaned on her poles and clipped into the ski bindings, toe then heel. Stomp. All she remembered from her beginner's ski lesson five years ago was to keep her knees bent and to keep the skis parallel. Like two french fries, the instructor had said.

She licked her lips—where was her ChapStick?—and pulled down her goggles. The world polarized: the sky a deeper blue, skiers' brightly colored parkas more vibrant, the snow more nuanced. She aimed toward the ski lift, the mobile scanner snug in her parka, and skirted the stage a crew was quickly erecting. Probably for the awards ceremony.

A kid swooshed across her path. Her skis crisscrossed, and she fell. *Dammit.* She struggled up, made sure her skis were parallel, stabbed the poles a few feet ahead, and pulled herself forward. She made it to the Coronet Express lift line. The chairlift was wide enough for four people, and a kid and her maybe-mother joined Alexa. They were two chairs away from liftoff when she spotted a commotion and bailed on her companions.

A stay of execution.

She recognized the reporter from the Papa Penguin's parking lot and an entourage of cameramen surrounded by ten or so curious spectators.

"We're pins and needles here at the Junior National Snowboarding Qualifiers finals and not for the reason you think. I'm Nancy Capaccio, News One, with a breaking story."

"What about?" a man called.

The reporter smiled in his direction, her eyes shrewd. "The JNS committee have just discovered many of this year's contenders attended a Papa Penguin's Pizza restaurant party, the very night it burned to the ground. One of the qualifiers, Dane Bui of Queenstown, was killed in the flames."

The crowd murmured. Alexa wondered who had leaked the information. A coach? A boarder? She slid backward and jabbed a pole into the snow.

The reporter continued. "The committee may strip medals from today's winners, who will be announced at two p.m. We'll have live updates then." She beckoned her crew to follow her and waved away questions.

The scandal had launched.

Chapter Fifty

Alexa studied the trail map sign before rejoining the lift line. Her choices from the summit were Black Bowl, Chimney Swoop, Hurdle, and Exchange Drop.

Her heart swooped, hurdled, and dropped.

Through the wide window of the departure station hut, she spotted computers, mechanical panels, a rescue litter, and a fire extinguisher. The lift operator stood under the shadow of the giant circulating cable wheel, watching skiers line up and slide onto the ever-coming chairs. If she fell, hopefully he would spring into action. She joined the line and beckoned him over. "Are you Mutt Stanford?" she asked while there was still time to bail.

"I'm Jake. Mutt's at the top."

She poled herself forward and watched a chairlift swing around, scooping up three riders. She was next on the chopping block. She followed the arrows to position herself, looped her poles over her wrist, braced, and looked over her shoulder.

A snowboarder wearing a swirl of fluorescent colors careened up into the spot next to her just as the chair came into view.

Their face was incognito: helmet, black ski mask, and goggles. Before she reacted, the lift seat bumped the back of her knees. With a jerk she plopped, scooched against the seat back, and reached for the T-bar as her seatmate got situated.

"Hold on." The voice was male. The boarder sat sideways,

one hand on the seat back, crowding her personal space—if that existed on a chairlift. He put out a hand to prevent her from pulling the bar. She fought an instinct to pull harder.

He reached down, wiped a clump of snow off his board, and then pulled the bar down.

They jerked forward and upward. The ground fell away. She held her breath; they were suddenly high in the air. She watched a skier below until he swerved out of sight. They approached a support tower, its bottom wrapped in bright-yellow padding, a ladder stretching up its side. She got the heebie-jeebies thinking about climbing it. Another tower loomed ahead. Her skis dangled precariously. What if one fell off?

She glanced at the snowboarder. The little bit of exposed skin around lips was free of stubble, so he was youngish. "Are you competing?" she asked.

He didn't answer. Maybe he hadn't heard.

The lift swayed. She craned her neck; the chair behind them held three skiers. She squeezed the safety bar. They juddered under the second tower. Bruce and Sammie had been stuck on this lift when the avalanche occurred. She squinted toward Greengates, wishing for her glasses. A faint line above the competition area delineated churned and wavy snow from smoother snow. Maybe it was the remnants of the avalanche.

When they jiggled under the final tower and jerked for a final climb, the upper hut came into view. She edged forward in her seat and lifted the bar. Again, the guy's hand prevented her from moving it. She pulled harder, panicked now.

No go.

Her seatmate's lips formed a smile. A canine overlapped an incisor. Eyetooth was another name for canine. People once believed that the eyeteeth were connected to the nerves of the eye. He finally let her lift the bar. She scooched to the edge of the seat, ready. A slick surface bumped under her skis, lifting them. She leaned forward and glided down the ramp, her seat-mate a blur to her right.

Her poles dragged, but she kept her balance and swiveled to a stop, proud. But crap. The next chair had arrived, and the three disembarking skiers careened toward her. She dug in with her poles, propelling herself out of the way just in time.

She let her heart rate decrease and got her bearings. Her seat-mate, a swirl of color, disappeared over a chute.

No. Thank. You.

She was downhill from the hut. A woman flew by as she turned sideways and lined up her skis. She put her weight on the lower ski and moved her upper ski a foot up the slope. Then she shifted her weight to that foot and moved her lower leg. Repeat, repeat, repeat. She breathed hard, warming up.

The hut was like a log cabin with a pitched roof. A tiny house. It connected by a walkway to the chairlift ramp. As she heaved closer, she spotted a man inside standing at the big window.

She waved. He didn't wave back. She watched a couple of kids zoom off the chairlift. Maybe nine or ten years old in short skis. They shot off like little rockets.

The ground leveled. She bent her knees and thrust forward, gliding behind the platform. When she reached the cabin, she clicked out of her skis. See? She had this. She leaned the skis against the cabin and took off the helmet and goggles. The door burst open, and the man hurled himself out as the chairlifts ground to a stop.

Alexa swiveled. There was a pileup. Two people's skis had tangled under the lift. One skier was on her butt, and the other was on hands and knees. One of her skis came off and headed down the slope. A boarder swooped by and snatched it up.

The lift operator helped the skiers untangle. He waited until the woman was reunited with her second ski. Then he jogged back to the hut and popped inside. The chairlifts resumed their cycle. The man resumed his spot at the window.

Alexa knocked on the glass. He motioned her in. Without taking his eyes off the lifts, he said, "How can I help?"

After introducing herself, she said, "I'm working on the Papa Penguin's investigation. Are you Matt Stanford?"

"Mutt. In the flesh." He glanced at her. Big brown eyes. Shaggy brown hair sticking out of a black knit hat, black ski pants, and a Coronet Peak parka. And big, well over two hundred pounds.

"You worked at Papa's, right?"

"Cooked the pizzas. Best on the South Island. I figured someone would be around. Didn't expect it to be up here."

"DI Pattie Katakana is in charge. She sent me to take your fingerprints."

He turned to her. "Am I a suss?"

She watched him closely. "The fire was an act of arson, and someone died."

He glanced at the TVs on the counter: one showed people getting onto the lifts at the bottom of the mountain, and the other showed skiers unloading. "I just learned it was Dane Bui, I mean like just now. Jake works at the bottom. He told me. Bui, he was a good bro. He bunked at my pad."

It was warm inside, and Alexa unzipped her jacket. "Why didn't you report him missing?"

He grimaced. "You think I'm not gutted?"

Alexa realized she had disregarded Bruce's order to not be alone with anyone on the list.

"I didn't know Bui was missing. Came to work early Friday morning. Then the frigging avalanche. Little busy, eh?" He paused. "Blokes don't keep tabs on each other."

A walkie-talkie squelched. He reached for it. "Coronet Peak Summit," he answered.

"Got a rider coming up, no safety bar."

He tossed the radio on the counter and hustled to the bottom of the lift ramp. Alexa watched through the window as three skiers lifted the safety bar and slid off the ramp, each peeling off at a different angle. Then a snowboarder arrived, safety bar already up, and hopped off. Mutt intercepted him, gestured toward the lifts, and spoke to the boarder.

Alexa read a sign posted on the wall:

SHOULD A CONDITION DEVELOP IN WHICH CONTINUED OPERATION MIGHT ENDANGER A PASSENGER, THE ATTENDANT SHALL STOP THE AERIAL LIFT IMMEDIATELY AND ADVISE THE OPERATOR.

If a rider didn't lower the safety bar, it would double the danger to stop the lift midair, she thought.

Mutt returned. "Kids think it's cool to ride with no safety bar. Most falls from lifts are because of that."

"The kid I rode up with didn't like it when I pulled the bar down." Alexa shuddered at the thought of falling from a lift.

"He got his warning, but don't know if it will do any good. Dane Bui was always up here. Practicing. Teaching. Hustling. The dude was too young to be on his own, in my opinion."

"He didn't want to move to Australia with his parents."

"I get that, but Bui fucked up Wednesday night and got kicked off the team." He leaned closer to the window. Alexa followed his gaze. An idiot had swiveled around and exited the ramp backward.

"Tosser," Mutt muttered. "Anyhow, the Bui was drinking heavily at the Papa's party. Taking up with the girls."

The warmth she had felt was gone. She zipped her coat back up. "Like who?"

He didn't answer.

"You know Autumn Ware, right? The American who works at the restaurant? Was she one of the girls he took up with?"

"Not my biz."

"Autumn said you helped her out a few weeks ago when some guy was bothering her."

"She said what?"

"This customer, an older guy named Jay Pierce, was harassing her. She filed a complaint with the Parrs. You walked her to her car."

"Autumn is full of shit."

What did that mean? "She said this Jay Pierce was at the party."

"No Jay dude was at the party. It was just kids. Autumn was probably the oldest one there. She makes things up for attention. I avoid her. Bui should have, too."

What else might she do for attention? Start a fire? Alexa pulled her phone out to text DI Katakana with this information. There was no signal. "What about Hannah Larrew? A CC Boarder. What's up with her?"

"Hannah is a contender. Might qualify for nationals."

"Do you know why she doesn't want to speak with the police?"

"Who does?" Mutt pulled his cap off and shook his head like a dog after a bath. "Graham and I thought the place was empty when he locked up. I swear we did."

He and Graham could have found the inebriated kid and saved him. Alexa imagined this would haunt him forever.

Enough talk alone in a hut with a big bear. Alexa extricated the scanner. "What time did you leave?"

"A little after one?"

"How did you get home?"

"I drove. Graham rode with me, but he didn't need a lift back. Dylan Parr, the owner's son, picked him up."

"In a Jeep?"

"Nah, yeah. Hold on." He pounced out of the door, moving fast for a big guy, and grabbed a snow shovel. Alexa checked the TVs. There was a pile of skiers at the bottom of the mountain, and the lifts were motionless. Out the window she watched Mutt heap snow onto the lower ramp, press it down, add more snow, and repeat. He used the back of the shovel to smooth it out.

Mutt bounded back to the hut. Once the lifts started again, he grabbed a water bottle and took a swig. Alexa had the scanner ready. "If you don't mind?"

He licked chapped lips. "Whatever."

His fingers were icy. His palms were calloused. One by one she collected his prints. There was no signal up here, so she'd have to check the results later. She packed up slowly, stalling. She was on top of a mountain, and every way down was perilous. The slushy snow of Appalachian Ski Mountain hadn't prepared her for this moment. "Does anyone ever ride the chairlift back down?"

Mutt grunted. "In emergencies."

Before she could declare an emergency, a shout penetrated the hut. A disembarking snowboarder had crashed into two women. They were a squirming pile at the bottom of the ramp. Mutt pushed the *Stop* button and bolted.

Chapter Fifty-One

Alexa stomped her boot into one binding, which reassuringly clicked. She did the other. *Click.* She adjusted her goggles. She threaded her wrists through the pole loops and glided to the other side of the terminal, past Mutt helping one of the women to her feet. Or skis.

A sign laid out the choices.

Black Bowl was a Double Black Diamond. That was the chute her seatmate disappeared over. Niagara Falls in a barrel.

Exchange Drop was also a Double Black Diamond. Gloomy Gus on a cafeteria tray.

The Hurdle was a Black Diamond. A black hole.

Chimney Swoop was Intermediate. Thank God.

The map depicted Chimney Swoop curving this way and that before joining Hurdle for the final leg. She recalled her ski instructor touting a back-and-forth path instead of straight down. *Will do.* Alexa followed a hilly trail on the treeless summit to the Swoop's starting point. Three men zipped by, talking and laughing as if being on skis were as natural as walking.

Then she was alone, her breath coming in cold misty puffs. She thought of Autumn. The American made things up. She had a record. She snared Dane Bui away from Breezy. Did Bui spurn her advances? Did she set fire to the restaurant in retaliation?

Did Breezy?

Why had Hannah done a runner?

She was on a ridge. Queenstown sprawled in the distance like a miniature train set. Lake Wakitipu looked like a sleeping giant. Or a lightning bolt. Other lakes were visible, too, blue gems. Larger whiter mountains beckoned on the horizon, one taller than all the others. Mount Aspiring was too far away to see from here, but the air was crystal clear.

So maybe not.

The glacier skull waved for her attention.

Enough stalling. Into the teeth of the wind, she pushed off. Chimney Swoop—wasn't that a bird?—descending gradually at first. She shifted her balance as she banked a curve, muscle memory taking over, the cold invigorating. She smiled, shifted again, dug the outer edge of her skis into the snow as she maneuvered around a hump. And then another. *Moguls*, she thought. What would her snowboard name be?

Glock the Jock.

Flexi Lexy, from years of yoga.

Whorl Girl.

Her skis sped across the powdery white snow, so different from North Carolina's ice and slush. Her turns were short and fast, and she kept her skis parallel. More short fast turns came up. Without intending to, she was speeding. Her poles flew behind her like skinny wings.

A bend came up. Then another. A bumpy patch stole her control. Where were the brakes? She dragged her poles, tried to slow, and crisscrossed her skis. She fell, a sliding heap of ineptitude.

But that wasn't the end of it.

The slope steepened, and she was still sliding, on her side, one ski backward, a pole catching something and wrenching her arm. She untangled and let it go. Lost it, like the ice axe in the crevasse.

Someone shot by, a blur, then gone. She wrenched her body over, belly down, and dug her elbows into the snow. Her skis, spread eagle behind her, dragged, decreasing her speed. She pressed harder, slowed more. Finally, she ground to a halt.

She looked over her shoulder and counted two ski tips. Amazing that the skis hadn't come off.

She pushed onto her hands and knees, panting, and assessed the damage. Down one pole. A sore wrist. A pummeled ego. How to get up? She pushed into downward-dog yoga position, butt in the air. She aligned the skis and nudged them forward, closer to her hands, tensed, and fell again.

She jabbed the remaining pole into the snow and turned so she was facing downhill and in danger of freaking out. *Fear is excitement in disguise*, she told herself.

Movement from behind caused her to jerk around. A boarder. Flying. She recognized the colorful parka. Her seat-mate must have finished his first run and come back for another. He headed straight for her, then swerved to a stop five feet in front of her, showering her with snow.

What the hell was wrong with him? She waited for a "Need help?" but it didn't come.

In a swirl of white and black, another snowboarder emerged. Red hair stuck out of his helmet. He stopped on a dime. Alexa relaxed; it was Cam. He offered her a hand, which she accepted, and then she was upright. They watched the first boarder disappear. "Who was that guy?" she asked.

"Tex?"

She forgot that she was only halfway down a frigging mountain. "That was Tex?"

Cam leaned his weight back to keep his board from sliding, lifted his goggles, and nodded.

"Congrats on the qualifiers. I watched you nail first place."

Alexa expected his eyes to reflect excitement or pride, but they looked lackluster.

"They'll take it from me because of the party."

He was probably right. "You were still amazing. The way you flew and flipped three times in the air."

"I saw him chuck it in the lake," he said.

What was he talking about? "Saw who chuck what?"

He scanned the slope as if checking that they were alone. "I fished it out. I have it."

"Fished what out?"

A snowboarder whizzed by so close, Alexa felt a breeze. Cam took off in his wake, leaving her clueless.

Chapter Fifty-Two

Alexa conquered the remaining hill at reckless speed and glided under a newly erected National Junior Snowboard Championship banner. "We Are the Champions" blared from loudspeakers. A crowd milled around the stage, holding drinks, the atmosphere lively and anticipatory. She clicked out of her skis and leaned them, and the one pole, against the rack.

Cam was nowhere to be seen. What had he fished out of the lake? The jerry can?

Close to the stage, young Luke from the Christchurch team danced around his coach, Mason, like he'd mainlined Five Hour Energy. Would he jump in the standings if Cam and the other winners were disqualified?

A girl with a dark braid, snowboard under her arm, threaded her way toward Luke and Mason. Alexa stuck her helmet on top of one of her skis, patted her chest to feel the scanner tucked inside, and ran. "Hannah!"

The girl froze.

"I'm glad I found you." She was still wearing goggles and lifted them up. "Are you okay?"

Hannah shook her head. "Not even."

Alexa made her voice friendly. "Why did you take off from the office? I need to take your fingerprints."

Hannah brushed snow off her Burton snowboard. "You're the police?"

"I work with the police, but I'm not a police officer. I like your board."

Hannah cradled it to her chest. "If you like to pop ollies and launch off rollers, this thing will have you flying. But I blew the big airs. I couldn't concentrate, kept thinking about Dane Bui." She paused, her cheeks bright red. "I've just been awarded a Prime Minister's Athletic Scholarship."

A teen in a Taranaki Shredder parka poked Hannah. "S'up, Hannah Banana?"

She smiled perfunctorily, and he sauntered away. "What if they find out about the party? They'll take away the scholarship. Bui never would have died if there hadn't been a party. Will I be arrested?"

The loudspeaker now blared Katy Perry's "Roar." A couple of women sloshing beers sang about dancing through fire. More people streamed from the lodge toward the stage.

"I don't know, but you have to face it, face the consequences," Alexa shouted. "Running off makes it worse."

Hannah's eyes teared up. "I let my parents and Coach Mason down. I don't know who I am anymore."

Jeez. Alexa ached for her. Like all the snowboard kids, Hannah was closer to childhood than adulthood. She pointed to a picnic table near the ski rack, and Hannah followed. Her fingertips were pink and unblemished. Her ski mittens smelled of snow and cold air. Alexa put the scanner away. "All done."

Hannah hefted her board and trudged away. She had no prints on file. Alexa checked Mutt Stanford's—they were clean as new-fallen snow. Her fingerprint list was officially a fait accompli. She called DI Katakana and reached her voicemail. "Cam Keeline has important information," she said. "He saw someone throw something in the lake. You need to speak with him."

She had a text from Bruce, only minutes old. Meet me mgr office.

She skirted a toddler in a pink snowsuit and fuzzy hat and rushed inside. After knocking on Mr. Johnson's office door, he opened it with a frown. "Now what?"

Past him, Bruce—dressed in ski clothes—and Tex's mother stood watching a TV monitor. The long-haired avalanche patrol guy—Heath—hovered behind them.

"DI Horne is expecting me," Alexa told Mr. Johnson. Bruce turned. His eyes were slate gray. She scurried to his side. "What's wrong?"

"It's video of the avalanche."

Mrs. Zafiro, businesslike in a pantsuit, didn't acknowledge Alexa. "Play it again," she ordered.

The avalanche guy rewound the clip and started it over. "It was filmed Friday morning from the Greengates viewing platform," Heath told Alexa.

Avalanche day. Alexa got a funny feeling in her stomach.

The clip had sound. An enthusiastic male voice—maybe the recorder—said "CC Zoe is off-camera, and SNO Z is up next. Let's see what this kid's got." A snowboarder in zebra-print pants rocked back and forth on his board, scooching sideways to the starting position. A flash of red hair spilled from his helmet.

"That's Cam Keeline," Alexa said. Now wasn't the time to share his strange message about something tossed in the lake.

Bruce pointed. "Look above him."

Denise, in bright pink, shone like a lighthouse beacon on the upper ridge. A boarder in SNO Z uniform cut across her path, throwing up a wave of snow. Denise covered her face and fell backward, landing on her butt.

What a jerk Tex was, Alexa thought.

Denise struggled to stand, though she was laughing. Tex, ten feet farther down now, cut diagonally across the slope, jiggled in the middle, and threw up more snow that didn't reach Denise this time.

Alexa checked Cam—he had turned perpendicular to the slope, ready to launch—then she watched Tex. He sliced across the crust again. This time his route caused loose snow to break off and glide innocuously down the slope.

Alexa held her breath.

The loose snow gained in bulk like a rolled snowman ball, and then a big plume of snow formed, and the entire slope beneath Tex ripped away with a gunshot sound. The video shook. The filmer screamed. Alexa skimmed down to Cam, who launched, but veered to the side, off-camera, as the mass of snow roared downward.

Then there were cries and crazy angles on the screen—faces, the sky, feet, spectators running—then it went blank.

Alexa grabbed Bruce's hand. She envisioned Zoe trying to outski the mass sweeping toward her. *"Okay physically. Maybe not mentally,"* her coach had said.

Mrs. Zafiro's voice was sharp. "Tex didn't know that would happen. It was obviously an accident."

Mr. Johnson had joined them. "The committee believes he knew skiing like that could start an avalanche. Our head of avalanche control can explain."

Alexa squeezed Bruce's hand and let go.

"Ski cutting is one of our tricks—well, methods—we employ to reduce slope-scale hazard by intentionally releasing avalanches," Heath said. "Sometimes it's better than explosives, but it's risky. We don't do it often, and when we do, we employ ways to reduce the risk. Have spotters, safe spots, beacons."

He rewound the clip and fast-forwarded to Tex cutting across the snow. He froze it. "The kid looks like he knows what he's doing, descending in that zigzag pattern. If you watch, you can even see him porpoizing, which loosens snow."

He played it in slo-mo. Halfway across the second cut, Tex jumped up and down on the board. Alexa guessed that was "porpoizing."

Mrs. Zafiro didn't buy it. "Tex is too big an idiot to know that. He was showing off for that girl."

Calling your child an idiot? Even if Tex was, Alexa was appalled.

Mrs. Zafiro stabbed Mr. Johnson with her eyes. "What's your responsibility? How did they get up there if that slope was closed?"

"Denise said they took the Greengates lift to the top and bushwhacked across," Bruce answered.

"To a closed area." Mr. Johnson shook a sheet of paper. "This is our rules of misconduct. I'm sure you understand why Mr. Zafiro is now banned from Coronet Peak permanently due to his reckless and dangerous behavior. You can share a copy of the video with your counsel."

The lines around Mrs. Zafiro's mouth deepened. "I brought Tex here merely to watch the awards ceremony. He's not skiing."

"Yes, he is," Alexa said. "I just saw him."

Mrs. Zafiro recoiled. "I'm late. How will I round him up? He doesn't have a phone."

"I'll send ski patrol," Heath said.

"That's hardly necessary." Mrs. Zafiro turned toward the door and stalked out.

Alexa almost felt sorry for Tex.

Bruce waited for the door to close, which it did with a bang. "What about my daughter?"

Mr. Johnson cleared his throat. "Sarah Sue, where they were found, and the top of Greengates, where the boy triggered the avalanche, were closed for safety reasons. She disregarded this." He referred to his paper rather than meet Bruce's eyes. "Misconduct will result in cancellation or suspension of privileges with no refund."

Bruce nodded.

"First-time penalty is a pass-suspension for ten days," he continued. "Your daughter and the boy may face more consequences, depending on the costs incurred."

"I understand," Bruce said. "She's on the slopes now, with her sister. I'll round her up."

He walked out, Alexa following. In the hallway he whipped out his phone and pushed a speed dial. His eyes darkened as he waited. After a moment he barked, "Denise, call me. Now." He tried another number, waited impatiently, and said, "Sammie. Where are you? Call me."

Alexa thought of how her phone hadn't worked at the top of Coronet Peak.

Bruce's thumbs were flying, sending his daughters texts. Finally, he met Alexa's eyes. "I'm going to find them." He headed toward the rental area.

Alexa caught up with him. "I'm off the arson case. I'll help."

The mention of the case stopped Bruce in his tracks. "There's been a development. The American, Autumn Ware. Senior Sergeant Fielding poked into her New Zealand employment history. There was a fire where she worked last. The Black Door Eatery in Lincoln. It started in the kitchen. In the middle of the night."

"Was anyone killed in the fire?"

"No deaths," Bruce said. "Maybe she didn't mean to kill Bui."

"Or maybe she meant to kill someone at the Black Door, and they lucked out," Alexa said.

Chapter Fifty-Three

Alexa and Bruce clipped into their skis and glided to the stage area. Alexa had snagged a new pole at the rental counter to replace the one she'd lost and felt balanced.

The music was off, and three girls stood on blocks on the stage. Sixty or seventy people watched a man in tight jeans and a glittery jacket prance back and forth on the stage, yelling into a microphone, "Last chance for a photo op before we get the blokes up here."

Alexa grabbed Bruce's arm. "There's Breezy O'Brien."

Breezy leaned down from the first-place pedestal as someone hung a medal around her neck. The second- and third-place winners, whom Alexa did not recognize, clapped politely. Breezy held up her medal for photographs. Lance and Kool Shima stood below the stage, cheering. Alexa was happy for Breezy, however long she would hang on to the medal. A news crew filmed the awards. Several judges watched with stony faces.

Bruce looked around. "Why aren't the girls answering their phones?"

"Mine didn't work on top of Coronet Peak," Alexa said.

Two snowmobiles whizzed by. Alexa figured it was the ski patrol, scouting for Tex.

"Make some noise for the slopestyle women's champions," the emcee yelled. The crowd hooted and cheered as they filed off stage.

The trend in ski apparel was vibrant bold colors, but Alexa didn't see any bright pink. Sammie's coat was red, but she was nowhere to be seen.

"Clear the stage for men's slopestyle winners," the emcee shouted. Music blared: "Jump" by Van Halen. The spectators hopped up and down. "They aren't here," Bruce shouted.

The music screeched to a stop. The emcee blathered about amplitude, trick difficulty, execution, and style. "Give it up for our third-place slopestyle winner, Wing Ozburn, Canterbury."

"Boom," someone yelled.

Bruce shouted in her ear. "Sammie is a beginning boarder. Denise wouldn't take her up Coronet Peak. I'll take Greengates, and you take Meadows Run. All good? You've got your phone?"

Alexa patted her pocket.

He hesitated, his eyes sapphire bright. "When we find them, I'll take Denise back to the villa. You can stay, ski with Sammie. None of this is her fault. Or yours."

It might be tempting fate to keep Sammie safe again.

Bruce glided away as a cheer erupted for the second-place winner, a Taranaki Shredder. The kid was all smiles and peace signs as he climbed the stairs to the stage. When the crowd settled, the emcee said, "This next boy will head to Internationals in November! Cam Keeline, NZ SNO Z, first-place slopestyle."

The audience roared "Cambo, Cambo."

Alexa decided to corner him when he left the stage and ask what he'd seen tossed in the lake. She clapped and clapped until she was the last one clapping.

No Cambo.

The crowd quieted. Kool and Lance craned their necks, searching for him. Had Cam ducked out, knowing he might lose the medal?

Alexa pushed off toward the Meadow Runs chairlift.

Autumn Ware was probably responsible for the fire and Dane's Bui's death, not one of the snowboard kids. That was a relief.

She counted her blessings on the way. Denise was safe. Sammie was safe. Bruce loved her. She was in New Zealand, beauty in every direction, Kool & the Gang serenading the Kiwis with "Celebration." She swiveled her hips to the music and almost fell.

At the base of Meadows Run, she scanned the chairlift line. Mostly younger kids and parents waited to board. She skied over to the sign. Meadows Run led to Gentle Annie, Rocky Run, Big Easy, and Little Easy. More her level, she conceded.

Past the chairlift she spotted a T-bar pulling people up a slope. In the line was a girl in a bright-pink jacket. Next to her, a girl in red.

Alexa called Bruce, told him where the girls were, and skied to the base of SloPoke, keeping an eye on them.

Denise appeared in a series of wavy turns, kicking up small wakes of snow, her body parallel with the board, her stance graceful. As the terrain leveled, she reached down for the lip of the board, tried some kind of trick, and lost her balance, tumbling. She got up laughing and turned to face the hill.

There was a red blur. Sammie zoomed straight down.

Denise waved her arms. "Turn! Turn!"

Sammie crouched, leaned back, and curved to the left and then right, slowing and then crashing, sliding on her butt, snowboard in the air.

Jeez, Alexa thought.

Sammie turned over on her stomach and pushed upright. She made it the rest of the way with no mishap.

"Boom." Denise fist-bumped mittens with her sister. "You did it!"

Away from their parents and friends, the girls were having fun together. Alexa hated popping their bubble but called their names and skied over to meet them.

Sammie's helmet was crooked. "Alexa! Did you see me fall?"

"You got right back up. I saw you come down, too, Denise. You were awesome."

Denise smiled before she caught herself. "I'm going again."

"Wait. Your dad is on his way. He tried calling you."

Denise's smile vanished. She wobbled on her board as she whipped a mitten off and found her phone. "Three times. He's going to kill me."

"There he is," Sammie said.

The three of them watched Bruce glide confidently over the level terrain, impressing Alexa. With no preamble he told Denise her ski pass had been revoked because of the avalanche incident. "You've got to leave. Come on."

"Denise is kicked out?" Sammie asked. "That's not fair."

"Denise broke the rules," Bruce said. "This is a consequence. You can stay and ski with Alexa. It's our last day here."

"But I don't want to. I want to go with you."

"Fine. But Denise will be confined to her room. No TV. No phone."

Alexa knew she shouldn't be hurt by Sammie's rejection, but she was. "I'll do a few runs and see you later," she told Bruce.

"God, Dad," Denise said. "You are so horrible."

Sammie undid her bindings and stood. "I want to switch to skis. I'm better on skis."

Chapter Fifty-Four

Bruce and Denise took Sammie inside to rent skis while Alexa waited by the stage. The awards ceremony was over. A parent photographed her two young children standing on the pedestals. People drifted by, some on skis or boards, some walking. Alexa spotted Kool Shima and waved her over. "Did Cam show up for his medal?"

Kool wrinkled her nose. "He ditched the awards. I guess what was the point if they're going to take the medal from him?" Her heart-shaped face looked pensive. "The season is over. I blew my backside nine and my parents' trust in me."

"You can earn that back," Alexa said. "You're what? Fifteen? You have more chances for qualifying. Cam, too, right?"

She shrugged.

"If you see Cam, tell him I need to talk with him."

Bruce and Sammie returned, minus Denise. Alexa asked Sammie how good a skier she was.

"I'm awesome."

"She's been skiing since she was three," Bruce said.

"Is she Black Diamond good?" Alexa asked.

"Yes," Sammie said.

"No," Bruce said. "Keep to the Intermediates." He studied Alexa. One eyebrow rose. "What kind of skier are you?"

"I've already been down Chimney Swoop." *Barely.*

"It's half-past three," Bruce said. "The lifts close at five. I'll see you back at the villa at five thirty or six?"

"Sounds good," Alexa said.

"Can we go out to dinner again?" Sammie asked.

"I'm cooking." Bruce kissed Alexa, who flushed as he walked to the lodge.

"Ew," Sammie said.

"I know, right? Let's do some easy slopes first so you can show me how good you are."

Sammie obliged. Helmets fastened, they glided to Meadows Run and rode the two-seater—safety bar firmly in place—to the top and skied Little Easy first, and then Big Easy. The gentle winding almost-empty slopes empowered Alexa. She focused on where she wanted to go, and her skis obeyed.

Sammie was faster. She waited at the bottom, a wide smile on her face. "Let's go up Coronet Peak now."

Maybe it wouldn't be as scary this time. Alexa followed Sammie back to the middle lift. Her hamstrings and glutes complained; she'd be sore tomorrow.

They waited as a group of four crammed onto a chair, the liftie standing by, looking bored.

"Our turn," Sammie said.

Alexa poled herself next to the kid, straightened her skis, and looked over her shoulder. The chairlift rounded the corner and scooped them up. Sammie pulled the safety bar down before Alexa had scooched against the bench back. They jerked upward, suddenly high in the air.

Clouds covered the sun now, giving the snow a grayish tint. Her ears popped; something heavy and pending in the atmosphere made her swallow. She looked over her shoulder. The chair behind them was empty. The one behind it was empty, too. It was late in the day, and the skiers were thinning out.

She felt the vibrations in every part of her body as they

passed under the first tower. Albert Einstein said everything in life is vibration. Alexa liked that.

"We practically have the mountain to ourselves," Sammie said.

Alexa's stomach belly flopped when she looked down. She squeezed the safety bar with both gloved hands and tried to relax. Skiing down Chimney Swoop the second time would be easier than the first.

"Denise is in love with Tex," Sammie announced. "She told me."

"Wow," Alexa said. She followed the path of a lone boarder until he was out of sight. Her skis clacked together, and she straightened them in the air.

"Mum said he got her in trouble."

The chairlift swayed and lurched, as if someone pushed it from behind. At what wind speeds did they shut chairlifts down? Alexa squeezed the bar tighter as they juddered under the second tower.

"Are you scared?" Sammie asked.

"A little."

Sammie patted her glove. Alexa could get used to Sammie Horne. Denise? It would take longer. "We're doing Chimney Swoop, not a Black Diamond," she reminded Sammie.

"I know."

The hut came into view. Mutt's large form watched from the window. He was probably thinking about Dane Bui, what he could have done to save him. They lifted the bar together. As soon as solid ground bumped their skis, she and Sammie slid off and away.

Mutt waved as she and Sammie passed behind the hut to the trail. She wondered if he'd be surprised if she told him about Autumn Ware. He was not a fan. She wished she could listen to DI Katakana interrogating Autumn.

Sammie zoomed ahead as if crossing the ridge were effortless. "Wait for me at the top," Alexa called. The view was different this time. Queenstown was hidden by clouds. A sliver of Lake Wakatipu looked like a serpent's tail, silvery and quick. Moisture coated her bare cheeks. She gazed up, alarmed.

"It's snowing," Sammie yelled.

They stood side by side, looking down. "Do I have to ski with you?" Sammie asked.

"Stop halfway and wait until I catch up. Then you can beat me down."

Sammie glided off and was gone.

Chapter Fifty-Five

The early part of the Swoop was gradual. Alexa felt slightly weightless as she leaned into the curves, graceful even, filling her lungs with cold, clean air, wishing Bruce were by her side.

Jeez. They were on a ski vacay and never skied together.

Like a crooked finger, curves summoned her forward. Knees bent, she conquered them at a clip, shushing left, then right, and then plowed to the side and stopped before the first drop-off.

In control. Of her skis and life. New Zealand had her hooked.

There were no other skiers around. The light was weird, flat, hiding ruts and moguls. Snowflakes smeared her goggles. She wiped at them with her gloves and took off.

A gnarly plunge caught her by surprise. She tensed, turned too quickly, and fell, this time landing uphill from her skis. It took effort to stand on an angle and brush off her humiliation. She panted, barely balanced, suddenly paralyzed. A pit formed in her stomach. *I can't do this.*

The thought of Sammie waiting for her halfway down—wait—wasn't she at least that far by now?

She looked over her shoulder. The slope was barren. Where was everyone? The pit enlarged to a crater.

Sammie is waiting.

She pointed her skis diagonally and cut across the slope, then back again, holding it together. She conquered the hill and curved back to where the Swoop merged with the Hurdle under the chairlifts. A flash of red caught her attention.

Sammie's parka. Sammie stood by the second tower, staring up. Alexa followed her gaze.

Dammit to hell.

A rider hung from a stationary chairlift, his legs, one with a snowboard attached, flailing. He was twenty or thirty feet in the air. The chair listed, and the other rider, jammed at one end and pressing against the safety bar, held him by his jacket.

Oh, my God. No one could survive that fall.

Alexa flew to Sammie's side.

"Help him," Sammie screamed.

She held on to the tower, released her bindings, and kicked off her skis. "Call 111," she told Sammie.

"I did."

"Good girl."

The snowboarder dangled near the ladder scaling the tower. His snowboard suddenly broke loose and crashed down, stabbing the snow three feet from Sammie.

It had nearly impaled her.

"Stand over here," Alexa cried.

Sammie was frozen, her eyes ocean wide. "It's Cam."

She was right. "Hold on," she screamed up. She recognized zebra pants and Tex's fluorescent coat. Cam and Tex had been riding together. Tex was leaning over, holding onto Cam.

Cam's legs stilled. One of his arms clawed at his neck; maybe the jacket was choking him. Tex had his other arm by the wrist.

Think fast.

She could climb the ladder and catch him if he swung over. She reached for the first rung, but hell, it was five feet high. Below it, thick yellow padding wrapped the base.

Padding.

"Help me pull this off," she called.

Sammie tripped trying to reach the tower. One of her skis came off and slid away.

The sound of a skimobile barely registered as Alexa yanked one of two Velcro straps. It scritched as the strap released. She yanked the other. The enormous mat released, falling forward, almost taking her with it. It was too heavy for Sammie and her to hold like a net. She dragged it under Cam, the back of her neck tingling as if he were going to crash on top of her. She jumped back.

Cam's scream was chillingly short.

Chapter Fifty-Six

He landed on his back, mostly on the mat, with a sickening bounce of his helmet. Alexa and Sammie dashed to his side. Alexa carefully pushed his goggles up. His eyes—deep reddish-brown—stared unblinkingly at the sky.

"You're okay, you're okay," Alexa said into them.

His left leg was bent backward at the knee. He moaned.

"Is he alive?" a voice called.

Alexa and Sammie looked up. Tex stared down, helpless, his face—stripped of goggles—white. Alexa nodded. Sammie was mute.

A flurry of Polaris snowmobiles arrived, one after another, in a deafening roar. Riders, some who had doubled up, jumped off and crowded Alexa and Sammie out of the way. They went about their ministrations quickly, talking into a radio, "lift incident," "fall from height," "possible fracture," and "conscious, not talking." They stabilized Cam's neck and kept asking, "What's your name, lad? What's your name?"

"It's Cam," Sammie called.

"Cam Keeline," Alexa added. "With NZ SNO Z boarding team."

"We're loading you up now, Cam," the leader said. Four of them gently lifted Cam onto a sled attachment. The Polaris with its fragile cargo disappeared down the mountain, the other crew members watching in silence. When it was out of sight, one said, "I can't believe he fell out of the goddamn chair."

Another squeezed a bundle of netting to his chest. "Aw fuck." He looked up. Tex had been watching all this time. "Dude! What happened?" he yelled.

Tex couldn't seem to form words.

"He's a witness," the guy said. "Get him down." He radioed for someone to start the lifts.

Another of the crew whipped out his phone. It was Heath, the avalanche guy. "Take pictures first. Everything needs to be documented."

"The kid is a goner," another said. "It's too high to survive a fall."

"Shut up," Alexa said. "You don't know that."

The chairlift hummed and jerked into motion, carrying Tex to the top of the mountain.

Heath recognized her. "The police, right? Was it you that called 111?"

"No." She pulled Sammie into her side, her arm around her. "Sammie did."

"Good on ya," Heath said.

"But he fell," Sammie said quietly.

Heath broke in. "You got the mat under him. Might have saved his life."

Sammie eyed Alexa. "It was her."

"Was the safety bar up or down?" Heath asked.

"Up," said Sammie.

"Down," Alexa said.

Sammie's eyes darted around. "I want to go home."

"I'll give you a ride, eh?" Heath looked at Alexa. "You'll have to make statements for the accident report."

The crew collected three skis and put them on another

snowmobile as Alexa and Sammie climbed on behind Heath. Alexa squeezed her arms around the kid, and even through the throttle of the engine, she felt Sammie's body shake as they whizzed down the ghost-town slope.

People gawked as they unloaded by the medical clinic. A siren blared. Sammie took her helmet off and covered her ears. Alexa caught sight of the flashing lights of an ambulance tearing away.

She took her helmet off, too, and called Bruce. "Sammie needs you. She's fine, but she needs you."

"What's happened?"

"Oh, Bruce. It's bad. We saw Cam, the kid from next door, fall from a chairlift. He landed right by us." She turned her back. "I don't know if he's going to make it."

———

They waited twenty minutes in the hallway for Mr. Johnson— the operations manager—and whoever else was in the office talking with Tex Zafiro. Tex emerged, with Lance, looking dazed, all swagger drained from him. "Is he okay?" he asked Alexa.

"I don't know. How did he fall?"

"He was fooling around, all of a sudden—damn—I tried to hold him."

"Does Cam's father know?" Alexa asked Lance. He looked horsewhipped and nodded gravely. He opened his mouth to add something, but Mr. Johnson motioned Alexa and Sammie into the office. A man in a Junior Nationals Organization blazer and a woman in casual clothes stared at them as they entered.

Sammie grabbed Alexa's arm. "Where's my dad?"

"He'll arrive any second. You don't have to say anything until he gets here."

"I just want to go home."

Mr. Johnson was solicitous, asking if they were okay and ordering hot chocolate for them. He made introductions as they waited. Names didn't penetrate Alexa's scattered brain, but the man was a Junior Nationals spokesperson ("a tragic ending to a riveting day") and the woman was co-owner of Coronet Peak ("never had a chairlift incident of this magnitude").

When Sammie had her cocoa and had taken a sip, Mr. Johnson gently asked her to tell them what she witnessed.

"I know his sister," Sammie said.

"Whose sister?" Mr. Johnson asked.

"Cam's sister. Lindsey is in my class. We're not like friends, but she's okay."

"If you could tell us what you saw?"

"Halfway down. I heard 'help.'" She blinked, several times, and when she stopped, her eyes seemed dull. Alexa worried she might be in shock. "I saw Cam. He was hanging on to the chairlift, kicking his legs, like trying to get back up. I called 111."

"That was so smart," Alexa said.

"It was, it was," the co-owner agreed. "Response time was under six minutes."

"Alexa came. She got the mat off, and then Cam fell. Did the mat save him?"

Alexa doubted the mat absorbed enough shock to save Cam.

"We don't know his condition yet." Mr. Johnson tented his hands. "What did you notice about the other rider?"

"His name is Tex. He was holding on to Cam."

"Did you notice anything unusual prior to the incident?" he asked.

Sammie looked confused and then jumped up. Bruce rushed into the office. "Dad. I want to go home."

He hugged her and kissed the top of her head, his eyes on Alexa. Constable Blume stood behind him.

It was an hour before they were released. Constable Blume was responsible for taking the official accident report. Alexa cornered him on the way out. "Have they found Autumn Ware?"

"She's in custody."

Chapter Fifty-Seven

The lights at Villa 5 shone, and Lance's SUV was parked out front. Why wasn't he at the hospital with Cam? Where was Tex? Mrs. Zafiro had mentioned he was spending the final night with his teammates. She looked through the glass panels but didn't see anyone. Kool and Breezy must be devastated. They were dealing with yet another shock that Lance was incapable of handling.

When would Cam's father arrive? What if Cam died? What if she never learned what he wanted to tell her? *I saw him chuck it in the lake.*

"Alexa?" Bruce broke her trance. He was holding the door of Villa 6 open.

Denise jumped off the couch. "What happened? Are you okay, Sammie?"

"Sort of." The kid sat on her butt, struggling with her snow boots. Denise took one foot and tugged it off as Sammie told her everything. "Cam might be hurt real bad, but maybe not. Alexa pulled this pad out and..."

"Is it true, Dad?" Denise interrupted.

"It's true. Cam has been rushed to the hospital." He hung up his jacket and helped Alexa out of hers.

Denise grabbed Sammie's second boot and yanked. "Tex was in the chairlift?"

"He saw it happen," Sammie said.

Alexa reverted to her trance. If only time could reverse to Thursday afternoon, before the avalanche and chairlift accident, before the fire and fatality, before this damn ski vacay turned nightmare. She would usher Sammie and Denise and Cam and Dane somewhere warm and safe. She felt faint, off-balance, and touched the wall to make sure it was solid. The shock of seeing Cam fall. His scream. Her helplessness.

"I wish Mum was here," Sammie said. "I talked to her all the way home."

Bruce looked at a loss. "You'll see her tomorrow, Sam."

"I'm starved, Daddy," Sammie replied.

The thought of food restored Alexa's equanimity. "We can order pizza," she blurted.

Denise glared at her. "Is that all you eat?"

"Wait in your room until I call you for dinner," Bruce told his older daughter.

Sammie started to follow Denise but then stopped. "Dad? What if I saw something, but I don't know if I did or if my eyes were playing tricks?"

Bruce considered. "Do you want to tell me? We can figure it out together."

She turned toward the bedrooms. "That's okay."

He had cooked up a batch of spaghetti sauce. He turned the heat on under the pan. Alexa loved him for the scent of garlic, oregano, sausage, onion, and—wait—was that green pepper and mushrooms? "Denise is right. I have a terrible diet."

He handed her a bag of lettuce. "Then you can fix the salad."

She rinsed and tossed and forgave him the rogue ingredients in the sauce when he poured her a glass of wine.

They sat on the couch. Bruce's arm tightened around her shoulder. "You'll never ski with me again, will you?"

She closed her eyes and saw Cam fall. They finished their

wine in silence. The girls were subdued over dinner. Afterward, back on the couch, Alexa couldn't keep her eyes open, even though it was only nine o'clock. She headed to bed first, leaving Bruce and his daughters space to debrief and snuggle. She called the hospital for an update on Cam. The ICU nurse clammed up when Alexa admitted she wasn't family.

I should have lied.

"But, ma'am?"

Alexa braced herself.

"He's alive."

———

A large form lurked in the doorway, backlit. Alexa blinked, struggled upright, not sure what was reality and what was dream. "Did you hear me?"

Bruce's voice. Bruce's body.

Her eyes widened, focused. "What?"

"Denise is gone."

DAY THREE, CONT.

14 NOVEMBER 1984

From everything I've read about North America's panthers, one would be on your back, its massive jaws clamped to your neck before you knew what hit you. That's how this fucking storm came. Four of us, descending in a straggle, blindsided.

Whiteout. Jesus, man. What happened?

I pressed my back against an ice wall. A sideways wind tried to push me off the ledge; I fought back with every muscle. Sank to my knees, then butt. I couldn't see. Ice crystals clogged my nose. My lungs constricted. Air was sucked out of me. The swirl and howl of it. I stretched my arms, hoping to touch Christian. Instead, nothingness.

Between howls, I heard voices. "Where are yoooouuu?"

Demons swallowed my response. The world went dark. I tried and tried to open my eyes. The left popped open. My right eyelashes were frozen together. Wanted to jerk off my goggles, didn't dare.

Half-blind, I felt something jab my thigh: my ice axe. I squeezed the shaft. Solid. I visualized where I was. We left summit twenty minutes ago. Crossed first ridge. Fought urge to get up and run. I hunkered down, pressed my pack into the rock, couldn't get my breath. Lungs froze from the inside out. Heard a keening wail. Me? The wind? Christian? I remember thinking what will happen to my stuff? My car? Rachel? My mum?

My right lashes let go. "Christian? Christian?"

Mouthful of ice and snow. Face between knees. Balled up.

"Help."

"Where are you?" I shouted.

"Over here."

I crabbed sideways, my pack scraping against the ice. Saw color. Yellow. "Zittydog?"

"Can't feel my hands," he said.

We hunched together, frozen blocks on a precipice, Zitty moaned until he didn't moan, until a lift in the light revealed Christian ten yards away on one side, then Bill's green coat. He's only ten feet from Zittydog. We were in a bad place: under a roof of ice cornices waiting to impale us. We flocked together like Arctic birds, stood on stiff, wooden legs, and inched our way to the base of the ice crux.

We were granted only a lull.

The blizzard kicked up again. We were against a snowbank. I dug out my shovel and saw. Caught a glimpse of my journal zipped in plastic and wondered if I died, if anyone would find it.

Zittydog, probably hypothermic, was on all fours. "Can't go on," he said.

Digging warmed me up. I shoveled snow. More, faster. I dumped it on C's tarp, and he and Bill pulled it away. I reached a harder layer. I cut with the saw. Blocks. Made a hollow mound. Then tunnel. I couldn't shovel anymore. C took over. Made it wider, made it deeper, added ventilation.

I crawled in and covered the snow with my space blanket. We helped Zittydog in. He and Bill don't have bags with them; they cached them to lighten up. What energy C had left turned to anger. "Asshole thing to do."

I put Zitty in the middle, and Bill and I crouched on either side of him and pulled my bag around the three of us. Zitty's nose looked frozen. I got him to talk—dog Dolly, graduate program in biology, no girlfriend. C huddled alone, silent as the storm was loud.

Chapter Fifty-Eight

"I'm going next door," Bruce declared.

Alexa threw the covers off. "I'll come with you. The kids know me."

Sammie appeared beside her dad. "I'm coming, too."

"Wait here," Bruce barked. "We'll be back in a second."

Alexa pulled on jeans and jammed her bare feet into her boots, grimacing at the cold dampness. She checked her phone: eleven forty. She threw on her fleece and followed Bruce to Villa 5. He pounded on the door.

She pressed her face against the glass as they waited. Light cast down on the dining table, strewn with outdoors detritus. There was no movement. Bruce pounded again. Kool padded into view. She looked at the door and screamed.

Alexa jerked back. Her face must have been distorted, grotesque. Lance rounded the corner behind Kool, bare-chested, eyes wide. He registered who it was and opened the door. "What now?"

"Where's my daughter?"

Lance looked confused.

Bruce pushed past him. "Denise!"

"Hey, man, you can't just barge in here."

Alexa suspected Denise was with Tex. She edged past Bruce and Lance and down the hall. The door to Cam's room was shut. She jerked it open and switched on the light, her heart pounding.

The beds were empty nests. The smell: dirty clothes, a sweet musk. Stuff was strewn on the dresser. An open duffel bag perched on the single chair, its contents spilling out. The sight of Tex's garish parka hanging on the closet knob stopped her cold. He'd been here since the accident.

"What are you doing?" Breezy crowded behind her. "Did Cam die?"

"He's alive. I'm looking for Denise Horne. Is she in your room?"

Breezy surveyed the beds over Alexa's shoulder. "She's gone, I guess."

Bruce strode down the hallway. "Where's Denise?"

Breezy shrunk back. All she wore was an oversize T-shirt, and her legs were bare. Kool followed Bruce. "She texted me to let her in. She had something to tell Tex."

"Where is she now?" Bruce's tone was calmer.

"I don't know. They were in there last I saw. I went to bed," Kool said.

Bruce extended his hand. "Let me see your phone."

Alexa tore past them and flung the front door open. Her heart stopped. The parking spot was empty and quickly being covered by new snow. "Bruce! They've taken the SUV."

"No way," Lance called. He did a quick search and discovered the key fob was missing. He collapsed on the sofa. "I can't take any more of this shit. I quit."

"You can't," Alexa said. "Breezy and Kool need you. Did you hear Denise come over? Or the car start up?"

He pointed to his ears. "Nah, man."

She wanted to toss him in Lake Wakatipu.

Bruce reached DI Katakana on his phone and filled her in. "Color and license plate number?" he shouted at Lance.

"Hell, man, I don't know. It's a rental. The paperwork is in the car."

"It's a silver Nissan Patrol," Kool said. "New."

Alexa remembered Sammie, all alone. "I'll go next door," she told Bruce. She slid out of one villa and into the other like a game of What's Behind Door Number Two. Sammie looked like a waif in tie-dyed PJs. "Did you find her?"

"Not yet. Let me put socks on, and we'll wait on the couch." In the bedroom Alexa tried to process. Denise and Tex missing. A repeat of yesterday.

She turned on the gas fireplace and slid next to Sammie on the couch, grabbed the throw blanket, and tucked it around them. "Is Denise in trouble again?" Sammie asked.

"She and Tex have taken Lance's car."

Sammie wiggled, agitated. "It's the middle of the night."

"Have you called her?"

"She doesn't answer."

Alexa put her arm around her. "Denise told Kool that she had something important to tell Tex. Do you know what?"

Sammie stilled.

Alexa stared at the flames, waiting.

Sammie rubbed her eyes with the heel of her palms. "When I saw Cam and Tex in the chairlift, they were shoving each other. The bar was up. I think..." She stopped and pulled the blanket up higher, to her chin.

"What do you think, Sammie?" Alexa asked quietly.

"Then Cam was hanging. It happened so fast, but Tex wasn't helping him. He leaned back instead of reaching for him."

A cattle prod zapped Alexa. "Did Tex push Cam?"

"That man said Cam is a goner."

"What man?"

"One of the rescue guys. Do you think Cam is dead?"

304 Sara E. Johnson

"Before I went to bed I called the hospital. The nurse said he was alive."

"Because of the mat. You saved him."

"I don't know if the mat helped that much."

"This is my fault." Sammie hung her head, hiding under loose dark hair, and pulled the blanket to her nose. Her voice came muffled. "I told Denise what I saw. She didn't believe me. She called me an idiot. Then she went to ask Tex, and she didn't come back like she promised. I waited a long time. I fell asleep and then she *still* wasn't here, and I woke Dad."

"We have to tell him what you saw."

Sammie found Alexa's hand under the blanket and grabbed it like a lifeline. "He'll be mad."

Alexa's thoughts took off. Cam saw someone toss something in the lake. Was it Tex? Is that what they scuffled about in the chairlift? Then Cam slipped?

Or was pushed.

She squeezed Sammie's hand. "Your dad will find Denise, just like last time, but he needs to hear what you saw, right?"

Sammie didn't reply.

Uneasiness slalomed from the left hemisphere of her brain to the right and back again, like Tex snowcutting, deliberately starting an avalanche. And who had been at the starting gate?

Cam.

Alexa threw off the blanket. "I'll be right back."

Next door, Bruce was grilling Kool and Breezy. She told him what Sammie had said. He raced back to the villa, leaving the girls bewildered. Alexa followed, not sure her information had registered except that Sammie had known Denise sneaked out.

"You should have come straight to me when she left," he bellowed from the front hall. "What were you thinking?"

Sammie cowered on the couch.

Bruce's loss of control rattled Alexa. "Don't take it out on her."

"Stay out of this," Bruce said.

She opened and then closed her mouth. This was not the time to defend herself. He was frantic. She pushed past Bruce and sat next to Sammie. "It's okay. Tell your dad what you saw on the chairlift."

In a plaintive voice she said, "Tex didn't help Cam." She shuddered. "He, it looked like he made Cam fall."

Her voice came out stronger now, as if the memory had solidified.

Bruce sat on the ottoman and put his hands on Sammie's knees. His voice was gentle. "That's why Denise went to Tex? To ask him about what happened in the chairlift?"

Sammie nodded, tears streaming down her face. "Denise didn't believe me."

There was a knock on the door. Alexa jumped up and let Constable Blume in. He walked to the dining table. "DI Katakana sent me to take a statement about the missing property."

"It's a missing girl," Alexa snapped. "DI Horne's daughter."

Constable Blume nodded. "She's in the stolen ute, right? We've got an APB out. We'll find them."

"How could I have forgotten?" Bruce slapped his own forehead. "I know where she is."

They stared at him.

"I've got GPS tracking on her mobile." He pulled out his phone and opened the app. Alexa saw his impatience. Then his eyes darted from the screen to Constable Blume's. "She's in front of Lakes District Hospital."

The location knocked the air out of her. "Call hospital security. Cam might be in danger," Alexa said.

"Daddy, do something," Sammie said.

Bruce's face froze in hardness. He stood and made a call. At the same time, Constable Blume called DI Katakana.

Alexa blocked that conversation out, concentrating on Bruce's, apparently to the hospital.

"Cam Keeline. The boy who fell from the chairlift. His life might be in danger. Check on him," he bellowed. Pause. "Now." After an eternity he caught Alexa's eye. "Does Cam have a brother?"

Father. Sister. "No."

"That's not his brother," Bruce said into the phone. "What about a girl? Denise Horne?"

His shoulders fell as he listened to a reply. When he hung up, his face was white. "Tex is at Cam's bedside."

"Where's Denise?" Sammie wailed.

"She's missing." Bruce ordered Constable Blume to stay and left the villa.

Chapter Fifty-Nine

Alexa fetched Kool and Breezy, knowing they would be upset and scared. They squeezed under the throw blanket with Sammie and channel surfed. Lance stayed in Villa 5, calling his superiors and Tex's mother.

Constable Blume drank the tea he had fixed. Alexa paced back and forth in the kitchen. "What's the latest on Autumn Ware?" she asked.

"She's not talking until the Department of State sends a solicitor. But we located this Jay Pierce bloke she claims was at the party. He wasn't. He was in Auckland."

"Was there evidence of arson at that other restaurant fire? Where she used to work?"

"Your tea is getting cold."

Alexa sat across from him and encircled the mug with her shaky hands.

"No evidence. Doesn't mean there wasn't, though."

Autumn as a suspect was circling the drain in Alexa's book.

Kool's head popped up from the sofa. "Cam might need his stuff. In the hospital."

"You can take it to him tomorrow," Alexa said.

Her nose twitched. "I can pack for him, like I did for Tex."

That smell—when Alexa poked her head in the boys' room—a sweet musk. A memory snagged in her mind. Whatever Cam had seen tossed in the lake, he had retrieved. *I fished it out.* New Zealand's lakes had a distinctive smell—cold recesses mixed with incoming rain and fir tree. She pushed back from the table, spilling her tea.

Constable Blume hopped up. "I'll get the paper roll."

"Kool? Can I see your Instagram posts from the Papa Penguin's party?"

Kool shuffled over, flipping through images. "Here's Dane," she said somberly.

Dane Bui guzzling a beer. He'd been brave trying to make it on his own. Alexa scrolled until she found the one she wanted: Tex Zafiro, his eyes reduced to slits, in Bui's face. "What were they mad about?"

"I don't know," Kool said.

The blanket fell to the floor as Breezy stood. She picked it up and covered Sammie, who appeared asleep. "Tex accused Bui of stealing his phone. At Nomads."

The Wednesday night party, where Bui was charged with intoxication and vandalism.

"Why steal a phone?" Kool asked. "It's all password-protected, and everything can be traced."

"Tex has a bad temper," Breezy said. "That's why he got kicked out of Rotorua Lakes. His mum found some alternative school that would take him."

Panic blossomed in Alexa's chest. "Did you leave Papa Penguin's in a group?" Bruce had asked Tex, but maybe no one had asked the girls.

"Kool and I left together. The boys were behind us."

"We ran down the middle of the road," Kool said. "It was freezing and spooky."

"You were drunk," Breezy said.

"*You* were. Cam skipped behind me. Like an idiot, but well, so Cambo."

"And Tex?" Alexa asked.

The girls shrugged. "Guess he was behind Cam," Kool said.

Constable Blume stopped mopping up the spill. "No group alibi. When you got back to the villa, did you see Tex then?"

The girls shrugged. "We went right to our room," Kool said.

Alexa gave Kool her phone back and checked her own. Nothing from Bruce. She popped next door in her socks, pounding for Lance to let her in. "Found the girl?" he asked.

She thought of Denise. If Tex set Papa Penguin's on fire and tried to kill Cam, what else was he capable of? "Did you reach Tex's mother?"

"Mrs. Z hung up on me."

"Hey." She had to be careful, to be lawful. She handed Lance her phone. "I'm going to look in the boys' room. Take a video of me from the doorway. I won't touch anything."

The light was on. She scanned the unmade beds, the night table and dresser, the floor, the open closet where six empty hangers looked skeletal and extra pillows and blankets lined the shelf. No jerry can.

A hard-shell suitcase stood upright. The luggage tag said Tex Zafiro. On the single chair in the room, a duffel—probably Cam's—spewed its contents.

Something dark, the size of a shoe, was wrapped in a translucent grocery bag. She leaned down and took a whiff. The bag smelled like lake. Something else, too. Something sweet and chemical. Alexa backed out, into Lance. She took her phone back and stopped the recording. "Don't let anyone enter this room until the police come with a warrant."

Chapter Sixty

DI Katakana answered Alexa's phone call. Before she could open her mouth, the DI said, "One of my officers found DI Horne's daughter. Dumped on the side of the road."

Alexa's knees buckled. Lance caught her as she staggered.

"She was wandering on Frankton Road. She's hysterical and half-frozen, but she'll be right. Tex Zafiro took her phone so she couldn't call."

Alive. Alive. Alive.

"She's in the hospital lobby. Come fetch her."

"Where's Bruce?"

The DI didn't respond. A radio belched. Voices. Finally, "In Cam Keeline's hospital room. With Tex and Cam's father."

Bruce. Tex. Cam's father. Cam. All in the same room.

"Looks peaceful through the door window, Mr. Keeline on one side of the bed holding Cam's hand, Tex on the opposite side, holding his other hand."

A standoff.

"DI Horne is talking to them like nothing is wrong."

Bruce had it under control. Alexa hung up and dashed back to Villa 6. "Denise is okay," she told everyone. "I'm going to get her." She ignored the clamor, slipped into boots, grabbed Denise's bright-pink coat hanging from the hook, and was out.

She drove to the hospital recklessly, her headlamps illuminating a fresh batch of snow, and maneuvered into the no-parking zone between Bruce's Subaru and two police cars. A security guard tried to block her entrance, but she shook the pink coat. "I'm here to pick up Denise Horne."

"Good, good. She's been wanting her mother." He pointed into the empty lobby. Denise, wrapped in a blanket, half rose at the sight of Alexa, then sank down again onto the bench. Before running to her, she asked the guard if everything was okay.

"The situation is under control," he said.

Denise's mascara was smeared. She shivered despite the blanket and wouldn't meet Alexa's eyes as she wrapped the coat around her. "Are you hurt?" Alexa asked.

"No."

Alexa took a deep breath, pressed the greenstone koru into the skin of her sternum—*thank you thank you*—and collapsed on the bench. The lobby was cold and vacant, due to the late hour—one o'clock in the morning—and luck: no car accidents, shootings, or heart attacks clicked and clacked across its vinyl tiles.

"I can't call my mum," Denise finally said. "Tex took my phone."

"You can use mine."

"She'll yell at me."

There had been countless times when Alexa, as a teenager, wanted to call her mother. Just to hear her voice, mainly. She couldn't recall the lilt of it. "After my mom died, I'd pretend to call her. You can do that."

"I was stupid. I know." Denise's chin dropped. "He drove like crazy. He wanted Cam to tell me that he slipped off the chairlift. That it was an accident. That's what he said."

Alexa found her hand. It was icy.

"When we were on Sarah Sue, he kept saying, 'Cam is up next. Cam is up next.' And when Cam got in position, he sliced back and forth. I asked him if he started that avalanche on purpose like that committee says. He slammed on the brakes and grabbed my phone. Then he opened the door and pushed me out. Right on the road." She rubbed her shoulder with her free hand. "He left me there. I didn't even have my coat. I had to walk."

It could have been so much worse. "You're safe now."

"Dad is in Cam's room. With Tex. No one will tell me what's happening."

"Your dad will find out the truth. We should go back to the villa. Sammie is worried."

"I'm not leaving without Dad."

Alexa handed Denise her phone. "Call Sammie. Let her know you're okay."

Twenty minutes later, DI Katakana and Bruce calmly escorted Tex through the lobby. His wrists were handcuffed.

Chapter Sixty-One

"Cam was intubated, so he couldn't talk," Bruce explained. He had his arms around all three of them on the couch, Alexa on one side and the girls on the other. Before they had parted ways at the hospital, Alexa told DI Katakana about the plastic bag in Cam's duffel and repeated what Cam had told her about fishing something out of the lake. The DI promised to start the warrant process.

"Intubated. What does that mean?" Sammie asked.

Everyone was too keyed up to sleep. "He had a tube down his throat to help him breathe. His eyes got big when I walked in. Tex said 'Hello, sir. I came to see if my friend was okay.'"

"But not really, right?" Sammie asked. "Tex isn't his friend."

"Did he ask about me?" Denise asked.

"No. He didn't mention taking the SUV, either. He had a chair scooched up to Cam's bed. I stood behind him so I could watch his movements. He actually introduced me to Mr. Keeline. He had convinced Mr. Keeline that he tried to save Cam, to keep him from falling. That he felt horrible. He told Mr. Keeline that Cam lifted the safety bar and lunged forward."

"He's a liar," Denise said. "Did he give you my phone?"

"He left it in the SUV. But for now, it's evidence. Cam kept blinking at me," Bruce continued. "I nodded to let him know I understood whatever he was trying to tell me. DI Katakana sent the attending physician in to tell us to leave. Everyone but Mr. Keeline."

Alexa imagined that had been a tense moment.

"DI Katakana arrested Tex in the hall."

"For pushing Cam out?" Sammie asked.

"That could come later. He was arrested for stealing the SUV."

Alexa hadn't updated Bruce on Tex's possible involvement in the fire. In her mind she saw Tex hanging back from the NZ SNO Zs, grabbing the jerry can before Graham and Dylan drove off, and torching Papa's. Intentional homicide sent a spasm up her back.

What she couldn't figure out was motive. Was it to rise in the rankings of the competition?

Maybe Cam noticed he was missing and found him tossing something in the lake. The jerry can or whatever was in the plastic bag. If only the warrant would hurry up and get here.

Denise brushed the hair out of Sammie's eye. "Tex asked me like three times what you saw. He wanted me to go get you."

Alexa and Bruce stared at each other.

———

Alexa tiptoed to Bruce's bedroom to update him. And to kiss him goodnight. She cracked the door but stepped back at the sight of him and Denise sitting on the edge of the bed, Denise's head on his shoulder.

"He hurt me when he pushed me out. And what he did to Cam? What made Tex that way?"

Bruce's sigh was audible. "I met his mother. She didn't seem to care about him. Think of all the people in your life who love you and show you love. Your mum and me…"

"But you and Mum are divorced."

"…Sammie, your grandparents, aunts, uncles, friends.

Maybe Tex doesn't have that. Maybe he doesn't have anyone to show him love or kindness or right from wrong."

Alexa thought about human behavior: the good, the bad, the ugly. Lots of people who grew up unloved or neglected matured into compassionate adults. Maybe Tex was born with less gray matter in his brain, less ability to empathize or control his actions or see consequences.

"Even if you know right from wrong," Denise said, "it's hard to be good."

"I know," Bruce said. "You just have to try."

She lifted her head. "I'll never trust another boy."

Bruce turned to face her. "You can despair over one person's actions and let it change your life. That's up to you. But Tex is one tiny part of all humanity, and most of humanity is good. Like you are. Like your sister is."

Like you are, Bruce.

DAY FOUR

14 NOVEMBER 1984

We hunkered for hours, wincing at the howls, like banshees on the warpath. One day slid into the next. When I could hear above the roar, I crawled out.

Next came C, then Bill.

I held my breath, blinking in brutal air.

Zitty crawled out. We helped him stand. He didn't look good, but we cheered. Bill got the Primus going, melted snow, made a hot sweet cocoa. We toasted our survival.

I knew at the time that was premature. We were alive, but we still had to get down.

We stuck together, Zittydog slow and clumsy, to the base of the ice couloir. They were headed back to Lucas-Trotter Hut, we to Colin Todd Hut via the Northwest Ridge. C hung back, talking to Bill and Zitty. Maybe apologizing for not sharing his sleeping bag. I don't know.

We rappelled a few steep sections, a few chunks of ice bouncing off my helmet. Then hours of tedium, me tensed up with every step, legs shaky, on the constant lookout for a depression indicating a crevasse. We reached the buttress by descending a series of ledges. C got a buzz going now. "No risk, no spark," he said. We used the rope to lower down from the gut. I worried about Zittydog making it.

My muscles were wooden. Don't mess up now. We stayed roped to cross Bonar Glacier, which went on forever. C made me stop and eat, and that helped. C hopped over a fissure, I did the same. C hopped over another. I stepped in his prints and slipped—Jesus—I'm at the lip and then I'm over, and I'm in fucking hell.

Ten feet down, twenty, twisting, falling, slamming.

I'm corked.

Chapter Sixty-Two

MONDAY

Alexa stumbled next door, where Constable Blume waited with the warrant in his hand. It was still dark out, but Lance and the girls bustled around, packing up.

"How's Cam?" Kool asked.

"I haven't checked this morning," Alexa said.

"We're stopping by the hospital on the way to the airport," Lance said.

A representative from the villa rental agency was waiting and accepted the warrant. "Have at it," he said.

On the cusp of the boys' bedroom, Constable Blume told her that Tex had been charged with car theft and misdemeanor reckless endangerment. "His mother refused his phone call. Can you believe it? Almost felt sorry for the lad."

Alexa went straight to the plastic bag. She held her breath as she undid the knot and opened it. The soggy black Burton ski glove reeked of lake and, on closer sniff, of gasoline.

A glove. Her eyes went to the dresser, but its mate was absent.

There had been hints. Tex had said, "My new gloves are shite." He had worn mismatched gloves when she asked to examine them, not to make a fashion statement, but because he had ditched one into the lake. "I think Tex was wearing this glove when he started the fire," she told the constable.

He whistled from the closet.

She packaged the bagged glove in cardboard. After the glove

air-dried in a lab, she—or a tech—would see what secrets it revealed.

Tex's suitcase was next. The wrinkled squirrel on his T-shirt studied Alexa inquisitively, paws crossed. A receipt stuffed in a pants pocket was for Alpine Swiss ski gloves at the Coronet Peak retail outlet, dated Friday morning. More evidence. "Where would he have ditched the petrol container?" she asked Constable Blume.

"The woods and parking lot were searched. Maybe the lake? I'll let DI Katakana know to search the shoreline," he said.

If they found the jerry can, it might be possible that the weave of the ski glove transferred a pattern onto its surface. There were forensic scientists who would swear a glove print was reliable evidence. Alexa was not among them. There was no research behind the variability in glove weaves. She could, however, use the glove print as a class characteristic. She sat on one of the unmade beds to think it through.

Class characteristics are common to a group, such as all men's Burton ski gloves. Alexa imagined testifying in court. "Whoever left this imprint was wearing a Burton glove."

She could hear the rebuttal. "Burton mass produced 150,000 men's ski gloves of this style and size in the last quarter. This doesn't prove young Mr. Zafiro had anything to do with the fire. Yada yada."

Individual characteristics, like fingerprints, were more conclusive evidence.

The jerry-can mount on the Parrs' Jeep Wrangler flashed in her mind. Tex would have had to undo a strap and rotate a handle to detach the can.

Fine motor skills are hard to complete in thick ski gloves. If he took his gloves off to wrestle with the jerry can, he may have touched the side panel or hood. Her words scrambled to catch up with her thoughts. She stood abruptly. "I need to dust the Parrs' Jeep for fingerprints. ASAP."

Her urgency was contagious. Constable Blume arranged to have the Jeep towed to a secure location.

Alexa chomped at the bit.

Chapter Sixty-Three

The Subaru was packed up when she returned. "We're off to the airport," Bruce said. "I'm flying with the girls to Rotorua. I'll be back in Auckland tomorrow."

She gave him a quick update.

"I thought that American started the fire," he said.

"I don't think it was Autumn Ware. I'll be back Wednesday at the latest."

"Stay in the villa."

The girls were waiting in the car, doors open. He kissed her in front of them.

"Ew," Sammie said.

Denise rolled her eyes.

She wanted to say something to them—a parting word of wisdom, a lauding of their bravery, a toothsome fact. Her mind blanked.

After a shower and a futile lip-gloss search, she made two phone calls: one to arrange dropping off the mystery incisor, and the other to Dr. McKenzie, who promised to have the glacier skull waiting.

She pulled into the parking lot of the DNA testing laboratory a half hour later. Until recently, extracting DNA from a tooth involved pulverization and decalcification. The process took a week or more. The new and quicker method was to extract it straight from the pulp chamber. The pulp would then be rehydrated and the genetic material retrieved.

Alexa hoped the DNA would match the friend Bill Gilroy had been hiking with.

Sally, the DNA analyst, was waiting. "Good to see you again. Did the gold miner get repatriated to China?"

They had teamed up to do a strontium isotope analysis on the molar from a skeleton during her last case. The result showed the deceased had grown up in south China. "He actually wanted to stay in New Zealand."

Sally gave her a speculative look. "Where did this tooth come from?"

"Blue Peak Glacier. A climber found a skull."

"I heard about it. Glaciers are melting all over the Southern Alps. When I was little, we used to park in the car lot and walk a short distance to touch a glacier. Not anymore. Now we're having funerals for them."

"Funerals?" Alexa no longer hated Blue Peak. Now she rooted for it.

"I'll let you know the results on Wednesday."

Sally was trustworthy—Alexa had seen her in action. Even so, it was hard to relinquish the mystery tooth and go meet Constable Blume at Earl's Garage.

Chapter Sixty-Four

A new forensic gizmo nestled in her crime kit: a SwiftLift Latent Print Developing Mitt. In the YouTube demonstration, a handsome police officer sprinkled black print powder on the white side of the mitt, patted it together to distribute the powder, and then brushed the mitt over the side of a car. Latent prints emerged.

High five.

The problem was that the car in the YouTube video was clean and white. Would the mitt work on a dirty silver Jeep? Snow, mud, and time might have rendered any fingerprints from Friday morning low in quality or destroyed.

As things stood, they had no irrefutable evidence that Tex set the fire. They couldn't detain him for stealing Lance's SUV for much longer.

Earl escorted them to the locked bay and turned on the overhead lights. Their quarry, the Jeep Wrangler, looked bound for adventure on its aggressively treaded Sahara tires.

Alexa and Constable Blume walked to the passenger side. Constable Blume watched her open the crime kit. "What are you thinking?"

"I'm hoping Tex pulled his gloves off to undo the strap and work the toggle. Maybe he touched the Jeep."

"But any fingerprints you find could just be from someone else, like Kipper Parr or the missus," he said.

"We have their prints on file for elimination." Her own, too. She had touched the door handle.

"Are you going to use cotton roll again?"

The last time she had dusted a car in front of the constable—who appreciated forensics—she'd used fluffy wads of cotton to spread the powder. "Something even better."

She pulled on gloves, cognitive of the constable's rapt attention. She opened a jar of midnight black Atomic CRP powder. "Perfect for metal surfaces," she explained. Then she removed a SwiftLift mitt and slipped her right hand in.

"A mitten?"

"It can dust the entire exterior of a car in ninety seconds."

"Sweet as."

When the powder was distributed across the mitt, she made light circular motions on the panel around the mount, down toward the fender, which had mostly protected the panel from splatter. The soft material caught on a clump of grit or mud. She moved a few inches and started again, moving back up. Just like in the YouTube, a palm print and three fingerprints emerged black against the silver paint.

The constable gawked.

She swiped the entire panel and some of the hood. Several more partials and prints emerged. She photographed and lifted them onto backing cards. The Queenstown Police Department lab had closed since she'd been here last. Forensic evidence went directly to Christchurch Forensic Service Center. Centralized labs cut down on error rate and bias.

Alexa packaged and signed off on the evidence and turned it over to Constable Blume.

"Should know by tomorrow," he said.

Chapter Sixty-Five

Alexa drove to the hospital satisfied with the performance of her SwiftLift. Dr. McKenzie's comment lured her forward: *Something is embedded in Mr. Gilroy's teeth.*

What could it be?

In the lobby, a man with red hair slumped on the same bench where she'd found Denise. The sight of him stopped her short. She waited for him to put his phone away and then approached. "Excuse me. Are you Mr. Keeline?"

He looked at her with hope.

"I'm Alexa Glock." She told him how she knew Cam and how he had helped her up when she had fallen on Chimney Swoop and how he had given her boyfriend's daughter snowboard tips. Finally, she said, "I was there when he fell."

"You saw it happen? Are you the one who pulled the mat under him?"

She nodded. "I got there when he was hanging. I'm so sorry I couldn't do more." She was afraid to ask. Her voice croaked. "How is he?"

Mr. Keeline's shoulders slumped. His eyes, the same southern-tea color as Cam's, pooled over. "He has a broken femur, but that will heal. His C6 vertebrae is shattered. He has no reflex activity from the neck down."

Alexa had a vision of an angel swooping down to catch Cam in her arms.

"The doctor hopes some reflexes will return, but Cam probably won't ever walk."

Her support kid would never fly again, either. She sat down.

Mr. Keeline continued. "His friend Tex? He thinks Cam jumped on purpose."

She winced at the word *friend*. "I don't think so. Cam tried really hard to hang on. Can he talk?"

He wiped his eyes. "They'll take the tube out later today."

Alexa trudged to the morgue and begged the skull to wrestle her thoughts from Cam.

"Ms. Glock," Dr. McKenzie said, "the skull is waiting for you." Her spirits lifted under his avuncular gaze. He had placed the skull on a tray, and it was like meeting it for the first time. Its brown color had lightened as it dried and now matched the color of the wispy hair. The eye cavities stared vacantly toward the overhead light, the right orbit cracked, and the lower jaw—the mandible—was missing, distorting the skull's shape.

Dr. McKenzie's eyes twinkled as he gestured to a microscope. The mandible with its embedded teeth was centered under the scope. "Take a look."

The implant used to tentatively identify Bill Gilroy was in the upper jaw, so that's not what the doc was excited about. She looked through the eyepiece and turned the knob until the bottom teeth came into focus, one by one. She marveled at how well-preserved they were and that, like his fingerprints would have been, these teeth were unique to Bill.

A spot of fluorescent green, trapped between the first and second molar, glistened through hardened tartar. She zoomed in and stared at the miniature shard. "I see it." She moved from the viewfinder and squinted. The speck was visible with her naked eye.

"Can you remove it?" Dr. McKenzie asked.

She retrieved her dental pick. Using magnification and the pick's sharp end, and holding the mandible with the gloved fingers of her left hand, she scraped. The tartar was like cement, reluctant to surrender its crystallized treasure. She gritted her teeth, switched to the hook end of the pick, scraped, and pried the scaly yellowish substance surrounding the speck like she was a dental hygienist. What was it? Thread? Glass? Grass?

She thought of the lapis lazuli trapped in the Blue Nun's teeth. What minerals were used to make green paint? Celadonite or glauconite? She made a groove, resumed her gentle scraping, and poked the speck loose. She nudged it into a clear vial and held the prize for Dr. McKenzie.

"Could be something he ate. Maybe candy," he said. "I'll send it to the lab."

Candy? Frozen all these years? Alexa thought back to her childhood. What green candy was available? Jelly beans. Sprinkles. M&M'S. Sour Apple Blow Pops. If it was candy, she would have a sweet-tooth story to tell Sammie.

The radiographs she proceeded to take confirmed the titanium implant matched the one the Wellington dentist implanted in William (Bill) Gilroy.

The retired dentist had said that Bill Gilroy's father was deceased. Maybe his mother was still alive. "What about the pelvis?" she asked. "Was the Search and Rescue team able to get it?"

"Weather deteriorated. They had to turn back."

Would she ever learn why it wore a red Speedo? "What about the foot?"

"Dr. Gladys Ball is with it in the autopsy suite. She's hoping you'll stop by."

The glacier archaeologist. They had spoken by phone when she was in the airport car-rental line.

"A reporter from *New Zealand Outdoor Magazine* wants to speak with you, too. A bloke at Wanaka Search and Rescue told him you were researching missing climbers. He thinks he has information about the remains. He's waiting in the lobby."

Pieces of the puzzle sifting into place.

Gladys Ball's hot-pink T-shirt peeked through her lab coat. Her honey-brown hair was swept back in a ponytail. Dr. McKenzie introduced Alexa.

"Call me Gladys, as long as you don't poke fun."

"Family name, eh?" Dr. McKenzie commented.

"Gladys is my grandmother. She's scaled the highest peak on five continents. She's shooting for Denali next."

Gladys Junior was mid-twenties, so Grandma Gladys must be up there. Literally. "We made a positive ID on the skull," Alexa said. "Bill Gilroy was last seen in 1984 below the summit of Aspiring. There's also a pelvis remaining on site."

Dr. Ball gestured to the remains. "The foot exhibits tissue preservation."

Dr. McKenzie rubbed his palms together. "What can you tell us?"

"I suspect the lads fell into a crevasse. Their bodies traveled in a trajectory that increased in depth and pressure through the years, thus crushing them and dispersing their bones." She took a breath. "Enter global warming. Glacial melt is speeding up. The foot and skull—and this nearby pelvis—surfaced as layers of ice melted."

Alexa peered at the foot bones. Muscle tendons and fatty residue clung to the ankle joint.

"The average temperature in the heart of a glacier is -0.13 degrees Celsius. This delays decomposition. That's why we have preserved soft tissue which finally thawed and now stinks."

Alexa's nose twitched. "Does the foot belong with the skull? Or with the pelvis?"

"DNA should answer your question," Dr. Ball said.

Alexa's next question was not unrelated. "Can the glaciers be saved?"

Chapter Sixty-Six

The reporter was thin, silver-haired with a prominent nose, and somewhere between sixty-five and seventy. He introduced himself as Steven Eckel, contributing editor of *New Zealand Outdoor Magazine*. "The remains on Mount Aspiring. You helped retrieve them?"

"Yes. We identified one person by his teeth. What's your interest?"

He looked toward the entrance. "Mind if we leave the hospital and talk at a coffee shop?"

Coffee and calories were a good idea. Alexa followed him to Life's a Grind. As she parked, she answered a phone call from DI Katakana. "As soon as our lad Tex Zafiro heard you lifted fingerprints from the Jeep, he confessed to starting the fire."

"But we don't know if the prints are compatible."

"I'm just reporting what happened."

Her brain scrambled for purchase. "Did he say why?"

"He said Bui stole his phone."

Her words didn't match their meaning. No one kills someone over a cell phone. "Say that again?"

The DI went quiet. Alexa turned the engine off, her hands shaking. Finally, the DI said, "Did you hear his mother refused to take his phone call? *Ko te whaea te takere o te* waka."

"What does that mean?"

"Mothers are the hull of the waka." Her voice quavered.

"When they are absent, and no one takes the helm, no one cares, there is a hole that never fills, a canoe that will sink."

Kill someone over a phone? Shove a teammate out of a chairlift? Push Denise out of a car? Tex's heinousness threatened to smother her. It was five minutes before she could enter the Grind.

She ordered a flat white coffee and a raspberry custard danish, the scents soothing, and selected a table by the window. Steven blinked uncomfortably when he joined her. His blue eyes were streaked with minuscule blood vessels. "From UV rays reflected off ice and snow."

They switched to a table in the windowless corner. Alexa ate half the danish, trying to fill the hole in her heart, waiting for the reporter to speak.

"I've devoted my life to the mountains and to writing about them."

She sipped the flat white patiently.

"I guided for eighteen years. Still do, occasionally. Wrote the *Alpine Safety Manual*. Did a lot of mapping. Climbed Mount Aspiring six times." His knuckles were scarred and rough, and he wore a wedding band. "Only once to the very top. I learned my lesson."

"What lesson is that?"

"The mountain absorbs every step a person takes during a climb. I guide differently now; to teach people to respect the mountains."

Alexa's pendant stirred. She fingered it through her blouse. "Why do you want to see me?"

"Do you know whose body was recovered?"

"We think we have remains from two people. We identified one due to a tooth implant he had. The police are tracking down his family members."

"Is it Bill Gilroy or James Welsh?"

Alexa sputtered her sip of coffee. "How did you know?"

He rubbed his sun-damaged eyes. "In November 1984, my cousin Christian and I spent the night at an alpine hut with two lads from Wellington—Bill Gilroy and Zittydog Welsh. We climbed Mount Aspiring the next morning—not together, but ended up summiting with them. That's the one time I stepped on the peak."

"Why is that?"

"The *tihi*, or peak, represents the head of the ancestors in Māori beliefs. To stand on it is disrespectful. Twenty minutes into our descent, a blizzard pounced out of nowhere, pinning us in place. We dug a snow cave. Six or eight hours we were crammed together. Zittydog—that was Jame Welsh's nickname—was in a bad way. When the storm settled, we started down again. We parted ways with the Wellies at the bottom of the ice couloir. I was relieved we made it that far."

"What's a couloir?"

"It's a steep gorge, notorious for deaths. The guys from Wellington were heading to the Lucas-Trotter Hut, and we headed to a different hut. I never saw them again."

"Bill had been in a car wreck," Alexa said. "That's why he had a tooth implant."

"He had a scar on his cheek." Steven squinted as if conjuring Bill's face. "I almost didn't make it to Colin Todd Hut. I fell into a crevasse. I thought I was doomed."

I know the feeling.

"Christian saved my life; he got me out. The next morning a ranger checked in on our hut. He said two climbers were overdue. Zittydog and Bill. I told him where we had last seen them. I learned later that they never found a trace of them. Man, tragic, I thought at the time. Could have been us."

Alexa thought the sad story was complete and ate the last of her danish.

"A few months later, Christian and I met up at a pub. All buddy-buddy-we-conquered-the-bastard reminiscing. After a couple beers, C bragged that he told the Wellies to cross Quarterdeck to get back to the hut. I didn't hear him do that." His eyes looked haunted. His left fingers had a tremor. "We'd been warned by a ranger to avoid the deck because a crevasse stretched across it. It would have been dark, I think, when they fell in."

Her stomach, just filled, hollowed. "Why would your cousin do that?"

"I don't know. Maybe because he thought they stole his scroggin."

"What's scroggin?"

"Trail mix. Nuts, M&M'S, raisins."

A spec of candy coating had been embedded in Bill Gilroy's plaque. Maybe green M&M'S had been his favorites.

"I think what really got to Christian was that Bill and Zittydog beat him to the summit."

His comment gave Alexa pause. Did Tex kill Dane Bui because of a phone, or was he angry that Dane beat him on the slopes? Cam had bested him, too. Did murder over trivial matters amount to king-of-the-hill contests of dominance?

"Did you report it to the police?"

He rubbed his eyes. "I didn't have any proof that's what happened. It could have been another storm, or an avalanche. Christian killed himself five years later."

Alexa let the facts sink in. Christian couldn't live with himself, and his cousin Stephen was atoning for him, all these years, writing articles and safety manuals and maps, guiding people.

"There are more bones on the glacier. A pelvis," she said.

"The Search and Rescue team are trying to retrieve it. This will sound weird, but the pelvis is wearing a red Speedo."

Steven drummed his fingers on the table. A slight smile played at his lips. "There was no quick-dry material back then. Climbers stripped down to skivvies or bathing trunks, Speedos sometimes, anything that would dry fast, to cross the rivers."

The mystery of the Speedo was solved. But there was something else she wondered. "Why do climbers do it?" Alexa asked. "Risk their lives in such unforgiving places?"

"The dancing with death? When I was young, it was about the challenge, the thrill of untrodden places, the way to feel I mattered."

Alexa waited.

"Now? It's spiritual. I am with the mountains, not against them. I bow my head. I do what I can to protect them. I am their parent, and they are mine."

She didn't quite get it, but his words, like a soft snow that coats the world anew, gave Alexa hope.

Chapter Sixty-Seven

ONE MONTH LATER

Bruce's mother said they'd had a late-season villa cancellation. He relayed this to Alexa as they talked on the phone. "The slopes close down next week," he said. "Let's go this weekend."

"Can we ski somewhere besides Coronet Peak?"

They settled on the Remarkables Ski Area. "A new tradition," Bruce said.

Alexa liked the sound of that.

When Friday came with no work interference for either of them, they flew together. En route, Bruce reported that the girls were processing all they'd been through in their weekly counseling sessions. "I'll be paying for therapy forever."

Alexa no longer panicked when she thought of Sammie and Denise. She knew them better now, and they knew her better. It was still up in the air as to whether Denise would be fined to help cover rescue costs.

"They went to visit Cam at his rehab facility," Bruce said. "He complained about how hard physical therapy was, but he's gained some arm mobility. No movement below the chest, yet."

Alexa leaned against the headrest as grief and anger duked it out in her head. It was small comfort that the fingerprints she had lifted from the Jeep Wrangler were compatible with Tex Zafiro's, and Cam had made a witness statement about seeing Tex toss a glove in the lake. He had been less sure about what happened on the chairlift, only saying that Tex lifted the safety bar. He stopped shy of saying Tex pushed him out. Maybe it was too traumatic for him to accept.

"Breezy visits him almost every day," Bruce said.

Alexa felt ashamed. "For a while I thought she set the fire. Did the Parrs press charges against the kids?"

"They let it drop."

She turned her mind to sharing the master bedroom with Bruce and the email she'd received from DI Katakana:

> *The Heli-Tours operator flew a SAR team to Blue Peak Glacier and retrieved the pelvis. DNA tests are pending.*

She announced that she wanted to stop by Heli-Tours to thank the owner, Kevin. They headed straight from Queenstown Airport. A CLOSED banner flapped over the entrance, but a familiar pickup truck was in the lot.

The building was locked. When Alexa banged on the door, a girl—maybe eleven or twelve—opened it. "My dad's business is closed."

"Is he around?" Alexa asked.

The girl shouted over her shoulder, "Dad."

Kevin appeared holding bibs and a parka. He handed them to his daughter. Alexa watched as he tried to place her.

"Blue Peak. I fell in a crevasse."

He cracked a smile. "Back for more?"

"I wanted to thank you. For taking the SAR team back and finding the pelvis."

"Your crevasse had widened instead of closed up."

Bruce shook his hand as Alexa introduced him. "Are you closing for good?" Bruce asked.

"Come in. Cold out there."

They stepped inside. Alexa scanned the counter. The

sunglasses were half-priced, dammit. The posters still hung on the walls: couples posing on glaciers, hikers crossing snowfields, climbers clinging to blue-iced cliffs, that ridiculous woman in a wedding gown on the edge of an abyss.

"Should have done it five years ago. I've sold the nine-seater. All I have left is the Squirrel. She's going to Auckland SAR after I take her out one last time. Gracie is going to take photos for a class project."

"It's a good thing and a bad thing." Gracie hugged the winter apparel to her chest. "Bad that we're using carbon emissions to get there, but good to show my class what the glaciers look like and how we can slow global warming, like Dad is going to stop flying up there. Maybe more helicopter companies will do the same thing. Want to come with us?"

"It's a bluebird day," Kevin said. He stared at his daughter with a sadness. "One last flight to the glaciers, to marvel and mourn."

To mourn made Alexa think of funerals. She had done a search and learned memorials for dead glaciers had taken place in Iceland and Switzerland. In Oregon, a black coffin containing melt water from the remains of Clark Glacier sat on the steps of the capital building, a black harbinger against white marble.

"The back seats are empty," Kevin said.

Bruce stared at Alexa, letting her decide.

The terror of falling and slipping rushed back. But so did a longing to face her fears. Besides, when did being afraid ever stop her from doing something?

They had to gear up in case of emergency. The sense of déjà vu made her hands tremble as she tightened her bootlaces. Before she came to her senses, they were aloft.

First there was the bird's-eye view of Lake Wakatipu and Coronet Peak. Her body throbbed and hummed as she leaned against the window. She knew more about the landscape now, how hard it was to climb. How it could preen one moment and jerk back the curtain in the next.

As the first winding river of ice unwound below, Bruce squeezed her hand. She wanted to tell him that the blue of the compressed ice reminded her of his eyes, but its color was a warning that the ice was in trouble.

Kevin began naming the glaciers as they revealed themselves. "There's Whitbourn. You can climb to a spur and cross it to Geikie Glacier."

"What's that one, Dad?"

He lowered the copter. Alexa watched its shadow skim across the cracks and crevasses. "Dart." They shifted direction, the air calm and seductive. "There's Hesse, half the size it used to be." They dipped and skirted the flank of a white sheep mountain. "There's Blue Peak, right below us."

The very glacier that had released its captives and toyed with her. She stared, dry-mouthed, as it receded.

"We're making one stop at twenty-two hundred meters," Kevin said. "You don't need to get out."

"Isobel, right Dad? I'm doing my report on Isobel Glacier."

"No crevasses where I'm setting down," Kevin added.

This glacier spread in a sweeping plateau. Gracie and her father quickly slipped out and didn't wear crampons. Alexa stayed buckled, watching them take photos and measurements.

Bruce sat quietly beside her; she could sense his yearning.

What am I waiting for?

The glare was intense. Alexa slipped on her sunglasses and nudged Bruce. They climbed out of the copter and forged a virgin path, the snow yielding to their weight. Hidden in the cold currents of air was the merest hint of spring. When she looked down, the individual snow crystals sparkled like diamonds. She scooped a bit of snow and stared at the crystals against her glove.

"What are you thinking?" Bruce asked.

"About snow crystals. They form when warm, moist air collides with a mass of cold air." She stared at him, wondering if he understood what she was saying. *Man sea, woman sea, merging.*

Behind his sunglasses, his right eyebrow arched.

Alexa pictured Cam flying into the air on his snowboard, facing his fears at dizzying speed, despite the fragility of the spine and the heart. She could fly, too. On top of a glacier—its lifespan dwindling like hers—she took Bruce's outstretched hand.

**IF YOU'VE ENJOYED *BONE CHILLING*,
READ ON FOR AN EXCERPT FROM**

"Johnson expertly balances her
lead's personal and professional
lives and maintains nerve-shredding
suspense throughout."
—*PUBLISHERS WEEKLY*
for *The Bone Riddle*

T
H
E **HUNGRY
BONES**

AN
ALEXA GLOCK
FORENSICS
MYSTERY

SARA E. JOHNSON

**ANOTHER EXCITING
ALEXA GLOCK FORENSICS MYSTERY**

Chapter One

"The mouth and hands of anyone at the scene are the biggest source of contamination," Alexa Glock replied to the question. "Wearing masks, barrier clothing, and gloves is crucial."

Professor Campbell, one of three on the interview committee, frowned from the upper-left Zoom box. "Anything to add?"

Alexa glanced at her image: behold the winner of the Bed-Head Hair prize. She refrained from taming it. "Protect the scene. Use disposable equipment when possible and sterilized equipment when it's not." This was Forensics 101 stuff.

Professor Campbell, whose specialty was DNA, leaned so close to her computer that Alexa could see her nose hairs. "Are you familiar with the Phantom of Heilbronn?"

Even though it was two a.m. in New Zealand, Alexa perked up. "She was Germany's most wanted woman. She left DNA at forty crime scenes, but in the end, it was found she didn't exist, and the DNA came from contaminated swabs."

"Aye." Professor Campbell relaxed into her seat and studied Alexa's curriculum vitae. "No PhD?"

"I have two master's degrees."

"No DMD?"

Most odontologists—Alexa's specialty—were Doctors of Medicine in Dentistry, so the professor was right to inquire. "My university created a special master's program because of a shortage." *Two years of nothing but teeth.* Should she share her motto with the professors? She tongued her top incisors and went for it. "Lips may lie, but teeth never do."

Lower-left box—Assistant Professor Abby Akintola, specialty bloodstain patterns—bared her teeth in a congenial smile, but Professor Campbell frowned. "If you joined the faculty at Abertay University in Scotland, we would expect you to complete a PhD."

Alexa liked a challenge.

Dr. Ben Odden, chair of the forensics department, upper-right box, seemed to be speaking.

"You're on mute," Dr. Campbell shouted.

A whimper came from the kitchen. Alexa's roommate's canine partner, Kaos, was stirring. His doggy dreams were interrupted. The apartment was open-concept, and there was no door to close.

Dr. Odden unmuted. "I see you submitted an article to *Forensic Science Today.* "Bacterium in Great White Shark Bite Lacerations."

"They've expressed some interest." If Alexa took a university position, she'd have more time for research and writing.

"What are you working on now?" Dr. Odden asked.

Alexa had a professional crush on Ben Odden. She'd devoured many of his published articles over the years and had used some of his cutting-edge techniques. It was a thrill to "meet" him. "The pink tooth phenomenon. I was recently involved in a case where the deceased presented a pink molar."

Alexa was chuffed by the interview committees' rapt attention, but she wasn't sure she wanted to leave her traveling forensic investigator job. Especially after her boss had called earlier.

"Your friend Dr. Luckenbaugh requested you. She received approval to exhume a Chinese gold miner, buried around 1900. She needs an odontologist. Can you get to Arrowtown tomorrow?" Ana Luckenbaugh was a forensic archaeologist who worked for a firm called Preserving Heritage. Alexa had already booked a flight. But first she wanted to ace this interview.

Kaos howled.

"What's that?" Professor Campbell shouted.

Alexa popped out of her Zoom box. She ran to the kitchen and opened the crate. Kaos jumped on her. "Down. Hush."

She ran back, the gangling dog at her heels. She pushed Kaos's butt down, whispered for him to sit, and slipped back into her chair. "It's my roommate's dog." She hated the sound of that. On the verge of thirty-eight and living with a roommate. "I'm looking into the relationship of pink tooth phenomenon and head position." She flashed back to her last away case. The deceased had been found head-down. The positioning had accelerated decomposition in his facial area. And possibly the PTP. The image of maggots in the corpse's orifices crawled into her head. She shook it away.

The interview went on for twenty more minutes. Kaos pushed his head into her Zoom box once and charmed the scientists, even Dr. Campbell.

"We'll be in touch," Dr. Odden said. "Maybe get you over to Dundee to check *oot* our facilities."

His Scottish brogue was sexy. Alexa clicked Leave Meeting. She took off the blouse covering her sleep shirt and realized her abrupt Zoom departure to fetch Kaos probably revealed her shortie pajama bottoms. *Did that constitute a flash?* She snorted, turned off the light, and laid on the couch, fingers buried in the remnants of Kaos's puppy fur. Did she want to leave New Zealand for a job in Scotland? In the darkness, skeletal remains of gold rush miners staked a claim on her thoughts. She pictured the teeth protruding from their jaws.

夏季

SUMMER

1880

Precious MaMa,

Our ship from Hong Kong almost sank in a storm, but we made it to Sun Gum Saan. Uncle Cheong Tam translated: New Gold Mountain. He told me to buy boots, woolen pants, a coat, and a hat. Five of us walked eighteen days, over bare mountains, rivers, tussock, rock to New Gold Mountain. White men think the gold is already gone. A little boy grabbed my queue and made pig sounds.

Shining rivers flow between this village and the many mountains. Uncle Cheong Tam and I built a mud hut along the creek where other Chinese stay. The birds, MaMa. They sing strange songs and keep me company. My rice bowl made the journey. You filled that rice bowl, MaMa; now it rests in my hands, the painted crane's wings spread.

Crane: the prince of all feathered creatures. Wings: your gift to me.

On my third day I found a nugget in Arrow River. My first Gold Letter for you: a seven pound cheque I earned from the nugget. More will follow and then I will come home, a rich man.

Faithful First Son, Spreading Wings,
Wing Lun

Chapter Two

WEDNESDAY MORNING

Natalie, in full uniform, hovered over her. "Kaos needs to sleep in his crate. He needs boundaries."

Alexa winced at the crick in her neck and tried to straighten her legs. The dog took up half the couch. "What time is it?"

"Five-thirty." Natalie held the dog's leash. "Come, Kaos."

He hopped off, tail wagging.

"I've got an away case in Arrowtown." Alexa stretched her legs. "I'll be gone for a couple days."

"Pack your puffer and beanie. What's the case?"

First she translated. *Puffer: warm coat. Beanie: hat.* Would she need them in May? "Something about exhuming a Chinese miner for repatriation. A benefactor wants to bring him home."

Natalie's young forehead creased. "There's a Chinese belief that a soul can only find peace if tended by family members."

Natalie was only twenty-seven yet possessed an elder's collected knowledge that often surprised Alexa. She also possessed a teenager's ability to sleep through dog howls in the middle of the night.

"That doesn't sound like a crime," Natalie said. "Why are you going?"

"Teeth are why." She thought back to the details Dan had sent in an email. "I'll measure the strontium isotope in the enamel to find out where it's from."

"Strontium isotope," Natalie repeated slowly. "What's that?"

Alexa stumbled to the kitchen to make coffee. "It's a trace

element found in rocks. It works its way into water, soil, plants, on up the food chain, so that animals and people consume it. The amounts of different strontium isotopes in your enamel vary depending on where you grew up."

"So my teeth can tell you where I grew up?"

Alexa added ground coffee to the French press. "You are *what* and *where* you ate."

"Sweet as."

Alexa beamed. "Then we'll extract DNA from the pulp chamber. See if it links either of the skeletons to the benefactor."

Natalie leashed Kaos and left. After a blissful cup of coffee, Alexa lugged the couch against the wall and did a twenty-minute kickboxing routine to her throwback playlist. She was psyched about the day ahead, but U2's "I Still Haven't Found What I'm Looking For" bothered her. *Shuffle, jab, cross, hook.* What if she *had* found what she was looking for? She loved her job. And maybe Bruce as well, the detective inspector she'd been dating. Her brother, Charlie, always accused her of running away from commitment. Said it was a pattern.

Jab, cross, undercut.

She showered, dressed, packed, and drove to work where she spent a couple hours in her cubicle at Auckland Forensic Service Center finishing reports. At noon she checked in with her boss, Dan Goddard.

"Ready to fly?" he asked.

Alexa tried to stem her excitement. "I just finished that robbery report."

"If a crime case comes up, I'll need to pull you away," he warned.

Even though it was a Wednesday, she felt like a kid on a Friday afternoon.

It was a two-hour flight from Auckland on the North Island

to Queenstown on the South Island. Her crime kit barely fit in the overhead compartment. She never left home without it. Alexa was glad the woman next to her was absorbed in her *NZ Herald* crossword. She opened her laptop and reread the email from Ana Luckenbaugh.

Kia ora Alexa,

The dig I've requested your assistance with is being funded by an elderly woman, Corrie Wong, in Guangzhou, China. Ms. Wong wants to spare no expense in repatriating her great-great-grandfather. He has been calling for her to bring him home. That's why I need your teeth expertise to see what we've got. We don't want to return the wrong remains.

My graduate assistant and I don't know why this skeleton was left behind (I will explain "left behind" when you get here). We've determined it's the remains of an adult male. I'm waiting for you to arrive before I examine the skull.

Shelby and I will pick you up at the airport. You can stay at our cottage.

—Ana

ACKNOWLEDGMENTS

Thank you to my Poisoned Pen Press editor, Diane DiBiase, who says of Alexa Glock: "She is one of my favorite PPP characters ever—even if she does have my hair." Diane's suggestions always make my books better, and her comments often make me laugh. (On a human pelvis wearing a red Speedo: "Well, then, whoever it was deserved to die—HA!")

I appreciate assistant content editor Beth Deveny for her fact-checking and editing. Likewise to Patience Bramlett and Bob Mitchell. Thank you to the Poisoned Pen Press/Sourcebooks cover team, who nail it with every book. Thanks to my agent, Laura Bradshaw of Bradshaw Literary Agency.

So many experts helped me with *Bone Chilling*. I thank them.

Dr. Heidi Eldridge, director of crime scene investigations at George Washington University, is my forensic consultant. Heidi said that it is sometimes surprising how well evidence can still be recovered after a fire and that it's often possible to recover fingerprints on charred surfaces under the char. I appreciated her crash course on class evidence (a glove weave) versus individual evidence (a fingerprint).

Jessica Smith, NC Senior Special Agent OSFM Fire Investigation Unit, offered her expertise on my fire scenes. About investigating fires, Jessica says, "I enjoy putting the pieces of a puzzle together." She also said, "Fire scenes are either the coldest or hottest (depending on the time of the year) and darkest crime scenes I have ever investigated." She helped me understand flashover, arson dogs, and proper protective gear, and I am grateful.

Dr. Leslie Anderson, Canterbury District Health Board forensic pathologist, advised me on the autopsy of the charred victim: "One of the only types of cases that doesn't have an overtly bad smell." She says it is a privilege to be the last doctor a person sees and to be able to speak on their behalf. Thank you, Leslie.

Tēnā rawa atu koe (thank you very much) to Tom Hoyle, publications and design editor for the New Zealand Alpine Club. Tom is in the process of doing a brand-new Mount Aspiring guidebook. He said Aspiring is the most climbed of all the three thousand m+ peaks in New Zealand. He helped me with maps, climbing routes, and understanding the climbing process.

My writing group is my village. Thank you to our facilitator, Nancy Peacock, and to Lisa Bobst, Denise Cline, Linda A. Janssen, and Ann Parrent.

Thank you, readers. When Alexa is alive in your head, I am happy.

My mom and sister, Jennifer, have been to all my book launches and always cheer me on. I love them for it.

To my husband, Forrest. Thank you for taking me to New Zealand, thank you for your support and love, and thank you for knowing there were no blue M&M'S in 1984.

ABOUT THE AUTHOR

Sara E. Johnson lives in Durham, North Carolina. She worked as a middle-school reading specialist and local newspaper contributor before her husband lured her to New Zealand for a year. *Bone Chilling* is the sixth Alexa Glock Forensics Mystery.